W9-AWD-081

Like unto Like

SOUTHERN CLASSICS SERIES
John G. Sproat, *General Editor*

Like
unto
Like

A NOVEL

Sherwood Bonner

with a new introduction by
Jane Turner Censer

UNIVERSITY OF SOUTH CAROLINA PRESS
*Published in Cooperation with the Institute for Southern Studies and
the South Caroliniana Society of the University of South Carolina*

Introduction © 1997 University of South Carolina

First published 1878 by Harper & Brothers, Publishers

Published in Columbia, South Carolina, by the
University of South Carolina Press
in cooperation with the Institute for Southern Studies and
the South Caroliniana Society of the University of South Carolina

Manufactured in the United States of America
01 00 99 98 97   5 4 3 2 1

Library of Congress Cataloging-in-Publication Data

McDowell, Katherine Sherwood Bonner, 1849–1883.
  Like unto like : a novel / Sherwood Bonner ; with a new
introduction by Jane Turner Censer.
    p.   cm. — (Southern classics series)
  "First published 1878 by Harper & Brothers, Publisher."
  ISBN 1–57003–184–3 (pbk.)
  I. Censer, Jane Turner, 1951– . II. Title. III. Series.
PS2357.L5 1997
813'.4—dc21   96-51295

TO HENRY WADSWORTH LONGFELLOW

O poet, master in melodious art,
O man, whom many love and all revere,
Take thou, with kindly hand, the gift which here
I tender from a loving, reverent heart.
For much received from thee I little give,
Yet gladly proffer less, from lesser store;
Knowing that I shall please thee still the more
By thus consenting in thy debt to live.

Contents

General Editor's Preface

Jane Turner Censer's sensitive introduction to *Like unto Like* accords Sherwood Bonner the long-delayed recognition she deserves as a major southern writer. A woman of extraordinary independence and determination, Bonner epitomizes the competing and often conflicting responses of women to changing perceptions of gender and race in the South of the late nineteenth century. In her own mind she never entirely resolved the conflicts, yet in her most important writing she dissected them with discerning skill. *Like unto Like,* thus, is both a traditional romance of reunion and a bold literary exploration into an uncharted realm of southern social politics.

* * *

Southern Classics returns to general circulation books of importance dealing with the history and culture of the American South. Sponsored by the Institute for Southern Studies and the South Caroliniana Society of the University of South Carolina, the series is advised by a board of distinguished scholars whose members suggest titles and editors of individual volumes to the series editor and help to establish priorities in publication.

Chronological age alone does not determine a title's designation as a Southern Classic. The criteria include, as well, significance in contributing to a broad understanding of the region, timeliness in relation to events and moments of peculiar interest to the American South, usefulness in the classroom, and suitability for inclusion in personal and institutional collections on the region.

John G. Sproat
General Editor, *Southern Classics*

Acknowledgments

I wish to thank the many people and institutions that aided in bringing Sherwood Bonner's novel back into print. I first discovered and read *Like unto Like* during a sabbatical leave provided by George Mason University. At Cornell University I relied on the extensive resources of Olin Library and the intellectual companionship of Glenn Altschuler and Michael Kammen while writing the introduction. I also found the University of South Carolina Press and the Institute of Southern Studies, especially Catherine Fry and John Sproat, to be extremely supportive.

I am grateful to many friends and colleagues for their help. Joan Cashin first alerted me to the dearth of women's fictional depictions of Reconstruction. Joel Williamson, Michael O'Malley, Rosemarie Zagarri, Lenard Berlanstein, John Inscoe, John David Smith, Jeffrey C. Stewart, and Jean and Michael Alexander all helped refine my approach to "reunion" novels and Bonner's writings. J. William Harris and James C. Turner gave detailed, thoughtful readings of the introduction that improved both style and substance. As usual Jack R. Censer read and commented at every stage of the project and, with Marjorie and Joel Censer, kept before me a sense of what happy endings can be all about.

Introduction

As the northbound train pulled out of the station in Holly Springs, Mississippi, in August 1873, twenty-four-year-old Kate Bonner McDowell had launched herself on a journey from which there would be no turning back. Her trip to Boston was both a headlong flight from the strictures of southern society and a defiant bid for a new role in life. Not only did she intend to complete her education in Boston, she also believed, rightly enough, that residence there would bring her into contact with the literary elite and allow her to reach her goal: to be an author. In Boston she would create a new persona for herself as the literary lady and author Sherwood Bonner.[1]

That the statuesque young woman with long auburn hair was traveling with no male escort violated current southern social conventions for women of her class and upbringing. But what made Kate Bonner McDowell's journey far more outrageous to her peers in the North and the South was her status as a wife and mother. Two years earlier, when Kate Bonner had wed Edward McDowell in a festive Valentine's Day event, she had apparently chosen her destiny. For a woman of genteel family to marry was to surrender any ambitions for achievement in the public world, literary or otherwise. A married woman whose husband was a meager provider might support herself and her family, as the example of women writers such as E.D.E.N. Southworth testified. But such women had always portrayed themselves as reluctant participants in the literary scene, not as aspirants to literary fame. It was Kate Bonner McDowell's insistence on additional education and a literary apprenticeship that showed her unseemly ambition and set her apart from so many other female writers, especially those of the previous generation.[2]

What kind of woman would knowingly risk uncertainty, disapproval, and even social ostracism in pursuit of literary fame? A stranger seeing Kate Bonner McDowell on the train might have thought her a pretty, conventional young woman of a privileged upbringing. She had been born in Holly Springs, only fifty miles south of Memphis, Tennessee, on February 26, 1849, to a prominent physician and his well-connected wife. Christened Catherine Sherwood Bonner, she always signed herself Katharine or Kate Bonner. As with many of her generation, the Civil War stood as a landmark in her early life. It interrupted her education when the Union's occupying army shut down Holly Springs's female seminary. Her short and unsystematic schooling also included a brief stint at a girls' school in Montgomery, Alabama. In postwar Holly Springs vivacious and intellectually thirsty Kate Bonner actively participated in the town's social and cultural life.

Still some events suggest that Kate Bonner was willing to challenge expectations for young women. A quick, lively child, she showed an early insouciance toward gender conventions when she wanted to drill with a group of girls who styled themselves Confederate cadets. Her father's refusal to allow her to participate reduced Kate to tears. Her mother, seeking to console her, made her an apron featuring the Confederate flag. This event, which she used in her novel *Like unto Like,* illustrated an early clash between the rigid gender roles her parents advocated and her own preference for a more flexible one. From her childhood on Kate Bonner wrote stories and verse easily and copiously; the diary she kept as a teenager shows her early interest in women's rights, as when she noted in 1869, "Regret more than ever that women are denied the privilege of voting."[3] Chafing against women's circumscribed roles, young Kate cherished literary aspirations. Much as the older New England author Louisa May Alcott had done, Kate experimented in writing sensational Gothic pieces for magazines and newspapers. Bonner's first stories, full of contrived plots and foreign characters, were published when she was twenty in the *Massachusetts Ploughman and New England Journal of Agriculture,* whose woman's department was edited by Nahum Capen, a Boston businessman.[4]

Bounded by small town life, Kate Bonner dreamed of the unconventional—of becoming an author or an actress. Yet her most realistic prospect seemed her romance with Edward McDowell, a tall slender young man from a Vicksburg merchant family with ties to Holly Springs and Galveston. Only a year older than Bonner, McDowell had attended an English public school during the war. In her diary Kate Bonner wrote romantically of knights and heroes, and this well-educated young man with similar literary tastes was her best candidate. First reaching a commitment in 1867, the two married in 1871.

Even before the marriage Edward McDowell was encountering problems finding a place in life despite the help of his well-connected extended family. In 1868 he had worked at an uncle's commission house in Galveston, and the following year he unsuccessfully sought his fortune in California. In the summer of 1870 he became a clerk in the store of yet another uncle in Holly Springs. When the couple's daughter, Lilian, was born ten months after the wedding, Edward was in the process of losing his position as his elderly uncle sought to sell the store. Kate was coming to see her marriage with Edward as a financial and emotional disaster.

While the birth of a child tenuously held the McDowell marriage together, Edward's financial difficulties destroyed Kate's faith in him. With aid from his extended family, he opened a store in Dallas, Texas, in late 1872 and moved his wife and daughter there in the spring. After a few months of loneliness there, Kate began to seek a way out. She had continued to write, and she shared her plans with elderly Nahum Capen, who had become somewhat her literary adviser. Her first scheme—to attend Vassar College in Poughkeepsie, New York—met with Capen's adamant disapproval because it would entail her leaving her child, even though Kate had both understated and underestimated the amount of family opposition she would face. She then created an alternative plan—to leave her daughter in Holly Springs and go to work and study in Boston—to which she later claimed her husband had assented. At the least Edward McDowell was willing to allow his wife to return to Mississippi that summer. She held steadfastly to her dreams of Boston, even when her incensed mother-in-law refused to care for young Lilian, packing her off to Dr. Bonner's house.[5]

When she arrived in Boston that August of 1873, Kate Bonner McDowell knew only Nahum Capen, whose family soon came to her assistance. With the help of the kindly literary man, she entered the tuition-free Girls' High School, found a boarding situation, and worked as his research assistant. Knowing that neither her father nor her husband would send funds, she spent a lonely, impoverished fall and winter, subsisting on her meager savings and small earnings. By the end of 1873, however, she had begun to make influential friends. Perhaps the most important acquaintance came about because of her determination and spunk. In December, describing herself as "a Southern girl away from my home and friends," she wrote a short note to the famous poet Henry Wadsworth Longfellow, asking for an audience. Significantly she included some of the same phraseology spoken by her heroine in *Like unto Like:* "I have come here for mental discipline and study—and to try to find out the meaning and use of my life."[6] Not only did Longfellow grant the interview, he quickly became both friend and mentor. Impressed by Kate Bonner McDowell's vivacity, ambition, and attractiveness, he would become her most stalwart supporter, emotionally and even financially. In 1875 he wrote a poem, "The Masque of Pandora," which not only described her beauty but also seemed to embody, in the encouragement given to Pandora, his hopes for this would-be author: "To build a new life on a ruined life / To make the future fairer than the past / And make the past appear a troubled dream."[7]

At the same time as she was gaining Longfellow's friendship and support, other doors opened. She found a secretarial position answering the correspondence of the well-known temperance lecturer Dr. Dio Lewis. The work in Dr. Lewis's office introduced her to the world of New England reform, which was linked to the world of literature in Boston. She met women her own age as well as local notables. Perhaps most important among these latter was James Redpath, the publicist and former abolitionist who later inspired the character of Roger Ellis in *Like unto Like*. Redpath, a fervent apostle and biographer of the abolitionist John Brown, would—like Longfellow—become an especially devoted admirer of Kate Bonner McDowell.

In the spring of 1874 she gained an additional position that served her literary purpose: she became a correspondent of the *Memphis Avalanche,* a Democratic newspaper. Over the next three years she chronicled New England manners and mores as well as the leading literary and political figures for a southern audience.[8] These pieces helped her find the perspective she would often use in her fiction: that of a detached observer amused and bemused by the people and activities she surveyed. While she wrote these articles as a self-conscious southerner among a different people, she cultivated the same gently satiric eye toward southern manners.

Thus, after a rocky beginning, Kate Bonner McDowell was successfully supporting herself in Boston. By 1875 she was also able to fashion her new literary persona, as she began to publish articles in a magazine, the *Cottage Hearth,* under the name of Sherwood Bonner. Her early articles in the *Massachusetts Ploughman* and elsewhere had appeared either unsigned or with the name Clayton Vaughn, while her letters to the *Avalanche* ran with the byline Katharine or Kate McDowell. Yet Kate had already shown distaste for Edward's surname. She had signed her first note to Longfellow "Katharine Bonner" and then to her embarrassment had to correct him about her marital status. As her biographer has astutely pointed out, Kate Bonner McDowell found her new name an excellent way out of her predicament. While she could not go back to being Kate Bonner, she would not have to bear the name of a husband who was at best a burden. The name Sherwood Bonner was "a part of her actual name, and it enabled her to present a new self which still encompassed that part of the old that she wanted to retain."[9] The masculine ring of the name Sherwood would also be an advantage in that part of the literary world which still tended to look upon literary ladies as part of what Nathaniel Hawthorne called a "damn'd mob of scribbling women."[10] As the writer Sherwood Bonner, she would be achieving the position that other southern women such as Mary Chesnut had so eagerly desired.[11] Sherwood Bonner was more than Kate McDowell's nom de plume. When she traveled to Memphis and Holly Springs in the summer of 1875, the *Memphis Avalanche* used the name to announce her visit. For the rest of her life, she would be Sherwood Bonner in public and Kate McDowell in private.

When Sherwood Bonner returned to Boston in the fall of 1875, she had come far closer to realizing her goal than any of her friends or family might have thought possible only two years earlier. She had published stories in the widely read *Youth's Companion* and *Lippincott's* as well as in the *Cottage Hearth*. Yet she was supporting herself only by combining secretarial and research work with her writing. Moreover, she was beginning to draw criticism because of her anomalous status as an estranged wife. Her own actions also caused her trouble. Perhaps her largest misstep came earlier that year when she penned a satirical poem entitled "The Radical Club," which parodied well-known reformers such as Julia Ward Howe, Bronson Alcott, and Elizabeth Peabody. Although the poem was published anonymously, rumor soon confirmed her as the author; and many prominent Bostonians were not amused. In addition, an interview with William Dean Howells, then editor of the highly regarded *Atlantic Monthly,* had gone badly: she would never realize her dream of publishing in the *Atlantic.*

While she had won an entrée into literary life, Sherwood Bonner found herself still struggling on personal and professional grounds. In 1876 she received a long-desired opportunity—the chance to visit Europe; she would be the companion of the poet and author Louise Chandler Moulton on a trip that lasted from January to October. During her tour she produced newspaper stories for the *Memphis Avalanche* and the *Boston Times*. Upon her return her family pressured her into a reconciliation with her husband in Galveston in April 1877. There she continued to write, producing short stories and working on a novel based on her own experience of becoming a writer, entitled "The Prodigal Daughter." She also penned a short story about a romance between a southern woman and a northern suitor which she called "Like unto Like." To Longfellow she described this story—the original version of which has not survived—as "a character study. There is no incident." [12]

Not surprisingly Kate Bonner McDowell's reconciliation with her husband was not successful. Perhaps her wariness about the whole affair was best illustrated by her unwillingness to take her five-year-old daughter, who had been living with Kate's father and aunt in Holly Springs, with her to Galveston. By July 1877 she herself was back in Holly Springs. She wanted to take Lilian with her to Boston, but Dr. Bonner insisted the child remain with him and his sister.

Again back in Boston, the literary lady Sherwood Bonner resumed writing. But her novel underwent a metamorphosis. Rather than complete the story of her own rebellion against social mores, she merged it with a radically expanded version of her North-South romance. Indeed, given her own experience in interpreting New England to a southern readership and writing local color stories about the South, it is not surprising that she attempted to put to use her understandings of character types from both regions. It also seems quite possible that the abortive reconciliation with Edward McDowell led her to add to the expanded story a feminist critique of marriage. In the spring of 1878 the manuscript of *Like unto Like* was completed. Longfellow read it and recommended it to Harper and Brothers, who accepted it and published it in September.[13]

Like unto Like reflects a number of literary and political currents. Bonner experimented with a mixture of literary genres and figures. Although she resorted to the vehicle of the romantic novel that women had been writing for much of the nineteenth century, Bonner was also open to newer, more fashionable literary techniques, especially local color and realism. Local color had entered American literature several decades earlier, especially under the influence of southwestern humorists such as Joseph Ingraham (the Episcopal rector of Bonner's home town), but it perhaps reached its zenith in the 1870s. When she first arrived in Boston, Bonner eagerly read the popular works of Bret Harte. While he used western locales, other local color writers set their stories in New England or the South, celebrating America's regional diversity by reproducing regional dialects and local customs and curiosities.[14]

Local color as Bonner produced it also drew on her reading of nineteenth century British literature. Authors such as George Eliot, Emily Brontë, and Elizabeth Gaskell not only included dialects and local customs in their writings, they also chronicled the lives of English villages and their inhabitants. While some of the characters were eccentric and broadly humorous, the English local color novel tended to be more domestic and less outrageous and violent than the American southwestern versions.

Another emerging development in literature—a turn away from sentimentality and sensationalism and toward realism—also was reflected in Bonner's writings. Best known of the authors symbolizing this change were William Dean Howells and Henry James, even though Howells combined his realism with an elevated moral tone. Bonner criticized the ending of Henry James's *The Americans,* but she may well have been influenced by it.

Even as Sherwood Bonner wrote a romantic story with realistic and local-color dialect elements, she was also utilizing a contemporary plot—the romance of reunion, symbolizing the rejoining of North and South. From the time of the Civil War on, northern and southern authors had produced stories in which an intersectional romance and marriage both symbolized and came to cement the political reunion of North and South. Union army officer John W. De Forest published the best-known specimen of this genre in 1866 with his *Miss Ravenel's Conversion from Secession to Loyalty.* In the hands of most popular northern writers, the reunion novel became a stock plot in which a dashing northern army officer won the affection and hand of a high-spirited southern beauty.

Historian Nina Silber has traced the gender implications of this scenario—how the submission of the southern beauty to the northern soldier first in love, then marriage, could parallel the South's being brought to heel in a newly reordered political union.[15]

The common view has been that southern women, when they wrote for publication, mainly produced poems and stories extolling the "lost cause" of the Confederacy. Recent research into these authors has found them to be more adventurous. Southern women who used the romance of reunion took a distinctively different perspective from either northern authors or southern male authors such as Thomas Nelson Page, who in the 1880s resorted to it to celebrate past plantation life. Bonner was only the first—although arguably the most talented—of a small group of southern female authors who gave a new cast to the theme of reunion, which even by the late 1870s was growing rather hackneyed. For these southern women the romance of reunion contradicted Confederate legitimacy by endorsing the northern victory in the Civil War. Some female authors such as Bonner went even further to undermining Confederate memorialism. Her keeper of the Confederate flame, Grandmother Herndon, is a lonely, almost psychotic figure, hardly the stuff of which myth is made. Other women characters observe "Decoration Day," but they grieve for individual sons or lovers rather than for the "lost cause." And while one former Confederate soldier in Bonner's story is a man of honor trying to make his plantation work, another had been a guerrilla who in the savagery of his patriotism never took prisoners.

The romances of reunion as Sherwood Bonner and other southern female authors conceived them had no southern men as romantic leads. Bonner did so obliquely: the northern hero had no southern competitor. Other authors such as Julia Magruder and M. G. McClelland in the 1880s juxtaposed northern and southern suitors as a way to critique southern mores and especially southern men. Like Bonner these women published with highly regarded New York firms and enjoyed considerable success in their day, writing romances that presented intellectually active heroines and challenged contemporary gender conventions. All of the southern "reunion" novels by women have a feminist "political" slant, but Bonner best and most fully articulates this emphasis on female autonomy. Sherwood Bonner's novel marks the emergence of a feminist critique of southern society a full generation before Ellen Glasgow and Kate Chopin published their better-known works.

Given her emphasis on women's autonomy and self actualization, one might question to what extent Sherwood Bonner had been influenced by the women's rights and woman suffrage movements. There seems little doubt that even from her youth she had wished to enlarge women's autonomy. In Boston she met women's rights reformers. While she wrote in a satiric manner about many reforms, she treated women's rights sympathetically. In a sketch of Julia Ward Howe published in the *Cottage Hearth,* she remarked: "Our Southern friends imagine that a woman who wants to vote, or stands on the platform to make a speech, of necessity unsexes herself, and must be bold, unwomanly, and false to her higher duties." Arguing that Howe in manner and deed showed such prejudices to be untrue, Bonner argued that those same people "would take the first step in that march of progress which is before them, that of acknowledging that a woman may read Greek and lead a suffrage party without being one whit the less what they apostrophize as the end and aim of feminine endeavor—a womanly woman."[16] Here Bonner also showed her determination not to allow woman's sphere and nature—womanliness—to be defined as excluding intellectual and public activity. In the mid 1870s Bonner also became friendly with Elizabeth Avery Meriwether, a leading reformer and advocate of woman suffrage in Memphis, and in March 1877 arranged for her to speak on the subject in Holly Springs.[17] These writings and actions all testify to Bonner's sympathy with feminism.

After accepting *Like unto Like,* Harper and Brothers rushed its publication, and Sherwood Bonner was unable to revise it as she wished. It appeared in New York as a 160-page novel in twenty-eight chapters, selling for 75 cents. Set in the fictional Alabama town of Yariba and in New Orleans, the story opens in 1875 as three young unmarried southern women contemplate the quartering of a troop of Union soldiers in their town. Only the heroine, Blythe Herndon, free-spirited though bookish, can face the situation with equanimity, though her coquettish friend Betty Page will in fact find numerous beaux among the federal soldiers. Only the most conventional of the three girls, Mary Barton, will be untouched by the Yankee "invasion," as her primary goal is marriage to the southern man she has long admired.

Bonner's major plot is a coming-of-age story that focuses on the vagaries of a romance that grows between Blythe Herndon and Roger Ellis, a former abolitionist from New England who had been a Union soldier during the war. Here the author has created a pair of intellectual lovers. Ellis seems a somewhat unlikely hero, fortyish and balding with radical social and political opinions. Blythe Herndon, by far the most unconventional person in Yariba, is bright and questioning at twenty-two despite the overprotective father who burns Henry Fielding's bawdy novel *Tom Jones* when he discovers her reading it. Bonner gives Blythe the desire that she herself had expressed on arriving in Boston, that of wanting to learn "the meaning and the use of my life."

A romance, and then an engagement, occurs between Ellis and Blythe Herndon. Her parents reluctantly consent despite the opposition of Blanche's grandmother, a bitter Confederate irreconcilable whose unbending hatred of Yankees has overridden even her belief in God. Roger Ellis becomes Blythe's guide not only to love, but also to a richer intellectual life. As Bonner puts it, "Blythe had certain theories about women that had been gently put down by the masculine beings of her life-long acquaintance; but Roger Ellis soon supplemented her budding views by wider and wilder ones that she readily adopted as her own." Over the course of the novel Blythe will come to perceive as a measure of her own provinciality her shock at egalitarian racial relations, notions of free love, and Ellis's past affair with a married woman.

Yet the romance quickly hits the shoals, as the author seems to be questioning whether her two leading characters are really alike. Can similar intellectual interests and a prickly relationship with society overcome different received beliefs and experiences? Yet despite Bonner's title and original conception of the work, the problems that the lovers encounter focus not so much on North-South distinctions as those of race and gender. While their differences over politics center around race, the politics of gender involve another form of equality and autonomy.

Roger Ellis's insistence on equality for the former slaves forms a major stumbling block in the courtship. The most concrete example of this comes in his championing of a young freedman, Bill—or Willy—Tolliver, who for an infant act of assertiveness has already been derisively nicknamed "Civil Rights Bill" by the local whites. Bonner here makes the conflict between Blythe and Roger lie in Reconstruction and the New South, not in the distant past. Agreeing with her fiancé that slavery was wrong, Blythe finds it much harder to accept his racial egalitarianism. Although Bonner was writing her novel as Reconstruction had ended and whites were disenfranchising African Americans, she gives Ellis the stronger arguments. As the couple quarrels about whether young Bill Tolliver will take meals with them, Blythe can muster little but sheer prejudice to justify her opposition. She tells Ellis, "my reason tells me that you are right. I agree with you entirely in theory, but—I will *not* sit at the table with Civil Rights Bill!" Blythe will have to decide whether her fiancé's radicalism on Reconstruction and race relations can be reconciled with her inherited opinions and her desire for family and community approval.

While the politics of race forms one barrier to romance, the politics of marriage also further complicates the story. Bonner's satiric approach to the romance creates a tension in the story. She was writing both a quest or coming-of-age story and a romance—a combination that with a female protagonist tended to lead nineteenth-century writers to hackneyed endings. Bonner wants her readers to perceive the danger lurking in marriage for a young woman such as Blythe, who is only beginning to understand life's potentialities. Bonner as the omniscient narrator notes that southern women "gather roses while they may; for, once married, their day is over, and they reverse nature's order by becoming caterpillars after they have been butterflies." Here and elsewhere the author, indicating the limitations of marriage as the primary goal for young women, hints at another world and other options for Blythe without ever clearly presenting these alternatives. Still the novel's presentation of marriage opens to question traditional gender roles.

Over the course of her courtship Blythe comes to realize that for a woman marriage—even to a man with radical opinions—will mean subordination. Significantly Blythe and Roger quarrel not over slavery or the outcome of the Civil War but over an event during the war that some historians have seen as deeply gendered—General Ben Butler's notorious "woman order." When, during the wartime occupation of New Orleans in 1862, hostile southern ladies spat at and otherwise insulted Union soldiers, Butler issued General Order 28, which stated that women insulting Union soldiers would be considered women of the street who were soliciting business. Butler sought to humiliate troublesome women by equating them with prostitutes, but many southerners considered the order as allowing and even justifying sexual assault.[18] Blythe is outraged when Roger Ellis defends Butler's past actions: "It is astonishing . . . how many ingenious ways those New Orleans women devised to torment our soldiers. Nothing but the most rigorous measures would have answered with them." Blythe retorts that she behaved in similar fashion to occupying Union soldiers and that the punishment was disproportionate to the offense. With masculine unconcern Ellis lectures her at length on the sacredness of the flag and patriotism "and, returning to the subject in hand, he declared that events had proved the wisdom of the order in question, as it had taught the women to behave themselves." Yet when Ellis calls Blythe "a desperate little rebel," she impassionedly corrects him. "'You mistake me entirely,' said the girl, proudly; 'it is not as Southerner I resent what you have said, but as a *woman*. I cannot bear it, Mr. Ellis!' and she made a sudden swift gesture of dismissal. 'I should like to be alone.'" While the language had not yet been coined, it was about the politics of gender that Blythe and Roger fought. While Roger believes they are arguing over the Confederacy, Blythe is asserting women's right to political positions and to public actions in support of them. Bonner deals with this subject of women and politics in yet another way when she shows Blythe rather futilely attempting to sort through the political opinions that the northern and southern men embrace.

As Bonner focuses on the romantic trials of her heroine, Blythe Herndon, she also depicts what has come to be known as the southern belle. According to Bonner: "The truth is, Southern girls like to flirt, and have a genius for it." Yet Sherwood Bonner, despite her own history of drawing male admirers, refused to view this kind of popularity as an answer to women's dilemma. Belatedly, in North Orleans Blythe enjoys a social whirl but finds it no more satisfying than her proposed marriage. Bonner also uses the parallel romances of Blythe's friends Betty Page and Mary Barton to show the limitations of romance: Mary represents a young woman interested in traditional roles of wife and mother. Long enamored of Van Tolliver who struggles to make his isolated plantation profitable, she is willing to bear the hardships of rural married life. Betty Page is a coquette; her marriage to a northern soldier will be one of social and financial calculation as she tries to choose the most comfortable position for herself. This is not the course that Bonner would advocate, yet she does not punish Betty Page, who is depicted as pleased with her marriage: "Oh, I love him well enough—not madly, you know. I'm not romantic. But then, neither is he. . . . We *suit* each other . . . and there's everything in that."

Blythe Herndon represents a break with the heroines depicted by other contemporary writers. While modern critics have found new power and force in numerous female characters of the nineteenth century, these heroines often drew their power from a steely piety and a resolve to be domestic muses and protectors of home, religion, and virtue. Augusta Jane Evans, whose *Beulah* (1859) and *St.-Elmo* (1867) probably made her the best-selling southern female author of the 1850s and 1860s, presented tempestuous, intellectual heroines who learned Christian resolution and forced their aspirations into domestic forms. Blythe has neither the steely piety nor Christian resolution of heroines such as Evans's Beulah Benton; even beside the March sisters of Louisa May Alcott's *Little Women,* Blythe appears quite uninterested in religion. Instead of curbing her heroine's will by God or man, Bonner wants to give it free rein.[19]

Neither did Bonner choose the other common manner of empowering females: creating antiheroines, or "dark women," whose evil nature gave them tremendous power over other men and women. Mrs. E. D. E. N. Southworth was a master of this style of writing, which probably was strongly influenced by the semipornographic police novels, and even other more highly regarded female authors such as Alcott thoroughly enjoyed producing such potboilers anonymously.[20] Bonner instead chose to create a naïve but intellectually alive and questioning woman in search of life's meaning.

As Bonner follows the ups and downs of the parallel courtships, she draws a sympathetic yet often satiric portrait of the southern townspeople of Yariba, setting forth a large cast of characters from different social classes and races. Profoundly provincial, insular, and anti-intellectual, Bonner's white southern characters find it hard to examine, much less question, their social customs. Some of these characters are in fact largely "types," meant to provide humor. Genial old Mark Barton, a provincial who sings the praises of Yariba and proclaims that "the man who couldn't live here couldn't live anywhere on God's green earth" is the familiar country squire of numerous English and American novels. His wife, similarly set in old habits, always calls him "Cousin Mark," as she had done in the days before their marriage.

Yet all is not sweetness and light in Yariba despite its picturesque beauty and characters. Regardless of their vaunted liberality the white folks are suspicious of other views. They are uncomprehendingly rude and often cruel to the former slaves, ordering them about peremptorily and joking about racial inferiority. Ten-year-old Bill Tolliver's nickname of "Civil Rights Bill" speaks volumes about the townspeople's stolid resistance to Reconstruction and racial equality. Bonner also retains a touch of the Gothic in some of her portrayals, especially those of the old regime and war which suggest male violence. Particularly tragic is the story of Blythe's sister, killed by her jealous planter husband, scion of a long line of hot-headed men—an episode based on the murder of Bonner's own aunt.

In this Gothic pantheon two of the older women, Blythe's and Bill Tolliver's grandmothers, stand as menacing wrecks of the Confederacy and the slave South respectively. Most ominous is Blythe's grandmother, bitterly unreconciled to the end of the Confederacy. So die-hard is she that defeat in war has destroyed her belief in God. With her hardness shown by her flashing diamond solitaire and her hatred of Yankees that seethes even when she is sleepwalking, she exhibits the cruel though tenuous hold of the old regime on the New South. Throughout the novel she and her dead guerrilla relative (who never took prisoners) symbolize the heavy hand of the southern past as well as death and destruction. Old Mrs. Herndon is willing to resort to bribery or even to selling her soul to stop Blythe's marriage to a Yankee.

More in the background but equally warped by the past is Bill Tolliver's grandmother Aunt Sally. Like Mrs. Herndon, Aunt Sally has a visage that testifies to her strangeness: "She was blind in one eye, and this gave a peculiar wildness to her expression, as the blind eye was fixed, blue, and glassy, while the other was black and rolling." Aunt Sally's blind eye extends to slavery and the old regime. Her references to herself as an "ole South Carliny nigger" and to the value of the old ways suggest that she has been twisted by slavery to become its defender. In a move reminiscent of slavery and its buying and selling of humans, she transfers her grandson over to Roger Ellis's keeping, not because of the education and advantages that Ellis wants to provide Bill, but because of the money he gives her. While Aunt Sally displays great superstition in her "cures" for her grandson, she transcends the stock figure. The calculation apparent in her subservience as well as her self-centeredness undercut Bonner's attempts at humor and ironically enough make her far more a person than merely a type.

It is in her portrayals of these women and their younger counterparts that Sherwood Bonner attempts and achieves most. She presents a variegated portrait of southern womanhood from the effervescent and intellectual Blythe Herndon to the self-centered belle Betty Page, obsessing about her "large" figure. Bonner also produces a handful of women whose lives show some of the special trials of being a woman in the postwar South; she focuses in particular on the widow Oglethorpe, arbiter of Yariba society, and on Blythe's grandmother, the lonely defender of the Confederacy. Through all this exploration of gender roles and conventions, Bonner maintains a feminist insistence that the future should hold great possibilities for her youthful heroine.

Bonner presents a Yariba where emancipation and Reconstruction have not empowered the freed slaves; they hold the same domestic roles of yore and are still treated with condescension and familiarity. Sherwood Bonner's cast of African American characters is not large; neither does she present them as active participants in Reconstruction politics and policies. Yet, for all that, she keeps race at the foreground of her story and presents a range of African American characters that goes beyond Aunt Sally Tolliver. To be sure, some of her African American characters such as Daddy Si, whose undying devotion to his long-lost sweetheart has not prevented him from having a string of wives, are humorous stock types. Yet her portrait of ten-year-old Bill Tolliver, "Civil Rights Bill," is an important attempt to create a sympathetic African American character. Indeed, the other fictional character whom Bill Tolliver most resembles is his contemporary Tom Sawyer, who had burst upon the literary scene only one year earlier. Like Sawyer, Bill Tolliver is mischievous, lively, intelligent, and enterprising. Bill enters the story as an errand boy whom the young white ladies order about with equanimity, yet an accident involving broken bottles at a picnic shows Bill "getting up a speculation" in a way that Sawyer might well have done. By the time of the New Orleans episodes of *Like unto Like*, Bill Tolliver no longer speaks in the dialect of Bonner's African American characters; familiar with the city, he has begun to acquire a new education and accent. While Bonner's use of Bill as a symbol for Reconstruction may have hampered her full development of him as a character, her novel shows a white southern writer groping her way toward a multidimensional portrait of an African American youth.

Bonner's depiction of Bill Tolliver and other African Americans is especially interesting given the characterizations of other contemporary white writers. Northern writers such as Constance Woolson and John W. De Forest, whatever their critique of southern whites, sketched only devoted African American servants who loved and kept afloat their incompetent former owners. At this time Mark Twain was changing in his racial attitudes—he had not yet produced Jim, the runaway slave in *Huckleberry Finn* who would be an admirable and complex character. Neither had George Washington Cable yet serialized *The Grandissimes,* the novel about creole New Orleans whose sympathetic depiction of African Americans has led Louis Rubin to label him as the only southern writer who defied the conservatism of his region to depict the essential humanity of African Americans.[21] In *Like unto Like* Sherwood Bonner broke new ground both in acknowledging the importance of race in southern attitudes and in creating a range of African American characters, some of whom transcended stereotype.

It is important to stress these characterizations by Bonner because they show a facet of her work that has rarely been recognized. The parts of Bonner's writings that have most often been reprinted are her dialect stories. Some of these are peopled with African American characters who are shrewd but illiterate and often unprincipled, while others, such as the "Gran'mammy" stories about the African American nurse who had brought up both Bonner and Bonner's mother, show affection and some subtlety in depiction. Bonner's own racial views remain cloudy; whatever her own prejudices and stereotypes she was able at times to depict complex African American characters. That her stories fostering the plantation mythology have remained in the public eye is as revealing of the nineteenth-century reading public as of the author.[22]

Bonner seeks an evenhanded depiction of Reconstruction and portrays a wide range of opinions through both her southern and her northern characters—although even the most moderate southerners are quite critical of Reconstruction. Her book stands in contrast to much late-nineteenth-century southern writing about Reconstruction that pictured a prostrate South being exploited and oppressed by unprincipled Yankees and ignorant former slaves. Occupied Yariba and even New Orleans present cozy scenes where southerners may be impoverished from the war but seem to have few other grievances. To Bonner, Reconstruction is a contest of opinions over the place of African Americans in political and social life, and she suggests that a commitment to white supremacy lies at the heart of white Southerners' resistance. Even Blythe, the most questioning of the Southerners, is touched by such prejudices. In the character of Matilda Roy, a poor white woman who has been deserted by her husband, Bonner shows a racism that is not restricted to the ruling elite. Roger Ellis procures a job at an orphanage for Mrs. Roy, only to see her scornfully decline it when she learns that her children would then attend a racially integrated school.

In her romance of reunion Bonner gives a different view of North and South and their reconciliation. A superficial reunion can perhaps be fairly easily achieved, as the self-interested marriage of a northern soldier and southern belle seems to symbolize. A reunion of hearts and minds remains more elusive, as different views of race relations and fundamental social values prove more difficult to reconcile. If John De Forest and other male writers used the romance genre to reinforce northern political supremacy and traditional gender conventions of female submission, in Bonner's hands it indicates the difficulty of obtaining true unions—political or marital— and further reinforces the feminist message.

Like unto Like appeared at a particularly desolate period in Sherwood

Bonner's life. In August 1878 in the midst of the yellow fever epidemic that had been devastating the lower Mississippi Valley, she rushed south to Holly Springs to remove her daughter and aunt to safety; she found her father and twenty-four-year-old brother Samuel fatally ill. That autumn she returned to Boston to find her book generally faring better in reviews than in sales. Contemporaries praised the book as "so original, so charming," "a brilliant, exceedingly interesting story" and compared its author to George Eliot. Of the major journals only the *Atlantic* was critical in a review that she mistakenly believed written by Howells. Yet the book was controversial to some. Paul Hamilton Hayne, then the foremost southern man of letters, declared himself shocked by both Sherwood Bonner and her novel: "How a Southern woman . . . could have patiently conceived such a personage as Roger Ellis, or at least lingered with such apparent pride, satisfaction and delight over the many traits of his ultra Radical nature, and many expressions of his ultra Radical belief, seems to be utterly unaccountable." Hayne accused Bonner of "selling out" to the Yankees or, as he put it, "yearning towards the tents of the Aliens." Yet even he admitted the novel was "very clever, sometimes brilliant."[23] The novel fared worse with the reading public. Although it was reprinted in London in 1882, since that time it has practically dropped from view, appearing in the form of brief excerpts in anthologies (two pages in one published in 1907 and six pages in another published in 1926). This has been so even though several volumes of Bonner's dialect tales were reissued in the 1970s.

Although disappointed with the sales of *Like unto Like,* Sherwood Bonner continued her quest for literary fame. Optimistically she told the editor of *Harper's Monthly* that she believed "a great future is possible. . . . In ten years I shall be an artist." But she did not have ten years. She worked, sometimes at a feverish pace, and published a fleet of short stories to support herself and her daughter, whose custody she had regained. She also shuttled between Memphis, Boston, New York, and Illinois, where in 1881 she divorced her husband. Only a few months after the divorce she discovered a painful lump in her breast, but her doctors assured her it was not cancer. Her health and financial problems continued, and in May 1882 New Orleans doctors told her that she was suffering from an advanced case of breast cancer and had less than one year to live. She died July 22, 1883, in Holly Springs while working on her autobiography.[24]

Her death did not close the drama and controversy that had characterized so much of Sherwood Bonner's life. While her friend and literary executor, Sophia Kirk, placed many of the stories written in the last year of Bonner's life, the autobiography was not among them. In 1886 a book entitled *The Story of Margaret Kent* became an instant best-seller as it chronicled the story of an unhappily married female writer who had a circle of male admirers. The novel appeared anonymously but was soon found to have been written by Ellen Kirk, Sophia Kirk's stepmother. Although the style is not Sherwood Bonner's, many of the incidents and characterizations of the first dozen chapters correspond to her views. Hubert McAlexander has convincingly argued that a literary theft occurred here; ironically Sherwood Bonner may have had her best-seller in a book never credited to her.[25]

Sherwood Bonner left an ambiguous literary legacy. Often she wrote what she knew would sell: dialect pieces, light romance, even melodrama. Her biographer has demonstrated that in her last years she sometimes engaged in a sort of literary opportunism—adopting the locale used by a George Washington Cable or Mary Noailles Murfree and then giving the story her own special twist.[26] But she also was a woman in search of literary excellence who was not granted the ten years that she thought would make her an artist.

Like unto Like fills an important niche as a southern white woman's assessment of the postwar southern social and political scene. Too seldom have we heard white women speak so publicly and directly from the late nineteenth century South and about the position of women there. Yet the romance of reunion as presented by southern women shows that the South of the 1870s and 1880s was far from monolithic in political and social views. Although female authors cannot simply be equated with women in general, research on other postwar southern women suggests that they too were questioning marriage and woman's place.[27] Bonner's novel is particularly interesting because its author explicitly deals with politics and female autonomy and criticizes the South—all themes that other southern female writers addressed more implicitly and discreetly.

Rich in characters and social history, Bonner's novel also has special significance as a commentary on Reconstruction and race relations. Although Sherwood Bonner at times resorted to stereotype, her African American characters in *Like unto Like* are also attempts to move beyond humor. With her uncommon knowledge and understanding of North and South derived from experience in Mississippi and Boston, Bonner could approach race and class with considerable insight. She chronicled with sympathy, understanding, and wit the problems that radical Reconstruction encountered in the South from rich and poor whites alike.

Both as writer and woman Sherwood Bonner complicates our understanding of the Reconstruction South. While a castelike prejudice poisoned whites' relationships with blacks, southern publications were not limited to Confederate panegyrics or paeans to the lost cause. A writer with a critical edge such as Bonner could be published, even though she encountered a public often indifferent, if not censorious. As her work shows, scholars need to shift their focus from decrying the lack of self-critical writing by southerners to explaining the limited impact of novels such as *Like unto Like* and writers such as Sherwood Bonner. How and why did southern literary history erase Sherwood Bonner? In her case her slip into anonymity likely came partly from the shortness of her career. With less than a decade of publishing and only one novel and one novella to her credit, Bonner left a relatively small corpus of work that could easily be characterized by the weaker stories or completely overlooked. Moreover, because she and other female writers used the genre of the romance, critics tended not to see their fiction as serious. Thus generations of historians and literary scholars have overlooked the importance of these women and their novels to the history of the late-nineteenth-century South.

While southern women may have been slower to participate in organized feminist endeavors, Sherwood Bonner often flouted convention to live the life she wanted, a literary life. Indeed, her life remains far more unbelievable and flamboyant than her fiction. Her biographer perhaps has best summed up the trailblazing role she played: "Twenty years before Kate Chopin wrote so powerfully of a woman's search for her self . . . Sherwood Bonner had explored another southern woman's awakening. Decades before Ellen Glasgow declared that what southern literature needed above all was 'blood and irony,' in her best work Sherwood Bonner had given it just that."[28] This new edition of *Like unto Like* will allow readers to share the rueful affection and critical insight that Sherwood Bonner brought to her exploration of southern society and the limitations it placed on young women.

Jane Turner Censer

NOTES

1. By far the best source on Sherwood Bonner is the excellent biography by Hubert Horton McAlexander, *The Prodigal Daughter: A Biography of Sherwood Bonner* (Baton Rouge: Louisiana State University Press, 1981), which unfortunately is now out of print. McAlexander not only gives a scrupulously researched account of her life but also includes interesting commentaries on her writings. He seems to have been the first critic to realize that *Like unto Like* is a coming-of-age story. Short biographies include William L. Frank, *Sherwood Bonner (Catherine McDowell)* (New York: Twayne Publishers, 1971), and entries in *Notable American Women* and the *Dictionary of American Biography*.

2. For information on women writers of the prewar period, consult Mary Kelley, *Private Woman, Public Stage: Literary Domesticity in Nineteenth Century America* (New York: Oxford University Press, 1984); and Nina Baym, *Woman's Fiction: A Guide to Novels by and about Women in America, 1820–1870,* 2d ed. (Urbana: University of Illinois Press, 1993). For information on southern women, consult Anne Goodwyn Jones, *To-*

morrow Is Another Day: The Woman Writer in the South, 1859–1936 (Baton Rouge: Louisiana State University Press, 1980); and Elizabeth Moss, *Domestic Novelists in the Old South: Defenders of Southern Culture* (Baton Rouge: Louisiana State University Press, 1992).

3. McAlexander, pp. 34.

4. Madeline Stern, ed., *The Feminist Alcott: Stories of a Woman's Power* (Boston: Northeastern University Press, 1996).

5. McAlexander, pp. 36–47.

6. Katharine Bonner [McDowell] to Henry Wadsworth Longfellow, Dec. 8, 1873, as cited in McAlexander, p. 53.

7. Henry Wadsworth Longfellow, "The Masque of Pandora," cited in McAlexander, p. 55.

8. McAlexander, pp. 58, 60–65.

9. Ibid., pp. 57, 66–68.

10. For this widely cited quote from Hawthorne, see Ann Douglas Wood, "The Scribbling Women and Fanny Fern: Why Women Wrote," *American Quarterly* 23 (Spring 1971): 3–24.

11. For Mary Chesnut's attempts to write fiction, see Elisabeth Muhlenfeld, *Mary Boykin Chesnut: A Biography* (Baton Rouge: Louisiana State University Press, 1981).

12. McAlexander, p.110.

13. Ibid., p. 114.

14. Local color was immensely popular in the 1870s and 1880s. A nuanced discussion of the several varieties of it can be found in Helen Taylor, *Gender, Race, and Region in the Writings of Grace King, Ruth McEnery Stuart and Kate Chopin* (Baton Rouge: Louisiana State University Press, 1989), pp. 15–20. For a New England version, see Susan Allen Toth, "'The Rarest and Most Peculiar Grape': Versions of the New England Woman in Nineteenth-Century Local Color Literature," in Emily Toth, ed., *Regionalism and the Female Imagination: A Collection of Essays* (New York: Human Sciences Press, 1985), pp. 15–28. An unsympathetic interpretation can be found in Ann Douglas Wood, "The Literature of Impoverishment: The Women Local Colorists in America, 1865–1914," *Women's Studies* 1 (1972): 3–45.

15. Nina Silber, *The Romance of Reunion: Northerners and the South, 1865–1890* (Chapel Hill: University of North Carolina Press, 1993). See also Joyce Appleby, "Reconciliation and the Northern Novelist, 1865–

1880," *Civil War History* 10 (June 1964): 117–29; and Paul Buck, *The Road to Reunion, 1865–1900* (Boston and Toronto, 1937), pp. 196–235.

16. McAlexander, p. 53–55, 69.

17. On Elizabeth Avery Meriwether, see Marsha Wedell, *Elite Women and the Reform Impulse in Memphis, 1875–1915* (Knoxville: University of Tennessee Press, 1991).

18. For Ben Butler and the women of New Orleans, see George Rable, "'Missing in Action': Women of the Confederacy," pp. 134–46, in Catherine Clinton and Nina Silber, *Divided Houses: Gender and the Civil War* (New York: Oxford University Press, 1992).

19. Baym, *Woman's Fiction*. For Augusta Jane Evans, see the new editions of *Macaria* (Baton Rouge: Louisiana State University, 1992) and *Beulah* (Baton Rouge: Louisiana State University, 1992), with introductions, respectively, by Drew Gilpin Faust and Elizabeth Fox-Genovese.

20. See, for example, E. D. E. N. Southworth, *The Hidden Hand, or Capitola the Madcap*, ed. Joanne Dobson (New Brunswick: Rutgers University Press, 1988); and Stern, ed., *The Feminist Alcott*. For the underside of writing in this period, consult David S. Reynolds, *Beneath the American Renaissance: The Subversive Imagination in the Age of Emerson and Melville* (New York: Knopf, 1988).

21. Arthur G. Pettit, *Mark Twain & the South* (Lexington: University Press of Kentucky, 1974), ch. 4, details Twain's evolving racial attitudes in the 1870s. Louis D. Rubin, Jr., *George W. Cable: The Life and Times of a Southern Heretic* (New York: Pegasus, 1969), pp. 96, 276.

22. See, for example, the treatment of Bonner in Catherine Clinton, *Tara Revisited* (New York: Abbeville Press, 1995); and Taylor, *Gender, Race, and Region*, pp. 85, 98.

23. Frank, *Sherwood Bonner*, pp. 140, 139, 137.

24. Noel E. Polk and James R. Scafidel, eds., *An Anthology of Mississippi Writers* (Jackson: University Press of Mississippi, 1979), p. 98; McAlexander, pp. 148–81.

25. McAlexander, pp. 213–21.

26. Ibid., pp. 185–200.

27. See, for example, Jane Turner Censer, "A Changing World of Work: North Carolina Elite Women, 1865–1895," *North Carolina Historical Review* 73 (Jan. 1996): 27–55.

28. McAlexander, p. 228.

Like unto Like

CHAPTER I

Between Sundown and Dark

Three girls were standing on a rustic bridge, looking down into the stream it spanned. Neither running water nor any other mirror ever gave back the glances of brighter eyes or reflected fairer faces; for these were Yariba girls, and Yariba was famed for its pretty girls even in this Southern land, where any out-of-the-way or in-the-way town held beauty enough for the servant of a wandering Titian to write *Est, Est, Est* above its gates.

At a little distance, higher than the level of the bridge, the town nestled, so shadowed by trees as to seem nothing but spires and chimneys. The stream flowed out from bubbling springs among rocks; over their jagged edges the water fell in light spray, through which rainbows shone on sunny days; along its borders were stretches of woodland reaching to low ranges of mountains that rolled away to the south in graceful sweep and outline, and were crowned now with lingering splendors of red and gold.

Lounging on a bridge within sight of mountains and sound of running water is perhaps as pleasant a way as there is of getting through a drowsy afternoon in spring; and these young idlers look much at their ease as they stand there, in the free, lazy attitudes natural to a people who live much out-of-doors and have a genius for repose. They have been talking in a depository sort of way, not having come to any subject to set their tongues going in earnest; as riders let their horses wander slowly through country lanes, before reaching a long stretch of road and striking spurs for a gallop. Their names were Betty Page, Mary Barton, and Blythe Herndon. This last young lady, it may be remarked, had been christened Emma Blythe; but the first name had been dropped, after a common Southern fashion, and she herself, except in moments of extreme dignity, scarcely remembered her right to a double signature.

"It is perfectly fascinating to watch that moss," said Miss Page, resting her hands on the twisted railing of the bridge, and peering into the water. "Doesn't it look as if the wind were blowing it behind plates of glass?"

"I can't look at it long without a shudder," said Mary Barton. "I always fancy that snakes are winding in and out through those waving stems."

"Your fancy doesn't go as far as mine," said Blythe, dreamily. "What are they but awakening serpents—these lithe darting tendrils all quivering with life, tipped with palest green, like little venomous mouths?"

"How absurd, Blythe!" cried Betty. "I'm glad I haven't a poetic turn of mind—particularly as I want some of the moss to take home."

"It's very ugly out of water."

"I don't think so. It would look lovely hanging from those tall vases by the parlor fireplace—ugly cracked things! they ought to be covered over with something. But how shall I get the moss? Mary, do look about you and see if there are any little darkies playing around here."

Mary gave the use of her eyes with cheerful readiness.

"Yes, there are half a dozen standing on their heads over yonder."

"Call one of them for me."

"I can't make out who they are, so far off."

"Never mind; just call Peter. It's a handy sort of name to exercise the lungs on, and some one of them will be sure to come."

"Wait a moment," said Mary, making a telescope of her two hands. "I think one of them is Willy Tolliver—'Civil Rights Bill,' you know."

"But I don't know. How did he ever get that ridiculous nickname?"

"How queer that Van didn't tell you! He thought it such a good hit."

Betty tossed her head. "Van and I have had better things to talk of."

"It was a good while ago," said Mary, with a slight flush, "when Willy was about three years old—pert and meddlesome as a monkey, ready to talk back to a king, if one came in his way. Colonel Dixon, from Hollywell, came to Yariba for a visit, and was staying at the Tollivers'. It was when the Civil Rights Bill was just before the public.*Colonel Dixon favored it as a measure of policy, but Mr. Tolliver opposed it, and they argued until everybody in the house was sick of the subject. One day they were playing croquet, and Willy, who was always under foot, took an unused ball and began a game of his own. In knocking it about, it rolled into the lines, and Colonel Dixon gave it a stroke that sent it flying. Willy was furious. He rushed up, with his mallet raised, crying, 'You lem my ball alone! I'll knock you down if you fools wid my ball any mo'!' The Tollivers only laughed—you know what easy-going people they are—but Colonel Dixon flushed up, and said, 'What's your name, you little rascal?' Then Mrs. Tolliver came out in her sweet, drawling voice: 'His name is Willy, but I think we'll have to call him "Civil Rights Bill."' So that's the name he has been known by from that day to this."

Betty laughed moderately. It was too great an exertion to do more. "I wish you would call him," said she; "it hurts my throat to scream."

Mary and Blythe exchanged a smile. Miss Page's selfishness was usually of this naïve character.

Willy was called, and Willy soon came, panting from his run, his lean figure showing through his ragged clothes like a dew-covered bronze. He was a lad about ten years old, with laughing black eyes, arched by eyebrows the shape of thin moons, flashing teeth, and a peculiar startled expression, due apparently to the fact that a lock of his crisp hair, wrapped with a white string, was drawn up tight from the centre of his head and pointed heavenward like an index-finger. This meant that Bill had a cold in the head; for when small darkies have colds their grandmothers say that their palates have dropped; and the lock of crisp hair tied up from Bill's crown-piece was supposed—on the principle of the potato-vine and the potato—to pull his palate up and afford entire relief.

Bill beamed expectantly on the young ladies, and Miss Page made her wishes known.

"Don't send him into the water while he is so warm," said Mary Barton.

---

*The Civil Rights Bill of 1866, for which Bill Tolliver was nicknamed, was an attempt by moderate Republicans in the U.S. Congress to guarantee some fundamental civil rights to former slaves in the South. The first federal law to define American citizenship, it also set out such basic rights as bringing suit and testifying in court and the ownership of property and indicated that the federal government would enforce these for citizens of all races. President Andrew Johnson vetoed the Civil Rights Bill, but the Congress overrode the veto on April 9, 1866.

"Lor', Miss Mary," cried Bill, "don't you be no ways consarned about me. Nothin' don't never hurt me. I'm one o'dem dat fire can't burn an' water can't drown. I stayed in de spring onct half a day, and dey pulled me out 's lively as a spring frog."

"Mind what I say, Bill!" said Miss Page, authoritatively; "go and sit down somewhere, and cool off before you go into the water. Then bring me the moss over to the stone bench. Come, girls, let us go. We've been dawdling on this bridge all the afternoon, and you know it's against my principles to stand up so long."

"Perhaps your feet are too small to bear your weight," said Mary Barton, with quiet mischief.

Betty's eyes flashed. She cultivated small tempers, as she had been told that she never looked so well as when in a passion. Any allusion to her size, however, called out real anger. The fear of being fat was, if I may so express it, the skeleton in this young lady's closet. She was a pretty creature, with a large and shapely figure, but she took no joy in her charming outlines, and never let herself be weighed. She had not heard of the Banting system, or beef and dry bread would have been "the chief of her diet;" and it was not the days of pilgrimages, or hers would have been long ago to the hill of Naxos, where the Greek girls went for the pebbles with which they repressed their blossoming bosoms.

"I was brought up to think personal remarks vulgar," said she to Miss Barton.

"What a vulgar set we must be," said Mary, frankly, "for Yariba people all talk to each other as if they were members of one family. But really, Betty, you are the first girl that ever objected to a compliment to her small foot."

This happy turn restored Betty's complacency. Two little dimples showed themselves at the corners of her mouth.

"Here we are!" said she, sinking down on the stone bench. "Now let's talk about our church-money. How much have you, Blythe?"

"Three dollars."

"I have five. I told mother I *must* have it; and there's nothing like being determined."

"So I think," said Mary Barton. "I knew when I joined the society that I would have to make what money I put into it, and *I* determined. I sent off to Altmann's for materials, and set to work crocheting sacks and baby-socks. I gave them to one of our old darkies to sell for me, and I've cleared—guess how much?"

"Two bits," said Betty, with a shrug.

"Fifteen dollars," said Mary, with calm triumph.

"Fifteen dollars! Impossible! Mary Barton, you are joking!"

"I cannot tell a lie," said Mary, laughing. "I did it with my little fingers;" and she spread them apart for inspection.

"You wonderful girl! But how you will cast the rest of us into the shade!"

"Oh, I sha'n't give it all to the church. I shall buy me a hat."

"How much you think of hats, Mary!" said Blythe, rather loftily.

"I own it. Visions of hats are forever floating about in my mind— sometimes brightly, sometimes dimly seen—

'Like silver trout in a brook;'

or according to the length of my purse. It is a positive pain to me to look shabby, Blythe."

"Why, you dear little smooth-feathered Molly Barton! you never look shabby. I have always thought you the freshest, daintiest girl in our set."

"Thank you, dear. But my old hat won't stand another making over; and I like to be particularly neat in the summer, when the army people are here."

"What are the army people to you?" said Betty Page. "If you are going to spend your church-money to dress for the Yankees, then I've my opinion of you."

"It's my own money, and I've a right to spend it as I please. I can say my prayers better if I know that the people in the choir are not criticising the top of my head. As for the army people—well, they have eyes, if they *are* Yankees. Besides, they say that nearly all the officers in both regiments are Democrats."

"And what if they are not?" said Blythe Herndon, indolently. "I am tired of this eternal harping on one string. I should think Yariba would welcome some new people. I don't believe any town was ever so dull. The men are as much alike as the four-and-twenty tailors who went out to kill a snail; and the women weary one's soul out with their inane talk about nothing."

"Well, Blythe, Mary and I don't pretend to be any cleverer than our neighbors, so our souls are not wearied out."

"Here's de moss!" interrupted a muffled voice, and Civil Rights Bill showed his black eyes from behind a great armful of dripping green. "Mos' thought de debbil was holdin' it down, had ter tug so hard to git it."

"Much obliged, Bill. You're a fine boy. Come over to our house to-morrow, and I'll give you some cake."

"How are all at home, Bill?" asked Mary.

"We'se all jes' tollerbul, Miss Mary. We'se purty much upturned on 'count o' some o' Mars' Jim's redikilous doin's. He's gwine ter take some o' dem Yankee officers to bode for de summer. Ole Mis,' she ain't so much upsot about it as mammy; but mammy says she ain't gwine to work herself to death for no *libin'* Yankees;" and Bill's emphasis seemed to indicate that she would have exerted herself tremendously had they been dead.

"Mammy knowed an ole 'ooman onct," he went on, "dat worked so hard dat she jes' dropped in her tracks one mornin' when she was fryin' batty-cakes, an' neber could have no fu'nel sermon nor nothin' pleasant, 'cause dar wa'n't no chance ter fine out if she died in de Lord."

"He will talk all day, Betty, if you encourage him."

"Here, skip along home, Civil Rights. We've had enough of you for one day. But, girls, do you really suppose it is true that the Tollivers have come to taking boarders—and Yankees at that?"

"I shouldn't wonder," said Mary. "They are very poor, I know."

"I would starve before I would do such a thing!" cried Betty.

"It would not surprise me," said Mary, with a certain solemnity in her manner, "if their coming to the Tollivers' should prove—a *wedge*."

"I hope it may," said Blythe, "I have no doubt there are gentlemen among the Yankees just as good as there are anywhere; and I should like every house in town to open to them."

Surprise and wrath struggled in Betty's eyes. Passion trembled in her voice.

"Blythe Herndon, if an angel from heaven had told me you could make such a speech, I would not have believed it!"

"They say that Yariba is almost the only town that has held out against them so long," said Mary Barton.

"And Yariba was always pig-headed," said Blythe, calmly. "During the war, mother says, the people never would believe in a defeat. And even at the last, when Lee surrendered, they would not believe it until the soldiers came home."

"And remembering Lee's surrender, you would have us receive these men?" cried Betty, passionately.

"Certainly. The war is ended; and besides, the soldiers are not to blame. They only did their duty in that state of life in which it had pleased God to call them," said Blythe, laughing.

"I suppose"—this with crushing emphasis—"that you would as soon marry one of them as not?"

"I haven't as much genius for marriage as some girls have," said Miss Herndon, with spirit, "but if you dare me to answer, I say—*yes;* and further, that I would marry any man I loved—were he Jew, Roman Catholic, Yankee, or Fiji Islander!"

"And I," cried Betty, "would throw myself into that water to-day, if I thought it ever possible that I could be a traitor to my country."

"The United States is your country."

"It is not. It is the South—the beautiful, persecuted South."

"'Little children, never let
Your angry passions rise,'"

sang Mary Barton, with the air of a peace-maker.

"Well, what would *you* do? would you marry one of these officers?"

"That is a question I will only answer to the officer. Look, Blythe, there are your father and mother."

Mr. and Mrs. Herndon approached the group slowly, walking with the lingering steps of those whose memories are brighter than their hopes. As boy and girl they had played by the spring near which they now loved to wander, recalling tenderly all the associations that made it dear; for they were still lovers, though a double score of years had passed since they first kissed each other by the beautiful waters that had seemed to murmur a blessing upon them. They stopped as they reached the girls, and Mr. Herndon lifted his hat with the fine air that distinguished him.

"What are you young ladies talking about?" he said, with courteous interest.

"Blythe has just been making a declaration of independence," said Mary, laughing.

He shook his head good-humoredly.

"That is dangerous. A true woman can no more be independent than the vine that clings to this rock."

"Oh, that vine! that vine!" sighed Blythe. "Can't my papa, the cleverest lawyer in the State, think of a new simile? Something might be made of a drooping corn-tassel."

"I am sure," said Mrs. Herndon, "your papa is quite right. I

7

don't see why any woman wants to be independent. It is so sweet to have some one to lean on. I don't believe I've so much as bought a bonnet without Mr. Herndon's help, since my first baby was born."

Mrs. Herndon had one of those sweet Southern voices over which age has no power. Hearing it for the first time, or the five-hundredth, it struck one's ear with surprise. Youth and fresh beauty seemed its fitting accompaniments. Coming from lips whose summer freshness had gone, it had an indescribably pathetic sound. Yet her smile was as sweet as her voice; and together they made it clear why her husband had loved her all his life, and had scarcely even noticed that the years, like harpies, had stolen from her all those charms that had once made a dainty feast for his eyes. He cared still less that an English classic was as foreign to her as a Greek one, and that she had a way of dating things from certain notable events in the lives of her children.

"I read something the other day," said Blythe, "that a Boston woman said—Fuller, I think, was her name—yes, Margaret Fuller: 'To give her hand with dignity, woman must be able to stand alone.' That seemed to me fine."*

"What does it mean exactly?" said Mrs. Herndon. "How can any woman stand alone?"

"There is a better line I would recommend to you, Blythe," said her father, "and to you all, young ladies. You may recall what one John Milton has said of woman:

'He for God only, she for God through him!'"

"That is beautiful!" said Mrs. Herndon, her voice falling like a soft bird-note into the air.

Blythe threw her head back with a listless impatience against the rocks. Her hand involuntarily fell into the heap of wet moss at her side, and a cold chill struck through her frame. But her soul was filled with fever and unrest.

"I wish," she thought, with sudden longing, "that I could find out the meaning and the use of my life."

---

*Margaret Fuller Ossoli (1810–1850) was a well-known Transcendentalist writer and editor from Boston, Massachusetts. Her own thorough education, her teaching, and her book *Woman in the Nineteenth Century* all made her a voice for the intellectual emancipation of women.

CHAPTER II

"Yes, We're a Good Breed in Yariba"

In its broad basin-shaped valley Yariba spread itself out, in an unabashed sort of way, like a seedy sunflower. With a happy disregard of time-honored laws, the town had been laid out at variance with the cardinal points, the streets running from north-west to south-east, bringing the corners of the houses where their fronts ought to be. The Yariba people pointed out this divergence from rule to strangers as "something different from the common run of towns," and were proud of it, as they were of everything pertaining to their village. They were by no means bishops who spoke ill of their own relics, these good people of Yariba; and, once among them, you were fairly talked into their own belief that their town was the finest on the earth's surface. This point or that might not please you; but, then, Yariba had so many virtues. You might deny the existence of any one of them, as you might chop off one of the heads of the hydra, only to have another rear itself at you.

In truth, it was a most engaging little town, with a natural beauty that the good, easy fathers who planned it had done little to spoil. Romantic lanes led from one part to another; mulberry, and catalpa, and poplar trees shaded the streets; the beaten sidewalks were fringed with long grass, that crept out into the road to the carriage-tracks—or wagon-tracks, I should say, to be exact, as Yariba carriages since the war "had left but the name" of their cushions and curtains behind, and were mostly used for hen-roosts. Flowers grew everywhere, telling their tale of the earth's fertility, like an orator's adjectives, in their wide and eloquent variety. They did everything but speak—these Southern flowers. They ran along the ground, they climbed over fences, they hung from sturdy trees in blossoms of bells, they floated on the valley streams, they rambled up the mountain paths, they sprang from between close-wedged rocks, and every wind that blew scattered their seeds on the outlying lands, until the very air had a "bouquet" as fine and subtile as that of sparkling wine.

Mingling their changeless shadows with the shifting shade of the oaks and elms that grew about them, the homes of Yariba lifted their weatherstained walls. There were few modern houses among them. They had been built for a longer use than that of the two or three generations who had lived in them. Massive, rambling houses they were, with tiled fireplaces in the finest of them, and mantels higher than a man's head, and hospitable doors always open, and generous windows fit to frame the mountain views on which they looked.

But the great beauty of Yariba was the Spring. It was indeed one of nature's wonders; an artery from her hidden heart laid bare. It was always called "The Spring," though in truth it was broken into numerous streams and water-falls, as it flowed down from the mountain where it had its source. Its culmination was at the base of a rocky hill, where there suddenly came forth a majestic swell of pure and limpid water into a stony basin it had hollowed for itself, deep enough to drown a giant, but so clear that one might fancy a child's arm could measure its depth. Then, bounding over rocks in leaps of foam, it reached a pebbly bed, and wandered away, a placid stream, ever widening, flowing gently through low meadow lands, until it turned into a canal once used for floating cotton down to the Tennessee.

Yariba people glorified in the Spring. It was something to show to strangers. It was a theme for poets. It was as useful as it was beautiful. Laundresses and lovers alike blessed it, for it served equally the one who washed, and the other who walked beside it. Every one enjoyed it with a pleasant personal sense of appropriation. Children were brought up to look on it as an inheritance. It was almost as good as family diamonds in every house.

The climate was delicious. Winter never came with whirl of wind and wonder of piling snow, but as a temperate king, with spring peeping to meet him, before autumn's rustling skirts had quite vanished round the corner. Yet there was not the monotony of eternal summer. Winter sometimes gave more than hints of power to the pert knaves of flowers who dared to spring up with a wave of their blooming caps in his face; and the peach-trees that blossomed too soon were apt to get their pale pink heads enclosed in glittering ice-caps, through which they shone with resplendent beauty for a day, then meekly died. Even a light snow fell at times; and everybody admired it and shivered at it, and said the climate was changing, and built great wood-fires, and tacked list around the doors, and piled blankets on the beds, to wake in the morning to find sunshine and warmth—and mud. But for the most part, the days, one after another, were as perfect as Guido's dancing hours.

As to the people of Yariba, they were worthy of their town: could higher praise be given them? They lived up pretty well to the obligations imposed by the possession of shadowy ancestral portraits that hung on their walls along with wide-branched genealogical trees done in India-ink by lovely fingers that had long ago crumbled to dust. They had the immense dignity of those who lived in inherited homes, with the simplicity of manner that comes of an assured social position. They were handsome, healthy, full of physical force, as all people must be who ride horseback, climb mountains, and do not lie awake at night to wonder why they were born. Their self-consciousness never took the form of self-questioning; it was rather a species of generous pride—for pride blossoms in as many varieties as if it were a seedling-bed. That they were Southerners was, of course, their first cause of congratulation. After a Northern tour they were glad to come home and tell how they had been recognized as Southerners everywhere—in the cars, shops, and theatres. They felt their Southern air and accent a grace and a distinction, separating them from a people who walked fast, talked through their noses, and built railroads.

In a town where every one had a grandfather the pride of birth was naturally very pronounced; and it was this, perhaps, that gave them strength to make a pride of poverty, when their time came to bear it.

They were proud of those qualities that the local papers—the local organs, may I say?—were fond of touching upon when they wished to give Yariba a "blow-out." (I speak with the exactness of a Pamela—that was their word.) The taste, the fashion, the refinement, the intelligence of her people—these were the songs they sung. Culture was not a word much in vogue; nor did it occur to the people that there was something to gather in other fields than they had gleaned. Their reading was of a good solid sort. They were brought up, as it were, on Walter Scott. They read Richardson, and Fielding, and Smollett, though you may be sure that the last two were not allowed to girls until they were married. They liked Thackeray pretty well, Bulwer very well, and Dickens they read under protest—they thought him low. They felt an easy sense of superiority in being "quite English in our tastes, you know," and knew little of the literature of their own country, as it came chiefly from the North. Of its lesser lights they had never heard, and as for the greater, they would have pitted an ounce of Poe against a pound of any one of them. The women of Yariba read more than the men; but the men were modelled after the heroes that the women loved.

Of course Yariba was not provincial. What small town ever was? It had its own ways, to be sure, that had sprung, like the flowers, from the soil. When a youth and maiden of Yariba promised to marry each other, they became possessed immediately of the one wild desire to conceal their engagement from all the world. They appeared no more together in public; they paid marked attention to other youths and maidens; they met at parties with a fine display of indifference; and they perjured themselves a thousand times over in their indignant denial of anything more than friendship between them. A girl was completely happy if she could send away for her *trousseau,* or at least have all her "things" stamped in the city; as, in so doing, she escaped the suspicion that always attached to one who invested recklessly in silk or linen at the Yariba shops. If forced to borrow an embroidery pattern, she was always careful to explain that she had promised to "work a band" for a friend. The number of people they could baffle or deceive became a point of pride with these mating doves. One young lady, whose engagement was not suspected until the invitations for her wedding were out, gained a fame that promised to become classic in Yariba annals; and not a school-girl in the town but vowed to do the same thing when her turn should come.

Another "way" of Yariba was to ignore, as far as giving them their title was concerned, the fact that there were any married women in the town. When a girl was married, the young men of her set went on calling her Miss Kate, Miss Janey, or Miss Ada, as the case might be; and the children of her intimate friends used the same affectionate address. Even when women who met after their marriage became in any degree intimate, their first advance toward sociability was to drop the *Mrs.*, and be to each other Miss Fannie, Miss Cora, or Miss Molly. It would have appeared a more simple matter to have dropped the title altogether, or to have given the proper one; but this was not the Yariba fashion. And whatever its origin may have been—whether caught from the negroes or the cautious habit of a conservative people who think change a mischievous innovation—it had a pretty and endearing sound, and is by no means to be confounded with the sharp abbreviations of the Northern tongue that makes "Mis' Cutter," "Mis' Overdone," and "Mis' Wicks" of the worthy women who have married the butcher and baker and candlestick-maker of their village.

Your genuine Southern provincial inhabitant has another characteristic that is probably one of all small towns—that of addressing every stranger who comes to the place, whether he be the Duke Alexis or a newly-arrived Esquimau chief, as if he were entirely familiar with all the genealogies of the best families and all the intricacies of town gossip. This was not objectionable, however, in Yariba, as it soon gave him the feeling that he was entirely at home in a large and warm-hearted family.

It was pleasant to hear Squire Barton talk about Yariba. Squire Barton was one of the Oracles of the Square. He had a purple nose, under which a cob-pipe appeared to grow, and a bushy white head, surmounted by a wide white hat. Nine months of the year he sat in a cane-bottomed chair, tilted back either against the post-office window, or under a huge tree that grew in the middle of the street, and out of which the Yariba people got a good deal of comfort as an ornament, as it was undeniably a very provoking obstruction. No one ever thought of cutting it down. Since their fathers had had sentiment enough to leave it, should their descendants be degenerate enough to destroy it, though it was a nucleus around which all the loungers in Yariba gathered, and at which all the cotton drivers from the country daily swore?

"Yes, we're a good breed in Yariba," Squire Barton would say. "The Lord didn't skimp the cloth when he made us. Don't know that we deserve any credit. Grew up in the woods. Got a free sweep to our souls. Look at a Yankee, now—shut up two-thirds of his time in a *room*—a hot, stuffy *room!* Why, his mind grows like it—full of angles, and dark corners, and cobwebs. But a Southern man's got all out-doors to grow in; so he is wide, and clear, and sweet-smelling. Liberal-minded, too—to a fault. Every man can have his own opinion, and nothing said about it. Now, here in Yariba—look at Lawyer Herndon! great man for poetry—likes Whittier—likes his slave poems—says so publicly, anywhere—just as soon say it as to roll off a log—always has said it. Twenty years ago they'd have lynched a man for that in some places I know of. But there is no Puritan blood in Yariba. *We* wouldn't have hung witches; and the man who couldn't live here couldn't live anywhere on God's green earth."

But—"in spite of all this, and in spite of much more"—the army people did not wish to spend the summer in Yariba. They grumbled over the order, and considered themselves an ill-used set of beings.

"It's a pretty place enough," said Captain Silsby, of the Third, to Mrs. Dexter, a lively little lady but recently married to the Colonel of the Thirteenth; "but, begging your pardon, so infernally dull!"

"I have heard," said Mrs. Dexter, "that the society in some of these old Southern towns is very good indeed."

"Society!" said her husband; "much we see of that! It is laughable to see the airs these Southern folks put on—and to old army officers, who would grace a king's palace"—this with an energetic frown.

"Yes," said Captain Silsby, languidly, "they seem to look down on us, you know. Pretty girls pass us on the street without so much as raising their eyelids."

"Proud little geese!" cried Mrs. Dexter, "they don't know what good times they miss! Never mind! let us be as gay as possible among ourselves. The colonel has promised me a ball-tent, and we can have dances every night. Elegant idea!"

"If there is anything that disgusts me with life," said Captain Silsby, "it is to dance with a man, with a handkerchief tied around his arm, making believe that he is a woman. And there are so few ladies in our camp, that it would have to be done at our parties. I would have given *my* vote to stay in New Orleans, if it had been as hot as Tophet."

"Soldiers can't have votes," quoth Colonel Dexter. "We've got to move like automaton chess-players, with somebody behind to do the thinking."

"Now I fancy," said Mrs. Dexter, cheerfully, "that the summer will turn out much better than you expect. The colonel and I are to board in a private family, you know, and in that way will soon make acquaintances. Yariba—I like its pretty Indian name! and you two may grumble into each other's ears, for I sha'n't listen to a word."

CHAPTER III

Mr. Tolliver's Grasping Greed

"Hark! hark! the dogs do bark,
The soldiers are coming to town;
Some in rags,
And some in tags,
And not one in a velvet gown!"

So sang Blythe Herndon in one key after another, as she rocked herself gently in a great wicker chair by the open window.

The gate, half hidden by two Osage orange-trees that grew on either side, gave a little click, and Mr. Herndon came in.

"Here is father, mother," said Blythe, in a surprised tone. "Can it be already noon? How the morning has slipped away!"

"I should think it would have dragged with you. You've done nothing since breakfast but sit in that rocking-chair, look out of the window, and sing."

"Oh, I've been dreaming delightfully! This is one of my happy days. What queer things moods are, mother! I often remind myself of one of your flannel jelly-bags, that takes the color of the stuff you pour into it."

"I don't know where you get your freakish disposition, Blythe. Mr. Herndon is just as even a man as ever lived—though he has a temper—and you are like him in the face. But it's been 'Simon says up' with you one day, and 'Simon says down' another, ever since you were a year old."

Mr. Herndon came into the room at this moment.

"Oh, father," cried Blythe, "they are really coming, aren't they?"

"They—who? I can't follow your mental processes."

"The soldiers—the enemy—the Third and Thirteenth Regiments from New Orleans?"

"Oh yes; they'll be here in a week—kits, cats, sacks, and wives."

"Wives!" echoed Mrs. Herndon, "why they've never been here before."

"There, my dear! Perhaps some new report of the charms of Yariba has reached them. At any rate, four or five ladies are coming."

"And will they live in camp?"

"I suppose so; though I believe one or two families are to board at the Tollivers'."

"So Civil Rights Bill told a true tale for once," said Blythe. "How glad I am they choose Yariba for summer head-quarters, instead of any other town on the road."

"They do that because no other offers such advantages."

"I should think they would find any of these stupid towns dull. I hope they will have the same bands they had last summer. It was so pleasant to be wakened by music, and listen to 'Annie Laurie' or 'The Mocking-Bird' from our front porch on moonlight nights!"

As she spoke an old lady entered the room. She was dressed all in black, and had the fine fragile look of a piece of Sèvres porcelain. She wore about her neck a gold chain almost as fine as a thread, from which hung a large open locket, framing the portrait of a bearded face under a soldier's cap. One noticed about her three points of light—her steel-blue eyes of a remarkable lustre, and the flashing of a single diamond on one of her nervous fingers. There was a touching dignity in her aspect. Her face had an expression of abstracted and unrested sorrow.

"What were you saying, Blythe?" she asked, in a voice faint and worn, as if to speak loudly were to compromise with her sadness.

"Nothing of any importance, grandmother, except that I was glad the soldiers were coming to make the town a little more gay."

It almost seemed that two sparks shot from the old lady's eyes.

"You are glad," said she, slowly, "and you are *my* grandchild!"

"But, grandmother, I can't feel as you do. I was so young during the war."

"You are not a child now, Blythe; and one might expect from you something more than a child's insensibility to tyranny and oppression."

"Well, well, mother!" interrupted Mr. Herndon, "Blythe didn't mean to hurt your feelings. It really isn't a bad thing for the town that they are coming. Barton says that it assures the success of our great enterprise."

The great enterprise was nothing less than an effort to run a street-car in Yariba. It had been projected three years back by some daring spirit, and one by one the solid men had taken stock in it. It had hung fire at election times, and while the crops were coming in, but in the interims it had advanced slowly. Six weeks of mud in the winter just past had given an impetus, and the rails had actually been laid in one burst of work. Now the car and the mule had been bought, the driver had been chosen, and the coming of the army people assured passengers.

"How charming it will be to have something to go about in this hot weather," said Blythe. "I'm afraid I shall get quite enervated by the luxury."

"It will be a gay summer for Yariba," remarked Mrs. Herndon. "What with the street-car and the Yankees, there will be something going on all the time."

"And besides all this," said Mr. Herndon, smiling, "Van Tolliver is at home."

"Is he, father? how long will he stay?" cried Blythe.

"Yes, he came last night, and intends to spend the summer, I believe. He's a great favorite with you young folks, isn't he?"

"Why, yes; but he is so much taken up with Betty Page that he isn't much use to any one else."

"I wonder if she will marry him?"

"I don't know. She likes him; but she is the last girl in the world to marry a poor young planter."

"Van will be a rich young planter before many years. Such a hard-working, clear-headed young fellow is bound to succeed. Let him once get a fair start, his mortgages paid off, and no girl could do better than to take him."

"I should like to know what he says to the prospect of Yankee boarders in the house."

"He probably feels it to be the disgrace that it is," said old Mrs. Herndon; "and, Lucy, I hope that neither you nor Blythe will go near Mrs. Tolliver this summer."

"Oh, mother, that is too much to ask. Think how good she was when Jimmie was born. And it isn't her fault, poor woman. You know she couldn't say anything if Mr. Tolliver chose to make the house head-quarters for both regiments."

It grew to be the general impression in Yariba that Mrs. Tolliver was a victim, and she was pitied as far as the outraged sensibilities of the people would allow.

"We are all so bound together here," said Mrs. Oglethorpe, "by so many ties of kindred, and association, and friendship, that one of us can't do a thing without reflecting on the others. Until now, the dignity of Yariba has been unimpaired, in spite of all we have gone through; and when it comes to one of our good old families falling so low, we must all feel the shock."

What Mrs. Oglethorpe said always had great weight in Yariba. Feeling ran high against Mr. Tolliver after this speech. The women held their heads more erect than usual, and looked at each other with eyes that said "the dignity of Yariba would have never been impaired by one of *us*." Old Mrs. Herndon said openly that Mr. Tolliver's grasping greed had brought it all about; and when he appeared at church, his bent figure leaning on a knotted hickory stick, his coat shiny with age, and his shoes tied with a leather string, all the ladies looked sadly on this monster of covetousness, and wondered how he could have done it. Finally, Mrs. Tolliver's friends hastened to call on her—for the double purpose of condoling with her, and of getting through a social duty before her summer guests arrived, that need not be repeated until after they had gone.

To their surprise, they found Mrs. Tolliver's eyes free from the least suspicion of redness, and her state of mind ignobly placid.

"Mis' Tolliver's affairs were getting so mixed," she said, in her gentle drawl, "that I had just lost all heart to live. Everything he went into turned out the wrong way. Rack and ruin all around, and not a dime to stop a hole in the roof. No ready money till Van's crop came in, and he writing in every letter for God's sake not to go in debt at the stores. When the Dexters asked Mis' Tolliver to take them, it just seemed as if the Lord had opened a door for us. Of course it's a trial—I don't say it isn't; but nobody can say it isn't perfectly respectable to take boarders, and it's all I could do in my position to help along. Of course Aunt Sally made a fuss about it; but I went out to her and said, 'You can just walk off this place any day you want to; but I'm going to take 'em, if I have to come to this kitchen and cook myself.' That brought her round short off. 'Lor,' chile,' she said, 'ain't you learned not to mind my tongue by this time? You go right along in the house, and don't you worry yourself about what goes on the table.' She's been as pleasant as a May morning ever since, and my mind's at rest; for there's no better cook anywhere than Aunt Sally, when she tries herself."

With these and similar details did Mrs. Tolliver entertain her guests. Their sympathy was a wasted offering. So they listened silently, and left her to the cheerful work of getting ready for her guests. She was a busy little woman, in spite of the fact that she spoke with a drawl and had long since given up the effort to say *Mister* Tolliver. She made the chambers of her house fresh and fragrant as the flowers with which they were adorned; Aunt Sally concocted a fruit-cake which, when it came out of the oven, was as large as her head in its best turban; Mr. Tolliver bought a new pack of cards; Van mended all the broken chairs; and Tom, the young son of the house, with Civil Rights Bill, set up a hitching-post in the yard for Colonel Dexter's horse, and striped it, like a barber's pole, with red and yellow paint.

Yariba was not on a railroad, and was five miles from any station. One soft afternoon, just as the sun began to tip downward, a bugle's piercing note woke the echoes in the hills around the town and startled it to sudden life. The ladies who were on the streets hurried home; small boys collected in excited groups; the shop-keepers came to their doors; the loungers about the square climbed upon shed-roofs, or stood in the high windows of the Masonic Hall, with field-glasses glued to the eyes of those fortunate enough to possess such aid; only Squire Barton remained tranquilly in his seat in front of the post-office, remarking that when fools kicked up a rumpus, wise men kept a steady head. And now a long blue line appeared in the distance, coming out from the forest's edge, and curving with the winding stream. Nearer and nearer it came. A gust of wind lifted the flag's drooping folds, and the Stars and Stripes, that the people hardly yet saw with composure, fluttered out in broad beauty as the soldiers came marching into town, while the band struck up the archaic air of "The girl I left behind me." Girls watched them from behind windows, and all the small boys collected around the drum, and kicked up the dust with ecstasy.

The camping-ground was the same that had been used for the two summers past by the regiments from New Orleans, and was a beautiful spot; a wide, level grove, heavily shaded by fine old trees. It was called "St. Thomas Hall Lot," and in its centre had once stood a military institute. Only the walls now remained; for it had been used as a small-pox hospital during the war, when the town was occupied by the Northern army, and was burned as soon as they left. Three or four graves were under one of the trees, and it was whispered that when the house was burned it held the corpses of three unburied men. Here was a hint for a fine ghost-tale; but, at least since the soldiers had been quartered there, nothing uncanny had been seen or heard.

The tents were soon pitched, and gave a cheerful picturesqueness to the dark grove. Not a Yariba boy but looked on the busy soldiers with envy; and when the preparations for supper began, they were speechless with delight, and could only testify to one another by silent nudges their appreciation of the joys of a soldier's life.

In the mean time the ambulance in which Mrs. Dexter travelled had reached the Tolliver gate; and that lady's pretty black head was thrust out eagerly, that her eyes might lose no time in taking their first impression.

She saw winding walks, rustic seats, and a wide frame-house set back from the road, surrounded by magnolia and mimosa trees; a house whose latticed porch and open doors hinted pleasantly of coolness and summer comfort. Large iron gates swung open to admit them.

"This is charming!" cried Mrs. Dexter, "this is delightful!" Nor did her raptures grow less warm as she ran lightly along the grass-grown walk, and the untrimmed rose-bushes caught at her flying veil as she passed. Mrs. Tolliver stood on the steps, and a warm welcome rose to her lips at sight of the bright young stranger, who was soon sitting in the parlor sipping a cup of tea, and glancing about her with quick, admiring eyes. In fact, those parlors were worth looking at. Faded tapestry hung on the walls, worked by fingers whose fairness no man living remembered. Old portraits of beauties in "baby-waists" smiled from under towering puffs of hair. On the tall mantel stood antique silver candelabra holding many colored wax-candles. Crossed above them were two rusty swords. The great open fireplace was filled in with branches of asparagus and althea boughs. The floor was uncarpeted, and here and there were fine, worn rugs. A chest of drawers, exquisitely carved, stood in one corner, holding heavy majolica vases.

Finally, when Mrs. Dexter was taken up-stairs and shown the two cool, high rooms that had been appointed to her, from whose windows she could see the mountains, the winding stream, and the soldiers' camp, she could not restrain longer her expression of pleasure.

"I am so glad to be here!" she said to Mrs. Tolliver, with bright impulsiveness; "to find that my lines are cast in such pleasant places for at least three months to come! We army people are so tossed about, that you don't know how much it means to me to come into such a haven as this beautiful old home of yours."

Mrs. Tolliver's heart warmed. "You must consider it your home, my dear," she said, "and try to be happy with us."

A week passed, and the Tollivers became more and more delighted with the strangers, who fell into their household ways as naturally as two children. Aunt Sally did not grumble at their presence, as many bright ribbons and red-bordered handkerchiefs found their way into her box; though nothing quite cast out a slight scorn that she felt at their liking for cold suppers, in spite of the trouble that she was spared thereby. Tom and Civil Rights Bill revelled in candy and cartridge-boxes. Mr. Tolliver saw his table well supplied from the Commissary Department, and found in Colonel Dexter an excellent partner at whist. Finally, Tom fell sick, and Mrs. Dexter, who had a medicine-chest filled with tiny phials, worked a miraculous cure with homeopathic doses; and then Mrs. Tolliver's heart was fairly won. It soon became the current report in Yariba that the Tollivers had all "gone" to the Yankees; nor were there wanting certain wise ones to say that they had foreseen all along how it would turn out, as they had expected nothing better from people who did not have firmness enough to resist temptation in the shape of a little money.

Chapter IV

Blythe Hears a Voice

Tom Tolliver was sick again; and Blythe Herndon, with a sun-bonnet on her head and a pot of jelly in her hand, ran across the street to see him, one bright morning, reaching the Tollivers' ever-open door just in time to see Mr. Shepherd's coat-tails vanishing up the stairs. Mr. Shepherd was the Episcopal minister; and as Blythe had not been to church for two Sundays past, she rather dreaded a flowing reproof from her pastor, and went into the back-parlor to wait until his visit should be ended. She seated herself in one of the deep window recesses, quite hidden behind the straight curtains, and picking up a battered volume of "Clarissa Harlowe," was idly turning its leaves, when she heard voices in the room. First the youthful treble of Civil Rights Bill, raised to a slightly patronizing pitch.

"Yessir, Tom's rele po'ly: been eatin' too many water-milions is what ails him. Der's some terrible bad boys in dis town, Mister Ellis. De oder night dey jumped inter Squire Barton's water-milion patch, an' plugged as many as fifty, I reckon, green an' ripe: et half de night, an' fotched away s'many as dey could tote. Tom didn't bring none home, but I knowed he was in de crowd, 'cause de seed was stickin' all ober his close nex' day."

"You, of course, were at home, sleeping virtuously in your bed," said a deep, amused voice.

"Me? oh, yessir! I don't like ter git broke o' my rest—it stops growin'. Mammy knowed a man onct dat slep till he growed as

23

high as de church steeple, an' neber had ter pay nothin' ter go ter de circus 'cause he jes' leaned ober an' punched a hole in de tent an' looked in. But you set down, sir; I'll tell Mrs. Dexter you are here."

A low laugh followed Bill's exit from the room, and the words, "Of all *gamins,* commend me to the African."

Blythe, in her window, liked voice and laugh. They were decided, easy, clear; of great sweetness for a man, and hinting at reserved power; so frank as to invite a child's trust, and imbued with the penetrating sympathy of fine music. The young girl, quick to receive impressions, felt that sudden thrill of recognition that comes now and then to the most guarded hearts in meeting a kindred soul. It was but a passing impression, for she was keenly alive to the awkwardness of her situation.

"What shall I do?" she thought. "It is too ridiculous to be hiding here, like a young woman in a play; but it will be still worse to make a sudden appearance, and have to explain."

The stranger took a turn up and down the room, and Blythe peeped out. There is little satisfaction, however, in gazing at any back out of marble; and all she saw was a tall form in a loose-fitting coat, and a swinging walk almost like a sailor's.

"How pretty and Southern this is!" he said; "these cool, high rooms, the old portraits, the narrow mantels, and the mahogany tables with their dishes of blown roses!" Then followed a deep whiff of satisfaction, as if he drew a breath with his face among the roses.

"How do you do, Mr. Ellis?" said a lady's voice, and Mrs. Tolliver came in, with Civil Rights Bill behind her. "Mrs. Dexter is out to-day, but she left a message for you in case you should call, and Bill does get things so mixed, that I thought I had better give it to you myself. She said that she wants to beg off from playing cards with Colonel Dexter and Mis' Tolliver this evening; and if you had nothing better to do, wouldn't you come up after tea and read German with her?"

"Certainly; I shall be most happy to do so. I am sorry to hear that your little boy is sick, Mrs. Tolliver."

"Yes, the poor child has been studying too hard." (Civil Rights Bill, in the background, rolled his eyes fearfully.) "He's got all the ambition in the world—too much, I'm sure, for a growing boy— and the hot weather coming on just prostrated him."

"I hope it will prove nothing serious, and that we shall soon see him over at the camp again."

Good-mornings were exchanged, and the gentleman went out. Blythe sprang from the window-seat, blushing like a rose.

"Why, Blythe Herndon! where did you come from?"

She laughingly explained, adding, "And here is a pot of jelly mother sent Tom. How is he to-day?"

"A good deal better, my dear. He is picking up quite an appetite. I know he will enjoy your mother's nice jelly. I always did say she hadn't her equal in Yariba for jelly."

"Do tell me, Mrs. Tolliver, who your visitor was," cried Blythe. "I had one peep at him, and noticed he was not in uniform."

"Oh no, he is not one of the officers. His name is Roger Ellis. He is a great friend of Colonel Dexter's, and his guest, I believe, for the summer. He has been somewhat out of health, I understand, and is trying camp-life to restore him. A very nice man he is. We've had him to tea a few times, and feel quite well acquainted."

"What a pleasant voice he has!" said Blythe.

"Lor', Miss Blythe!" cried Civil Rights Bill, who had been leaning in a jaunty attitude against the mantel, "he ain't no match for you; he's too ole an' ugly.

> 'He's got no wool on de top ov his head,
> De place whar de wool ought ter grow,'"

and Bill broke into song.

"You Bill! what have I told you about singing in the house?" cried Mrs. Tolliver, with wrath in her gentle face. "It seems to me, the more I talk to you the worse you get. I did think, when Mrs. Dexter came, you'd behave a little better; but no, on you go, just as much of a wild Indian as ever. Go right out of this house, and tell Aunt Sally if she doesn't whip you, I will!"

Bill moved out placidly. "He's a mighty good gentleman, anyhow, Miss Blythe," he said, with a nod. "He gave me a silver dime; an' you can't pick up dimes in every horse-track in dis town."

"And now, Blythe," said Mrs. Tolliver, impressively, "what do you think I have to tell you? Mrs. Oglethorpe has called!"

"What! Do you mean, she has called on Mrs. Dexter?"

"Yes; that's just what I mean. It came on me like a thunderclap. When Bill said she was in the parlor and had asked for Mrs. Dexter, I didn't believe a word of it. But I went in, and there she sat, all dressed up, with her lace shawl looped as an overskirt, and a spick-and-span new bonnet on; though I'm pretty sure she made it herself, for I recognized the feather. 'I've come to call on Mrs. Dexter,' she said, with that smile of hers. 'I noticed what a stylish little woman she was in church Sunday, and I think it my Christian duty to reconcile.' So I sent Bill up to Mrs. Dexter with her card, and everything went off as pleasantly as you please."

"I suppose every one will call now," said Blythe, deeply interested.

"I suppose so. Mis' Tolliver says the people in this town follow Mrs. Oglethorpe's lead like so many sheep."

"What are you two talking so earnestly about?" said a gay voice at the door. "You have the air of conspirators. How do you do, Miss Blythe? I haven't had the pleasure of shaking hands with you since I got home."

"I'm very glad to see you back, Van," said Blythe, giving her hand cordially to the tall young man who came forward. "I hope you are with us for the summer."

"Yes; unless things go wrong at the plantation."

"I have just been telling Blythe about Mrs. Oglethorpe's call," said Mrs. Tolliver.

Van laughed, and drew his mother toward him in a protecting sort of way. "Never was any little woman so pleased as this one," he said, gayly, "when my Lady Oglethorpe vouchsafed to be gracious. She went about the house all day smiling to herself as if she had heard some particularly good news that none of the rest of us had a share in."

"You needn't laugh at me, Van. Of course I was pleased; for Mrs. Dexter is just such a winning, social, lovable woman that I wanted her to have a pleasant summer here in Yariba, and not feel herself neglected. And Effie Oglethorpe, you know, when she does take anybody up, makes people all see her way."

"True, mother; she has some secrets worth learning. And really, Miss Blythe, Mrs. Dexter is all that mother says, and more—a charming little creature, a perfect school-girl in her ways."

"And Colonel Dexter—how do you like him?"

"If I were writing a novel," said Van, "I should call Colonel Dexter the Man with the Eyebrows. They are long and heavy and grizzled. One of them grows up stiff and straight as a holly-leaf, giving that half of his face an expression of perpetual surprise; and the other droops over his eye like a weeping-willow, and makes him look suspicious and fierce on that side."

"Don't you listen to him, Blythe," said Mrs. Tolliver; "Colonel Dexter is a very fine man. Mis' Tolliver says he doesn't know anybody who plays a better game of cards, when he gives his mind to it. And he just worships his wife."

"He is twenty years her senior," said Van, "and I don't think he has quite got over his surprise that she married him. To make amends for her sacrifice he is doing his best to make a spoiled child of her, and suffers the usual inquietudes of those who have such darlings on their hands."

"Mother and I have both been wanting to call on Mrs. Dexter," said Blythe, "but we have put it off from day to day, partly from laziness, I suppose, and then, you know—grandmother."

"She doesn't soften at all, does she?"

"Not the least in the world; and I believe this summer she is harder than ever, perhaps because she sees that people are not so bitter as they have been. I have never known her spirits to be so low as they are now. She is never exactly cheerful, you know, but last winter she seemed to take a little more interest in things than she had since the war; but all that is over. Mother says she looks almost as broken down as she did the first summer after Lee's surrender, when she used to walk in her sleep so much, and we were all afraid she would lose her mind. Many a night I have watched her pacing up and down the hall, wringing her hands, all in white like a ghost, until I would get so frightened I had to hide my head under the bedclothes to keep from screaming."

"Poor soul!" said Mrs. Tolliver. "If William had been spared she wouldn't have felt so. I'm sure I don't think I ever could have had them in my house if Van had been killed."

"I don't think Uncle Will's death made any special difference; it's the 'Lost Cause' grandma mourns. I can't understand it. I think it is a great deal better to forgive and forget; don't you, Van?"

"I don't want to forget," said Van, throwing back his head with a spirited action peculiar to him. "We made a good fight for our rights, and I'm glad and proud to have been in it. But as for bearing any malice against the men that whipped us—not I. The war ended, I would just as soon have shaken hands with General Sherman as with Joe Johnston."

"Or with Grant as with Robert E. Lee?"

"No," said the young man, with a sudden reverence in his tone, "for I should have knelt to Lee."

Mr. Shepherd's step was heard on the stair, and Blythe rose to go. "I told mother I should be gone five minutes," she said, "and here I've spent half the morning!"

"Let me walk home with you," said Van. "I had been intending to call at your house to-day."

Mrs. Tolliver watched the two figures as they strolled down the curving walk, until called from her agreeable contemplation by Mr. Shepherd's voice.

"Aha!" said that gentleman, "I have caught you, have I? Confess, now, Mrs. Tolliver, that you were looking after your boy, and thinking to yourself that no other woman was ever mother to so fine a young man."

"Perhaps I was," said Mrs. Tolliver with a smile; "at least I think I might think it without going very far wrong. Here come Colonel and Mrs. Dexter. Stay and see them, won't you, Mr. Shepherd?"

"I shall be glad to do so. I should like to cultivate my acquaintance with the Dexters. Evidently they are people worth knowing."

Mr. Shepherd, who was a distinguished-looking man with curling gray whiskers, had a very fine manner, and a great deal of it—so much, in fact, that it seemed to be always oozing out, like moisture from damp clay. Mrs. Tolliver felt that the Dexter star was in the ascendant, as he bowed profoundly over Mrs. Dexter's hand.

"Oh, Mrs. Tolliver," cried that vivacious little lady, "this is the most beautiful country in the world! We've had the loveliest walk—all along the Spring and half-way up the mountain. I tore my dress frightfully on a blackberry-bush—only see what a rent! I gathered heaps of wild flowers for you, but they withered before I got half-way home, and I had to throw them away. The colonel says we can have the ambulance any day for a picnic up the mountain. Elegant idea, isn't it? We will go just as soon as Tom gets well. We must have walked ten miles to-day, and I'm tired half to death."

"She walked too far, I'm sure she did," said Colonel Dexter, anxiously, to Mrs. Tolliver. "I begged her to turn back before she got so tired, but you know how wilful she is."

"I like to be tired, colonel; you know I do; it gives me a good appetite."

"You poor child, you must be hungry now," cried Mrs. Tolliver. "You ate scarcely any breakfast, and dinner won't be ready for two hours. Let me get you something. I think Aunt Sally's light-bread is just about done. Don't go, Mr. Shepherd"—as that gentleman rose—"you know there's nothing you like so well as a slice of hot bread and a glass of buttermilk." Mr. Shepherd sat down. "I can give you some of Mrs. Herndon's jelly, too, for a treat. Blythe brought some over to-day for Tom. Just look at the color!"

She held the jelly up to the light, then hurried out to prepare the luncheon, while Colonel Dexter established his wife in an arm-chair, put a footstool under her feet, inquired if she would like to be fanned, and pulled the curtains together to keep the light from her eyes.

"There, there, colonel! you give me the fidgets. Mr. Shepherd, can you tell me if the young lady we met walking with Mr. Van Tolliver was Miss Blythe Herndon?"

"Yes; they left the house together, and you came in immediately after."

"I thought her quite pretty—unusual looking."

"Blythe often produces the effect of beauty," said the minister, cautiously, "particularly in animated moments. But her face is spoiled by its dissatisfied expression. To my mind the predominant characteristic of beauty should be serenity. Look at Miss Page's face, for instance. It is the most harmonious one I know."

"Miss Page? Is she the young lady with the black hat, who sits two pews in front of the Tollivers?"

"Pardon my inadvertence; I had forgotten you had not met her. It is she whom you have noticed in church."

"She is Van Tolliver's sweetheart. I've seen them smiling at each other during prayers. I hope she is nice enough for Van. I've fallen quite in love with him myself, haven't I, colonel?"

"In a way, Ethel, in a way," said the colonel, with an apologetic glance at Mr. Shepherd, "but we all like young Tolliver. He is a fine fellow."

"He is a type of a class that in another generation we shall see no more," said Mr. Shepherd.

"Hey! eh! how's that?"

Mr. Shepherd settled himself in his chair.

"There has been in the South," said he, "a race of men who might have been the descendants of knights and feudal barons; a race so peculiar in a new country that it has been caricatured until one hesitates to use such words as 'knightly' or 'chivalric' in describing those proud and gallant men who stand out the most romantic figures in the history of our century. Blood and circumstance combined to give them the most fascinating and heroic qualities—personal daring, resolute will, and inflexible pride. Surrounded from their cradles by obsequious attendants, they gained a royal ease of manner which was matched by an exquisite courtesy. No sordid cares ever obtruding upon them, their generosity was as lavish as their hearts were warm. They held landed estates, and were princes in their own domains."

"You mean the Southern planters," cried Mrs. Dexter, beginning to understand why Mr. Shepherd's admirers said he "talked like a book;" "but were they not, as a class, rather lazy and arrogant?"

"Lazy? no, indeed! Look at their superb *physique,* gained by continued and violent exercise in the open air. No people ever equalled them in powers of physical endurance, unless the English, whom they were not unlike. Arrogant? well, perhaps a little arrogance was inevitable; but it was more than counterbalanced by an open-hearted frankness and a delightful gayety of temperament."

"Whatever his race or class," said Mrs. Dexter, keeping steadily to the subject in hand, "I'm sure Van has all of its virtues and none of its vices. Do you know, colonel, Mrs. Tolliver was telling me, the other day, that he went into the war when he was only eighteen, and fought all through without a furlough!"

"I think that fight not worth as much as the one he has made since," said Mr. Shepherd. "He rushed off to Brazil just after the war, and lived for some years in an adventurous sort of way, not dreaming that his family would ever need his services, for Mr. Tolliver was a rich man even when the war closed. He lost all his money, however, speculating in cotton, and trying to carry on the plantation under the old rule. Van came home to find the place mortgaged heavily, and ruin dangerously near. He went to work at once, and has shown the manliness and self-denial of a true hero, working all alone, as, between ourselves, his father's advice is only valuable as pointing out a road not to take. In short, Van Tolliver, like thousands of other young Southern men, a Sybarite in days of ease, has proved himself a Spartan when necessity came."

"Now it's all ready," said Mrs. Tolliver, opening the door of the next room. "I waited a little while for Bill to finish churning, so that I could give you some fresh buttermilk. The bread is just out of the oven."

She cut into the brown smoking loaf with a sharp knife, and the fresh, sweet smell filled the room.

"How perfectly charming!" cried Mrs. Dexter. "Fancy, colonel, what they would say at home to cutting into hot bread in this reckless manner."

"I wish Van were here," said Mrs. Tolliver. "He will never eat cold bread, and it seems as if he is never in the house at the right time to get it hot."

At this particular moment Van was making long strides toward the home of the young lady whose beauty was characterized by serenity; for he had permitted himself one luxury in all these years, and that was to fall in love with Betty Page.

CHAPTER V

Mrs. Oglethorpe Feels It Her Duty to Reconcile

"Dry your sweet eyes, long drowned with sorrow's raine,
Since, clouds disperst, suns guild the air againe.
Seas chafe and fret and beat and over-boile,
But turn soon calme againe as balm or oile.
Winds have their time to rage, but when they cease
The leavie trees nod in a still-born peace.
Your storm is over; Lady, now appeare
Like to the peeping spring-time of the yeare;
Off then with grave-clothes; put fresh colors on,
And flow and flame in your vermilion.
Upon your cheek sat ysicles awhile,
Now let the rose raigne like a queen, and smile."

We may be sure that it was not to one of those oasis types of whom the Bible speaks as widows indeed, to whom Herrick addressed this audacious and charming "Comfort." No; it was to some artless creature, who needed only a little decent encouragement, as the laughing poet knew, to "flow and flame in her vermilion." Her type is perennial. In Yariba she was called Effie Oglethorpe. This lady had been for many years a—very—resigned widow. Her husband had been a pleasant man, with a fine talent for spending money. She loved him and mourned him, and had never said even in her most secret soul that his loss was her gain; but she believed very devoutly that God ordered all things for the best. If her husband had been alive he would have gone to the war; with anxiety and dread weighing upon her, she would have wept oftener than smiled; and it was smiles, not tears, that had won her protection-papers from this general and that, during the four years' fight. As a widow, too, she could plead prettily for her "fatherless babes," without impairing her standing as a Southern matron in hot-headed Yariba. She could even bewitch the "Vandals" who held the town, looking very lovely in her black bonnet with the white frill inside, with no fear of tales being told an angry husband when he came home. Finally, when the end came, and bankruptcy, like a great devil-fish, drew in one Southern family after another, she remained secure. She came out of the war with slight loss beyond that of her slaves, and as her wealth had always been in goods rather than chattels, in the midst of

> Poverty to the right of her,
> Poverty to the left of her,

she flourished like a thrifty plant. In her little establishment things went on much as they had always done. "Aunt Betsey" cooked in the kitchen as she had cooked for twenty years past; and in the house Aunt Betsey's grandchildren grew up as her children had done, trained by the mistress to habits of neatness and obedience. Mrs. Oglethorpe's maid, Peggy, was a model—capable, industrious, polite; everything, in fact, that a girl of sixteen ought to be, if we except a certain picturesqueness of moral character, at which Mrs. Oglethorpe, figuratively speaking, winked. "We can't expect *everything*," she said, philosophically.

There is always a leader in a country town, and it was Mrs. Oglethorpe who timed the music of the Yariba orchestra. This was due in part to her social position and easy circumstances, but more to her tact. Men and women in her presence seemed to gain what they had lacked—the old, a touch of pink on their cheeks; the young, a softened grace; the silly, wisdom; the wise, other charms than wisdom. She reflected people like a highly polished mirror, that gives back an idealized likeness. It is not, perhaps, so fine a thing to be a mirror as a diamond; but we look at the diamond once and are satisfied, while we want the mirror, as we have the poor, always with us.

The news that Mrs. Oglethorpe had called on the Dexters acted on the Yariba people with the force of a galvanic battery on a frog's legs—a figure suggested by Squire Barton's remark, that "it made them hop like sixty." After the first shock the ladies of her own church upheld her nobly; but the Baptist congregation "wondered at it" for a week, and the Methodist sisters said it all came of being an Episcopalian, and having no real feeling about anything; although the undertaker's wife, a notable woman at prayer-meetings, remarked that she thought she should call herself, as it was only right that "our set" should pay some attention to strangers. And at last all Yariba reduced its dignity to the size of a pocket-compass, and decided to follow in the forgiving steps of its leader.

The next piece of news was that Mrs. Oglethorpe was going to give the Dexters a dinner-party, to which the Bartons, the Pages, the Herndons, and the Tollivers were invited—a report that Squire Barton confirmed in his own idiomatic way.

"Yes," he said, cheerfully, his hands in his waistcoat pockets, his linen coat flying out breezily at the sides, "Effie Oglethorpe's going in for the Yankees hot and heavy. Nobody but the Lord knows why—and he won't tell. We're invited, and we're going. I want to see the thing through. Hot weather for black clothes; but I can't let down to a light coat before the Yankees—honor of Yariba, you know. Going to wear my swallow-tail, white cravat, gloves, maybe; though I tell Molly that it doesn't make any difference about gloves. Summer-time and kid gloves are like oysters and sugar—don't go together, you know. Besides, they won't fit. I've got the real Barton hand—pudgy—can't fit a glove on it. Can any gentleman give me a light?"

Lighting his pipe, he added reflectively, "Molly takes after her mother's side. Very good people—but it was the Bartons had the blood. I'm sorry Molly hasn't got the Barton hand; it shows breed."

In no house had Mrs. Oglethorpe's three-cornered note of invitation made a greater commotion than at the Herndons.

"Dear Miss Lucy"—she wrote,—"I fear you will think I have indeed *gone over to the enemy* when I tell you I have invited the *Dexters* to dine. The way it all came about is this: it seems that Uncle James Paxton—who lives in Natchez, you know—was an old classmate of Colonel Dexter's. Running down to New Orleans just before the troops were ordered here, he met *Colonel D. quite by accident.* They shook hands, talked over old times together, and when Uncle James found out they were coming to Yariba he wrote to *me* asking me to pay them some *attention*. He said that Colonel Dexter belonged to the real *blue blood* of Boston, and that his wife had been considered one of the *beauties* of New York. I did not know exactly what to do; but when I saw that she was a church-woman—and very *high*, I noticed—I determined to *reconcile*. I called; found her very pleasant, though not to be called a *beauty here in Yariba*. I have invited them to dine next *Thursday*, and I want you, Mr. Herndon, and Blythe to meet them. Tell Blythe I have not invited any of *our* young men except Van Tolliver, as they could not *assimilate* as readily as we can *seem* to do. But there will be a Mr. Roger Ellis, a friend of Colonel Dexter's, and Captain Silsby, of the Third, both of whom have called with Mrs. Dexter, and are very pleasant men. Be sure to come—*all of you*. Ever yours,

"Effie C. Oglethorpe."

Mrs. Herndon read the note aloud to Blythe, who listened with sparkling eyes.

"Shall you go, mother?"

"No, dear; it will be too gay for me. My party days ended when Nelly died. Dear! dear! almost the last one I ever went to was at Mrs. Oglethorpe's, and was given to Nelly as a bride. But you shall go, Blythe—you and papa."

"Lucy Herndon, do you mean what you say?"

It was the grandmother who spoke. Pale and silent as a spectre, she had glided in and stood by Blythe's side a worn, wan figure, by the side of which youth and beauty had a cruel look.

"Why, yes, mother," said Mrs. Herndon. "I do think it time that Blythe should see a little more of the world than Yariba affords. These may be very desirable acquaintances."

"So that is how you feel about it!"—the thin hand on which the restless diamond flashed touched and covered the open portrait on her bosom—"and I look on every Yankee that lives as my son's murderer; their hands are stained with his blood!"

"Oh, mother, I am sure it is wrong to feel so! Why do you not talk to Mr. Shepherd about it?"

"Mr. Shepherd—and what new thing could that time-serving man tell me? That is a weak thought, Lucy—but you were always weak."

"I'm sure I was strong enough to let my husband go to the war."

"You let him because you could not help yourself. He had my blood in his veins, and thanks to that he made a good fight. I gave all I had—one son's life—and night and day I prayed—prayed as the women all over our land were doing—to a God whose promises we trusted. But we were conquered; and never, never, so long as life holds in this feeble body, shall another prayer cross my lips!"

"Mother! what are you saying?" cried Mrs. Herndon, with a half-frightened look.

"If there had been a God," she said, drearily, "he would have heard—he would have been just—he would have spared his people."

"I dare say Napoleon was right when he said that the Lord was on the side of the biggest battalions," said Blythe, flippantly.

Mrs. Herndon looked from her daughter's young, pettish face, to the fixed, cold one beside it, and sighed.

"Blythe, you wring my heart by your irreverent way of speaking. And, mother, don't you see how wrong it is to speak as you do before the child?"

The old lady seemed not to hear the question, but turned to her granddaughter. "Emma Blythe," said she, with a slight, solemn gesture, "I have something to say to you. I suppose it is natural for the young to desire a gay life. I have often heard you longing for a winter in New Orleans. I will give you one, if you will promise me to have nothing to do with these army people, no matter how eagerly your friends may take them up."

"But, grandmother, I do not understand—"

The grandmother held up her hand, upon which the diamond that seemed part of herself had sparkled as far back as Blythe's memory could reach.

"You know, Blythe, what this is to me. My husband put it on my finger sixty years ago. But I will give it to you—ah, gladly, as I sent my boys to fight for their country! It is valuable. It shall be sold, and the money is yours for a winter in the most beautiful city in the world."

"Why, grandmother!" cried Blythe, half annoyed, half touched. "As if I would let you sell your ring! No; I can give up this party. I suppose I shall live through the disappointment."

But she turned to the window to hide sudden, swift tears. "I never wanted anything so much in all my life," she thought.

"We will refer the whole matter to your father," said her mother; "what he says about it is sure to be right."

As it happened, Mr. Herndon had met Mrs. Oglethorpe in town before he came home, and had accepted her verbal invitation. Be-

sides this, he prided himself on being a man of reason without prejudices, and was really pleased at the thought of making new and
agreeable acquaintances. He was not a man to be turned from a
purpose by any woman's entreaty; and to his mother's sad little
prayer that Blythe at least should stay at home, he returned a good-
humored but firm negative. So it was decided that Blythe should
go. She felt guilty to be so glad, and considerately turned her face
from her grandmother, that she might not see its rosy blush and
smile when the important question was settled.

In the afternoon Betty Page ran in glowing with excitement.

"Have you had a note from Mrs. Oglethorpe?" she began.

"Yes; and I see that you have had one too," said Mrs. Herndon,
laughing.

"Shall you go, Miss Lucy?"

"Oh no, I am too old. I have got used to running in the ruts,
and it would jar me to pieces to get out of them. But Blythe and her
father will go."

"I think it shameful of Miss Effie Oglethorpe!" cried Betty. "Of
course every one will take them up now."

"But I suppose you won't go, of course," said Blythe, slyly.

"Perhaps I shall."

"Oh yes, Betty, I would if I were you," said Mrs. Herndon.
"Get what pleasure you can while you are young enough to enjoy it."

"*Pleasure!*" cried Miss Betty, scornfully. "I hope, Miss Lucy,
you don't think I would go for *pleasure!* But there are two rea-
sons—"

"Let us have them."

"For one thing, mamma says it will never do to slight Mrs.
Oglethorpe's invitation—that I may be left out some time when it
won't be pleasant; and you know she does give the nicest parties of
anybody in Yariba. However, I pay no attention to this," said Betty
loftily. "I am independent, and don't run after my Lady Oglethorpe,
as other folks do."

"But your other reason?"

"Is this: There is a Captain Silsby in the Third, who, I take it, is
a very conceited jackanapes, and Mrs. Oglethorpe has invited him.
He has, it seems, so fine an opinion of his own sense that he thinks
himself qualified to pronounce judgment on people of whom he
knows nothing. Tom Tolliver heard him talking to that silly little
Mrs. Dexter about Southern girls. He said that they were as pretty

as Christmas dolls, and about as wise; that he had never met one capable of shining in cultured Northern circles. What do you think of that?"

Both Blythe and her mother thought very ill of it. Southern matron and Southern maids exchanged glances that would have reduced Captain Silsby to the condition of a withered leaf had he fallen under their fire.

"What impertinence!" cried Blythe.

"What ignorance!" said her mother.

"It's only a case of sour grapes," said Betty. "Southern doors haven't opened to him as freely as he wished."

"He can't meet anywhere a more elegant woman than Effie Oglethorpe," said Mrs. Herndon judicially; "and I do hope, girls, that you will feel the responsibility resting on you, and do credit to your country."

"That is why I want to go," said Betty, with delightful ingenuousness—"to let him see what one little town can do in the way of girls."

"Will your mother go?"

"No; you know she never goes anywhere."

"Blythe and Mr. Herndon will call by for you, then."

"I was just going to ask if they would. Now the great question is, What shall we wear? Do you think my old black silk would do trimmed up with mamma's black lace, and with fresh ruches and roses?"

"Why, yes; but why do you wear black in the summer?"

"Because I look thinner in it than in anything else. I don't want them to think me as big as Mount Sano. Now, Blythe, what shall you wear?"

"I think," said she, laughing, "that I am thin enough to venture on my white muslin."

"Oh, Blythe! you know we shall go into the room together."

"Yes."

"Then don't wear white. We shall look like a hearse!"

"I haven't anything else that will do."

"I don't care for you to wear your white muslin," said Mrs. Herndon, with unwonted energy. "It is a short, shabby thing. I have always said that you should open Nelly's trunk some day. You shall do it now."

"Oh, mother!" cried Blythe, with a thrill in her voice.

Mrs. Herndon got up, and moved restlessly about the room.

"She was just your height and complexion," she said, gently. "It will bring her back to me to see you in her pretty dresses. Perhaps it has been wrong to keep them from you so long. But *she* had worn them; she had been—so happy in them."

Blythe sprang to her mother's side, and saw the tears streaming over her face.

"No, no; do not give them to me," she cried. "Let them stay where they are."

"It is right you should have them, my Blythe. It will not grieve me. Fifteen years ago, dear children, since I packed them away, and it seems but yesterday! I will get the key, and you may look over them together."

She left the room, and Blythe turned to Betty with tears in her own eyes.

"I know what a trial this will be to mother: and oh! Betty, I feel as if I hardly dare touch those things, much less wear them."

"It isn't as if you remembered her, Blythe. You were scarcely more than a baby when it all happened. And I think she would like for you to be happy in her clothes."

Mrs. Herndon re-entered the room with her bonnet on. "Here is the key, girls. You can take whatever you choose. I am going to spend the afternoon with old Mrs. Goodwyn, who is sick."

"You see," said Blythe, under her breath, as her mother left the room, "she won't even stay in the house."

"Well, that is a good thing," said Betty, cheerfully. "She can get used to the idea a little while she is away. Come now, Blythe. You know everything will be out of fashion, but I will come over and help you gore and ruffle every day this week, if you want me."

So they went to the unused room up-stairs, where Nelly's guitar, her books, her little favorite ornaments, were packed away; and, half-frightened, half-curious, they turned the key in the trunk's rusty lock, and lifted out dresses fine and faded, yellowed lace, ribbons, and dainty slippers. Trembling hands had laid them there; hot tears had stained them from blinded, burning eyes, that had thought never again to know a look of joy. But the flowers of fifteen years had bloomed over Nelly's grave; the fair, fair face was remembered only as a dream by the sister who had wept when she found it too cold for her kisses to warm. Soon Blythe and Betty breathed more evenly; ceased to speak in whispers; even laughed over some quaint bit of finery. Their time had come for life and love; the dead were to them but as pictures on the walls.

The days of preparation passed gayly and happily for Blythe. She sang over her work, and even the sight of her grandmother's face could not depress her spirits. At last something was going to happen in her life! She had long since exhausted all that Yariba had to offer in the way of entertainment—or thought she had—and had come to feel very much bored with the monotony of things. It would have pleased her to do something very startling to give the village a shock, but the meanness of opportunity had hitherto prevented. As yet she had done nothing more dreadful than to grieve Mr. Shepherd and her family by going to the Methodist church— that they called a "meeting-house"—several Sundays in succession; an exertion for which she scarcely felt herself rewarded, as she gained nothing new beyond an impression that it was less elegant to take up the collection in red-velvet bags than on silver plates. Perhaps if Blythe had been more popular among the young people she would have absorbed herself more happily in the usual interests of a girl in her father's home; but she had never been a favorite. She was called literary. This was an unfortunate adjective in Yariba, and set one rather apart from one's fellows, like an affliction in the family. Blythe's claims to the word, indeed, might not have been allowed in a Boston court, though she had read all the novels in Yariba, and thousands of old magazines; and had written the graduating compositions for half the girls in her class. There was a certain likeness between these efforts, as of a family nose or chin; still, they had won her great reputation. Then, too, she had written a Carrier's Address in poetry for her brother Jimmie, beginning,

> "Though our Greeley is dead and our nation in grief,
> And our future looks dark without hope of relief,"

which had been printed in gilt letters, and was framed by more than one admirer of native talent.

The young men of Yariba were more than ever shy of Miss Blythe after this performance, though they were rather proud of her too, and always pointed her out to strangers.

Blythe's face was pretty enough to have neutralized the ill effect of her mental gifts; but she was indifferent, and neglected ordinary courtesies. On one occasion some callers were announced to her as she was reading an interesting book. She decided to finish her chapter before seeing them, and by the time it was finished she had forgotten their very existence. Mrs. Herndon was not at home, and after waiting an hour, Jimmie Herndon strolled in, with the cheerful remark that he supposed sister Blythe had forgotten about them. She was up-stairs crying over a book! It was, perhaps, natural that those young men did not call on Miss Herndon again. Blythe had a power of sarcasm, too, that did not add to her popularity; and she was openly intolerant of mediocrity and narrowness, without suspecting her own arrogance. Never troubling herself to study character, she had an irrational contempt for most of the people of her acquaintance; and, by virtue of her high aspirations, her vague and lovely dreams, she felt herself their superior.

And yet Blythe—my Blythe—I should wrong her not to speak of her charms. The ingenuous young face—the sweet, cold, innocent eyes—the generous heart, quick to resent an injustice or a wrong—the glancing play of her bright mind—the matchless, the unsullied purity of her heart—the humility of her imperious nature before the ideally beautiful or the great—these might have won forgiveness for worse faults than she owned. So far, life, love, passion, have been to her like close-shut buds of roses of whose sweetness she has dreamed. Has the sun dawned in this fair summer's sky that is to warm them into bloom?

CHAPTER VI

A Southern Olive-branch

"Yes, madam; if I had my choice of the whole world, I would choose to live in America; of all States, just this good old Southern State that I'm living in now; of all towns, Yariba, of course; of all streets, that wide avenue fronting the sun that runs along by the church; and of all houses, the big square white house at the head of it, that my grandfather built, and lived in until he was carried out feet foremost, and that I live in to-day."

Squire Barton was speaking to Mrs. Dexter. The wax-candles were lighted in Mrs. Oglethorpe's drawing-room; her guests were nearly all assembled.

"I wonder what Cousin Mark is saying to Mrs. Dexter," said Mrs. Barton, in an aside to Mrs. Oglethorpe. "You know there's never any telling how he may break out. I cautioned him, before we came, to remember we were going among strangers; but I don't believe it has done the least good."

Mrs. Barton was a person of fixed habits. She had called her husband Cousin Mark before she married him, and continued to do so after. She spoke gently, slowly, and with great precision. She was always more or less oppressed by anxiety as to "Cousin Mark's" behavior, and when they were in company together, she spent most of the time in trying to catch his eye; an attempt he persistently baffled, from a very natural desire not to draw in his horse as he was leaping.

"How charming to meet a contented man!" said Mrs. Dexter

to the squire. "I think I must have stumbled across a descendant of Diogenes."

"I don't say I have a contented disposition," he returned, gravely; "but the man that couldn't live in Yariba couldn't live anywhere on God's green earth. We're a good breed of people here."

Mrs. Dexter's laugh rang out so gayly that the colonel, who was talking to Mr. Shepherd across the room, turned his surprised eyebrow upon her. Squire Barton caught the look, and a sudden recollection dawned in his own face.

"Beg your pardon, sir," he said, "but can you tell me where you were in the spring of '74?"

"Where was I?" repeated the colonel, somewhat fluttered by this sudden question. "With my regiment, sir; with my regiment, down at Jackson Barracks."

"Never saw such a likeness in my life!" said Squire Barton, slapping his knee. "Molly, you remember the man I hit in the eyebrow?"

Molly, sitting by the window, in a white dress, with deep pink roses in her cheeks, said, "Yes, papa;" and Mrs. Barton exclaimed, "Never mind, Cousin Mark; it isn't worth talking about."

"But, wife, there is a most extraordinary likeness. Good joke on me! Mrs. Dexter was taking Molly down to New Orleans, and some book peddler on the cars put a book into her lap not fit for ladies' eyes. I saw the title—threw it at his head. General idea was good—execution faulty. The boy had gone some seats off, and I hit an unoffending old gentleman on the eyebrow. Stiff-looking old customer. Wonderful likeness to the colonel. Explained to him, of course, that my theory of the case did not originally include his eyebrow—apologized like a gentleman, and he was good enough to overlook it. Said he appreciated the spirit of the thing, and would not regard the mere matter of detail. Very well put, wasn't it?"

Mrs. Dexter laughed again. Colonel Dexter coughed a few times, and continued his talk with Mr. Shepherd.

"You think, then, that the negro race is doomed to go under?"

"Not a doubt of it, sir," said Mr. Shepherd, calmly. "They were fitted to live in just the position they held—no other. Contact with a superior race had elevated, refined, christianized them; but left to themselves, with their irregular passions, unclean habits, and inborn shiftlessness—there's no other word for it—they'll die off, sir, year by year, just as fast as graves can be made for them."

"Inborn shiftlessness," said Squire Barton; "you're right there, Shepherd. Did I ever tell you about that old nigger of mine, Pris Dowdy? He's got a little place in the woods, where he raises a crop, and could do well, if he wanted to. He gets out of corn every year, and comes begging to me before the winter is over for money to buy corn. Last fall he varied the thing by coming just as winter set in. 'Look here!' says I, 'what's become of all your crop?' 'Lor', marster, my crop failed dis year.' 'Failed! why, there hasn't been as good a corn year since the war.' 'Dat's so, marster, but to tell you God's truth, I forgot ter plant.' Now, what can you do with a nigger like that?"

"Kill him and use him for a fertilizer," suggested Mrs. Dexter. "Elegant idea!"

The colonel frowned slightly. Even to him it sometimes occurred that his adored wife was a little flippant.

Roger Ellis and Captain Silsby now entered together. Mr. Ellis was a tall, loosely-built man, a little bald and a little gray, with humorous, kindly gray eyes, and strong, plain features, capable, perhaps, of expressing a high degree of emotion. Captain Silsby produced a more dazzling effect, with his blue coat and gold lace, his brown eyes, Greek nose, and little curled mustache. One felt instinctively that his had been a victorious career on the gentle fields where croquet-balls clash, and that he had been a hero in the ball-room strife. His manner was languid, his bow perfect. Mrs. Oglethorpe gave them seats near the window in whose recess Mary Barton and Van Tolliver had already established themselves. Mary, who had been having a highly satisfactory talk with Van about the way he spent his time at the plantation, only reconciled herself to the interruption by making comparisons very much to the advantage of the young Southerner. Captain Silsby and Mr. Ellis were pleased with her; for she talked as easily and sensibly as if she had been an ugly girl instead of a pretty one. She looked at them with innocent, candid eyes; thinking triumphantly, "Van has a shabby coat, but he is head and shoulders above either of *you*;" which was rather a hasty judgment on Miss Mary's part, after a five minutes' acquaintance.

"What a pretty woman our hostess is!" said Captain Silsby, in his lazy tones. "Would it be indiscreet to wonder how old she might be?"

"Don't you know that a man is as old as he feels, and a woman as old as she looks," said Mr. Ellis.

"But a woman is as variable in her looks as in her temper," said

Mary Barton, "so that rule won't do: a fit of the blues or a dull day will add ten years, sometimes, to a woman's face."

"Speaking of ages," said Ellis, with a smile, "I am reminded of what a queer little darkey said to me the other day. I had asked him how old he was. 'If you count by what my granmammy says,' he replied, 'I'se gwine on ten; but if you count by de fun I'se had, I reckon I'se about a hundred.'"

"That sounds like Civil Rights Bill," said Van Tolliver.

"So it was. 'My name's Willy,' he said, 'but dey all calls me Civil Rights Bill.'"

"He is a bright little shaver," said Van, "but fearfully spoiled."

"And no wonder," cried Mary Barton; "you all laugh at him, Aunt Sally whips him, and he gets no training at all."

"Nicknames play the deuce with a fellow's prospects sometimes," remarked Captain Silsby. "I knew a fellow whose chances in life were all ruined because he was called Snookery Bob."

"And they are often so inappropriate," said Mary. "I had a friend who, as a child, was so thin that her family nicknamed her 'Bones.' She grew up to be very fat, but they go on calling her Bones all the same. Ah! here is Mr. Herndon, with Blythe, and Betty Page."

Mr. Herndon stood in the door-way, and on either side a smiling vision of youth—Betty Page, all in black, a lace scarf draped over her long, plain skirt, and caught on the shoulders with roses; her arms, smooth and firm, and purely white as a magnolia petal, bare and unadorned; her piquant face was composed to an expression of dignity: Blythe in a dress of some green, shimmering stuff, brocaded with a silver thread, that clung close to her slender figure as the calyx of a moss-rose to its bud. Her hair in a golden plait encircled her small head, and gave it an air of elegance and distinction. Both girls had in their beauty an element of strangeness that seemed to the Northern eyes a foreign grace; but was only that distinguishing and indefinable charm of the high-bred Southern girl, that seems to come up like an exhalation from the earth and wrap her in its waving lines.

"Let us be a little late," Betty Page had said; "our entrance will be all the more effective." And, in truth, as they came in all the other women felt themselves suddenly pale and dim, like candles burning in a room into which the sunlight is suddenly thrown.

"By Jove!" cried Captain Silsby under his breath, "what gloriously pretty girls!"

Van Tolliver started forward, but Mr. Shepherd had been too quick for him, and was already leading Betty Page to a seat. He liked this young lady—both her serenity and her sauciness. She was pleasant to look upon and to pet, as preachers may.

Blythe sat down contentedly near Mrs. Barton, and answered abstractedly the remarks of that lady. Blythe never talked unless she liked to, and was rather proud of this indifference. To-night her heart was in a flutter of expectation. She had recognized Roger Ellis in a swift glance, and she felt only his presence in the room. It was enough to sit quietly, catching an occasional tone of his voice, and hope dreamily that he would talk to her before the evening should be over. A girl's first fancy needs as little as an air-plant to live on.

Mrs. Oglethorpe had this evening a novel feeling of anxiety as to the success of her entertainment; an anxiety such as Vatel might have felt in compounding a broth of unknown ingredients. She was glad when Peggy appeared in a much-beruffled white apron to announce dinner, where a valuable ally awaited her in the shape of certain wine-bottles that had lain for years in the Oglethorpe cellar, and whose supply seemed as inexhaustible as the cruse of a certain other fortunate widow. We may believe, however, that she drank home-made blackberry for every day, and only brought out her cobwebbed Madeira on high-days and holidays.

Blythe had the happiness of being taken in to dinner on the arm of Mr. Ellis. His first remark was to the effect that a restaurant-keeper at the North would make his fortune if he could give his customers such gumbo soup as was served at Southern tables; his second was an aside to Peggy—"No wine, please; but I should like a glass of buttermilk."

Blythe felt that these remarks fell somewhat short of the heroic standard; but his eyes and voice and smile held a fascination for her, and she waited a moment of inspiration.

Colonel Dexter was almost as desirous as Mrs. Oglethorpe that the dinner-party should go off well. It was the first olive-branch that a Southern hand had extended, and he was disposed to hug it to his bosom, not on his own account, but that his gay little wife might have a pleasant summer. He was therefore in a mood of anxious amiability. He was dressed in a full suit of citizen's clothes, as if determined to hurt no one's feelings; and he praised the South in labored terms, as if it were dead and he were repeating its eulogy.

"And what do you think of Yariba?" asked Squire Barton, cheerfully. "You've been here, going on three summers—time enough to find out an open-hearted, out-doors people like ourselves."

"Now, Cousin Mark," said Mrs. Barton, "it isn't fair to ask the colonel what he thinks of the people, for 'praise to the face is open disgrace;' and of course he can't say anything but praise right here in a nest of Yariba folks."

"My dear Mrs. Barton," said the colonel, "it might indeed be indiscreet to say all I think of the intelligence and refinement of the people of Yariba; but I may say that though I have been in many towns, I have never seen one so beautiful as this. Here, as the poet says, 'Every prospect pleases'—"

Mrs. Dexter's tinkling little laugh interrupted this flow of eloquence. "The colonel doesn't know the next line," cried she, in a stage-aside to Van Tolliver—

"Every prospect pleases,
And only man is vile."

The colonel's face became red, the younger guests laughed, and Mrs. Barton thought that Mrs. Dexter was almost as bad as "Cousin Mark."

"One great beauty of Yariba," said Mrs. Oglethorpe, "is its situation. Our forefathers couldn't have chosen a prettier spot."

"The largest springs of fresh water in the United States are here," said Mr. Shepherd; "and nothing is more natural than here, where 'He watereth the hills from his chambers, and sendeth springs into the valleys which run among the hills,' that a human settlement should early form, and afterward grow up into a type of the highest Southern culture and refinement, and one, too, eminently distinctive in its character. Not even in England can be found more individual forms of provincial life than those which existed in some of our Southern States before the war. The climate, with the languor of a lotus-fraught atmosphere—the blood of the old Cavaliers showing itself in the easy grace and fiery spirit of their descendants—the accumulated wealth of generations—all had a share in producing and establishing a form of culture noted for its subtle tastes, its native elegance, and its aristocratic tendencies."

"Culture," said Roger Ellis, easily, "that's a word worth defining. In the South it is, as you suggest, a matter of refinement, social gifts, birth, and wealth. In the North its meaning is more complex."

"It is a difference of dress," laughed Mrs. Dexter, "with the women, at least. A Southern woman of culture is sure to be a dainty and fashionable lady; but in the North culture is compatible with a frowzled wig and a poke bonnet. I remember one queer-looking lady from Boston, who used to visit us, who could out-talk all the learned professors and literary folk my father invited to meet her; but she would come into the drawing-room with her overskirt wrong side out, and would often leave the dinner-table with her napkin still tucked under her chin."

"She belonged to what I should call the semi-cultured class," said Mr. Ellis; "people of one idea. They embarrass one terribly. I was once presented to a demure-looking girl at a ball, and she covered me with confusion by asking quite loudly if I could advise her as to the best Chinese grammar, and what was my opinion of the language. I knew no more about Chinese then than I do now; but I felt that she scorned me for my ignorance, and I crept out of her circle as soon as I could. Many of our most elegant women, however, are also the most cultured. For types of Northern and Southern culture take Madame Le Vert and Mrs. Julia Ward Howe. Madame Le Vert, I take it, was the very flower of Southern culture. She spoke half a dozen languages passably, shone in a ball-room as its belle, and was gifted with a sort of divine tact that brought friends and lovers to her feet. Contrast her with Mrs. Howe, a society queen, as far as she chose to be, but beyond that a profound student, an original thinker, a poet, and a reformer."

"I acknowledge," said Mr. Herndon, somewhat coldly, "that Madame Récamier always seemed to me a woman of finer culture than De Staël."

"The old life of the South has passed away," said Mrs. Oglethorpe, who did not quite like the turn that the conversation was taking. "It only remains for the genius of a George Eliot to grasp these old materials, and from their wreck build a memorial of its glory in a Southern 'Middlemarch.'"

"What a tremendous thing the man will have to do who writes the American novel!" remarked Mr. Herndon. "He must paint the Louisiana swamps, the sluggish bayous, the lazy Creole beauties; the Texas plains, with their herds of cattle and dashing riders; the broad, free life of the West, and that of the crowded Northern cities; the skies of California, the mountains of Carolina. Where is the man who can do all this?"

"He will have to be a peddler," said Captain Silsby, "or a book-agent: no other fellow could get over so much ground."

"He was here the other day," cried Mrs. Oglethorpe; "he called himself a bread-maker. He had travelled the country over teaching his noble art—one of the lost arts, he called it. He had, indeed, found one woman in Tennessee who could make good bread; but had the salvation of the South depended on three righteous bread-makers, it could not have been saved."

"And did you have him teach you?" asked Mary Barton, with interest.

"Yes; he was such a persuasive rogue that I yielded. I kept him here two days. He used half a barrel of flour, ate a ham and a turkey, charged me five dollars, and found out the history of myself and my grandfathers. The questions that man could ask! He kneaded the dough, pale and pensive as if he had a secret grief, and gently dropped one question after another into the ear of whoever would stop to listen. I did not suspect him at the time, but now I feel that he was an author in disguise, collecting material for the American novel."

"'Gin there's a hole in a' your coats,
I rede ye tent it!
A chiel's amang ye takin' notes,
And faith he'll prent it!'"

quoted Mr. Shepherd, with a fine accent.

"And what of the bread?" asked Mary, who liked to hear all of a story.

"None of us could eat it. It is piled up in the sideboard, and I'm sure I don't know what to do with it."

"You must do as we did in Texas with the onions a neighbor sent us," said Mrs. Dexter. "Day after day a little tow-headed boy would come in making the air fragrant around him, and drawl out, 'Mam' says she don't reckin yer got no gyardin wuth talkin' 'bout, so she sent yer a mess of ing'uns.' Of course we had to return our thanks."

"In the practical shape of sugar, coffee, or canned fruit," interrupted Colonel Dexter, "my wife used to feed half the neighborhood. She let herself be imposed on by everybody—too generous by nature. I guess she has some Southern blood in her veins—"

"Never mind that, colonel; let me finish my story. We couldn't eat those onions, nor give them away; so we used to bury them in the garden and cover them over with leaves, like the babes in the wood."

"I respect this down-trodden vegetable," said Mr. Shepherd, in the midst of the laugh that followed. "Cut up raw with cucumbers, dressed with pepper, vinegar, and salt—the very look of such a dish is enough to give one an appetite."

"Or an indigestion," said Captain Silsby. "It depends entirely on the person who looks."

"And how charmingly Warner talks of the onion in 'My Summer in a Garden,'" said Mr. Ellis. "He declares it, in its satin wrappings, the most beautiful of vegetables, and the only one that represents the essence of things. It can almost be said to have a soul. You take off coat after coat, and the onion is still there; and when the last one is removed, who dare say that the onion itself is destroyed, though you can weep over its departed spirit? There is fine humor for you!"

"Warner?" said Captain Silsby, who disliked general conversation—in an aside to Betty Page—"who is this Warner? Some Southern fellow who runs a garden?"

Betty's eyes sparkled. As it happened, she had read the delightful book to which Mr. Ellis had alluded. Van Tolliver had sent it to her the year before for a Christmas present.

"Is a prophet without honor in his own country?" she asked, "or is Captain Silsby affecting ignorance because he is talking to a Southern girl?"

The captain received this shot without wincing. "No," he said, placidly, "but I don't take to books; never did. I could hit a bull's-eye in the centre before I knew my letters."

"You were born after your time. You should have lived in the Middle Ages, when the priests had all the learning, and the gentlemen hunted, fought, and signed their names with a cross-mark."

"Yes, that would have pleased me well enough, except that I should have been dead now; and I wouldn't have missed being alive to-day, and at Mrs. Oglethorpe's dinner-party, for anything the past has to offer," said the captain, with low fervor. Betty was not such a novice, however, as he supposed, and she went on eating her salad with admirable composure.

"Are you a great reader, Miss Page?"

"I am very fond of reading," said Betty, with dignity.

"I shouldn't have thought it," said the unabashed captain, looking at her with such serious sadness in his handsome eyes that she could not avoid a smile. "That's the specialty of Boston girls, you know: that's how they know so much—pick up things out of books, don't you see?"

"Oh yes, I see," said Betty, showing her dimples bewitchingly.

"I had a dreadful experience once with a Beacon Street girl, who had been educated at Vassar College. Fancy—she sent me to the Athenaeum to find out all I could about Protoplasm!"

"Hercules himself would have groaned at the task."

"A classical allusion! Miss Page, I begin to be afraid of you. But let me ask you a few direct questions, please. Are you fond of dancing?"

"Oh, very."

"And of riding?"

"Yes, indeed."

"Do you sketch, paint in water-colors, or write poetry?"

"No—no—no."

"You like the opera and the theatre?"

"Yes, though I almost never have a chance to go to them."

"I am relieved. You are neither strong-minded nor a blue, or you wouldn't confess to such civilized tastes. And let me beg of you not to read too much; it is bad for the eyes. Leave books to students, and disappointed folks, and homely women who can't be heroines. You Southern beauties ought to live your own romances. Apropos of dancing—do you glide?"

"Oh, I have heard of that new waltz-step," cried Betty, all ardor and artlessness, "but I don't know it at all."

"Let me teach it to you. It's my strong point—any fellow in the regiment will tell you so. You have just the figure for it. It's a rhythmical sort of thing—stately and slow: you can dance it to a hymn-tune. You can learn it in two or three lessons. I'll have the regimental band to play for us."

The regimental band! This suddenly recalled to Betty the fact that it was "the enemy" with whom she had been conversing so amicably. She said, in her coldest tones, "Thank you; I will not trouble you;" and turned her attention to Mr. Ellis, who was speaking.

"Ellis is a great talker," murmured Captain Silsby. "Do you ever notice, Miss Page, that a man who is reckless as to the tie of his cravat is apt to be fluent of speech?"

Miss Page made no reply; but the captain, gazing earnestly at her profile, saw a slight curl of her pretty red lip, and he registered a mental vow to teach this young lady the glide waltz, and several other things, before the summer should be over.

"What have you all been talking of, Van?" whispered Miss Betty sweetly, to her neighbor on the other side.

"Emerson, Hawthorne, and the towns about Boston," rejoined the young Southerner, briefly. "Perhaps it's just as well for you to listen as to get it second-hand from me."

"I believe Concord has been quite a home of genius, has it not?" Mr. Shepherd remarked, in a tone of easy patronage.

"Yes," said Mr. Ellis, "and the little town is disposed to give itself airs. They tell a good story of a stranger, who, after strolling half a day through its quiet streets, seized the first living creature he met—a small boy, of course—and said, 'Look here, sonny, what do you people do here in Concord?' and the youngster, in the fine shrill voice of youth, replied, '*We writes for The Atlantic Monthly!*'"

"That reminds me," said Squire Barton, untying his cravat that he might laugh freely, "of two old fellows here in Yariba—General Boxley and Colonel Plummer—vain as turkey-cocks, both of 'em. They met one day on the square, took their hats off, and began to puff their own praises like two frogs swelling at each other. The general, he said, 'My friends all tell me that I resemble Napoleon Bonaparte—in my power over men, dogged pluck, military genius, and brilliant achievements.' 'Yes,' says the colonel, thinking to flatter the general, against his turn, 'and they do you no more than justice. There is a close resemblance. For proofs, look at your campaign in Mexico, your distinguished generalship in the late war.' Then he coughed a little, and went on: 'It has often been said of me that I have a face like Lord Byron's; the general contour is the same, and the color of eyes and hair identical.' This was too much for old Boxley.

"'Humph!' said he, 'the devil looks about as much like Byron as you do.' 'Yes,' says Plummer, jamming his cane down hard; 'and I told a fool a lie when I said you were like Bonaparte!'"

Every one laughed but Mrs. Barton; she, unhappy lady, could only hope that the gentle exhilaration of the wine would prevent any one from wondering what there could have been in the anecdote Mr. Ellis had told, to remind "Cousin Mark" of the one with which he followed it.

Mrs. Oglethorpe felt all her cares at rest. Conversation flowed with undiminished gayety during the two hours from the gumbo to coffee. When she re-entered the drawing-room, it was with the air of one who led her forces from a victory.

"Take Mr. Ellis to see the roses, Blythe," said she, with her charming smile; and Blythe, feeling that Mrs. Oglethorpe had a very happy way of guessing what people would like, led the way out of the heated room into the coolness and stillness of the summer night, where June roses bloomed under the stars.

"Mrs. Oglethorpe has the finest roses in Yariba," said Blythe. "Let us gather the full-blown ones, for they will be all shattered by morning, and she likes to keep the leaves."

She took off her wide straw hat and, knotting the strings loosely, hung it on her arm.

"This will do for a basket," said she, smiling.

"This is idyllic," cried Roger Ellis; "it is like a dream. I shall grow strong and well here. To gather roses by the moon's light in a girl's straw hat, is an experience that doesn't come into every man's life."

"Is that a help in making you 'strong and well?'" asked Blythe, with mischief in her voice.

"Oh, it is the peace and quiet and simplicity of everything. It is just what I need. My nerves had begun to play the deuce with me. I was overworked—tired out. But this out-of-the-world little town, with its cool breezes and mountain views and roses, is like a strain of gentle music between two acts of a melodrama."

"Have you never been South before?"

He laughed. "Yes, more than once. But you wouldn't have gathered roses with me then, Miss Herndon."

"Why not?"

"I travelled through half the Southern States, penetrating to the most remote plantations. I rode on horseback or walked through barbarous regions where my life would not have been worth a minute's purchase, had it been known who I was. My friends and companions were found only in the negroes' cabins; and it is the one thing in my life of which I am proud, that I helped many a poor wretch to freedom who, otherwise, might have died waiting on the slow mills of the gods. So you see, Miss Herndon, twenty years ago your father would have set his dogs on me; and perhaps I am a little too frank to win the good-will of your father's daughter to-night."

"Indeed, Mr. Ellis," said Blythe, "I am more liberal-minded than you think. I should have been an abolitionist had I lived at the North; and, in fact, I think I should have been one even at the South. I have a very strong sense of justice. Oh! see—isn't this lovely?"

She held toward him a wide, firm rose, dewy, sweet, and of a dark rich color.

"It looks black in this light," she said, "but it is a beautiful crimson in the day. It is a splendid rose. 'Giant of Battles' it is called. I won't pull the leaves off; you must see it in all its beauty when we go into the house. Wait here one moment. Let me see if the 'Malmaison' bush is in bloom."

Ellis stood still for the pleasure of watching her, as she ran along the walk, tripping back in a moment, and coming toward him, like an exquisite fair spirit in the moonlight that had turned the roses dark.

"There are only buds," said she; "we must leave them to open."

"Are you mortal?" said Ellis, abstractedly, "or am I dreaming of a Southern garden and a fair-haired spirit?"

She gave him a little prick with the long thorn of a rose she held in her hand.

"Now you are more unreal than ever. You remind me of Shelley's Hymn to Pan. Do you remember the last four lines?"

"No," said Blythe, regretfully.

> "'Singing, how down the vale of Menalus,
> I pursued a maiden and clasped a reed.
> Gods and men, we are all deluded thus!
> It breaks in our bosom, and then—we bleed.'

Henceforward those lines are sacred to Miss Blythe Herndon. See, there is blood on my hand. But you were telling me what a liberal mind you had."

"Yes," said Blythe, "I am liberal about everything. Mr. Shepherd calls me the young person of the opposition, because I'm always against the common ideas of things. But about the war and its results, I think you'll find most Southern people free from ill-feeling. As Van Tolliver says, we are not sorry we fought, but we are willing to shake hands now that it is over. To be sure, there are a few people who still hold to the old prejudices—my own grandmother, for instance."

"It is hard for the old to change."

"Yes, that is it. Grandmother did not want me to come to-night. She offered me her diamond solitaire if I would stay away."

"And you resisted?" said Ellis, thinking to himself that there was no feminine grace so attractive as *naïveté*.

"Mr. Ellis," said Blythe, impressively, "when I want a thing very much, no price is too great to pay for it; and when I am determined on doing a certain thing I can't be bribed from it. If I had been superstitious, now, I might not have come."

"How is that?"

"Because," said Blythe, "when mother was fastening my dress a tear fell on it."

"And was your mother opposed to your coming?" said Ellis, thinking that Miss Blythe must be a young lady of spirit.

"Oh no, indeed; but this dress was my sister's, and this is the first time it has been worn since she died, fifteen years ago. All the evening I have been wondering how she felt and looked the last time that she wore this pretty green gown."

She shivered slightly, and Ellis glanced beyond her slight figure, half expecting to see a slighter, fairer form, clad in pale and flowing green, glide along the silvery paths.

"It is growing cool, I think," said Blythe.

"Let me go after a shawl for you."

"No, we shall be going in soon."

"Put on your hat, then. You ought not to stand with your head bare."

He handed her the hat, and she put it on, at the instant breaking into a ringing laugh. Ghosts fled. There stood a lovely blushing girl, over whose face and neck a cloud of rose-leaves was falling.

"Oh, Mr. Ellis! how could you forget?"

"How could *we* forget, you mean."

"All our labor gone for nothing."

"Never mind; there are other nights in June, and the world is full of roses."

Later in the evening, when they had gone into the house, Ellis noticed that the red rose had clung to Blythe's hair. He said to her with a quizzical smile, "I think you must let me have my rose now. You have showed me its color splendidly."

"What do you mean?"

"Didn't you know that it was in your hair? I have been admiring for some time the effect of crimson on a cloth of gold."

Blythe laughed, blushed, and gave him the rose. She rather hoped he would keep it; but just before they left, her father engaged Mr. Ellis in an animated discussion about labor-reform, and Blythe noticed that as he talked he pulled the petals from her rose, and threw them on the floor. A young girl, however, who has started out to make a hero of a man is not easily discouraged. "He is a manly man," thought Blythe, "and has no foolish sentimentalism about him. I like him all the better."

Chapter VII

A Serious Word from Van

When Captain Silsby asked Van Tolliver, a day later, to take him to call on "that handsome Miss Page," Van did not refuse, though he anticipated a rival in the Yankee captain. He knew the quick effect of Miss Betty's charms. The Pages had not always lived in Yariba, and Van had not seen her until his return from Brazil, five years before, when Betty was sixteen. Coming from a land of full-blown tropic beauties, he decided at once that God had never made anything so pretty as this young girl, with her cream-white skin and clear gray eyes. He fell in love at first sight, made love* to her at the second, and at the third had won her promise to "think about it." She had been thinking of it, more or less, ever since. She had finally allowed herself to become engaged to him; but the engagement was very much like a magician's ring, that never gets itself so much entangled with its fellows that it cannot be disengaged at pleasure. To Van, however, it rang true steel, although their nearest friends did not suspect that matters had advanced so far. Betty liked Van—she thought him a charming fellow; but she was by no means prepared to bury herself on a Louisiana plantation. "If I were thirty years old," she thought pensively, "I don't suppose it would matter much what became of me; but as young and pretty as I am, it does seem a pity to waste myself on Van."

---

*"Made love" in the nineteenth century meant only that a man had initiated a courtship and "paid addresses" to a woman.

Unconscious of his sweetheart's fluctuating fondness, Van wrote a note requesting that he might bring Captain Silsby to call, and sent it by Civil Rights Bill. The young lady was not at home, and Bill, after calling at several of the neighbors' houses, found her at Mrs. Herndon's.

Blythe and Betty had each found a good deal to say to Mrs. Herndon about the dinner-party.

"It was pleasant," owned Betty; "but you know how Mrs. Oglethorpe is; if she invited a set of pea-sticks and barber's poles to her house, she would manage to make them enjoy it."

"I am glad everything went off well," said Mrs. Herndon. "Mr. Herndon said he was proud of you both."

"You ought to see Captain Silsby," continued Betty. "He is so handsome, and rather fascinating, too. But I remembered—and I snubbed him beautifully, didn't I, Blythe?"

"I didn't notice," said Blythe, abstractedly; "he isn't worth thinking about. He is the sort of man that says sweet things to every girl he meets. But Mr. Ellis—he is a *man,* mother!"

"Yes," said Betty, "an oldish man in a baggy coat, who drank buttermilk instead of wine, and asked for it, at that."

"He wanted to compliment our Southern drink," said Mrs. Herndon, smiling.

"And suppose," retorted Betty, "that at my first dinner-party in Boston I should ask for a piece of pumpkin pie, by way of complimenting their Northern pie!"

"Nonsense, Betty!" said Blythe, impatiently.

At this moment Civil Rights Bill came in with—

"Lor', Miss Betty, I'se been a huntin' you high *an'* low. Here's a note Mars' Van done sent you."

Betty read the note and handed it to Blythe.

"*Would* you see him?" she cried, with a brave show of perplexity about the eyes, and unconscious dimples in the corners of her mouth.

Blythe laughed. "There is my writing-desk in the corner," said she; "of course you will write that your principles, patriotism, etc., etc., forbid your receiving one of the men who fought against the Southern flag, etc., etc., unless, indeed, Betty, your principles are like beauty—only skin deep."

"Principle hardly seems involved in this matter," said Betty, with dignity; "it is only a question of whether or not I would hurt Van's feelings."

"Oh, I see," cried Blythe; "you think Van would be hurt by your receiving this officer. That's a noble thought, Betty."

Betty flashed one look at Blythe, then wrote a stately little note: "Miss Page's compliments to Mr. Tolliver and Captain Silsby. She will be very happy to see them this evening." After which her remarks became irrelevant, and she went home.

"Mark my words," said Mrs. Herndon, impressively, "Yariba is *coming out!*"

"You speak as if Yariba were a widow," said Blythe, with a gay laugh.

It soon became evident, indeed, that the day of Yariba had come. After Mrs. Oglethorpe's dinner-party there was no further question of whether the Yankees should be "received." There were still left certain "irreconcilables," like old Mrs. Herndon, and in a few cases entire families poised themselves on their patriotic toes, in the difficult attitude of belligerents; but for the most part Southern doors and Southern hearts were opened. A warm hospitality was extended. The officers' wives were found to be delightful acquaintances; and as for the officers themselves, they were so agreeable that the Yariba girls began to regret what they had lost in the two summers past. Never in its old and prosperous days had Yariba been so thoroughly alive. The young men thought this a fine opportunity to display their chivalry, and vied with each other in courtesies to the summer guests; which was no inconsiderable magnanimity, as the latter had more time and money at their disposal than the home-bred youths, and could easily throw them into the shade in the elegance of their attentions to the Yariba belles.

Among these Miss Betty Page took a foremost rank. She had less to say now of the "enemies of her country." She began to make sharp distinctions between Democrats and Radicals.* Yet when Colonel Van der Meire, of the Third, a very outspoken Republican, invited her to ride, she accepted without hesitation. "It was only for the glory of the thing," she explained easily, "not that I have relapsed in my principles in the least."

Betty's principles, I fear, were nothing more than her opinions; and the opinions of the young were not unlike the icicles that hang from house-eaves—quickly formed, fantastic in shape, and easily shattered.

Van Tolliver was not an exacting lover: he liked to see his "dear girl" enjoy her triumphs, and was proud of the admiration that she

---

*That is, a distinction between Democrats and Radical Republicans.

excited; but when people began to say that "Betty Page meant to marry one of the officers," he thought a serious word from himself might not come amiss.

"After all," said he, one day, "it isn't a bad idea to announce engagements as soon as they are made."

"That's the way they do at the North," said Betty, balancing a flower lightly on her finger. "Captain Silsby told me all about it. The moment a girl is engaged everybody who ever heard of her has to be told the good news. Then she must be congratulated in great form, and her lover has to be her escort wherever she goes, just as if she were married."

"How very disagreeable!" murmured Van.

"To be sure it is! to go poking about with a bridled horse, while the free wild ones are rushing by, daring you to lasso them."

"Upon my word!" cried Miss Betty's "bridled horse," "that is a vigorous simile to come out of a lady's rosy mouth!"

"Well, well, Van, our good old Southern fashion doesn't need to be changed."

"It is all right for you to stand up for it, Betty. If the officers had known that Miss Betty Page had promised to marry Van Tolliver, it would have spoiled her fun for the summer. These army men never pay attention to engaged girls."

"What stupid times the poor things must have!" said Betty, maliciously, "particularly if their engagements are spun out like a Chinese play."

Van flushed deeply. "Betty, you are cruel!" he exclaimed. Then, coming to her side, he clasped her hands impetuously, and said, "Believe me, darling, I realize how much I have asked of you. Often, when I am alone down on the plantation, I question myself whether I have not been selfish in condemning you to these dull years of waiting. But then, I think, I will hold my dear by so light a fetter that she will never feel its weight; and when at last I can ask her to come to me, I shall love her so utterly that she cannot regret being bound. And now, understand, dear, that I trust you absolutely. I know you will do nothing to imperil our love."

"You must not listen to what people may say of me," said Betty, with wise forethought. "Remember how the Yariba detectives like to talk."

The Yariba detectives, so named by the young people of the place, were the gossipy old gentlemen who lounged about the square, and exchanged remarks that answered for wit concerning the passers-by.

"Squire Barton is just as bad as any of them," said Betty. "He sits out there by the post-office, and watches the girls' feet as they lift their dresses at the crossing opposite. And do you know, Van, when it is muddy, he actually goes over and measures the tracks, and puts down the length in a little note-book, with the initials of the girl—and then he shows that villanous little book to any of the young men who want to see it."

"Fatal book! Who knows what fortunes it has made or marred! But I sha'n't listen to any gossip about you, Betty, be sure of that. Only, my dear girl, don't you think it would be well to give them no occasion to gossip? You make people misunderstand you by the gayety and impulsiveness of your manners. Now if you could be a little more like Mary Barton. She has animation enough, but she never loses a certain gentle reserve that to me is the greatest charm a woman's manner can have."

Betty's color rose. "I think we have talked enough," she cried, "when you can tell me to my face that you prefer Mary Barton's or Mary Anybody's manner to mine!"

Van perceived that some one had blundered, and hastened to make his peace with all the lover's flatteries at his command; and his "serious talk" had about as much effect on his vivacious sweetheart as might have been expected by one who understood that young lady better. Betty was fully convinced in her own mind that her friends Mary Barton and Blythe Herndon were having a very dull summer; but, had she only known it, their lives were fuller of excitement than her own.

There are to be no mysteries in this story, and it may as well be said at once that Mary Barton had been in love with Van Tolliver all her life. Those nearest and dearest to her had never suspected her secret; but Mrs. Dexter, whose bright black eyes had been given her for something more than to see a church by daylight, had divined it when she first saw the young people together. Mary herself could scarcely have told when it had begun. She had played with Van as a child: he had been her hero ever since she could remember. When he came back from Brazil and pretty Betty Page had won him with a glance, she gave no sign. But she learned the brave lessons of hopelessness, and made of her life a sweet and serene model that all disappointed maids might do well to imitate. Not even to her own soul did she ever tell over the story of her love. She called herself Van's friend; but, until this summer, with instinctive wisdom, she had kept as much as possible out of Van's way. It happened, however, that Mrs. Dexter took a great fancy to Mary; and, as this little lady's fancies were obstinate, Mary soon found herself occupying the position of her intimate friend. This threw her a good deal into Van's company, as he and Mrs. Dexter were sworn friends and allies. She liked to visit at the Bartons; and would come tripping in on moonlight evenings with, "The colonel and the rest of them are playing cards: Van and I ran away from the stupid folks." Then she would chatter gay nonsense to Squire Barton, leaving Van and Mary to talk to each other. Or, in the fair summer mornings she and Van would call for Mary to walk; and Mary, fresh as the morning's roses, would tie on her hat, and the three would ramble up the mountain as gayly as children, while Miss Page was still sleeping. Or, Mrs. Dexter would take Mary home with her to spend the day or evening, and invite charming young officers to meet her, and give Van the opportunity of admiring the young girl's graceful self-possession and gentle dignity among the strangers with whom she was thrown.

All this was pleasant. That it was not prudent Mary had quickly decided; but, with a new feeling of recklessness, she yielded to the current, and for the first time in her life shut her eyes to the future. Nothing happened worth the telling; but her days were not so colorless as they seemed to Miss Betty, the belle.

It would have pleased Mr. Herndon to have seen his daughter much admired; but, with his mother's silent, bitter presence in the house, he could not give her the advantage of his courteous hospitality; and, as I have said, Blythe was not well enough liked by the young men of Yariba for them to make any special effort to include her in their summer gayeties. But Roger Ellis had been to see her more than once, and she was satisfied. She liked him. She said to herself with a little thrill of pride, "He is old, he is ugly, he is a Radical; but—I like him." Blythe had advanced far enough to know that the word *radical* had somewhat more than a political signification, but her ideas were vague. He had been an abolitionist— that was well and good; she would have been the same had she been grown-up enough to understand the question before it was settled. He did not go to church, but passed his Sundays in the woods reading and dreaming; that was a fine and independent thing to do! "I should like to do it myself," thought Blythe, "if only to give Mrs. Oglethorpe a shock." Blythe had certain theories about women that had been gently put down by the masculine beings of her life-long acquaintance; but Roger Ellis soon supplemented her budding views by wider and wilder ones that she readily adopted as her own. She began to think it very nice to be a Radical, and to wonder if she had not been one unconsciously all her life. For the rest, Roger Ellis charmed her as a brilliant and witty talker, and a man of wide experience in many worlds. "He is a very improving friend," she thought; "and it is pleasant to find a man now and then whom one can look up to."

And Roger liked Blythe. She was part and parcel in the summer delights. She seemed to him divinely pure, and she charmed him as a fresh opening soul always charms a man with poetic tastes—and forty years. But she was no more to him than the flowers that bloomed or the birds that sang in this holiday time; for Roger Ellis believed that the better part of his life lay behind him.

CHAPTER VIII

An Eccentric Fellow

It was a hot day. The square was deserted except for a few men who stood in the shade fanning vigorously, and some cotton wagons whose black drivers were stretched out drenched and dreaming on top of their loads. As mail-time approached, a small crowd gathered in front of the post-office, where Squire Barton sat, smoking and talking, with his chair tilted very far back, and a silk handkerchief spread over the top of his head.

"About these army men," he said; "I can't say that I think they are any great shakes. Not but what I like 'em—am glad they're here—fine thing for the town; but Lord! they're a lazy lot. Nothing to do but to lie around camp and plan how to have a good time. Why, I'll bet you, the laziest tramp that walks would be perfectly willing to be a responsible man if he could be an army officer. It would be in his line, don't you see? But they are awfully down on tramps. That stiff old Dexter says there ought to be a whipping-post for their benefit in every town. If it wasn't so hot I'd have given him my opinion, and a hint about fellow-feeling, you know."

"You had better not," said Mr. Herndon, who was standing near with Mr. Shepherd, waiting for the mail to be opened. "They say that Dexter is a fighting-cock."

"I hope they can all fight," said the squire; "that's what we keep 'em for. If they can fight as well as they can flirt, they'll do well. Upon my word, you can't turn a corner on a dark night but what you run against a pair of love-makers. Officers, indeed! I call 'em sappy boys.

Remind me of Werther—eh, Herndon? 'Sorrows of Werther,' you know. I read that book when I was an s.b.—sappy boy, you know—myself."

"Not much like Werther," said Mr. Herndon, laughing, "for however much they may sigh, and pine, and ogle, they don't blow their silly brains out at the end of a summer's campaign—not by any manner of means—not while there are 'fresh woods and pastures new,' where they can graze."

"That's so," assented the squire; "it's touch and go—love and leave. Well, the life is demoralizing, any way you take it. I wouldn't put a son of mine into the army any more than I'd put him into the Chu—" The squire checked himself suddenly and began to cough, as if he had swallowed some smoke the wrong way. Mr. Shepherd, however, only said, with immense dignity,

"There is a great deal of truth in what you say, Barton. The tendency of army life in times of peace seems to be lowering rather than elevating. It seems to be a sort of irony of fate that those who of all others have the most opportunity for reading and thought, give the least time to it. With more advantages than any other isolated class of men, they are, taken as a body, the best mannered and worst informed men among us." So saying, Mr. Shepherd passed into the office, and one of the loungers, nudging another, remarked, "They say that Shepherd has soured on the officers since Silsby cut him out with Betty Page."

"Shepherd's head is level," said the squire, severely, "just as level as if his coat-tails were as short as mine. But as for these army fellows, they can't have any bowels, you know. Now—take two lieutenants, for instance, first and second. They may be good friends, but how in thunder can the second forget that the first has the best pay, and that if anything should happen to No. 1 it's so much the better for No. 2? Stepping-stones—that's how they look on each other. Halloo, judge! want to be smoked?"

Judge Rivers, a dignified old man, stopped within range of Squire Barton's pipe, and in a moment his head was enveloped in the clouds of smoke.

"That fellow Ellis came along one day," said the squire between his puffs, "and saw me smoking the judge. You never saw a man look so astonished! Finally he burst out—wanted to know 'what the devil I was doing.' I was so full of laugh I couldn't tell him; but the judge made out to let him know that he got a friend to smoke him now and then, because it made him sick to smoke himself."

"I haven't time to stop longer today, squire," said the judge, touching his hat; "much obliged, sir."

"That Ellis," continued Mr. Barton, "is as queer a chap as ever crossed a wagon-track. They don't make his sort here in Yariba. I told him one day what Jack Hill said to Lawyer Herndon about the nigger. Didn't you ever hear that? Why, Herndon went into Jack's office one day and found him fiddling. Herndon's a great fellow for poetry, you know; so he comes out—'That strain again'—then something about the south wind over a bed of violets—'stealing and giving odor.' 'Oh, hush!' says Jack, 'that's too much like a nigger!' See? Stealing and giving odor—good, wasn't it? Well, Ellis he grinned a little, and then he said, 'Sir, the mistake you gentlemen of the South have made for a good many years back, and will make for a good many years to come, is in not knowing how to spell the word *negro*.' Said I, 'Well, for out-and-out Tom-foolishness, Mr. Ellis, that puts "the drinks on you."' I reckon he is a little cracked: there's something wrong about the fellow."

"He's a bloody Radical, that's what's the matter with him," said a voice in the crowd.

"He is a good fellow, though," said the squire, peaceably; "and as for being a Radical, now just suppose Yariba had been one of those little towns tucked under Boston's wing, what would *we* have been? Let us be thankful for our mercies."

While this talk was going on, a scene was being enacted at the soldiers' camp that had likewise resulted in the remark that Roger Ellis was a queer fellow.

Three or four young officers were in Captain Silsby's tent, tri-fling over a game of cards, bored with themselves and life on this hot July afternoon. Mr. Ellis was lying on a cot in one corner, apparently asleep. A woman appeared at the door of the tent wearing a long green sun-bonnet that concealed her face entirely. "I want ter see the colonel," said she.

Captain Silsby looked up at the sound of a woman's voice. "Come in, madam," said he, "come in."

Now, among this young man's accomplishments, he excelled in the noble art of quizzing. He gave a sign to his companions as the woman seated herself.

"My name's Roy," she said.

"A royal name," said Silsby, gravely, "and borne by one, I doubt not, graced with royal virtues."

Mrs. Roy belonged to that class that the negroes despise as "po' white trash," known in this particular region as "mountain sprouts." She was tall and jaded-looking, with a figure bent like the leaning tower, that excited continual wonder as to how it sustained itself at such an angle. Her head was very small, and was adorned with a yellow bow and a high horn comb. Her hair was tied up as securely as if each particular hair had been a convict, and was twisted round in a hard little knot like a cotton-boll. Her face was tinted in dim yellow, and the skin had a crumpled look on the forehead and around the eyes. Her nose was long, with a mole on each side of it; her mouth was drawn down at one corner, apparently by a small stick that she held between her lips, that she removed now and then and plunged into a small tin box that hung at her belt by a steel chain.

"I didn't come on no friendly errant," said Mrs. Roy, fanning herself severely with the green sun-bonnet.

"Madam, you grieve me," said Silsby. "It is so seldom that my tent is graced by one of your lovely sex, that I can hardly bear such a cruel announcement."

"Be any of you Colonel Dexter?"

"We are all Colonel Dexter. That is to say, we all, with him, represent equally the honor of the regiment. What can we do for you?"

"It's about my chickens," said Mrs. Roy. "I had as purty a little brood as anybody could a-wanted. I meant ter save every one of 'em for layin' hens, so's ter sell eggs Christmas-time."

"Count not your eggs before they are laid," said Silsby.

"Well, I kept a-missin' them chickens. I suspicioned rats; but they went so fast that I made up my mind to set up some night and watch fur the thief; and no sooner had the moon gone down than I saw two Yankee soldiers jump the fence, grab a chicken apiece, and git away befo' I could more'n holler at 'em."

"In faith, my comrades, there's a moving tale!" cried Silsby. "All her pretty chickens and their dam—did I understand you to say dam, Mrs. Roy?"

"I didn't come here to say cuss-words nor to hear 'em. What I want is pay for them chickens!"

"I am a lawyer, madam," said one of the others, "and I will gladly take the case. In the first place, you must prove that you had the chickens. To do this it will be necessary to produce their tail-feathers, which of course you have kept?"

Mrs. Roy rose, her yellow face turning a brick-dust red. "You are all a set of rascals alike!" said she. "I was a fool ter expect any jestice from a set of low-down Yankees!"

She went out of the tent, followed by a laugh. But Ellis, who had, perhaps, not been asleep, sprang to his feet and seized his coat.

"You carried your *fun* a little too far, boys. Remember, she is a woman."

"I'll be shot if he isn't going to follow her!" cried Silsby. And then it was that they all united in declaring Roger Ellis the "queerest fellow out."

He soon overtook Mrs. Roy, and spoke to her with genuine respect in his tone. "Pray excuse those young men, Mrs. Roy. They don't mean any harm by their thoughtlessness. The best thing for you to do will be to speak directly to the colonel. He is boarding at Mr. Tolliver's. I know that you will be paid at once for your chickens, and if possible the thieves will be punished. The colonel exacts the strictest discipline."

She looked at him questioningly; but not the poorest, meanest of mankind could look in Roger Ellis's face and doubt him.

"I'm sure I'm obleeged to you," she said. "I was afeard you might be a-makin' game of me, like the others. I saw through 'em the minute they begun it; but I had to sit there and stand it, for I'm a po' lone woman, wuss'n a widder, and I'm used ter hard things. Them chickens was about all I had ter count for the winter. The 'Piscopal Church gives me my house-rent, but I have ter scratch round ter keep from starving."

"Do you ever do any sewing?" inquired Ellis.

"Yes, sir, when I can git it; but I'm free to confess I ain't as good at the needle as some."

"I am needing some shirts, and if you could make them for me it would really be a great convenience," said Ellis, who had his own way of doing a charity.

"I'll be uncommon glad to make 'em, sir, and will do the best I can. Shell I come for the stuff?"

"No, do not trouble yourself; I will either bring or send it. Where do you live?"

"In the little green house behind the depot. You will know it by the hollyhocks growin' in the yard, and the shetters bein' blown off."

He lifted his hat to her as politely as if she had been the prettiest girl in Yariba; and Captain Silsby, who had watched the interview from his tent door, declared, with a shake of the head, "He's deucedly eccentric; there's no other name for it."

CHAPTER IX

Roger Ellis

Roger Ellis was a man nearly forty-five years old. Life had given him some hard lessons, but as yet he had become neither cynical nor practical. He thought, with Hamlet, that the world was out of joint; but instead of calling it a cursed spite, that he must do his part toward setting it right, he went to work with a cheerful confidence in ultimate results that nothing could shake, because it was not alloyed with any hope of personal gain. He had helped in the realization of one of his bold dreams—the abolition of slavery in America. He had been one of the devoted band whom the fiery eloquence of a Garrison and a Phillips*had stung to apparently hopeless effort in the old days when men's hearts beat in their bosoms like mad birds dashing against prison-bars. Roger Ellis, with all his young, quivering, violent sensibilities, had thrown himself into the cause, more sacred to him than the war for the Holy Sepulchre to the crusading knight. This was the happiest time of his life, for it gave him memories of which he was proud. With the war came opportunity of gaining open and honorable distinction. He enlisted as a private, but he came out with a colonel's eagles. Since the war he had indulged his tastes in various ways. He had founded an orphan asylum, collected a library, and lectured a few times on unpopular subjects. He had still been a man of action, however,

---

*William Lloyd Garrison (1805–1879) and Wendell Phillips (1811–1884) were two of the most prominent abolitionist leaders in Boston.

and had worn himself out in leading forlorn-hope bands along the rugged path of "reform." Many of his schemes were quixotic and impracticable; but of the many human souls that had appealed to him for help, none ever breathed his name without blessing it. This power of helping the weak or the oppressed, and the overflowing of his own glad vitality, prevented Roger Ellis from being a sad man, though in truth he had suffered much. In his hot-headed youth he had fallen in love in an impetuous way with a beautiful woman some years his senior, who had jilted him eventually for a suitor with more money and less enthusiasm. Since then he had loved many times, but, as it happened, never worthily. In the Northern city where he had lived, chance had thrown him among a set of people who talked more sentiment, and felt less, than any others on God's earth; a small coterie, semi-literary, semi-fashionable, who had nothing real about them except their self-indulgent bodies. Having a good deal of leisure time on their hands, they easily talked themselves into the conviction that they were blighted beings, misunderstood by the world, and defrauded by fate. But their appetites remained unimpaired, and wit and laughter shed a transitory gleam over their consolatory lunches. To see them in their full glory, however, the "conditions" must be favorable, and not dissimilar to those the canny spirits demand when they "materialize"—shaded rooms, morbid sensibilities, a good deal of faith, and but little sense of humor. Their great subject of constant discussion was "love." They tossed it about among them like a ball of tissue strips, until it was a soiled and worn-out thing. Every one was either the lover or confidant of some one else; so a chain of sympathy bound them all together, and they canvassed each other's affairs with generous openness. They talked a great deal of purity and duty, but—they defined terms. Naturally they had much to say about affinities, and they believed constancy, like human perfection, a divine possibility. The unforgivable crime in their calendar was to love more than one—at a time. A series of impassioned affairs they called growth.

Roger Ellis, to his credit be it said, in this morbid and magnetic atmosphere had never experimented with his own emotions. And now how remote all his past seemed! He was growing light-hearted as a boy in this sweet Southern town, where the people never vexed themselves about problems of life, but lived on happily and heartily as the villagers in a Provençal poem.

As the moon neared its full in the month of July, a moonlight picnic to Mount Sano had been proposed. An ordinary day-excursion had been first planned, and it was Mrs. Oglethorpe who lifted this into a higher region of romance by suggesting the mysterious beauty of the woods when the moon was at its golden full. Betty Page declared it was because Mrs. Oglethorpe knew she hadn't a picnic-complexion that she made this change of plan; but she and all her friends were delighted with it. They felt that cold indeed must be the hearts that could resist the combined influences of pretty faces and the moonlight. The truth is, Southern girls like to flirt, and have a genius for it. And never are young people more let alone in their affairs of the heart than those of a Southern town. Their parents jog on in the comfortable conviction that when the right time comes "the children" will marry where their hearts incline, as they did before them. No scheming is thought of, though a mild wish may cross a mother's heart that her girls will marry with the neighbor's boys over the way, instead of falling in love in a family at the other end of town. As for the girls themselves, expecting to marry as confidently as they expect a coming birthday, they stave off serious declarations as long as possible, and gather roses while they may; for, once married, their day is over, and they reverse nature's order by becoming caterpillars after they have been butterflies.

The young men lost no time in arranging details, and Roger Ellis started out in the afternoon to offer his escort to Blythe Herndon, going through the woods in a roundabout way, for the pleasure of watching the sunshine flicker through the leaves and breathing the sweet odors of the forest. A country road wound along the edge of the woods, like a rough, red line. As Ellis reached it he heard a sound of crying, and looking in its direction, he saw a doleful little figure. It kicked at the red clods of clay, it rubbed its fists into its eyes, it indulged itself in various exhibitions of a frank rage. Roger Ellis stopped, and waited for it. Then he gave it a cheerful slap on the shoulder.

"Why, Civil Rights Bill! what is the matter with you?"

Bill gave a jump. "Why, Mars' Ellis! you gimme as much of a start 'sif a bee had stung me."

"All the better, as it has made you stop crying. Now, what's the trouble?"

"I want ter go ter the moonlight picnic," said Bill, with a fresh sob.

"Why?" said Ellis, with a stare of surprise.

"I always like ter go whar there's folks an' carryin' on," said Bill, "an' I ain't never been to a moonlight picnic in all my born days."

"Neither have I, Bill, and I want to go. Your desire, after all, is quite natural. Well, why can't you go?"

"I meant ax Mars' Van ter let me ride one o' de mules; but now he's done gone an' got mad at me, an' I'm afeard to ax him. He sont me wid a note to Miss Betty Page, ter go wid him ter de picnic, an' tole me ter hurry so's ter git dar befo' anybody else. An' I jes' streaked it like lightnin' 'cross de short cuts, 'cause I seed dat Yankee captain's orderly ridin' along de road, an' I thought like as not he'd have a note for Miss Betty. An' I got dar fast, an' Miss Betty had done read Mars' Van's note befo' de orderly come up wid his'n. Den Miss Betty writ an answer, an' I tuk it ter Mars' Van, an' he read it; an' den he said, kind o' vexatious-like, 'Why didn't you git dar five minutes sooner, you lazy little scamp? You let dat Yankee orderly git ahead o' you, an' Miss Betty has to go wid de captain 'cause she got his note fust.' An' den I said, 'I clar ter God, Mars' Van, I streaked it like lightnin' roun' by de short cuts, an' Miss Betty she had read your note befo' dat Yankee orderly had so much as knocked at de do'.' An' den he says, 'Bill, if you don't stop tellin' lies de debil 'll git you;' an' he pulled my years, an' mammy she whupped me, an' I can't go ter de picnic, an' I donno what ter do."

Another wail finished this affecting narration, and Ellis said, "Well, well, Bill, your woes can be mended, I think. Come along with me. I'm going to ask Miss Blythe Herndon to let me drive her in a buggy to this famous picnic, and I shouldn't wonder if she were willing for you to go with us, if you can curl up in the bottom of the buggy, and make yourself as small as Alice was after she drank out of the little bottle in Wonderland."

"What was dat, Mars' Ellis?" said Bill, looking up with curious eyes.

So as they walked along Mr. Ellis told him of the little maid's quaint dreams; and Bill listened and laughed intelligently, forgetting his grievances and even their possible cure, becoming more and more convinced that Mr. Ellis was an "awful funny man, an' a powerful good one."

It was nearly sunset when they reached Mr. Herndon's, and Blythe was walking in the yard among the flowers.

"Two petitions!" said Ellis, as they shook hands: "first, may I have the great pleasure of driving you to the moonlight picnic next Thursday?"

"You may," said Blythe, laughing.

"Second: would you object to Bill in the bottom of the buggy? he wants to go to the picnic: he says, feelingly, that he's never been to a moonlight picnic; and if you don't mind—"

"Oh, I don't mind," said Blythe, carelessly, though she felt that Civil Rights Bill wriggling about in the buggy would rather take the sentiment out of things. "That is," she added, "if Bill has a clean jacket to wear."

"I can war my burial close, Miss Blythe," said Bill, with great animation. "I kin steal 'em out o' de drawer while mammy's asleep."

"His burial clothes!" cried Ellis.

"Don't you know," said Blythe, "that the darkies always like to have a clean suit laid away for them to be buried in?"

"I wonder if Mrs. Dexter would call that an 'elegant idea?'"

"I mus' go arter de cows, now," said Bill. "Good-bye, Miss Blythe. It's mighty good in you to take me along wid you. I'll take keer o' your basket, to pay fur it."

Bill ran off, and Ellis said, "So this day hasn't been lost, Miss Herndon, for we've made one person happy. I'm tremendously happy here," he went on. "Do you know that I am hungry three times a day?"

"And that is the reason?"

"Oh, it helps. And then everything is so serene, so wholesome. I really think of investing in a Southern farm and spending the rest of my days here."

"Oh, Mr. Ellis, you would be dead in a year."

"You seem to have stood it longer than that."

"I've lived on hope. Heaven knows it has been dreary enough. Do you know, Mr. Ellis, that I've never been *anywhere?*"

"Not even to New Orleans?"

"Not even there. I think I could not endure life if I did not feel that somewhere there was a great satisfying, splendid world that some day I was to enter."

"A great splendid world—yes; but whether satisfying, is another thing. Still, our Northern cities will be a revelation to you. Boston, with its wealth of tradition; New York, with its magnificent rush of life; and Chicago, that modern miracle, which fire blotted out in a night, and work, with more than a magi's art, restored in grander beauty in a year. It makes the wonders of the Arabian Nights mere commonplaces—the miracles of Palestine mere school-boys' feats."

Blythe shivered a little, but she felt that it was something very much out of the common run of things to have a friend who spoke in this off-hand way about the "miracles of Palestine."

"Oh, for a modern Homer," she cried, "to sing the rise of Chicago, and dim with its noonday splendors the rush-light glories of the siege of Troy!"

He joined in her laugh. "But the truth is," he said, "I never get used to the wonders of work, and I hope I never shall. They keep alive my love and reverence for man; a sentiment, I believe, which is to take the place of that reverence for the Unknown which has failed to do what its teachers hoped for it."

"I fear, Mr. Ellis," said Blythe, demurely, "that your natural talent is not for religion."

"I don't know about that. My natural instinct is. I drew in religion with my mother's milk. I am of Scotch descent, and my religious training was of the strictest. How well I can remember my fervent belief in a God, and my unspeakable fear of him!"

"And now?" said Blythe, quickly.

"Now," said he, laughing, "I call myself a radical thinker; and of course every radical thinker says that man can think out only forms of man—that what the Greeks called Jupiter, and the Jews Jah, or Jehovah, were neither more nor less than their conceptions of ideal manhood. Calling their God the Lord God, and the like, imposes on the multitude, who bow and close their eyes; but to the radical, who stands erect and never shuts his eyes nor his ears, they are only idols—as wretched in the realm of high thought as the South Sea idols are wretched in the world of art."

"I don't quite follow you, Mr. Ellis. I have always thought myself rather liberal in religious matters. I never believed that Cicero and the rest of them went to hell; and sometimes I have even doubted if there could be a place of eternal torment. Yet it is only logical, if you deny that, to deny heaven, isn't it? Oh, how confusing it all is, when one begins to think!"

"Yes, and that is why so few people are willing to think," said Mr. Ellis. "They call themselves conservatives. Conservatism is the creed that teaches that it is better to bear the ills we have than fly to benefactions that we know not of. It is the Song of the Shirt trying to drown the noise of the sewing-machine in the next room."

"And a radical, a true radical, I suppose," cried the young girl, "is one who has thought his way through every tangled problem—whose nature is opened out in every direction like a rose."

"That's a very pretty thought," said Ellis, looking kindly at the fair, bright face. "I don't believe any one before you ever compared a radical to a rose. But, my dear child, there are very few pure types. Every good man has some evil trait, every bad man some good; so every radical has some conservative element in his character. And we are such inconsistent creatures! If a bullet should come whizzing by us this second, I should certainly say Good God! though I might have denied the existence of a God the moment before."

"But you don't quite do that!" said Blythe, under her breath.

"No; oh no! I do not trouble myself much on this subject—life is too short. I only know that I am here in a world full of work. And I know that I need bow my head or even lift my hat to no man I have met yet—except one, and he was hanged—for having lived a life honestly devoted since boyhood to earnest efforts to make the world a better place for the weak to live in than when I entered it. But come, these are not the subjects for the hour. Tell me what you have been doing with yourself to-day?"

"One moment," cried Blythe, "what do you mean—who was the man who was hanged?"

"John Brown," said he, gravely.*

---

*John Brown (1800–1859) was an abolitionist who, as part of a planned slave insurrection, led an abortive attempt to capture the federal armory at Harper's Ferry, Virginia (now West Virginia). Captured and put on trial, Brown was hanged.

CHAPTER X

Moonlight on Mount Sano

"Rarely, rarely comest thou, Spirit of Delight!"

Van Tolliver had not "wasted in despair" because he could not take Miss Betty to the picnic, but had offered his escort to Mary Barton, as that young lady had expected, after hearing through Blythe Herndon of his ill-success in another direction.

"Which would you prefer, Miss Mary," asked Van, after her demure acceptance of his invitation, "to go in a buggy, or on horseback?"

"On horseback, by all means," said Mary, with animation; for she was conscious that her little figure never looked better than when she was riding; while—was not Betty a little too fat for this form of exercise to suit her?

The day of the picnic was without a cloud, and at sunset the party started out. As they passed through the town, the country-people, whose mules were hitched around the courthouse, stopped their "trading" and came to the door, with the clerks, to comment upon them. From every gate children and darkies gazed after them. It was a great event in Yariba.

"I hope this horse meets with your approval," said Roger Ellis, as he handed Blythe into the buggy. "It is a Yariba horse. Mr. Briggs assured me it was the finest in his stable. I don't think he will run away with us."

"Mr. Briggs's horses seem to lack that flower of all fine natures—soul," said Blythe, with a laugh; "or shall I call it spirit, since the first word is monopolized by the Yahoos?"

"But Mr. Briggs is a happy man to-day, for not a knock-kneed animal is left in his stable, and his pocket-book is plethoric with an unwonted fulness."

"The finest horses I ever saw," remarked Blythe, "were a pair of blooded Kentucky bays—superb creatures. A young fellow from California, who was visiting in this part of the country, had bought them to take home with him. It was an experience to ride behind those horses, they were so full of fire. I asked their owner once, when we were having a drive, what he would do if they ran away— for he had acknowledged he couldn't hold them—and what do you think was his answer? He pulled a loaded pistol out of his pocket, and said, 'I would put a bullet through their heads.'"

"What a man for an emergency! And you went driving more than once with the loaded pistol, and the wild horses, and the young man from California?"

"Oh yes; there was always the chance of an adventure, and that is what I have pined for all my life."

By this time they had driven out of the town and were passing the fine old places in its suburbs, at great distances from each other, with stretches of wild land between. One of these attracted Roger Ellis's particular attention, and he drew up his horse a moment to observe it. The house was a large massive brick house, with generous doorways and many windows, and round-headed chimneys that shot up above the tops of the elms and the shining gloria mundi, whose thick shadows rested on the ground in wide black masses that flowed together like waves. It was set in a square sloping on all sides to the south, and this was enclosed by a brick wall twelve feet in height, built with buttresses and surmounted by a coping of flagstones. At the north and west corners were the lodge-gates, buttressed and battlemented in unison with the architecture of the wall.

"What a remarkable old place!" said Ellis. "Who is living in it?"

"It is the county jail," said Blythe, speaking in a somewhat constrained voice. "The jail proper was burned during the war, and this property was bought at auction by the public officers."

"A jail in the midst of birds' nests!" cried Ellis, as a flock of martins rose with a whir of wings and darkened the evening sky. "But I wonder that its owner could give it up. It isn't a haunted house, I suppose? It looks as if it might have a history."

"It was deserted for some years, I believe," said Blythe, "and was finally sold by a distant heir, who had never seen the place. All the immediate family were dead. But let us go on."

Ellis saw that for some reason the subject was not agreeable to Blythe, and he asked no further questions. Touching the horse lightly with his whip, they drove along the road, that soon began to grow narrower and more steep.

"Look at the sunset!" said Ellis; "is it not worth a dull day's living to have such a sight as that at its close?"

As he spoke they were ascending the spur of the mountain, which, clothed in the sombre hue of the pines, stood like a sentinel in dark livery of green before the kingly peak now folded about with royal robes of crimson and purple. In the golden west great cloud-gates of pearl and amethyst and jasper stood apart, through which the sun shot lances of fire, like beams from some divine Titanic furnace, upon the mountain's top, where they rested in a blessing of color, making, with the blue of the dim distant hills and the purple of evening's deep shadows, "the sacred chord of color— blue, purple, and scarlet, with white and gold," given to Moses on the Mount for the Tabernacle of Divine presence. Below them, as both Roger and Blythe looked back, to lose no beauty of the picture, lay the round valley from which they had come up, its streams, like silvery veins, intersecting and giving life to woods and fields; the cross-crowned spires of its town glittering and seeming to tremble in the air; its swelling fields of plumy wheat and bearded grain waving their rich bread-promise to the land. Far to the south, in an opening among the low, blue mountains, lay an expanse of the Tennessee River, shining like a fair page of silver. The scene was one of Nature's masterpieces, where with prodigal hand she had thrown together color, form, beauty, and grandeur for earth's completest glorification.

"Ah, the kinship of kings!" cried Ellis. "See how the sun flings his rich gifts into the mountain's lap, and the mountain answers back with every hue reflected from gracious curves and quivering woods. Why should poems ever be written, when Nature speaks in such eloquent magnificence to all who have hearts to understand her various language?"

"I think that the most splendid thing about sunsets is their constant variety," said Blythe. "It is not merely that no two are ever just alike, but in each glorious spectacle there are such swift, wonderful changes as we see in dreams. Look at those clouds, now. Do they not seem to take new forms and colors with every breath? Do you know that I always sympathized with poor old Polonius? I don't think there was a bit of hypocrisy in his finding the cloud first like a camel, then 'backed like a weasel,' and finally, 'very like a whale!'"

"You read Shakspeare?" said Ellis, with a pleased look; "and do you enjoy him?"

"Why don't you ask me if I enjoy the shining of the sun," said Blythe, a little piqued at the question.

Ellis smiled. "You seem such a child to me," he said, apologetically. "And the other Elizabethan writers—are you familiar with their works?"

"Why no," said Blythe, ingenuously. "Papa found me reading in a volume of the British drama one day, and he took the book away, saying that those plays were not fit reading for a lady."

"The happy fortune of being a woman," said Ellis, "ought not to deprive any one of the opportunity of appreciating some of the finest things in the English tongue. You ought to study an age of which Shakspeare is king, and understand that greatest man better by knowing his contemporaries. They were giants whom none have touched, though many have made for themselves paths beside their footsteps. In reading them you will find grace, fire, passion; passages to make you weep, and such as will make you smile with mere pleasure at their beauty; and further, you will find your very feeling for the beauty of words increased. Of course it is not necessary to go through them all."

"Tell me some of the finest," said Blythe, "and I will read them first."

"Oh! I haven't them at my fingers' ends. But I will make out a list for you of those you may read entire, and mark selections from others that would be as unintelligible to you as operatic music is uninteresting to me, except for the 'airs' that come in from time to time. You will like Ben Jonson best of all. He had a rich mine of soul—rare Ben—and from its depths he drew the gold of virtue, the dark copper of vice, the varied jewel-forms of beauty. In him, as in Shakspeare, you find the essence of human nature, humanity in its heights and depths, that can never be studied too long or too tenderly."

"There are three volumes of old English plays on the top shelf of the bookcase in the library," said Blythe, "with a lot of other books, that I've been forbidden to touch ever since I can remember."

"Poor child! And did you never disobey orders?"

"Once only. It had rained for a week, and I had read everything I could lay my hands on. I was so bored that I was desperate; and one day I stood on a chair, reached up to the top shelf, and took down the first book my hand touched. What do you think it was?"

"I am a Yankee—but I can't guess."

"Tom Jones," said Blythe, lowering her voice. "I took it to my room, locked the door, and plunged into it. But one day when papa and mamma were out, I went down to the sitting-room to read it by the fire. They came home suddenly, and I had only time to thrust it under the sofa-cushion. Now, if you can believe it, I forgot all about that book and left it there. It was found the next morning before breakfast, and there was a scene! Papa scolded, mamma cried, I cried, and it ended by the book being thrown into the kitchen fire. To this day I have never known whether Tom married Sophia!"

Ellis laughed heartily, with a lively remembrance of Mr. Herndon's fine and gentle manner.

"Papa never liked me to read any novels," said Blythe; "and, indeed, he was strict in every way. As a child, I used to think him unjust, and we were all terribly afraid of him. I don't know why; for he was not often angry, and hardly ever punished us. But papa is a very impressive man;" and Blythe gave a light laugh. "Once, I remember, when I was a very little girl, I was studying my spelling-lesson, and I came to the long, hard word 'abolitionist.' I spelled it out, syllable by syllable, and then asked my father its meaning. 'It is a name for a Yankee rascal,' he said, 'who believes that a negro is as good as a white man, and who would set all our slaves free if he could get a chance.' This was such a new idea to me that I stopped to think about it. At last I stunned my family by the remark, 'Well, I think I am an abolitionist. I don't see that we have any right to make slaves of people because they have black skins, any more than because they have crooked noses.' Then I saw my courtly papa in a white heat. He did not use many words to tell me I was a young idiot, who would come to some very bad end unless I restrained the vanity of having opinions opposite to those of older and wiser folks; but what he did say can only be likened to the whipping that a certain father once gave his son when he saw the salamander; and it impressed the occasion quite as faithfully in my memory."

"It was your sweet, pure, true nature that spoke," said Ellis, feeling a strong inclination to give Blythe an appreciative kiss; "but tell me, did you ever change?"

"Oh! I put the subject out of my mind; and then, of course, when the war came I had to take the side of my people. The question of slavery was not the only one involved, you know; and even with that outsiders had no right to meddle. Oh, pardon me!" cried Blythe, with her quick blush. "I forgot—"

"That I was one of the outsiders? Why, I like your frankness, my dear Miss Herndon. Besides, you were too young to understand the questions at issue."

"I don't know about that. I was always a strong believer in State's rights and secession. This country is too large for a single government."

"I see," said Ellis, with a smile, "that you have listened intelligently to the political talk of your father and his friends."

"I am not a chameleon," said Blythe, proudly.

"No," he said, "or you could not be near me without taking what's the color of loyalty."

"True blue, I suppose?"

"Or that of the life-blood."

> "'And like a lobster boiled, alack!
> I'll blush with love for Union Jack!'

if I know you much longer," murmured Miss Blythe.

"So you read Hudibras, too! Bless me, child! aren't you wasted in Yariba?"

"I am wasted with pining to be somewhere else. Oh, for a prince and a flying horse!"

"They will come," said Ellis; and something almost like sadness stole into his voice. He did not for a moment fancy himself the prince on the flying horse; but it did occur to him that it would be "pretty, though a plague," to see Blythe's face when her prince should first take her in his arms. What a face it was! a little cold and sad, perhaps, in repose, but with what a charm of swift blushes and changing expression!

The road wound along, "up-hill all the way," and the surroundings grew milder and more beautiful. Little mountain streams sprang to meet them with a gurgle of welcome. Rhododendrons stretched across the road, and Blythe gathered handful after handful of the leaves, bruising them for their sweetness and throwing them away. At last the road, that had been narrowing gradually, like a prima

81

donna's sustained note, dwindled to a narrow foot-path, and they got out of the buggy. An army wagon had been sent on in advance, the soldiers busied themselves in taking charge of all the horses of the party. Mary Barton and Van Tolliver had just dismounted— Mary brilliantly pretty in her close black habit, and Van as gay and debonair as if he were not wondering how far Betty Page's flirting propensities would carry her under the favoring influences of the moonlight.

"We are the last of the party," said Mary. "We will find the others on the flat rock on top of the mountain. Shall we lead the way?"

Blythe and Mr. Ellis followed slowly, their senses on the alert for enjoyment. Rocks, streams, ferns, mosses, and giant forest-trees were mingled here in a wild union of strength and beauty. There were fresh and delicate woody smells, and lonely, lovely bird-notes rang high above the sound of falling water, that hurried through its rugged chambers to the spring in the valley below. The gray twilight began to be pierced by sharp darts of silver, like mysterious thrills of life stinging through a half-torpid soul. Light laughter soon broke through nature's musical silence, and they came upon their friends grouped in various attitudes of picturesqueness about the mountain's top. Then for a while there was a confusion of voices, until Mrs. Oglethorpe made a gesture for silence, and commanded Blythe Herndon to tell the legend of Mount Sano, that none of the strangers had ever heard. And Blythe, who was wrapped in a scarlet cloak, leaned close upon the indented rock, and, fixing her eyes on the vague, vast mountains dimly defined against the moon's gold, told the legend, almost like a Corsican improvisatrice chanting a *ballata*.

"Long ago an Indian chieftain made his home upon this mountain—the lesser hills his hunting-grounds. Monte was his dark-eyed daughter, whom many suitors came to woo. Two of the boldest outstripped all others; but to one she gave promises and love, to the other refusal and scorn. He, stung by jealousy to madness, swore a fearful oath that he would yet win Monte, the dark-eyed maid. Then he summoned to his aid all evil souls. One gave him fiery eloquence, another giant strength, and a third the wild beauty of the beautiful lost gods. One day, when the wind blew high, he met the Indian maid, and beguiled her to a lonely spot, where the high trees kissed the clouds; and here he stretched his arms to her, and wooed her with such rushing fire that the heavens darkened and the earth seemed slipping away. Then he assailed her with threats, and fear seized the soul of the maiden, and almost she consented to his fierce will; when from a hidden place in the arching rocks behind her came a whisper low and strong as distant thunder—'*Monte, say No!—Monte, say No!*' Strength came to her with that deep murmur, for the Great Spirit himself had come to her aid. 'No!' she cried, in a voice that rang through the forest like the stroke of steel on steel, and the winds ceased to rage, and the warrior with a cry of wrath fled from the sight of her face, and neither in the council, nor by the wigwam fire, nor on the hunting-ground nor battle-field, was he ever seen again of man."

Ellis had watched Blythe with amazement. "What an actress the child is!" he thought; "or is it unconsciousness—that pose against the rock, the musical monotone, the abstracted gaze? Miss Blythe, you're a study!"

"The legend disappoints our notions of Indian vengeance in having no bloody sequel," remarked Mrs. Oglethorpe; "but all its romance is preserved in the name it has given to the mountain— *Monte Sano.*"

"I don't altogether like it, you know," said Captain Silsby, "for I don't believe the young ladies of Yariba need any prompting to say No."

Whereupon Betty Page, breaking a large leaf from a bush near by, fanned the captain with an air of saucy solicitude not wholly agreeable to one young man of the company.

They had supper on the flat rock, and with champagne, cold chicken, and jokes, in which a little wit went a great way, filled up the next hour. Civil Rights Bill was treated to his first glass of champagne, and he entertained the company with the story of the Tar-Baby,* and joined boldly in the songs that were sung. They wandered about in groups of twos and threes, while the moonlight bathed everything in floods of ethereal yellow, as if some gay angel were holding a buttercup under the mountain's chin. Everybody declared this the most unique and delicious picnic of any season; and finally it brought to Blythe Herndon what she had wanted all her life—an adventure. It was due to Civil Rights Bill, for whom

---

*The Tar Baby is a character in one of the most famous Brer Rabbit stories, which drew upon an African American tradition of animal trickster folktales.

the excitement and champagne had been too much. He was sleeping composedly on Mr. Ellis's feet, as Mr. Briggs's staid horse was jogging homeward, when—what dream came to him? That I cannot tell, but he gave a cry as wild as the Indian lover's howl of rage, and jumping up as if the bottom of the buggy had been a rearing horse, he sprang out into the road. Mr. Briggs's horse now proved himself the possessor of more spirit than he had been given credit for, by running away, upturning the buggy against a stump, throwing out Mr. Ellis and Blythe on opposite sides, and dashing off to town unimpeded by aught but some fragments of harness. There was a crash as if the world were coming to an end; for Bill, with brilliant thrift, had gathered up the empty wine-bottles to sell in town; and they broke with a tremendous clatter about the ears of the dislodged pair.

Mary Barton was off her horse in a twinkling.

"Oh, Blythe, are you hurt?"

"Not at all. I hope my new hat isn't;" and Blythe put her hands to her head. Mr. Ellis sprang across the road.

"Are you sure you are not hurt?" he asked, anxiously.

"Indeed I am sure; but I am afraid poor little Bill is in a bad plight. Do step back and see about him, Mr. Ellis."

I believe, in that moment of unselfish thought for another, Roger Ellis became her lover. He turned and hurried back, to meet Bill limping toward him.

"Somepen's done happen," said that youth: "seems to me I'se flew all to pieces!"

Blythe was still sitting on the roadside when they came up. "Oh, my gracious!" cried Bill; "dars my spekilation done broke all to smash!"

They all laughed; and Blythe, declining the offer of Van's hand, sprang up. But alas! a bit of a broken bottle had imbedded itself in the soft earth, and as Blythe started forward she stepped on its jagged edge. Of course, her shoes were thin—your true Southern girl is fond of a cloth gaiter with a paper sole.

"Oh, my foot!" she cried.

"Is your ankle sprained?" cried Ellis.

"No, my foot is cut—on Bill's—speculation," said she, faintly.

"Oh, you little imp!" cried Van, looking toward Bill as if he longed to shake that small sinner, who crept crying behind Mr. Ellis.

"It isn't his fault, Van," said sweet Blythe.

Fortunately, Mrs. Oglethorpe's buggy came up at this moment, and Blythe was helped into it. They were not very far from town, and Mr. Ellis and Bill walked the rest of the way—or rather, Mr. Ellis walked, for bearing as long as he could Bill's sobs, and seeing that he could scarcely walk from lameness and excitement, he took him in his arms and carried him home.

Chapter XI

Three Visits

Although his bones ached on waking, the morning after the picnic, Roger Ellis arose earlier than usual, with a brisk sense of having a great deal to do. His first care was to go into town to a dry-goods shop and ask over the counter for a piece of muslin. Some fine organdies were shown him.

"Not this," said Ellis, impatiently; "I mean such stuff as shirts are made of."

"Oh! a bolt of domestic," said the clerk, with an easy and superior smile.

The cotton cloth purchased, it was sent to Mrs. Roy's, where Ellis soon followed it, having no difficulty in finding the "little red house with the hollyhocks in the yard and the shetters blown away."

Mrs. Roy was looking forlorner than ever, in a comfortless room to which the sunshine that poured in gave only an added look of desolation. The floor was bare, and the boards were loosened or broken in several places. A cracked looking-glass hung above a pine table, while some red ribbons on the table and a box of prepared chalk, with the top of a stocking hanging out of it, indicated that Mrs. Roy still sacrificed to the vanities. Two empty barrels stood in one corner, and upon a board stretched across them was placed a water-bucket of obtrusive blue, in which a well-seasoned gourd floated. A half-moon of water soon formed around this in splashes, as the Roy children at play in the yard seemed to be con-

sumed with an inward fever, or afflicted with a burning desire to
see the stranger, for they filed in one after another during his call,
drinking like young horses, with the gourd at their lips and a stream
pouring to the floor, as they peered at Mr. Ellis.

"Take a cheer, sir," said Mrs. Roy, advancing a loose-jointed,
split-bottomed chair. "I'm sorry to have you see me in sich a po'
place; but the Lord knows that I'm thankful nowadays to have a
rooft over my head."

"Are you a widow?" hazarded Ellis. The question unlocked the
fountain of all her woes.

"Our heavenly Father knows I'm wuss off 'n if I was a widder,
which I am not, by reason of havin' a husband which is a rascal,
an' him the father of my po' children, an' a saddler in very good
business when I married him."

Mrs. Roy now began to weep, and Ellis, not knowing what to
do, gave a sympathetic murmur that seemed to encourage her to go
on.

"Pappy an' mammy didn't want me to marry him," she said,
wiping her eyes and taking a pinch of snuff; "for all we wus plain
people livin' up the mountain in a plain way, an' him a saddler
ownin' his shop an' movin' in good society too, bein' a church
member. Howsomever, aginst that he had a sort of repitition for
bein' a fast man, an' mammy she said from the first that there wasn't
no part of him she liked to see so well as the back of his head. But
marry him I would, for I had a sperit of my own in them days,
though broken it is now. Well, he brought me to town, an' for a
while I wus as proud as a peacock. Jim wus a liberal man with his
money, an' we didn't want for nothin'. He give me a silk gown too;
and I wus so foolish about that man that I wasn't satisfied with
namin' my first boy after him—Jim; but when the next one wus a
girl, what did I do but name her Mij—an' that ain't nothin' but the
name of Jim turned back'ard. Here, you Mij! stop a-sloppin' that
water an' come an' offer Mr. Ellis a drink."

Mij approached, hanging her head and holding the gourd in
such a way that its contents flowed through the handle in a thin
stream to the floor, and looking rather pretty with her elflocks and
shy, black eyes. Mr. Ellis welcomed a diversion, and tried to make
talk with the child; but the mother said,

"Now, Mij Roy, you jest go on out to play. Don't you see I'm
busy talkin' to Mr. Ellis?"

"Well, sir, more children come, an' I kind o' lost my health, and Jim he got ter stayin' out late at nights, sayin' he had extry jobs. Well, things went on, an' I wus as unsuspectin' as the unborn babe, till Dan Rice*come to town with his circus. I wanted to go the wust sort, for everybody had been crackin' it up for the finest show ever seen in these parts. When the night came, an' I was lookin' for Jim to take me, he said he wus powerful sorry, but he couldn't go no way he could fix it, for he had to work in the shop till midnight. I thought I ought ter be thankful for havin' sich a hard-workin' husband, so I give up the circus without makin' any words. But after Jim went off I got to wonderin' why I couldn't go with some of the neighbors; so I ran over to Bet Chalmers to see if she was goin'. She an' her husband was just ready to start, an' I just went right along with 'em. The tent wus packed when we got there, an' the clown wus carryin' on as ridikilous as you please. Mr. Ellis"—and here Mrs. Roy's bitter monotone fell to a deeper key, and she leaned toward her companion, speaking with the emphasis of one who hardly expected to be believed—"*I never want to go to another circus again as long as I live!*"

"'I shall never be friends again with roses;
I shall hate sweet music my whole life long,'"

thought Roger Ellis—"that sounds rather more poetic; but isn't the sentiment just the same?"

"I wus a-settin' there laughin' fit to kill at the clown," continued Mrs. Roy, "when Bet Chalmers caught hold of my arm, an' she said, 'Why, Matildy Roy, there's your husband!' She wus a-pintin' over to the six-bit seats, Mr. Ellis—the finest seats in the tent—and I looked, and there sat Jim, with a girl named Ann Eliza Lowe beside him—snuggled as close as if they'd a been twin hicker-nuts—*drinkin' out o' the same glass o' lemonade—eatin' off the same stick o' candy*—befo' the eyes o' the whole world! I didn't see much o' what went on in the ring after that. I just sat there an' watched 'em; and God knows I never want to go through no wuss hell 'n I did that night!

"Well, I made it hot for Jim when he got home; but it didn't seem to do no manner o' good. After that things went from bad to

---

*Dan Rice is an amalgam of the names of two of the most famous minstrel entertainers, Dan Emmet and Thomas D. Rice.

wuss; he spendin' his money on Ann Eliza Lowe, an' the children goin' in rags.

"I tried to forgive him; I prayed on my knees for strength to forgive that man; for I said, 'My father is dead, my mother is po', an' if I *don't* forgive him what'll me an' my children do for bread?' So I did forgive him, time and time agin, till I waked up one fine day to find Jim Roy gone—gone the Lord knows where, with Ann Eliza Lowe; and from that day to this nobody in this town has sot eyes on either one of 'em."

"How long ago did this happen?"

"It's been mor'n a year; an' a han'-to-han' fight it's been to live," said Mrs. Roy, sighing heavily. "I ain't got no hopes of his ever comin' back, for when a man has once broke loose there ain't no gittin' him in the traces agin."

"Ah, well, your children will grow up to be a comfort to you," said Ellis, cheerily; "in the mean time don't lose heart. Have you seen Colonel Dexter about your chickens yet?"

"Oh, yes, sir; he paid me handsome for 'em, and his wife guv me a real fashionable alpakky, as good as new. I'm free to confess that some Yankees is mighty clever folks."

Ellis laid a bill on the table as he rose to go. "A little advance pay for the shirts," he explained. "I have ordered the stuff sent to you."

"I think I can suit you, sir," said Mrs. Roy. "You're just about Jim's build, and I made all his shirts."

A fresh burst of sobs seemed imminent, and Ellis hurried his good-bye, though he stopped to make acquaintance with the sallow-faced children in the yard, and to invite them over to his tent to a tea-party, consisting entirely of candy and fire-crackers.

Mr. Ellis next turned his steps in the direction of the Tollivers'. He met Tom in the yard, and inquired after Civil Rights Bill.

"So you had a spill!" cried Master Tom. "What fun! Bill is sick, I believe: anyhow he has been in bed all day."

"I should like to see him."

"Come on," said Tom.

He took Mr. Ellis through a gap in the fence to the back yard, and pointed out a little cabin.

"Lift the latch and the door'll fly open," he said, and vanished.

Ellis rapped at the door.

"Who dat knockin' at my do'?" cried a voice.

Ellis pushed the door open. "Grant you grace, mister," said

an old woman, rising to meet him, and dropping a funny little courtesy, as if somebody had pulled a cord in her spinal column. "I wouldn't a' spoke so sharp, but I thought it was Tom Tolliver up to some of his tricks."

Aunt Sally was an imposing figure. No one knew how old she was. She said she had lived a hundred years, but she was as straight as if she had been strapped to a board. She wore a wide calico gown that reached to her ankles, covered with pale, staring flowers, a handkerchief knotted on her bosom, and her head was tightly bound in a snow-white turban. She was blind in one eye, and this gave a peculiar wildness to her expression, as the blind eye was fixed, blue, and glassy, while the other was black and rolling. Her mouth gave a cavernous impression of vastness; it was toothless apparently, save for one long fang, and when she spoke or laughed she showed its entire roof and her thick red tongue to its roots.

Mr. Ellis inquired after Bill.

"Bill's asleep jes' now," said Aunt Sally. "He's been a-sufferin' right smart. Got a powerful heap o' bruises: I've been a rubbin' him with yearth-worms."

"With *what?*" cried Ellis.

"With yearth-worms," repeated Aunt Sally, showing him a glass full of wriggling bait for fishes. "Dey's mighty good for stone-bruises and any kind o' limb trouble.

"Bill always was sickly," she went on. "He had a spell o' terrified fever las' summer dat I thought would lay him out, sure. I nussed him till I thought I'd drop. But lor'! I'se an ole South Carliny nigger, I is, wid a backbone; none o' your limpsy Alabama trash!"

"How long have you lived in Alabama?"

"Oh, for de bes' part o' my life. Ole mars' when he died he lef' me to dis branch o' de Tollivers. But it was jes' like drawin' eye-teeth to leave ole mis'—sho's you born it was. All de Tollivers is good stock, but none ekal to de Carliny stock. Ole mis' she brought me up from a baby. She nussed me, an' tucked me in nights, an' fed me outen a silver spoon. I never had no humpin', nor dumpin'. I never had but one whippin' in my life, an' dat was give me by a miserbel mean ole overseer. He jes' stretched me out like a rabbit for breakin' a little yearthen pot on his table. Lor'! wasn't ole mis' mad when she heerd about it! Dat overseer was sent a kitin' off de place, an' 'twarn't more'n a year befo' dat very man was hung at de crossroads. I went to de hangin', an' it was a fine sight, sho's you born."

Ellis began to find Aunt Sally alarming.

"Ole mars' honeyed me up mightly arter dat whippin'," she went on; "couldn't do enough for me. One mornin' I felt kind o' droopin,' an' I said, 'I want a drink, Mars' Dare.' He says to me, 'How much whiskey could you drink, Aunt Sally?' says he. 'Try me, Mars' Dare,' says I. 'Come along,' says he. He tuk de key to de sto'-room, an' when we got dar he pulled de plug outen de whiskey barrel, an' let out a brimmin' glass o' liquor. I tossed it off, an' he says, 'Have another?' 'Yes, sir.' So I drunk dat. 'Nuff?' says he. 'Lor,' Mars' Dare, you're jokin'!' He gim me another—dat made three; I drunk dat, an' hel' out de glass. 'Good God A'mighty!' says he, 'ain't you never goin' ter be satisfied?' Well, he poured out two mo' glasses; an' de las' glass I said, 'Len' me your knife, Mars' Dare.' 'What you want wid it, you crazy ole critter?' But he handed it out, an' I scraped my finger-nail in dis glass, an' den, de Lord be praised! I had my fill. 'Some o' you watch dat ole lady,' Mars' Dare said to de niggers roun' de house; 'she'll keel over befo' long.' But, bless you, I went roun' straight as a preacher all day."

"Pray how large were the glasses?" cried Ellis.

"Oh, 'bout de size of a pint cup," said this terrible Aunt Sally. "All dat whiskey might a made some fool niggers drunk; but it jes' seemed to me as if wings was sproutin' out o' my shoulder-blades."

At this moment Bill awoke, in great surprise at sight of the visitor. "My eyes! Mr. Ellis, is dat you?"

"You Bill! dat's no way to speak to de gentleman. Tell you, nigger, whar I was raised no white gentleman ever spoke to me without I made my low obedient."

Fortunately the voluble Aunt Sally was called out at this juncture, and Ellis had an opportunity to talk a little with Willy, whom he found fevered and restless. A paper of oranges made his eyes brighten, and, with the promise to come again, and a silver *pourboire* for Aunt Sally, Mr. Ellis's second visit came to an end.

"And now for the reward of duty!" he said to himself as he walked away, "sweet Blythe!"

Dinner, however, and a freshened toilet intervened before this visit. Roger even looked in his mirror, as he dressed himself, with a certain odd interest. "If I were ten years younger," he muttered, as he brushed his curling light hair and wished it more than a fringe to his head.

Blythe was in the cool latticed parlor, her foot bandaged and on a stool, and half a dozen magazines strewed around her. In her cool white wrapper she looked as fresh and smiling as the May, as she leaned back in the loveliest and laziest of attitudes, sipping iced lemonade, and reading by turns.

"How comfortable you look!" said Ellis, as she gave him her hand with a bright, beautiful smile. "And how are you to-day?"

"Very well; my foot scarcely pains me at all."

"Have you seen the doctor yet?"

"Oh yes, and he tells me it may be a month before I am able to walk. Papa is more concerned about it than I am. He thought it so improper to fall out of a buggy with a lot of bottles! He was very much annoyed this morning by the men on the square crowding around him to ask how his daughter was after her dreadful accident; and his first care was to rush to the editor of the *Advocate* to tell him not to make a paragraph of the 'shocking affair.' Papa never willingly gives gossip any food. I believe he would like for us all to be drowned at sea to avoid the sensation of a funeral in the family."

"How well you bear the thought of a month's confinement!" said Ellis, thinking Blythe looked charmingly pretty as she threw her head back and laughed at her own nonsense.

"I will tell you a secret. I am, in the flesh, the laziest creature in the world; but I have an intellectual consciousness that laziness is contemptible. So my two selves are constantly at war; I am torn by conflicting desires. But now I'm at peace; for it is my plain duty to do nothing but lie on the sofa, read novels, and drink lemonade. Can you suggest any further amusement, should these finally pall upon me?"

"You might learn the signal language," said Ellis, laughing.

"What is that?" said Blythe, with lively interest.

"It is a method of communication invented by the officers of the Thirteenth. All the ladies in camp have learned it, and amuse themselves signaling from one tent to another on rainy days."

"I should like to learn it. Do you think I could?"

"You need only a handkerchief and a memory. It is a little like talking with the fingers, you know."

"Ah, yes, I begin to see into it. But it must take a great deal of practice before one can do it at all well."

"You shall have all the practice you want," said Ellis promptly. "Your window overlooks at the camp. I shall take some tall tree as my station, and climb it every morning just at the hour when Daniel—or was it Peter?—went out on the house-top to pray. Then I shall inquire how you have passed the night, when I may come and see you, whether you've any commissions for the humblest of your servants, and a thousand other things, that you must answer at length—for practice."

"I fear it will be a severe tax on my intellect," said Blythe; "and I shall read fewer magazines than I supposed I should."

"I brought you some books to-day, by-the-way," said Ellis, "some odd volumes of Hawthorne. You were saying that you were not familiar with his books?"

"Except the 'Marble Faun.' I know that by heart."

"Take the 'Scarlet Letter' next. It will mark a date in your life. I do not know whether I could be so greatly moved again as I was when I first read the 'Scarlet Letter.' Never did a book so profoundly impress my imagination. I have thought since then that it is the one matchless flower of American literature. I was quite young when I read it; but I half fear to read it again, as it seems to be a law of life that the same delight shall never be tasted twice by the same lips."

"Is Hawthorne your favorite American author, Mr. Ellis?"

"No, I think not; though he, in my judgment, is *the* great artist of America. His style is consummate art—the work is fused in his genius and is a perfect unit. You must admire it as a finished product of his mind; not stop, as you do in reading some very clever authors of a later date, and pick out plums in every paragraph to admire separately. Such a style may be art, but it is mosaic art; high sometimes, but the highest never."

A ring at the bell was heard, and a moment later Betty Page and Captain Silsby came in.

"How is your foot, Blythe?" cried Miss Betty. "What a thousand pities it should be hurt just now! Did you know that the officers were going to give us a ball in Masonic Hall?"

"How soon?"

"In a week or two—as soon as I learn to glide. Captain Silsby is going to give me a lesson to-night. You must learn, Blythe, just as soon as your foot gets well."

"Is it very hard?"

"Let us show the step, Captain Silsby," said Betty; and the young lady and the officer placed themselves opposite each other.

"It is very simple," said Captain Silsby, speaking with more animation than usual. "The great thing is to *remember always to keep one foot behind the other*. If you let them go apart you are lost. Then it is only a continued forward and back—come to me—go away"—and the captain balanced lightly to and from Miss Betty Page.

"Only two steps?" said Blythe.

"Yes; the third is a rest. Now see how it goes to music."

Beans! beans! Bos- ton baked beans!

he hummed agreeably. And to see the blonde and languid young officer advance on the first beans, retreat on the second, and rest on Boston, while Betty followed his movements with flushed gravity and pretty, awkward steps, was a sight to win a smile from the weeping philosopher.

"Never mind," said Blythe; "while you are gliding I shall be learning something very mysterious and delightful—the signal language."

"What is that?" said Betty; hardly waiting for it to be explained before expressing a violent desire to add it to her accomplishments. "You will teach me, won't you, Captain Silsby?"

"For what other purpose was I born?" said the captain.

"Do you dance, Mr. Ellis?" asked Betty.

"No, indeed. I should be at a loss to know what to do with myself in a ball-room."

"You ought to learn. Come over this evening, and have a lesson with me."

"Thank you, Miss Page, but I fear nothing short of standing on a hot plate would make me dance in this year of my life, and I have an engagement for this evening. Willy Tolliver is sick, and I promised to look in on him."

"Willy Tolliver: who is he?"

"I believe you call him Civil Rights Bill."

"Oh!" said Betty, with a look of wonder in her gray eyes. "Captain Silsby, I think it time we were off."

"Don't go," said Blythe, hospitably.

"We must," said Betty. "Captain Silsby is invited to our house to tea, and if we are late there's no certainty that Aunt Lissy will keep us any hot muffins."

"So much the better," said Captain Silsby. "Who wants his constitution undermined by these delicious hot abominations, that you Southern folks eat at an hour when you ought to be virtuously supping on cold bread and apple-sauce!"

"And yet I notice that you Yankees never decline these 'hot abominations.'"

"True, but the goblins rend us afterward."

"How proud you are of being a dyspeptic!" said Betty. "You allude to it as constantly as Squire Barton does to the Barton hand, and with the same complacency."

"On the contrary," said Silsby, with an air of sentiment, "I deplore it now more than ever, as it seems to place a gulf between us. On every other point there is such harmony. Still, as the years roll on, a persistent course of hot muffins and pickles on your part may unite us in feeling."

"Don't you think," said Mr. Ellis to Blythe, in a stage whisper, "that their conversation is taking a very personal turn? Would it not show a delicate sympathy if I were to wheel your chair to the farthest window, and read to you in a loud voice?"

"For shame, Mr. Ellis!" cried Betty. "Now we are really going. Good-bye, Blythe dear; I shall see you to-morrow."

"Don't you think their hearts are beginning to tip a little toward each other?" said Ellis, after they had gone.

"It hardly seems possible. You've no idea how bitterly Betty spoke against you before you came. She and I almost had a quarrel because I said I hoped the officers would be received. But I suppose she can't resist the temptation to amuse herself."

"She would find it very amusing to marry Silsby," said Mr. Ellis, with a laugh; "and she isn't one to trouble her head about consistency. Now, you have been consistent all the way through."

"Yes," said Blythe, proudly; "I am not influenced by my feelings or fancies."

"I have an artist friend," said Ellis, gravely, "and some day I shall get him to paint me a new Goddess of Reason. She shall be standing in the moonlight in a Southern garden, with rose-leaves falling about her, and one red rose clinging by its thorns in her golden hair."

"I am afraid you are laughing at me," said Blythe; "but, indeed, I am reasonable in all things. Only try me."

"Perhaps I shall, some day," he answered.

CHAPTER XII

Ah Dio! Morir si Giovane!

When Blythe Herndon came home from the moonlight picnic, with her foot bandaged in half a dozen handkerchiefs and a green veil, and the doctor had declared that she must stay in the house for a month, the grandmother secretly rejoiced. Since Mrs. Oglethorpe's dinner-party, the bitter old lady had known no moment of peace or rest. She had said nothing; and, to do her family justice, none of them realized how she suffered. She moved among them paler and more spirit-like each day; at a sudden word pressing her hand to the locket on her bosom, as if it were her heart in pain; and all the while her hurt, hostile soul was throbbing with one desire—to save Blythe. She had never before concerned herself about the child's future. Blythe might have married the poorest or idlest young fellow in Yariba—she would scarcely have come out from her abstracted living to know what was going on; but the fear of a lover's liking between one of her name and blood and an abhorred enemy stung her to life. The accident to Blythe she hailed as fortunate, as it must keep her aloof for a time from the gay doings of the summer, and would lessen her chance of meeting a possible lover. But the grandmother had counted without—Roger Ellis. Scarcely a day passed that he was not at Mr. Herndon's. He was not a society man, and perhaps but for the accident that kept Blythe a prisoner, she would never have been more to him than a bright vision of the summer; but in her isolation she almost seemed dependent on him, and this was a thought too enticing for him to resist. So the days passed, and these two natures drew near to-gether, each finding in the other a strange charm.

Blythe was the purest woman Ellis had ever met; Ellis the clev-erest man Blythe had ever known. To her he was a stimulant; to him she was a rest. He lent her books and read her the poems that he loved best; he delighted her with stories of distinguished men and women he had known, who had seemed to Blythe as remote from every-day life as the vast shades of a Dante's dream; he opened to her a new world in literature and the arts; he told her of his own life and its loneliness; finally, he talked to her of herself, with such luminous appreciation of the fine elements in her character that Blythe must have liked him from mere gratitude. He drew her on skilfully to tell him of the little events of her simple life. She told him of her childhood and its wild pranks, varied by occasional efforts to be good, one of them lasting a whole day, and resulting so successfully that her papa bought her a gold ring as its souvenir; of one mad freak when, in a passion of rebellion against an unjust punishment, she packed up her best Swiss dress and some bread and ham in a satchel and ran away to seek her fortune, only to be brought back and punished, alas! instead of being petted into rea-son; of her beautiful pony, Jet, that her papa gave her when she was eight years old, and of the many times she had tumbled off his back without telling, for fear of being forbidden to ride. Then she told him of her romantic and dreamy girlhood; of the secret passion she had cherished for a knightly being whom she had seen riding at a tournament under the name of Glendower; of her confirmation when she was thirteen, with ten other girls, all dressed in white, with white veils—only she had on brown gloves, and was mortified because the others were bare-handed, and she pulled them off dur-ing the ceremony, and her mother scolded her afterward for doing so; of one cruel experience during the war, when a French boy, named Paul Lemoiner, a ward of Mr. Shepherd's, formed a com-pany of girls and taught them to drill; but her father said it was unlady-like and wouldn't let her join them, though she shed rivers of tears and her mamma had made her an apron of stars and bars; of her young-lady life, that had been disappointing, because she had realized no ideals; of her longing for action, adventure, life. In short, Blythe Herndon, whom the young men of Yariba called cold and sarcastic, and who was apt to talk above their heads, seemed to Roger Ellis adorable because of her simplicity, sweetness, and docility; and truly, if love may be likened to the kingdom of heaven, Blythe prepared herself to enter it by becoming as a little child.

Roger Ellis found means, too, to make himself acceptable to other members of the family. There was a sunniness of nature about him that made most people warm and expand in his presence. The children clustered around him like flies about a honeypot; Mr. Herndon invited him to tea, and laid down political laws to which Ellis listened deferentially as he watched the changing expression of Blythe's face; Mrs. Herndon made him sweet little rambling confidences, "quite as if I were her son," thought Ellis, with a flush of joy. One, indeed, he failed to win; though he lost no opportunity of a gentle or a genial word to the silent little lady in the long black dress, with the diamond flashing on her withered finger. He could see that he advanced not one step. She did not conspicuously absent herself from the family circle when he was present; but in Roger Ellis's presence she turned the locket that she wore so that the face touched her bosom: his eyes should not profane it by a look.

There came a time when a high proof of the family friendship was given him—he was admitted to the confidence of a family sorrow.

Calling one morning as usual, he was met at the door by a servant, who, instead of asking him in, handed him a note that he read standing there.

Dear Mr. Ellis,

This is an anniversary day for us, and a very sad one. We never receive any visitors. Pardon me for not telling you yesterday, but I did not think of the date when I made an engagement to see you. Please come to-morrow.

Your friend,
Blythe Herndon.

The next day, when he called, Mrs. Herndon was in the room. "I was sorry Blythe did not see you yesterday," she said, as she shook hands. "It isn't necessary that she should shut herself up because I do. She is too young to remember. I have told her to tell you about it, and you will understand that we did not mean to fail in either courtesy or kindness toward such a good friend as yourself."

She left the room, and Blythe said: "I told mamma I knew that you would not take the least offence at being denied, but she said I had better tell you."

"My dear Miss Blythe, of course I had not thought of the matter again, except to sympathize in your sorrow. Pray do not tell me what it will give you pain to speak of."

"No, it will not do that exactly; as mamma says, I am too young to remember. It is about my sister Nelly. I have spoken to you of her?"

"Yes, the very first time I ever saw you, you told me that you were wearing her dress, and that she died fifteen years ago."

"It is a dreadful tragedy," said Blythe. "Nelly was very beautiful, very wilful, and had had her own way all her life. We have a picture of her that I must show you some time. Her eyes were dark, but her hair was as light as mine; and you never saw anything so pretty as her neck and arms. When she was sixteen years old she met a young man named Roy Herrick, who had just come home from college. He was brilliant, handsome, and rich. The Herricks were a fine family—none better in the State; but there seemed to be a drop of bad blood in their veins. Nearly all of them met with violent deaths. Do you remember that beautiful old place on the edge of the town that I told you was now used for a jail?"

"Yes, perfectly."

"The Herricks lived there, and it was the finest place in the country. Roy's father and grandfather had been men of cultivated tastes, and they had filled the house with pictures, bronzes, and lovely articles of *vertu*. Roy Herrick was the last of his name—his father had been killed in a duel. In each generation there had been some tale of blood. Roy was very handsome—dark and tall, with wild, melancholy eyes, and the finest shot, the boldest rider, the richest planter, in the country. It was no wonder poor sister Nelly loved him; and he loved her from the time he saw her first on her way home from school. In one month they were engaged. Father and mother bitterly opposed the match, for he had the name of being a wild young man—and this dreadful family record! But they were so determined! They pleaded, and wept, and threatened to run away, and at last consent was wrung from my parents. But there wasn't even a servant on the place who was not frightened at the thought of the marriage. Every one was oppressed by presentiments. I have a distinct remembrance of seeing our negroes running with waving firebrands to frighten away a whip-poor-will that had perched on a tree near sister Nelly's window. They said it boded death. But they were married, and the prayers and love of all who knew them went with them to their home—they were so young, so beautiful, so happy.

"We paid them a visit, a month or two after their marriage, at that beautiful house, which I cannot pass now without a shudder. It was like fairyland inside; and they were like two gleeful children. Their servants were never tired of telling my mother of how their young master and mistress adored each other. One curious thing he had done. He had taken offence at some people staring at them, one day, when they were gathering flowers, and he had a high wall built round the grounds. I believe sister Nelly was rather proud of this as a sign of his jealous love.

"One winter day she rode in early to spend the day with us. About four o'clock he came after her to take her home. It had turned colder during the day; the wind was blowing, and my mother begged them to stay all night. Roy said it was not possible for him to do so, but that Nelly might, if she wished. Then we all got round her, begging her not to go. I remember so well how he stood by the fire striking his boot lightly with his riding-whip, smiling at sister Nelly, and the answering look of fondness that she flashed back at him as she threw her arms around mamma's neck and cried, 'Do you think I would stay away from my husband all night?' So they rode off laughing and waving farewells as long as we could see them.

"The next day we children were playing in mamma's room, having a pillow fight on her bed, when suddenly our old black mammy rushed in shrieking out, 'Oh, Miss Lucy! Miss Lucy! Miss Nelly's dead. Dat man's done killed her and himself both!'

"My mother sprang past her to the porch. There stood a man from the plantation, his horse reeking with foam, and he told us, as well as he could for his choking sobs, that when they went into the house that morning to make the fires, no answer was returned to the knocks at the bedroom door. They waited an hour, and knocked again without reply. Then they became frightened, broke open the door, and there were Roy and Nelly—*dead*. She was in bed, looking as if she were asleep—with a shot through her heart. He was lying on the floor, with a pair of pistols by his side.

"Oh, that fearful day! I remember my mother walking up and down the hall, not uttering a sound or a cry—only wringing her hands, and myself creeping after her, afraid to speak to the mother with the strange new face. I don't believe she shed a tear until our poor old mammy caught her in her arms and begged her to cry. Then she broke down."

Blythe paused, and wiped away her own tears.

"He must have been insane," said Ellis, in a low voice.

"Yes, there is no other explanation. The servants said they had been more than usually fond and gay that evening, after reaching home: they had heard them singing together. They had been married six months. She was not quite seventeen years old."

"And you have always kept the anniversary of her death sacred and apart from other days?"

"Yes, and it is the saddest in the year for us all. Mamma scarcely speaks—certainly does not smile. She stays for hours by sister's grave. Mamma is Episcopalian, you know; but she is very High-Church, and I believe she prays for their souls."

A moment's silence, and Blythe said, "It was cruel to sadden you by this story. We have many bright family anniversaries, and I hope you will be here to help us celebrate some of them. All our birthdays, of course, and mamma's and papa's wedding-day. Papa tried to inaugurate one anniversary of gloom dating from the fall of Vicksburg, but he gave up the effort about the third year after the war."

"I shall forget all my old anniversaries," said Ellis, "and begin anew from this summer. There are so many white days I want to remember!"

"And I," said Blythe, with a smile, "shall choose for my one day of memory the tenth of last June."

"The tenth of June? That was before I knew you. May I ask what are your associations with that day?"

Blythe was in a very gentle and softened mood.

"It is the day I first heard your voice in Mrs. Tolliver's parlor, and I knew we should be friends," she said, with so sweet a look in her blue eyes that Ellis forgot the sad story he had just heard in a bewildering rush of hope.

CHAPTER XIII

I Will Make Much
of Your Voices

"For goodness' sake, wife, get me a fan!" cried Squire Barton, as he entered his house one day at noon.

"Sit down, Cousin Mark, and let me fan you."

"Warm!" said the squire, as he submitted to this delicate attention—"it's warm enough to give a fly the blind-staggers! Old Convers will have a sunstroke if he doesn't look sharp—walked home with his wig off."

"Are there many ladies out to-day?"

"Oh yes—enough to bring on a storm to-morrow. Saw Mrs. Herndon, Effie Oglethorpe, Betty Page—pretty much everybody!"

"I hope you remembered to ask after Blythe?"

"Of course I did. I'm not a brute beast."

"And how is she?"

"Oh, mending slowly. She has been hoping to get out Decoration-day, but her mother seems doubtful. Foolish affair, that picnic! Some of Effie Oglethorpe's nonsense. Such airs and graces as she puts on! Buying a spotted veil this morning—peeping at herself in that old cracked looking-glass in Convers's shop. Reckon she wishes we decorated the soldiers' graves by moonlight. Moonlight picnic, indeed!"

"Oh, Cousin Mark, let the young folks enjoy themselves!"

"Young folks! Well, if Effie Oglethorpe isn't forty-five, I'll kiss my elbow!"

"Just my age," said Mrs. Barton; "but I'm sure she looks ten years younger."

"No she doesn't. If you dressed out as she does, and put flour on your face—"

"Flour! oh no, Cousin Mark."

"It's too hot to argue," said Mr. Barton, sleepily, "but I saw it on her nose. By-the-way, young Tolliver nearly knocked me down this morning."

"Nearly knocked you down!"

"Well, he wanted to do it—just because I hinted to him mildly that Betty Page was making herself ridiculous by the way she was carrying on with these Yankees."

"I know what your *hints* are," said his wife, "and I don't wonder Van was offended. I don't see what Betty has done to call you out on the subject. She only amuses herself as any gay young girl would do."

"Humph! what should you say to our Mary standing at the gate and signaling to an officer riding by on horseback, or holding a long conversation with one a hundred yards away, by means of a handkerchief tied to the end of a stick?"

"Things get exaggerated so, Cousin Mark; and, after all, it was only a bit of fun."

"D—n such fun!" said Cousin Mark, with brief pertinency.

Van Tolliver had, indeed, been much cut up by Squire Barton's remarks, which, as may be supposed, were more forcible than delicate. Again he determined on a remonstrance with his capricious sweetheart; a determination that he carried into effect on his next visit.

"I do not like this signaling business," he began.

"Don't you, Van?" said Miss Betty. "I think it is great fun. I can do it so well; a great deal better than Blythe Herndon, for all she is the clever girl of Yariba. Captain Silsby says that he never saw any one learn it so quickly as I have done."

"Captain Silsby—always Captain Silsby! Whatever he may say, I say it is not lady-like."

"But *I* do it."

"You are but a girl, and your judgment is often at fault—you know it is, Betty."

"Yes, I think it is," said Betty, calmly. "It was one day, for instance, when we were gathering chestnuts in St. Thomas Hall lot, and I said 'Yes' to a young man who might have been your double, except that his expression was more winning than yours is now."

"What a day that was!" cried Van. "I shall never forget how lovely you looked in your white dress—"

"All stained with coffee that Tom Tolliver spilled on it."

"And your lovely eyes—"

"Red with crying, because I pricked my fingers with the chestnut-burs."

"Don't tell me that you regret it, Betty," he cried, heedless of her interruptions.

"How can I help regretting it, when I see that you do not love me now as you did then."

"Not love you! Have I not proved my love? Have I ever looked at another girl? I wish I were an eloquent fellow, Betty, that I might make you realize my love better than I can do with my plain words. I found a little poem in the odd corner of an old newspaper, the other day, that seemed to me a pretty expression of love; though I don't care much for poetry, as a rule. But this seemed to express so exactly my feeling for you. It was called 'A Sigh.' Should you like to hear it?"

"Yes, Van, if it isn't *too* pathetic."

"Listen, dear:

> 'Never to see her nor hear her,
> To speak her name aloud never;
> Yet hold her always the dearer,
> And love her forever.
>
> To see how, day by day, clearer,
> She blights both hope and endeavor—

["God grant you may never do that, my Betty!"]

> Yet absolve her, bless her, revere her,
> And love her forever.
>
> To sleep and dream I am near her,
> To hate the daybeams that sever,
> To think of death as a cheerer,

And love her forever.
Never to see her nor hear her,
To speak her name aloud never;
Yet wilder, tenderer, dearer,
To love her forever.'"

"Van, I am not worthy of that!" cried Betty, with a sudden burst of candor; "indeed, I am not! I do think the best thing you could do would be to give me up."

"Give up my pretty Betty, and all the dreams and hopes that cluster about her! I am not quite ready for that. You don't know, darling, how my love for you has grown in these years of absence. I took a little thought of you in my heart when I went down to that grim old plantation four years ago, and there, in the long, hot days, through the lonely nights, that little thought has grown until it is intertwined with my very heart's fibres: to tear it away would be to tear myself to pieces."

Betty replied to this very sweetly; and, on leaving, Van was conscious that his visit had been an extremely satisfactory one, although, looking at it impartially as a "remonstrance," it did not appear to him a success. As the impression of her witcheries wore away, his annoyance at the "signaling business" returned, and meeting Roger Ellis shortly after, he resolved to enlist his help in putting a stop to it.

"Pardon me," said he, "but I believe you originated this—infernal—signal language, that the Yariba girls have taken up as if it were a new crochet stitch?"

"Why no," said Ellis, laughing; "it 'growed' of itself, because the time was ripe for it. But I taught it to Miss Blythe Herndon, as a possible means of amusement while her foot kept her a prisoner."

"That was all well enough," said Van, "but it has been turned into a vehicle for coquetry, and it is really so undignified—"

"Yes, I see. It can be overdone and Miss Page certainly has overdone it."

"It is not necessary to mention any names," said the young Southerner, stiffly.

"As you please," said Ellis, good-humoredly.

"But you will help me put a stop to it all?"

"Oh yes, I'll 'never do so any more!' And I will promise that Miss Blythe Herndon shall not. She has never played the child's game with any one but me," said Ellis, with a light laugh, through which there ran a thrill of pride. "It was only a child's game; but I am sorry if it has caused you the least unpleasantness," he added so frankly that Van could do no less than meet him on his own ground.

"I must apologize," he said, "if I have seemed rude; but I have been very much annoyed by hearing this matter discussed with a free tongue by the men about the square. If women only knew how men talked, how their little frivolities would drop away!"

"And how uninteresting they would become!" said Ellis, laughing. "But I doubt, after all, if that result would follow. It isn't the women that care for men's gossip, but it is the men who are afraid of each other."

"You say 'the men' as if you belonged to another order of beings yourself. Should you not care if any one dear to you had been lightly talked about?"

"If she deserved it, the trouble would be too deep for mere words to affect me one way or another. If not, evil speech would affect me no more than the wind that blows—not so much, in fact, for the wind that blows sometimes gives me catarrh."

"I can't go with you," said Van; "it would be almost easier for me to close the coffin-lid over the woman I loved best, than to have her fair fame ever so lightly breathed upon, though she were innocent as the stainless Una."

"How serious you are!" laughed Ellis. "Come, tell me what you should do, if you had a wife, and she, like the lady in the poem, should run away with a handsomer man?"

"I should kill her!"

"Now see how different men are. I would give her a divorce, say 'Bless you, my children!' and start the new husband in business."

"It is easy to jest."

"Oh, I am in earnest, I assure you: but perhaps it is because I am a radical, and believe in every human soul—and body—having a right to itself. At any rate, I should never try to keep a love that was going from me. For the law of love is liberty."

Van had a defined opinion that this sentiment was an outrageous one; but looking into Roger's kindling face, the eyes twinkling with humor and kindliness, it was hard to feel any way but warmly toward the man whose soul it indexed. But on leaving him, the Southerner reviled himself secretly for having yielded to Roger's personal charm, and a vague distrust of him crept into his mind.

The most important day in the Yariba summer was now near at

hand—that appointed for the decoration of the soldiers' graves. The strangers joined with the townspeople in friendly preparations; everybody talked reconciliation at a tremendous rate; and the Sunday before Mr. Shepherd preached such a beautiful sermon on forgiveness, that every woman in the church felt that she must invite the Yankees to a tea-party during the week, by way of showing her Christian grace. Van Tolliver, Mary Barton, and Mrs. Dexter made wreaths together in the wide front hall at Mr. Tolliver's during the afternoon preceding the great day.

"What is the order of exercises for to-morrow?" asked Mrs. Dexter.

"We are to be on the grounds at three o'clock," said Van, "and young Greyson is to give us a speech. Then somebody will recite 'The Conquered Banner,' and Mr. Shepherd will make a prayer."

"All that is so elaborate," said Mary Barton. "I think it would be much nicer to have no fixed ceremonies, but just to let the people go when they liked and decorate the graves. There would be more sentiment about it—don't you think so, Van?"

"Yes, I do; but then it would be a pity to deprive Greyson of the chance to air his eloquence. I don't doubt it has been his one thought since Christmas."

"This Mr. Greyson seems to be the clever young man of the town," said Mrs. Dexter, laughing. "I hear his *promise* spoken of in a vague, large way, as if it were a sugar-plantation in Texas."

"He is a cousin of Blythe Herndon's," said Mary; "and they do say that Blythe helps him to write his speeches."

"What! is she brighter than he is?"

"Oh, I don't suppose it is true; but every one has a great idea of Blythe's talent."

"She is a pretty girl," said Mrs. Dexter, "indeed, almost elegant, except for a little air of thinking herself superior to the other people."

"Yes, Blythe always had that. But when I was at Mr. Herndon's the other day, I thought I had never seen her manner so soft and sweet; and she certainly might have been excused for being very irritable and impatient, shut up as long as she has been."

"By-the-way, I wonder if Mr. Ellis isn't falling in love with her," cried Mrs. Dexter. "He ought to do so, I am sure, after tipping her out of the buggy: all the laws of romance demand it."

"I should be very sorry to see Ellis in love with any one of the Yariba girls," said Van.

"What, Van!" said Mrs. Dexter, in a pathetic tone, "are you still so bitter against 'these horrid Yankees?' What are you going to do about Miss Page, who will certainly marry Arthur Silsby—if she can?"

Mary glanced apprehensively at Van, but his face was impassive.

"If Miss Page did Captain Silsby the honor of accepting his proposals," he said, "there is no reason why she should not marry him. He is a gentleman, and a pleasant fellow. But Ellis is the sort of man that ought to be labelled dangerous."

"What *do* you mean? Colonel Dexter thinks the world of him. He is a most generous and unselfish man, and, I'm sure, a very brilliant one."

"That may be; but he seems to have no moral sheet-anchor."

"How do you know that?"

"I can hardly tell; but I have gathered it from certain expressions he has let fall. He avows himself a free-thinker, you know, and he has a specious way of talking that might easily blind the judgment, especially of such an impressionable young creature as Blythe Herndon."

"You must learn to be tolerant, Van."

"Tolerant—I hope I am; but I do not like to hear the adjective 'free' prefixed to such words as love or religion."

"Free religion?" said Mary, innocently; "what does that mean? Free from what?"

"From God, as far as I can understand it," said Van, dryly.

"Ah well, Van," said Mary, "you needn't fear that Blythe will fall in love with Mr. Ellis. I have heard her describe her ideal hero too many times. And besides, I do believe it would kill old Mrs. Herndon."

"What an implacable old lady she is!" said Mrs. Dexter. "I meet her sometimes in my walks, and actually it seems to me that her whole form *shrinks* as I pass by."

"She had a son killed in the war, you know; and she gave everything she had to the Cause—melted her silver, sold her books, and used to spend all her time—even Sundays—making lint for the hospitals. She had no more doubt of our final success than she had a doubt of her own existence."

"Does it not seem strange," said Mrs. Dexter, "that all over the land people can be praying for the entirely opposite results, and all with a firm faith that their especial prayers will be answered? It makes one doubt, at least, whether it is any use to pray at all. But I must not talk this way before Van! He will be declaring that I am as bad as Mr. Ellis."

"Mr. Ellis!" said Mrs. Tolliver, appearing at this moment—"are you talking of him? Well, now, I've such a funny thing to tell you. I have just been in the kitchen watching Aunt Sally make a rum omelet for Mis' Tolliver—he isn't very well to-day, and if I didn't watch Aunt Sally she would drink the rum—and she was telling me about Mr. Ellis. You know the night of the moonlight picnic, when they all were spilled out of the buggy? Bill got hurt. On the way home he began to cry and complain, and what does Mr. Ellis do but pick him up and bring him home in his arms!"

"No!" cried Mary.

"Yes; Bill told Aunt Sally himself. Of course it may be just one of his tales. You ought to hear Aunt Sally tell it. She is mightily disgusted—says Mr. Ellis is the sort of white man that is made out of scraps."

"I hope Bill was a little cleaner than he usually is," said Van.

"Well, he wasn't, for he fell into a mud-puddle."

At this Mrs. Dexter laughed heartily. "How like Ellis!" she cried; "it is lucky it wasn't daylight, and on the public square, for he would have gloried in doing the same thing with all Yariba looking on, had he felt that the interests of humanity required it."

While Mr. Ellis was thus being discussed, the gentleman himself, with neither of his ears burning, was talking earnestly with Blythe Herndon. The young girl's chair had been wheeled out on to the front porch, and Ellis sat on the steps, his head showing finely against a background of Madeira vines.

"It is too bad that I can't go out to-morrow," Blythe was saying; "but I owe it to my own imprudence. I tried to walk too soon, and have been thrown back a week."

"I believe you girls look on this as the most festive day of the year," said Ellis, smiling. "I saw Miss Page in town buying ribbon and flowers."

"Yes, Betty means to have a new hat. We all like to look our freshest and brightest on Decoration-day. It has got to be a sort of fashion."

"I wonder," said Ellis, slowly, "if I might ask a favor of you, Miss Blythe!"

"One? A dozen!" cried Blythe.

"Wait until you hear what it is. Have you ever noticed those four unmarked graves under one of the large trees in St. Thomas Hall lot?"

"Indeed I have," said Blythe, "and with real sympathy, Mr. Ellis; wondering what hearts had been desolated by the mystery of their deaths, what love was sighing to spend itself on their poor graves, unnoticed or scorned here in an alien land."

"Who or what they were," said Ellis, thanking her with a quick look, "we can never know. Enough that they were loyal men who gave their lives to their country. To-morrow I shall take their graves under my care. I could do this alone; but for some reason I should like for you to be associated with me in it. I want you to make me some wreaths and crosses—will you do it?"

"Of course I will, Mr. Ellis. Did you think so meanly of me as that I would refuse?"

"No, Blythe, no. I understand your generous nature too well."

Blythe colored bewitchingly—he had never called her Blythe before—but what more he might have said was prevented by the appearance of the grandmother. She glided by them with averted face, and passed into the front yard, where she stood plucking the dead seed-pods from a rose-bush with quick, nervous motions, the great diamond on her finger shooting little angry sparkles of light. Mr. Ellis perhaps felt a menacing influence, for he stayed but a little longer. As soon as he left, the grandmother came back to the porch where Blythe sat.

"I am sorry I can't offer you my chair, grandmamma," said Blythe, breaking off a gay tune that she was humming under her breath.

"I do not wish to sit down. Emma Blythe, have my ears played me false? Or did I hear that man asking you—my grandchild—to make wreaths to put on the graves of those vile murderers in St. Thomas Hall lot?"

"I don't know about vile murderers, grandmother. There are some soldiers buried there whose graves I shall be very glad to decorate. Poor fellows! I should think anybody would feel sorry for them. And besides, only see how generously the army people are acting about Decoration-day. Betty Page says that they are all going. And I know that Mrs. Dexter has been making wreaths with Van Tolliver and Mary Barton all day."

"Oh, you blind, foolish girl! Because these people, for the sake of having something to do, plunge into this excitement as they would into any other, you think them very fine and magnanimous. What do you suppose is in their hearts? They mingle with us to exult over us—to spy out the nakedness of our land. To-morrow they will laugh at the tears that flow. The touch of their feet will pollute the sacred ground where our dead lie. And yet you must grow sentimental over the graves of those wretches who helped to make our land the ruin that it is—robbers, cut-throats—"

"Spare the dead, grandmother."

"Spare the dead!"—and the old lady flashed a swift lightning glance upon her—"then shall I tell you what I think of the *living?* Of this Roger Ellis, who comes here day after day with the assurance that only his kind have—this bold-speaking, bold-looking man, who recommends himself to you, God knows how—"

"Stop, grandmother, stop!" cried Blythe, her face in a flame, her eyes illuminated with anger. "I won't listen to you! You shall not abuse my friends! I will put my fingers in my ears. How cruel of you, when you know I can't get away! You don't know Mr. Ellis. I won't hear you abuse him! I won't—I won't! If you begin again, I will sing 'MacGregor's Gathering' just as loud as I can scream it! There!"

The grandmother raised her hand as if to still a tempest.

"It would be too much, perhaps, to expect good manners from you, Blythe, after this summer's association," she said quietly, and passed into the house, leaving Miss Blythe to repent her undutiful outburst at leisure.

CHAPTER XIV

Decoration-day

Decoration-day in Yariba had very much the air of a village festival. Children danced about, scattering flowers as they passed; families from the country greeted friends in town with cordial effusion; young men and maidens smiled at each other over the funeral wreaths they bore. The presence of the army people gave to the day a new element of excitement; and one can scarcely tell which to admire most—the generous tact with which they were made to feel that their society was a pleasure, not an intrusion, or the warm sympathy with which they entered into the feelings of the day, and listened to the sad little details that every gravestone suggested.

It was a time to revive old memories. When Mrs. Meredith was seen entering the gate, leading her fair-haired boy who had never seen his father's face, and followed by an old negro man who had been her husband's body-servant and borne his body off the field, the story was told again of the gallant officer's bravery and daring; how he held a besieged town, and, when summoned to surrender, flung back the proud reply, "Mississippians *never* surrender!" and had fallen madly fighting, with his face to the foe; how his young bride had not even worn mourning for weeks and weeks after he died, but had gone about in her gay bridal garments, whose brave colors emphasized so pathetically her wild grief and isolation that no one dared speak of her dress, until at last mourning-clothes were provided for her, and now she would never wear any other; how the first time she had appeared in church after her widowhood it was to have her baby christened, and how everybody cried as she stood there, motionless as a figure in black marble, holding the milk-white babe to whom his father's name was given; how she had locked her piano, nor touched it in all these years; had never kissed any one on the lips; and had sold her diamonds to buy the fine tomb that was now the chief ornament of the burying-ground. It was a tall monument, in the centre of a level plot, with an urn at the four corners of the square, to-day heaped and running over with flowers. Close by its broken shaft the fair-haired boy set a flag-staff, from which drooped folds torn and riddled and stained with blood. It was his father's flag, brought here this one day of the year as a sacred relic. Old Ned, the colonel's servant, stood by it all day, telling over tales of the war to one after another who came— tales that year by year gained in breadth of richness and detail, as imagination lent her smiling aid to memory.

Another widow was talked over very tenderly. This was Mrs. Ross, who had sent her six sons to the war, and had seen them, one by one, brought back to her dead—even to the youngest, the slight lad who had looked like a masquerading girl in his gray soldier-clothes. But nowhere in all the country round was there a brighter and cheerfuller little woman than this mother bereaved of her all. Her house was gay with flowers; she wore soft, light colors; her eyes were smiling, and her withered cheeks were fresh and pink. She talked of her boys as if they were in the next room; she never put away their belongings, and they lay about the house as if six riotous young men were coming and going through its rooms. The active little lady would use Charley's whip on her drives; drink her milk-punch out of Tom's christening-cup—Tom was the baby; lend Eddy's books, scribbled over with his marks; read Joe's letters to choice friends, laughing heartily at their jokes; or snatch up Egbert's cap to crown her beautiful gray head when she chased the hens in her garden, or ran over to a neighbor's with a Charlotte-Russe or a dish of ambrosia. All the young people loved her; children crowded the house; those in trouble went to her for comfort, and those who had sinned found rest in her divine charity. But to one person living her heart seemed closed—to the young girl who had been engaged to her Walter, and who, after years of mourning, had married an-other. Decoration-day was to her the happiest in the year. She bubbled over with happy talk. "Only think how blest I am!" she would cry. "All my boys here—not one dear body lost to me, buried in some far-off grave. God knew just how much I could bear."

It was pretty to see the bright-faced old lady stooping among her graves, twining around each gravestone the flowers that he who lay beneath had best loved.

All this was kindly gossip; and there was none less friendly save a half-suppressed whisper of Miss Pointdexter's heartlessness when that tall and dignified young lady moved about with an indifferent air, not putting so much as a flower on poor Ralph Selph's grave, who had died with her name on his lips. None knew that in the early morning before the stars had gone from the sky they had looked down upon this girl kneeling at her lover's grave, weeping wild, hot tears, and laying on it, with her flowers, new vows of constancy that gave to him her youth, her bloom, her heart, herself, with all the absoluteness of a royal gift that it would be degradation to take back.

Mr. Greyson got through his speech creditably; then a youth, with an eloquent gesture in the direction of Colonel Meredith's battle-flag, recited "The Conquered Banner." He had a voice of music, and sobs resounded as he spoke. Indeed, it will be long before a Southern audience can hear that poem without the accompaniment of tears.*

> "Furl that Banner, for 'tis weary,
> Round its staff 'tis drooping dreary:
> Furl it, fold it, it is best;
> For there's not a man to wave it,
> And there's not a sword to lave it
> In the blood that heroes gave it;
> And its foes now scorn and brave it:
> Furl it, hide it, let it rest.
>
> Take that Banner down; 'tis tattered,
> Broken is its staff and shattered,
> And the valiant hosts are scattered
> Over whom it floated high.

---

* "The Conquered Banner," whose lyrics are presented here, was a popular postwar poem written by Abram Joseph Ryan (1838–1886), who had been a Catholic priest and a chaplain in the Confederate army. Father Ryan was often called the poet of the Confederacy for his many commemorative poems.

Oh, 'tis hard for us to fold it,
Hard to think there's none to hold it,
Hard that those who once unrolled it
Now must furl it with a sigh.

Furl that Banner, furl it sadly:
Once ten thousand hailed it gladly,
And ten thousand wildly, madly
Swore it would forever wave;
Swore the foeman's sword could never
Hearts like theirs entwined dissever,
Till that flag should float forever
O'er their freedom or their grave.

Furl it, for the hands that grasped it,
And the hands that fondly clasped it,
Cold and dead are lying now;
And the Banner it is trailing,
While around it sounds the wailing
Of the people in their woe:
For, though conquered, they adore it,
Love the cold dead hands that bore it,
Weep for those who fell before it,
Pardon those who trailed and tore it,
And, oh, wildly they deplore it,
Now to furl and fold it so.

Furl that Banner; true, 'tis gory,
Yet 'tis wreathed around with glory;
And 'twill live in song and story
Though its folds are in the dust.
For its form, on brightest pages
Penned by poets and by sages,
Shall go sounding down through ages,
Furl its folds tho' now we must.
Furl that Banner, softly, slowly;
Touch it not, unfold it never;
Let it droop there, furled forever!
For the people's hopes are dead."

A prayer followed the poem, that had the good effect of calming the excited nerves of the listeners. This concluded the ceremonies of the day, after which the people broke into groups that soon became cheerful. Betty Page wandered off with Captain Silsby to the graves on the side of the hill, where the unknown soldiers of the hospitals were buried, and the two sat down to rest under a tree at the end of a long row of graves.

"Our regiment," remarked Captain Silsby, who had made a mental vow not to talk about dead soldiers, "is the best drilled in the brigade; but I don't suppose you understand enough about tactics to appreciate that."

"Oh yes, I do. I think it is beautiful to see you drill your company. It moves like a machine. I wish you would give another skirmish drill. I never saw anything so pretty as a skirmish drill."

"I will have one in your honor. Haven't you a birthday, or something, coming off soon?"

"Oh, I can have a birthday at any time."

"Very well; appoint your day, and we will have a skirmish drill, with all the town invited, and you for the queen of the occasion."

"How charming! How kind you are!"

"Now, Miss Betty—as if I wouldn't go to the ends of the earth to please you!"

Betty thought it would be interesting at this point to coquet a little.

"I am sorry for one thing," said she, artlessly—"that the Thirteenth has so many more handsome men than the Third. Now, your company is so ill-assorted. There are some tall, some short men, two or three with blazing red heads, one that has had the smallpox, another with a broken nose—"

"By Jove!" interrupted the captain, "how closely you have examined my company!"

"Well, I've been invited to see it drill often enough. Now, Captain Tucker's company is made up of such straight, fine, soldierly fellows, all of a size. I like to hear him drill them. He is the only one of you who pronounces clearly. Upon my word, for a long time I thought that you all said '*Shoulder—humps,*' when you jerked out your order; but Captain Tucker says 'Shoulder arms' in a natural, easy way that any one can understand."

"If there is a company in either regiment that is poorly disciplined and drilled, it is Tucker's," said Captain Silsby, with a little heat.

"Then the Thirteenth's band," continued Betty, calmly, "is so much better than yours."

Captain Silsby looked moody.

"But your caps are nicer," said the *naïve* Miss Betty. "I think the crossed rifles in front are ever so pretty."

"Do you really? Now, that's lucky. I happened to have a duplicate of mine. I sent it on to New York, and had a pin put to it."

He drew a little box out of his waistcoat pocket and handed her the ornament.

"Wouldn't it make a good scarf-pin?" he said.

"Very good, indeed."

"Won't you wear it? Do say Yes. It would please me so much!"

"It would please me, too," said Betty, sweetly.

"Put it in now, in that floating black thing you have around your neck."

She pulled out the faded rose at her throat—Van had given it to her—and tried to fasten her scarf with the rifles. There was some difficulty with the clasp.

"Let me fasten it," said Silsby.

He disengaged the pin, that had caught in the lace. His hand almost touched her chin. She blushed, and allowed her eyelashes to flicker on her cheek.

At this moment Van Tolliver and Mrs. Parker passed on the other side of the tree. They saw, but they were not seen, for Betty and the captain were entirely taken up with each other.

"So I enroll you in the Third," said Silsby, gallantly. Van passed on with one glance of fire; and Betty—constant and consistent Betty—coquetted in peace at the side of a Southern soldier's grave, and felt not the slightest desire to throw herself into the waters of Yariba Spring.

Late in the afternoon Blythe saw Mr. Ellis on his way to St. Thomas Hall plot, with the wreaths and crosses she had made. Civil Rights Bill was with him, and when they reached the graves the two laid the flowers reverently upon them. Then Ellis stretched himself out under a tree that grew near, while Bill sat on the ground and watched him respectfully.

"You poor little atom, you!" said Ellis, "it was for you they died. Do you understand that?"

"No, sir," said Bill, promptly; "dey died befo' I was born."

"So did Jesus Christ," said Ellis. Then, seeing the child's

bewildered look, he said, "Listen to this, Bill, and tell me what you think of it:

> 'In the beauty of the lilies Christ was born across the sea,
> With a glory in his bosom that transfigures you and me.
> As he died to make men holy, let us die to make men free,
> As his truth goes marching on.'"

Bill's great black eyes were fastened on Ellis's face: his little dark face looked puzzled.

"Won't you say it agin, Mars' Roger, please, sir?"

"This time I will sing it for you, Bill."

His voice rolled out in the wild, sweet tune that illumines the stainless words, like a red light thrown on a crystal carving; and as Bill listened—who knows why?—two sudden tears sprang to his eyes and rolled over his face.

"Why, you poor little child," said Ellis, "you've got a soul, haven't you? What do you think of the song?"

"It's like being in de woods early in de mornin' befo' sun-up," said Bill, brushing away his tears and looking ashamed, "an' hearin' de hounds way, way off, bayin' long and clear. Seems s'if when I hear dat I can't keep in my skin. I mus' run or jump, or climb trees or swing from saplins."

"And should you like to do that now, Bill?"

"I'd ruther hear you tell some mo'," said Bill, timidly.

And late into the twilight the two sat there, and Ellis talked to the child, in whom he felt a constantly deepening interest.

It happened that night that Ellis could not sleep. Between eleven and twelve he got up, left his tent, and wandered some distance into the woods. His path wound upward, and finally he turned to look back at the camp—so white in its waving shadows—and the graves he had decorated touched with little gleams of silver as the moon shone on white flowers. As he stood there he saw, or fancied he saw, a figure moving among the trees. His blood thrilled tremulously; for he was not without a certain fine chord in his nature that would have echoed to a spirit-touch. He watched closely: yes, a figure was emerging from the shadows.

> "'Man or woman,
> Ghost or human,'

I must find out," he muttered. The apparition advanced slowly—

slight, all white—as if the vagrant moonbeams had taken shape and slid to earth. It reached the flower-covered graves, stooped, lifted a wreath, and the next instant, with a fierce gesture, stripped it of leaves and flowers and threw it to the ground. Ellis sprang forward with a hoarse exclamation, only to fall back with a look of horror; for it was no outraged Southern ghost that wrought this deed, but a breathing spirit of revenge that Ellis dared not touch. It was Blythe's grandmother—and she was asleep. Yes; in her sleep the tireless brain, the embittered heart, had sent the unconscious body on its errand of hate. Ellis could not turn his eyes away. He seemed to himself in some awful dream. Her face was fixed and livid; her eyes wide open; the wind blew her white hair and her white dress gently about her; the diamond on her finger flashed like a little demon's eye. One after another she gathered the wreaths, tore and trampled them.

"Blythe's grandmother!" he whispered, as he held himself in a leash, that he might not spring forward to save the graves from sacrilege.

At last the wild work was done and she glided away. Ellis then rushed forward, and picking up the poor, defaced flowers, tried to restore to them a little beauty. Again he laid them on the graves; and, with sleep banished for the night, he went back to his tent to ponder through all its hours on the implacable heart shut in the breast of this frail old woman.

CHAPTER XV

So Long as Blythe Is Willing

During the week following Decoration-day Van Tolliver paid Miss Page a visit, and Blythe Herndon took a walk; events not of a pronounced nature, perhaps, but of more than sufficient importance to those of whose lives these torn pages give a fragmentary glimpse. It is not necessary to dwell on the distressing details of Mr. Tolliver's visit, in which a graveyard scene was adverted to with lively frequency. At its close Van flung himself out of the house, with the air of one who only awaited a convenient opportunity of falling on his sword, and at the gate nearly fell against Mary Barton, who was just coming in.

"What is the matter, Van?" she cried, her heart giving such a leap that her face grew as white as his own.

He seized her hands.

"I am going away, Mary," he said. "I am going to the plantation. I must crawl off with my wound, like any other hurt animal. I have been a fool—the victim of my own conceit. I have dreamed of a love great enough to bear poverty and court isolation. I have found out that *it is too much to ask of any woman!*"

"There is such love, Van; there is! Do not let one girl's falseness destroy your faith in it," cried Mary, the blood rushing to her face in a crimson torrent.

"I will believe it, Mary," he said, more softly, "for I have known you. In your spirit there is no guile. Thank you for all you have been to me this summer. Good-bye, dear. I shall not see you again."

He wrung her hand, and hurried away, leaving Mary so agitated, that, except for the fact that she had been long accustomed to control her emotions, she must have turned back and gone home. She found Betty sewing some beads on a velvet jacket, her beauty characterized by as much serenity as usual.

"Did you meet Van, Mary?"

"Yes, I did. What have you been doing to him, Betty?"

"Nothing much. You know Van has been in love with me a long time."

"Yes, and I was sure you were engaged."

"Well, we were—off and on," said Miss Betty, "and now it's off for good and all."

"Oh, Betty! Betty!"

"He is so provoking!" said Betty, threading her needle. "He began at me about flirting with Captain Silsby. Then when I convinced him that I was an injured innocent, he declared that he would forgive me on one condition—and what do you think that was?"

"I cannot imagine."

"That I would marry him now—in three weeks' time—and go down to the plantation to live. I told him it was too much to ask of any woman."

"Not if the woman loved him, Betty."

"Love goes where it is sent," said Betty; "and it will be an uncommonly long time before I send mine to Van's plantation."

"How about Captain Silsby's tent?"

Betty laughed. "The captain doesn't talk love to me," she said; "he is all the time leaning toward sentiment—about like the tower of Pisa toward the earth—but he never quite falls into it. So I reserve my heart, and don't lose my sleep."

"I hope Van Tolliver may not," said Mary, in a low voice.

"Oh, Van will survive. He and I never were really suited, you know. He wouldn't let his wife dance round-dances for a kingdom. Poor Van, I hope he will marry some nice girl; but she will have a stupid time of it."

Much more did Miss Betty say, and Mary listened quietly, only hanging out two flaming little signals of emotion on her cheeks. She walked home with flying steps, and for the rest of the day manifested an extraordinary activity. She made a cake, put fresh flowers into all the vases, told stories to the children, and finally read aloud to her father until he was half asleep. Could it be that she feared to be alone with her own heart? And why, when she should have been quietly asleep, did she bury her face in her pillows as if to shut out some sound? Was it that the stars laughing in at her window, the moths beating against it, the rustling trees, and the wavering shadows, had all found voices, and were ringing in her ears, like a silver bell, the sweetest word to which lips can ever give utterance—hope?

It was a great day for Blythe when she took her first walk after her accident. She had never been in-doors so long before, and she passed through the square with a slight feeling of surprise at finding everything so unchanged. Still, the sunbrowned young men in linen suits and the countrymen in jeans chatted together; the black-faced old "uncles" lounged about; the patient mules stood around the courthouse; the cotton-wagons were being unloaded; the shops hung out their faded ribbons. Blythe stopped to buy a Chinese fan, and to kiss half a dozen young lady friends; then she passed out of this prosaic world into that other world of shade and coolness and pleasant sounds where the Spring gurgled a welcome. Here, with a new pleasure, her eyes dwelt on the giant rocks whose faces were covered with graybeard moss and whose feet rested in the silent pool. She walked to the bridge, and stood for a while watching the waving spears of moss, then raised her eyes to take in the evening's quiet beauty. The sun's face had disappeared, but the trail of his golden garments rolled in fiery forms along the blue floor of the heavens. The light fingers of the wind lifted and dropped the leaves in play until all the forest moved like a gently swelling sea. Down the stream, where it turned suddenly, like a broken silver bar, stood two mild-faced cows, ankle-deep in the shining water. Waiting for them to drink, was Billy Tolliver on the shore, giving utterance now and then to the melancholy and musical "Soo-oo cow—soo-oo-e—soo-oo-e," with which the darkies call the cattle home. The final interest was given to the picture when Roger Ellis came walking out of the woods and stopped to talk with Civil Rights Bill. He soon caught sight of Blythe on the bridge, and hurried to join her.

"How delighted I am to see you!" he said. "I did not know you were to be out to-day."

"Nor did any one," said she, with a smile; "but mamma and papa had gone to the country, grandmother was asleep, so I had no one's leave to ask but my own."

"And it does not hurt your foot to walk?"

"Oh, not in the least. I was very tired of staying in the house.

And how pleasant it is to see the woods and the water again," said Blythe, directing a frank glance toward Mr. Ellis, and meeting a look of passionate love that he made no attempt to conceal. For the languor of the summer evening had stolen into his veins; he scarcely dared speak lest his voice should break with tenderness.

As a bunch of grasses under a burning-glass quivers faintly before breaking into flame, so the sweet disturbance that precedes love agitated the maiden's heart as her eyes met his ardent glance. Her color fluctuated; her hands moved nervously.

"Let us go and sit on the stone bench and watch the moon rise over the water," said Ellis, gently.

"Mrs. Oglethorpe gave a little party last night," said Blythe, as they seated themselves. "Were you there?"

"No," said Ellis. "I am not very apt to go to such gatherings. I am like Rousseau, at once too indolent and too active to enjoy them."

"I don't understand exactly," said Blythe, looking interested.

"'The indolence of company is burdensome,' quoted Ellis, 'because it is forced; that of solitude is charming, because it is free. In company I suffer terribly from inactivity, because I must be inactive. I must sit stock-still, glued to my chair, or stand like a post, without stirring hand or foot, not free to run, jump, shout, sing, or gesticulate, when I want to—not even allowed to muse—visited at once with all the fatigue of inaction and all the torment of constraint; obliged to pay attention to every compliment paid, and compelled to keep eternally cudgelling my brains, so as not to fail when my turn comes to contribute my jest or my lie. And this is called idleness! Why, it is a task for a galley-slave!'"

"How little some people appreciate their blessings!" cried Blythe, "and what a dull, blind soul Rousseau must have had, to feel thus in the most brilliant and delightful society of the world! Why, do you know, my idea of perfect bliss is to be a society queen in Paris!"

"Heaven forbid such a life for you! And you would not like it as much as you fancy."

"Why not?"

Ellis's eyes twinkled. He took Blythe's fan from her lap, and, holding it up like a book, began, in a sing-song tone: "Three dear little boys went sailing to the west in a great balloon, accompanied by their teacher, who held advanced ideas, and taught by the natural method. 'Oh, see that splendid world!' cried one of the dear little boys, pointing to a gorgeous mass of floating color thrown like a blaze against the sky. 'How I wish we could go nearer to it!' 'We will sail thither,' said the teacher, with a wise smile. And when they had sailed into it, it was only a cloud of cool, gray mist, and the dear little boys were all chilled to the bone, and had to take three little nips of brandy, while the teacher, still smiling wisely, applied the moral."

Blythe's laugh rang out gayly. "Oh, Mr. Ellis, if the moral of your charming allegory is that I must stay content in Yariba, it is wasted on me. I cannot tell you how I long for life, movement, action. I am so tired of this place!—the quiet streets, the hills and the streams, and the moss eternally waving. I want to get away from it all. Nothing ever happens here. And only think—there are people living here who are old, and who have never been out of Yariba! Fancy having written against one's name in the book of fate only this:—was born—married—died."

"It is enough if you had said, was born—loved—died."

"It is the same thing, is it not? But love could not fill my life."

"Sappho thought it the only thing that could fill hers. Do you know her ode 'To the Beloved,' the most incomparable piece of writing in any language?"

"I have never read it. Repeat it to me, please."

Blythe! Blythe! what a chance you have given your lover.

My heart swells toward my unconscious heroine with sudden, half-pathetic tenderness. What a revelation awaits her! Farewell now to the fancies and dreams of her past! Never again will she lift eyes so innocently cold! Never again will she see silvered water flowing beneath a pale sky and a great white moon, but that a voice sweeter than singing will echo in her ear the rhymed cadences of Sappho's song:

> "Blest as the immortal gods is he,
> The youth who fondly sits by thee,
> And hears, and sees thee all the while
> Softly speak and sweetly smile.
>
> 'Twas this deprived my soul of rest,
> And raised such tumults in my breast;
> For, while I gazed in transport tost,
> My breath was gone—my voice was lost.

My bosom glowed; a subtle flame
Ran quick through all my vital frame;
O'er my dim eyes a darkness hung;
My ears with hollow murmurs rung.

In dewy damps my limbs were chill'd,
My blood with gentle horrors thrill'd;
My feeble pulse forgot to play,
I fainted, sunk, and died away."

His voice, low, resonant, and clearly musical, seemed to strike the very keynote of the young girl's being. The delicate voluptuousness of the poem set her heart to beating as tumultuously as if each word had been a lover's kiss.

Roger Ellis watched her face as it shone in the moonlight, and it dazzled him like the page of an illuminated book. Wild words trembled on his lips; but, with a woman's first impulse to hide an unwonted emotion, Blythe sprang to her feet.

"I must go home," said she, hurriedly; "it is growing late."

"It is chilly, too," said Ellis, drawing her hand through his arm.

"Yes; I hope we shall find a fire at home. I like a light blaze these August evenings."

"May I come in?" said Ellis, as they reached the gate.

"Certainly."

The fire in the parlor was burning low. Blythe knelt down by the woodbox and began to replenish it.

"Let me help you," said Ellis.

"You could not," said Blythe, laughing. "Making a wood-fire is like writing poetry—one must have a genius for it. About a year ago I made the acquaintance of a lady from the North, who soon began to question me about my accomplishments. When she found out that I was neither a musician nor a student, and detested fancy-work, sewing, and house-keeping, she looked at me over her spectacles and said, 'My poor child, Will you tell me what you *can* do?' And I answered meekly that I could make a very good woodfire. Fancy her disgust!"

She turned her laughing face, and looked over her shoulder at Mr. Ellis. The pine kindling, breaking into a blaze, deepened the red of cheek and lip and brought out the glory of her Titian hair. He was so near her that he could touch her shoulder with his hand.

"Blythe!" he said, in an unsteady voice.

She felt herself drawn gently toward him, and before the light smile could leave her lips, or a protest reach them, he had made them his own with a kiss. She sprang away from him, and stood crimson—trembling—afraid—ashamed.

"What does it mean?" her lips formed.

"It means, dear," he said, quietly, smiling a little, but still in that curiously unsteady voice, "that you must light the fires of my life for me. Will you be *my* Vesta, my darling, my own?"

Blythe had often imagined herself as playing a very poetic and satisfactory part in a love scene; but, alas! when the occasion came, four of her five wits went halting off. She could only droop her lovely head and say nothing.

"How beautiful you are!" he whispered. "Look at me, darling!"

She raised her eyes. She saw a dark face glowing with love; deep, passionate, yearning eyes that, resting tenderly on her, filled slowly with tears.

Tears—how they thrilled and startled her! Impulse, generosity, and a divine tenderness swept her toward him. He opened his arms with a glad, proud gesture, and she was drawn to the lonely heart that believed itself at last to have found a home.

"Blythe!" he cried, passionately, "never was woman loved as you shall be! I shall make all your Southern lovers tame to you."

"I haven't any Southern lovers."

"Let them come, then; and if any man can love you more than I, he is more worthy of you, and I can give you up."

"How can you talk of giving me up," whispered Blythe, "in the first moment that you know you have gained me?"

"Because, my darling, I accept with a kind of doubt the good the gods bestow. I hardly meant to tell you my love, but it was stronger than myself. It seemed to me that I should hold back when the beautiful young life, with its bright mind, its sincere heart, its great need of love, its greater power of loving, came near to mine; for perfect love is perfect self-sacrifice, taketh no thought of its own desires, looketh only to make more serenely happy the mate that it yearns for. And then I was so much older than you; I had seen and suffered so much: my ambition had burned to its embers; a great career was no longer possible—"

"Hush! hush!" cried Blythe, "do you think I should have liked you had you been an immature boy? I hate young men. I want to look up to my—"

She stopped short with a wide blush.

"To your husband, Blythe—sweet Blythe Ellis! Was there ever a more delicious little name! Darling, let me hear you say that you will be my wife."

"Yes," said Blythe softly, "I will be your wife—God willing."

"And I," he cried, pressing her hands to his lips, "will be your husband, God willing—or God *not* willing—so long as Blythe is willing!"

Steps were heard in the hall. "There are father and mother coming home," said Blythe. "Oh! what will they say to this? I had forgotten about your being a Northern man, and all that!"

"Miss Capulet, your Montague does not fear either your father or your mother. But, child! child! how your grandmother will hate me!"

"She cannot, when she knows you better."

Ellis had never told Blythe of the scene at the soldiers' graves: he thrust its ugly, ghostly remembrance from him with a shudder.

"Well, well," he said brightly, "we will hope for the best. Now, dear, how soon shall we announce our engagement to the wondering public of Yariba?"

"Announce our engagement?" cried Blythe, "why, never! We Southern people don't do that sort of thing. No Southern girl would have it known for the world that she was engaged."

"Why not, Blythe?"

"Oh! it would take away all the romance—every one would be talking about her, and none of the other young men would pay her any attention: and the engagement might be broken, or she might not be in earnest when it was made. One of the girls here was engaged to eleven at the same time."

"Blythe, you alarm me. it seems that engagements in this country are as numerous and as honorable as duels at Heidelberg. May I be so impertinent as to ask your record?"

"I am twenty-one years old," said Blythe, proudly, "and you are the first sweetheart I have ever had—the only man who ever kissed the tips of my fingers."

Then he said a thousand tender and flattering things to her; and her vanity, like the slave that ran by the emperor's horse, kept pace with the swift rush of his words—so convincing is the magnificent unreserve of a strong soul. And if any one had said to Blythe, in this delicious hour, that Cleopatra was loved more madly, she would have put away the thought in scorn, as Roger Ellis poured out a wine for her drinking pressed from his life's experience, sweet and rich as a cup of the gods offered to eager human lips.

CHAPTER XVI

The Grandmother's Last Stake

"Oh, the shame of it! the shame of it!"

It was night, and the grandmother was alone in her room. A few hours since she had been told of Blythe's engagement, and in the same breath her son had added that he had consented to the match and approved of it; and Blythe's mother with tears had begged the old lady to try and be reconciled to her child's lover. She had said nothing; words were idle, even had the offence not been too monstrous for expostulation. But when night came and she shut herself up in her room, she made her moan in a terrible and deep despair. What could she do to prevent it? Nothing—nothing—nothing! "I am so old and helpless and weak," she murmured, wringing her frail and fevered hands. "I have no brain to plot or plan. God help me! I can do nothing." She started at the sound of her own words, and a sudden gleam of light passed over her face. How dare I tell the strange train of thought that awoke in her brain? Since the day that the news came of Lee's surrender she had ceased to pray; she thought that she had ceased to believe in a God. She had gone no more to church, and had refused to listen to the ingenious arguments with which Mr. Shepherd, in common with other Southern pastors, tried to excuse God's failure to meet the wishes of the Southern people. But now, as she walked up and down the room with noiseless steps, an old faith stirred within her, mingled with the daring impiety that had grown to be her second nature. In short, Mrs. Herndon was making up her mind to forgive God the past, if he would grant her prayer for the future. She flung herself on her knees by the bed, humbling herself at last, and prayed—prayed that God would do what she could not—prevent this loathed and hated marriage. She pleaded with God for this proof of his power, and promised him her soul as a reward.

"Grant me this, O God, and I will strive to see thy justice even in the ruin thou hast brought upon this wretched country. I will love and serve and worship thee all my days. Hear me, God! Fulfil now the promises made unto thy people, and listen to the voice of my despair."

Thus far into the night she prayed, while tears burned along her cold cheeks, until at last her voice grew hoarse, her eyes dry and dim, and she crept to bed a pale, faintly breathing image, exhausted with emotion but strong in a new-born hope.

From that time the grandmother seemed a changed being. Her face grew even more rapt and far-off in its expression; she spoke little, and never in her old tone of bitterness; the family thought her almost reconciled to the thought of Blythe's marriage. With her new gentleness came a physical change. Her voice gained a fuller tone, her form a firmer erectness; she fancied that the strength of youth had come back to her, upborne as she was by the excitement of her strange inner life. Morning, noon, and night, whether kneeling alone or moving among her people, she prayed. She resorted to prayer as a stimulus, and such was her fervid will that it never failed to leave her in a state of exaltation. She rarely spoke to Blythe of her engagement, but the young girl in her presence became dimly aware of a strong opposing influence; and sometimes, after the novelty of having a lover had worn away, and her mind was in a languid state, if she happened to be standing by her grandmother when Roger was coming toward her, she would feel as if the air about her had condensed to a force that pushed her with a gentle steadiness in an opposite direction. It was a strange feeling—one that was instantly overcome by an effort of will; but she was vaguely conscious that if she should yield to it, the movement of her body would follow its guidance as surely as if she were an automaton pushed about by human hands.

But all this was so trifling as to be hardly remembered when Roger was near; and the weeks drifted by that opened a new world to Blythe and glorified an old one to her lover. Ellis remembered these weeks afterward as the most perfect of his life. He was aroused from the unworldly happiness of the sweet days by letters requiring his immediate return to the North. He saw at once that he must go; but, he hoped, not alone. Strolling through the woods with Blythe, he told her of the necessity of leaving her within a few days, and after pleasing himself for a while with her surprise and distress, he said:

"And now, Blythe, for a test of your character! The time has come when I am to see where your unlikeness to other young women ends and likeness begins."

"Am I unlike other girls?" said Blythe, demurely: "tell me how, please."

"What an outrageous bid for flattery! Well, then, I have seen handsomer women than you are, but none with such witchery of hair, and eyes, and mouth. I have known cleverer women, but none with so lovely an enthusiasm, and not one so shy in her tenderness, so delicate in her expression, so pure in her soul. Blythe, my child, you dazzle me sometimes. I want to shade my eyes when I look at you."

Blythe laid her hand lightly across his lips. "No more of that, Roger. You make me feel ashamed that I am not better. Now for the test of character!"

"What I wish to know, Blythe," he said solemnly, "is, how much you are held in the bondage of fashion."

"Not very much," she said, laughing, "as I make all my own dresses."

"And very pretty ones they are," said Roger, looking her over with an approving eye.

Blythe was singularly pretty to-day. She had on a white dress, and as she passed through the hall she had caught up a short red cloak that hung on the rack, and had tossed one of her brother's hats on her head—a broad, soft straw, under which her peach-bloom face shone with exquisite delicacy.

"Now, I like this dress particularly," continued Roger, touching her flowing white skirts. "Don't you think it would make a very pretty wedding-dress, Blythe?"

"This!" cried Blythe; "why no, dear. Don't you see it is *thick*?"

"So it is!" said Roger, with an air of surprise: "how stupid of me not to notice that! Of course, a wedding-dress shouldn't be thick."

"Unless it is silk or satin, or something of that sort, you know."

"Certainly," said Roger, with easy assurance—"silk, or satin, or bombazine—"

"*Bombazine!*" and Blythe gave a laugh that must have startled the birds.

"Come now, Blythe, don't lead a man on to his ruin and then laugh at him. Tell me, darling, how long would it take to get up the proper and conventional wedding-dress?"

"Oh, that depends! If you were to order it from a city dressmaker, she would probably keep you wasting in despair for weeks and weeks after the time she promised to let you have it. If you made it at home, and called in all your neighbors to help, you might have it ready in a week."

"A week!—I can stay just a week longer," said Roger, with deep meaning in his tone. But Blythe was deaf to his hints.

"Only a week!" she sighed. "Let us not think of it, Roger. Who knows if we shall ever meet again?"

"Blythe, don't you see what I am driving at?" cried Roger. "I want to take you with me, my darling. I want to be married right off, as you Southern folk say. Oh, my love, say yes, I implore you!"

The color flew out of Blythe's face and into it again. "It is impossible!" she said, breathlessly.

Then Roger set to work to convince her of how possible a thing it was; and, of course, it was not many minutes before she began to yield, and not an hour before she had quite consented to marry him in a week's time, if her family would hear of such a sudden arrangement.

Ellis lost no time in preferring his request to Blythe's father, and that gentleman promised to think it over; and it was discussed at length in the family circle. Mr. Herndon did not "like things done in a hurry;" and Mrs. Herndon "could not bear to think of the poor child marrying without anything to put on." Still, as tender parents should, they waived these little prejudices, and were about to announce their consent, when—the grandmother spoke.

"Emma Blythe," she said, quietly, "I shall say nothing of the indecent haste of marrying a man whom you scarcely know, and leaving your home with him; I shall say nothing of the suffering in store for you when you, a Southern girl, find yourself among enemies and strangers; but I shall make a prayer to you. Do you remember, my child, eight years ago, when I had that long siege of illness—rheumatic fever?"

"Yes, grandmother."

"Do you remember how constantly you were with me? how you rubbed me, nursed me, tended me? how you listened when I told you of my sorrows, and did not weary of my groans? how you read to me, sung to me, wept over me?"

"I remember it all, grandmother," cried Blythe, tears rushing to her eyes. "Why do you speak of it now?"

"I appeal to that memory, dear, because Blythe the young lady has loved me less than Blythe the child. It may be that it has been my fault—I have been cold, and harsh, and unloving—though you, of all others, have always been nearest my heart. But the ghosts of those that are gone come like a cloud between me and the living. I have little joy in my life. I have fallen on evil times. My days are numbered, Blythe. It will not make you happier when I am gone to think that you refused my last request."

"And that request, grandmother?" said Blythe, trembling.

"It is not to give up your lover, child," she said, with a slight, cold smile; "do not look so alarmed. It is only that you will defer your marriage six months. Is it too much to ask?"

"No, grandmother, it is not; I will do as you wish," said Blythe, mastered by the influence that seemed to be closing like bands around her, and ready, too, to make a sacrifice that seemed so small to one whose wishes she had treated so lightly from the beginning.

"You promise—solemnly?"

"I promise—solemnly!"

A long, quivering sigh escaped the old lady's lips. She leaned back in her chair and closed her eyes. Mr. and Mrs. Herndon warmly praised their daughter's docility, and commended the moderation of the grandmother's demand. But neither heard them. The one was lifting up her soul in passionate gratitude to God, the other was wondering what her lover would say when she told him of her promise.

What he did say was something under his breath that Blythe did not hear; then—"I knew she would injure me," he said, with a strange look on his face. He remembered the tearing hands, the trampling feet.

It was now Blythe's turn to argue; and though she did not quite succeed in convincing her lover that delays were not dangerous, she brought a smile to his lips, and with a judicious kiss made him forget that she was—Mrs. Herndon's granddaughter.

Blythe was a little dissatisfied with herself that she did not feel this disappointment more keenly. And, to tell truth, she had been a little dissatisfied with herself almost from the beginning of her engagement. She was perhaps more unlike other women than Ellis had imagined. Her imagination was highly sensitive; she could not read an impassioned love scene without a thrill of the blood; she believed ardently—or thought she did—in the theory of "All for love and the world well lost." Then why, in the very moment when her lover clasped his arms about her and told a rosary of kisses on check and brow and lip, did she feel a vague sense of something missed? What was the little mocking inner voice that, even at the moment of her highest feeling, questioned the reality of her emotion—even ridiculed it? Was this all she should know of the passion for which empires had been thrown away? Or was love something that must *grow* until every lesser feeling should be pushed out by its spreading roots?

Mr. Ellis, it is needless to say, did not dream that Miss Blythe was becoming an analyst and critic. Many a delicious thought had come to him of her sweet impassioned Southern nature, for her self-surrender had been absolute. Had it not been so, her disappointment would at least have been longer in coming. After all, it was scarcely more than a breath on a mirror; her admiration for her lover was unbounded; she was proud of his love; and she would have become his wife at the time he wished, with high hope and happiness, had God and her grandmother so ordered it.

Roger Ellis left Yariba with strange reluctance. He could not account for it. He should be back in a few weeks; Blythe would write to him every day; and yet an oppression that he could not shake off fell upon him as he drove over to the station and looked back upon the little town among its hills and springs. Once back at the North, however, his natural buoyancy asserted itself. He announced his engagement to a few of his intimates with peculiar complacency; indeed, he could scarcely help talking of Blythe, for he seemed to draw in thoughts of her with his breath.

"I do not worship her"—it was only to himself he said this—"nor even adore her. I see her faults. I am too old a man to be blinded by my passion as a youth might be; but I love her with reason and devotion, and I am as much her friend as her lover."

And then Mr. Ellis, being in a hotel, rang for pen, ink, and paper, and wrote this letter to his lovely Southern sweetheart, whom he did not worship nor even adore:

New York, August 15th.

I reached here yesterday morning, my darling, and intended to write a day sooner, but I was hurried by business until late in the afternoon, and when evening came was dragged off to some patriotic tea-party by friends whom I could not well refuse. When I got back I was all tired out, and had no wish to write to you. No wish—for I cannot give the dregs of my life, even of a day, to her who has given the richest vintage of her life to me. I lead a charmed life. I am encompassed round about with the glory of your love. I see the cares and sorrows of humanity as trees, walking. I am young again with the ripeness of a power which boyhood cannot know; and I find it all needed to express the richness and fulness of my love for you. My own, my beautiful, I thank God for you. I bless you as his most perfect symbol of love. I am grateful for my life, because you have shone with all the splendor of your heart and mind across it. For your bright intellect, I love you; for your pure heart, I love you; for your beautiful body, type of a beautiful spirit, I love you; and I love you because to me you have been the most beneficent and most radiant soul that has ever brightened my life with its pure effulgence. Darling! I kiss you as I would kiss a messenger of God sent to compensate me for all the wrongs I have endured without a murmur, and for all the sorrows whose history only my secret sighs have told. I love you, Blythe, heart, soul, and body—with my heart, soul, and body I love you. Fate itself I defy; for be its decree what it may—hear me, *God,* who made us both!—body and soul I am *hers,* and hers only, now, henceforth, and for aye. Amen. For I love you! I love you!

My own, my mate, my beautiful one! to me the rustle of your garments is sweeter music than earth yields to the spell of genius; to touch your hand is to open the doors of a heaven fuller of more exquisite joys than any Elysium that the Greeks or the Hebrews ever dreamed of; to me your face is a revelation of goodness which no other writing of the Infinite declares.

I love you!

I take your bright face between my hands once more, and gaze into your glorious eyes and kiss them tenderly, and with a love that even the most perfect kiss can never express. I kiss your forehead, shrine of a brilliant and noble intellect, and I kiss your white hands, as I would kiss your feet, with a pure and manly love which is too genuine either to exalt or debase itself, and too sincere to see homage of a servile kind in any form of acknowledgment of an absorbing and overwhelming and inspiring affection.

I love you!

For your sweet sake I love your people whom I hated; for you I abjure all enmities that a life of warfare has brought forth; for you, my queen, my royal and glorious mate, I love whatever can be loved in the life and thought of your countrymen; I abjure all but honor and honesty, and these I cannot give up, because without them I should not be worthy even to *say*—I love you!

For you, flower—and the fairest flower of the South! I bless the South. I shower benedictions on the people against whom I urged endless and remorseless war. For you, except to kneel to its Baal, I shall do all I can to serve it. I shall ever thrill with a mystic delight when I hear the very name of the South.

I love you!

I shut my eyes, and see again the pure and stately maiden whose voice has been my most heavenly music since first I heard it—whose eyes have thrilled me with the most celestial pleasures I have ever known—whose heart and soul have inspired me with a joy and hope and gladness that I never yet knew, nor believed could be.

I bless you!

I love you! and I am ever and forever yours.

R. E.

It was Blythe's first love-letter; and well I know the changing cheek, the rosy blushes, the quickened sense, with which she read. How the lovely little bosom throbbed when she kissed the scattered sheets and placed them against her tender heart! How nature's soft glory moved her soul to a mysterious delight as she walked by the spring with shining eyes! How she started half in fear if one spoke to her suddenly, as if the refrain of her ardent letter were a shouting Greek chorus that all the world might hear! After all, there is a wonderful charm in *first times;* and Blythe never felt again quite this same tumult of emotion on reading a love-letter, though a new one came every day, and there was no falling off in their sustained fervor. But they made her very happy; and the grandmother, watching her soft, contented face, redoubled her prayers, thinking desperately of the widow and the unjust judge, who was wearied into clemency by much pleading.

CHAPTER XVII

Miss Page's Strategy

"I was sorry to see you come," said Betty Page; "but oh, how much more sorry I am to see you go!"

Miss Betty was standing on the front porch, with a watering-pot in her hand, while Captain Silsby was sitting in a dejected attitude among her geraniums. They were discussing the marching orders that had just been received by the two regiments.

"You look a perfect image of sorrow," said the captain, wishing that he knew how much the young lady did care.

"I'm sure," said Miss Betty, "I could scarcely sleep last night for thinking of it. How dull the winter will be without you! No more serenades, nor picnics, nor germans, nor rides—"

"Shall you miss nothing more than these?" said Captain Silsby, faintly reproachful, with his head a little on one side.

"Oh, certainly! There are Captain Simcoe's jokes, and Major Bullard's songs, and the visits of my friend Mrs. Dexter, who is just coming through the gate now, by-the-way, as you will see if you look from behind that pillar."

"How very annoying! It seems to me that I never have a quiet word with you of late. I must have one long evening before I go. When shall it be?"

"To-morrow, if you like. I am engaged for this evening. How do you do, Mrs. Dexter?" and she ran down the steps to shake hands. "Won't you come in?"

"Let us stay out here awhile," said Mrs. Dexter; "I always like to see the flowers just after they have been watered. Don't let me drive you away, Captain Silsby."

"I was just on the point of going," said the captain, bowing himself off with easy grace.

"There is one thing that young man can do well," said Mrs. Dexter, as the gate closed behind him—"or perhaps I should say two things: he knows how to enter a room and how to take leave; but for the rest—" She shrugged her shoulders expressively.

"Now, see my ignorance!" said Betty, artlessly. "I thought that he was one of your finest specimens of Northern culture."

"He has good manners, as I have said," returned the little Northern lady sharply, "but he is a frivolous, lazy fellow, without any object in life except amusement. Then he isn't sincere," she went on, with a touch of Betty's own artlessness. "He is always making love to some girl who happens to be near him. Of course, each one thinks that *she* is the one to whom he will be constant. I have often felt very sorry for the deluded creatures—who are not to blame, of course—for he usually selects simple-minded girls, who have not had enough experience of the world to understand a man of Silsby's stamp."

"How lovely of you to be a sort of dictionary of his character!" said Betty, sweetly, "and how infinitely he would be obliged to you if he knew about it! No doubt he would manage to return the favor in some way."

("She will tell him," thought Mrs. Dexter, biting her lips in vexation, "and there isn't a man who dances the german who knows my step so well. Ethel Dexter, what an imprudent creature you are! But this girl is too aggravating!")

"To tell the truth," said she, sociably, "I believe Van Tolliver has spoiled me for all other young men."

"Is Van a paragon of yours?" said Betty, lazily picking the dead leaves off a geranium-bush.

"Indeed he is. I admire him in every way. He looks like one of Vandyke's heroes, with his dark face under that broad hat he wears. Then he is so noble, manly, earnest, self-sacrificing! By-the-way, he has invited us to make him a visit. I am so anxious to see a Southern plantation! We are going to stop for a few days, on our way down to New Orleans. Elegant idea, isn't it?"

"Yes, for those who like that sort of thing. I think a plantation the dullest place in the world."

"I do not agree with you. It gives a man great dignity to own large estates. There is a noble pride about his way of living—so different from our rough-and-tumble army life. The only trouble about Van is that he must be lonely at times. But I don't know any one who is good enough for him to marry, unless it is Mary Barton. She is a great favorite of mine."

("You malicious thing!" thought Betty.)

But she only said, with the faintest possible trace of imitation, "Elegant idea! Hadn't you better suggest it to Van? I don't believe it has ever entered his head."

"Don't be too sure of that," said Mrs. Dexter, smiling mysteriously. "Van may have had little love affairs with one girl and another, but when it comes to a question of marriage he is too wise not to appreciate a charming, well-balanced girl like Mary Barton."

"It has not been my observation," returned Betty, "that well-balanced girls hold any particular charms for men. However, Mary is a dear good girl. She would suit admirably as the mistress of a plantation. She is naturally domestic."

("She is worth twenty times as much as you, you little goose.")

This mentally, as Mrs. Dexter rose, saying, "Is your mother here? I must go in and say good-bye to her."

Betty led the way in, feeling that she had kept up her end of the plank nobly in this feminine balancing; and as Mrs. Dexter and her mother talked, she formed a plan. "The little cat gave me a hint, in spite of herself," she thought.

Accordingly the next day Miss Betty asked Blythe Herndon and Mary Barton to stay all night with her. Then she wrote pretty little notes to different officers of her acquaintance, inviting them to spend the evening; and she set out a table with ambrosia, and syllabub, and fruit-cake, for their entertainment; and when Captain Silsby arrived, in a mood of parting tenderness, he found the parlor filled with company, and Betty heartlessly gay. He felt himself to be an injured man. There was no chance to be sentimental, so the noble captain sulked. It was not long before he rose to go. "Goodbye, Miss Betty," he said, with a sad attempt at dignity. "I suppose I sha'n't see you again."

"You are not going so soon?" cried Betty, with charming surprise. "I thought you promised to spend a long evening."

Captain Silsby bowed stiffly, and murmured something that

nobody heard. Then he stepped into the hall, to reappear in a moment with—"Miss Betty, may I have a word with you?"

He was standing by the hat-stand in the hall, his fair mustache pressed hard upon his lower lip. Betty excused herself, and joined him. But before he could speak she took up Captain Simcoe's cap and placed it jauntily on her black braids.

"Does it become me?" she said, with the very spirit of mischief dancing in her eyes.

"I do not like you in it at all," said the captain; "and if you were my sister I should say you were not—ladylike."

"Lady-like!" cried Betty, with a pretty scorn. "Don't you know, Captain Silsby, that it is only people who are *not* ladies who must be lady-*like?* and Betty Page can never be merely *like* what she is— a lady by the grace of God—though she put a soldier's cap on her head, and gives you a military salute in saying, 'Good-night and good-bye.'"

She raised her hand in a mocking salutation, tossed the cap upon the stand, and was back in the parlor before the mortified captain could reply. He went back to camp much more in love than he had yet been, which proved the wisdom of Miss Betty's course; and that astute young person, when alone in her room, nodded to her image in the mirror with great satisfaction. "If he *means* anything," she thought, "this won't change him; if he doesn't, he can't boast of his conquest of Betty Page!"

And the two regiments marched away from Yariba, followed by as many good wishes as if they had been a lot of brides. Good wishes from all save a pale old lady, who stood on a high veranda, pressing a locket to her bosom, watching them with long glances of hate; and who said, as the last glimmer of their blue ranks was lost in the forest, "Now I can breathe a breath of pure air!"

CHAPTER XVIII

An Elegant Idea

"So this is Laurel Station?" said Mrs. Dexter; "and it is here that Van is to meet us."

"There he is now," cried the colonel. "Look sharp, Ethel!— short stop, you know. Are these all your traps? This way."

Van was on horseback, looking more like a knight than ever. He lifted his hat as heads were thrust from the car windows and eager salutations called out, for all the army people had liked the young man.

Springing off his horse as Mrs. Dexter and the colonel appeared, he greeted them with delighted warmth.

"I have a spring-wagon here for you," he said. "You will find it very comfortable, Mrs. Dexter. Colonel, I would offer you my horse, but he is really such a vicious beast— Steady, Tempest!"

"Thanks, thanks; I prefer this, I assure you," said the colonel, helping his wife into the wagon drawn by a pair of frisky young mules.

"This is Daddy Ned," said Van, waving his hand toward a white-haired old man who stood at their heads, "who will drive you with the skill of a Roman charioteer over the devious ways that lead to the plantation."

They started off, Mrs. Dexter looking with interest on the little Southern town, that seemed too lazy to hold itself upright; for the houses were rickety, the fence-rails tumbled over each other, the men leaned up against things: very brown men some of them were, who had lived "i' the sun," until hardly to be distinguished, save for their lazy air of command, from their brethren whose color had been burned in before the light of the sun had touched their faces.

Van's home was fifteen miles away, but the drive was full of interest. His Northern guests were surprised at the variety of scenery in a low, flat country. Now it was a wide, still sheet of water, with reedy grass growing along its edges, and tall white flowers and lance-like spears in shining shadows on its surface; now a long, slim, curling stream winding through willows, and kissing weeds whose faces blew lightly together across its dividing line; and water again—thick, red, muddy creeks, their intolerable color broken with little green islands as round as footstools. Nor was human interest lacking. Smiling darkies just out of babyhood, whose rags fluttered breezily about their small persons, as if they were young trees in full leaf, and whose appearance suggested that they must have been dipped in tar before having their clothes stuck on, shouted "Howdy?" as they passed; old "uncles," standing knee-deep in withering broom, gave them cheerful greeting. Cabins dotted the road at wide distances, over which broad banana-leaves drooped heavily. By one poor little house, in a fenced-in plot, was a poor little grave. A dwarfed magnolia grew beside it, stiff-leaved and shining glossily—stern sentinel for a grave so pitiful and small that it seemed to beg some weak, soft tribute of flower or clinging vine.

Then there were the trees—the strange trees weighted, whether in green leaf or dry leaf, with the long, dim moss that gave sombreness and mystery to the woods. Fancy could run wild among them. Here a long line of them green-topped with bare, dead trunks, about which the moss has wound itself coil on coil: like paralyzed bodies, with living, miserable heads that know death is slowly creeping up to them. Some grew in a bold erratic way, that in their youth may have been a daring grace; but they were old, and dry, and leafless now, and the very moss was cruel, for it hung from them in a shreddy sort of way, leaving their ugliness unshaded and bare. Others made one think of young widows; the moss draped them heavily, like deep dark weeds, but little budding, tender leaves were shooting from every limb, like furtive glances and half-checked smiles.

"We are nearing home now," said Van.

As he spoke, a turn in the road revealed a queer figure standing on the edge of a stream. It wore a short skirt, from which a pair of man's brogans obtruded, a short sack, and a battered hat, under which could be seen long twists of hair coiled in a knot. Evidently it was not meant for a scarecrow, for as it peered into the water it gently agitated a fishing-rod.

"Van, Van, see that thing!" cried Mrs. Dexter. "Can you tell me what it is?"

Daddy Ned broke into a grin, and Van laughed as he said, "Oh, that is old Uncle Si', one of the characters on the plantation."

"A man? But the hair!"

"Thereby hangs a tale. When Uncle Si' was young, he fell in love with my grandmother's waiting-maid, who, poor girl, walking out one day when the Big Muddy was up, fell in, and was drowned. In his affliction Si' made a vow never to cut his hair again, and he has kept his word. On the plantation he is held up as a model of constancy, and the beauty of it is that he has had about as many wives as ever Solomon had! This does not at all impair his reputation as a widowed and grief-stricken soul; as old Aunt Mely, my cook, said to me: 'Lor', Mars' Van, he jes' takes up wid dem foolish women to 'stract his mind; but all dat po' soul longs fer is to meet Sally on de oder side of Jordan.'"

"Delightful Uncle Si'!" cried Mrs. Dexter; "he ought to be put into a book."

"Our land begins here, colonel," said Van; "but I am forced to let all these outer fields lie idle. They are gradually eating themselves up; but I am hoping that when Government gets hold of them they will be sold to a good class of emigrants who will improve the country. For myself, I shall attempt nothing more than a small farm of two or three hundred acres. My father nearly ruined himself by trying to make things go under the old plantation system."

A few moments more of rapid driving brought them in sight of the house—a great rambling structure, with wide piazzas on either side.

"So this is your home, Van," said Mrs. Dexter, softly; "where you were all born, I suppose?"

"Yes, and where we are all buried," said Van, pointing out a heavily-shaded enclosure with chilling glimpses of marble. "Some afternoon I will take you to our family burying-ground, and if you like you may sit on the flat tomb of my great-grandfather, and I will read you the epitaphs and tell you stories of the dead and gone Tollivers."

Mrs. Dexter began to say "Elegant idea!" but her husband

turned his fierce eyebrow upon her in time to prevent the seal of her favorite phrase upon Van's suggestion.

An old black woman met them at the door with a very fine courtesy.

"This is my old Aunt Silvy," said Van, "who keeps house for me, and makes coffee that the gods might be proud to drink."

Aunt Silvy received the praise with dignity.

"Supper's about ready," said she; "but I suppose the lady would like to freshen her dress a bit after her ride."

"Yes; show her to her room, Aunt Silvy."

Mrs. Dexter followed Aunt Silvy upstairs, quite impressed by the good bearing and gentle speech of the old servant.

"Do you never go to Yariba, Aunt Silvy?" she inquired.

"Oh no, ma'am; Mars' Van couldn't get on without me to see to him."

"Mars' Van ought to get married and have a wife to see to him; don't you think so?" said Mrs. Dexter, sociably.

Aunt Silvy relaxed a little from her dignity.

"Yes, ma'am, it would be a mighty pleasant thing to see Mars' Van with a wife, and he deserves a good one if ever a boy did. I'se been thinking he was in love with somebody up in Yariba; but when he come home this time, and I asked him after his sweetheart, he kind o' lifted his eyebrows and said he didn't have any sweetheart. 'But you us'ter have,' says I. And with that he took his egg out of his cup—he was just beginnin' breakfast—and he says, 'True, Aunt Silvy; and this egg used to be in the cup.' Then what does he do but throw the egg out of the window, where of course it broke all to pieces, and says,

'An' all the king's horses an' all the king's men
Can't set Humpty Dumpty up again.'

I thought it was a mighty curious way for the boy to do; but I wasn't brought up to question folks, so I wouldn't say nothing more to Van, for all I nursed him, and love him like my own."

"All the secret, I fancy, is that he was smitten with some pretty girl who wasn't worth loving, and he found it out," said Mrs. Dexter, lightly; "but his heart isn't hurt a bit."

Her trunk had been sent up by this time, and at the unaccustomed sight of woman's finery Aunt Silvy grew still more cordial.

"I'll wait on you myself, honey, while you are here," she said.

"Mars' Van wanted me to call in one o' the young slips for your maid, but they're all as triflin' as cotton-seed butter—wishy-washy. What do they know about waitin' on a real lady? I'm powerful glad you're come, and I hope you'll stay a long time at the old place." And so she talked while Mrs. Dexter made herself fair before the mirror.

This accomplished, they went down to the dining room—a great barn of a room, so dimly lighted that a white dog coming to meet them from a dark corner, loomed up with such sudden large ghostliness that Mrs. Dexter gave a little start and caught Aunt Silvy's arm. At the farther end was cheerfulness—cheerfulness in the shape of the lamp with its gay shade, a smiling waiter, moon-faced and yellow, Van, beaming with hospitality, and a round table upon which was spread a Southern supper: Broiled chickens; waffles brought in hot every five minutes, crisp and brown, with drops of golden butter in their dimples; Sally Lunn, light and white (blessed be the Sally who first gave to its particles local habitation and a name!); batter-bread—a delicious mingling of eggs, milk, and meal, known only unto a Southern cook; water-melon preserve, with elaborate green embroidery on its leaves and hearts; cream—goblets of cream; and coffee to make a Turk doff his turban—such is a Southern supper, that no one enjoys more than a Northern man. Colonel Dexter was not proof against its temptations, though he declared that he ate in the spirit of the soldiers who buried Sir John Moore. "I bitterly think of the morrow," he said. "Yes, Aunt Silvy, another cup of that coffee, if you please. I'm in for it, anyhow."

The week went by trippingly. The three friends rode, walked, and talked in great harmony; and the last day but one of their visit Mrs. Dexter put a secret resolve into execution.

Colonel Dexter had gone off fishing with Uncle Si'; she and Van were on the porch watching the sunset.

"Are you glad we came to see you, Van?" she began, sweetly.

"Indeed, I am. It has been like a draught of wine. I believe I was getting a little out of heart."

"You have no need to do that, I am sure. Isn't the plantation doing well?"

"Better than it has done since the war. And now there is strong hope that our political affairs will be happily settled—for a Democratic president will be elected beyond a doubt, and this infernal carpet-bag government overthrown—I think that the future of our whole country looks bright. Already it seems to be waking from an awful dream."

It was by no means Mrs. Dexter's intention to discuss the state of the country, so she said, heartily: "Well, Van, if this election will make you average more cotton to the acre, I shall certainly pray for it. I want you to be rich."

"Oh, in another year I can give the old house a coat of paint," said Van, lightly.

"You had better wait until you are married; then give the place a thorough going over, as we say at the North."

"It might be a long waiting," said Van, compressing his lips.

"But why, Van? Do you not mean to marry?"

"Of course. I think that is part of a man's duty."

"What a cool way of putting it! Have you no dreams? no ideals of wife and home?"

"All men have, I suppose."

"Tell me what yours are," said Mrs. Dexter, very softly.

"There isn't much to tell—only what any decent man looks forward to."

"But, Van, if you wouldn't mind, I should like to know what your ideals are."

The moon was rising; the hour was propitious. Mrs. Dexter was very winning; Van was but a man.

"Don't expect any romance from me," he said. "I'm a very practical fellow. First, a home. Now you may think me supinely content, but I do think the life of a country-gentleman on his estate the finest and freest in the world. I ask nothing better than to re-new this old place, and live here soberly, generously, and to the good of those around me, all my days. And the wife—a woman not so beautiful that all her soul is sucked into her face, but not ugly, you understand—fair, fresh, and tranquil, with tender eyes, and lips sweet to kiss. She must be even of temper; not so gay as to pine in the quiet of a country home, nor yet so simple as to chronicle the small-beer of her country life when she goes to town. Well read, but not learned—without ambition—well bred—a lady to her fin-ger-tips—unselfish, without knowing that she is so—of a sweet reti-cence of soul—with no small coquetries—loving her home, her husband, and the little heads that nestle in her bosom— But I'm only generalizing: any man's ideal wife would be all this."

"You may have described the ideal wife of any Southern gentle-man," said Mrs. Dexter, quietly; "but Van, you foolish fellow, don't you know that you've described Mary Barton?"

Silence. Mrs. Dexter dared not look at the young man, whose boots were just visible to her as he stood leaning against a pillar.

She fell to watching a vagrant cloud in the western sky, and tried to look as if she hadn't said anything. Finally Van remarked very naturally, "Here come the colonel and Uncle Si'. And do look at that string of fish!"

The little lady breathed freely. She had said it; she lived; and she began to talk volubly about the fish.

The subject was not renewed; but she could not control her eyes. At the very moment of their parting she gave Van one swift look that asked a thousand questions.

Van smiled. Then he leaned forward until the corners of his brown mustache almost touched her cheek. And as the train with a wild shriek came rushing into the station, he whispered,

"Elegant idea!"

CHAPTER XIX

Mr. Ellis as the Good Samaritan

"Come, you long, yellow thing!" said Blythe, holding her plait of golden hair between her eyes and the sun, "be very sleek to-day; for somebody may stroke you before the sun goes down."

Mr. Ellis had written that this was the earliest day on which she might expect him, but it was five days later before he came. Blythe was not looking for him, and had gone out with Betty Page; and he met the two girls walking arm-in-arm down the street.

Blythe wondered if she were blushing as he came up to them. His face was beaming. He looked at his love with a proud glance of possession that threw her into an agony lest Betty Page should observe it. Indeed, it was hard for Roger Ellis to keep such a secret. When he looked at a woman he loved, his face took everybody into his confidence.

"How long have you been here, Mr. Ellis?" she asked, in a tone of polite friendliness.

"Only an hour, Blythe. I took a room at the hotel and went directly to your house—to find you away."

There was no doubt about Blythe's blushing now, but it was not a blush of pleasure. Betty Page stared; but Mr. Ellis, with fine unconsciousness, after telling Blythe that he should see her after tea, lifted his hat and passed on.

"What does it mean?" cried Betty, as soon as he was out of hearing.

"Mean? Nothing," said Blythe, blushing furiously.

"Then why are you blushing? And he called you Blythe! And his tone was so assured! Why has he come back to Yariba? Blythe Herndon, I do believe—"

"Yes," cried Blythe, desperately, "you are right. I am engaged to Mr. Ellis. But, Betty Page, if you betray me, I'll never speak to you again on earth!"

"He is the blackest of black republicans!" said Betty, solemnly; "forty-five years old, and *bald*. Blythe, how *could* you?"

"He is the noblest and the cleverest man I know! And I should thank you, Betty Page, to speak more respectfully of him."

"Oh, good gracious, Blythe, you needn't fly out! I'm too surprised to be respectful. I don't see why you want to marry him. He is so peculiar, you know. He carried Civil Rights Bill home in his arms the night of the picnic. And he doesn't make anything of stopping on the street to kiss a black baby."

"What of that? I dare say you've kissed many a black person."

"To be sure; I kiss my old Mammy Ann to this day. But I don't do it to show off, as Mr. Ellis does."

"Betty, how *dare* you speak so!" cried Blythe. "Mr. Ellis is a philanthropist, I would have you know. He spares no effort to elevate the human race."

"The reason that I thought the baby-kissing was for show-off," said Betty, calmly, "was that I never yet knew a man who would kiss a white baby if he could get out of it; but, of course, if he is in the stupendous business of elevating the human race, any little eccentricity is accounted for. No wonder he is bald. By-and-by you'll be having a mission, Blythe. I hope it won't take your hair off!"

Miss Page's remarks rankled in Blythe's bosom, and she received her lover with less dissolved tenderness than he had expected.

"How *could* you?" she cried, waving him off as he came toward her with outstretched arms; "how could you speak to me, look at me in that way?"

"How could I do otherwise, my beautiful Blythe? I haven't seen you for a century!"

"Of course, Betty guessed everything."

"Hadn't you told her? I thought you girls always made confidants of each other."

"I have no confidants. And I was very averse to any one knowing of this affair."

"This affair! Good heavens! Blythe, you speak as if this were the first of a series."

"I do not know how you can jest, Mr. Ellis, when you see how annoyed I am."

"Darling, forgive me, and put yourself into my place a moment. I had not seen you for so long a time. You don't know how I struggled with the desire to clasp you to my heart before Miss Page's eyes. I haven't done it yet, by-the-way—and I'm not a patient man. What a pity, dear"—and laughter twinkled in his eyes—"that Nature did not give you a pair of eyebrows like Colonel Dexter's; then, as I came up, you could have turned the fierce one toward me, and I should have been warned to be discreet. Blythe, don't you think if you had been wandering about purgatory a long while, you would have beamed rather effusively on the golden-haired angel that met you at the gate of heaven? Blythe—"

He spoke her name in the low, passionate whisper that she had not learned to resist. As she swayed gently toward him, he caught her in his arms and rained such kisses as she had dreamed of on cheek, and brow, and lip.

"I must forgive you," she murmured, at last; "but, Roger, dear, do try to be more discreet."

"I will. Blythe, do you know that your cheek is like satin?"

Blythe glanced into the mirror over the mantel.

"I wish you had been a dark man," said she, regretfully. "Your eyes are gray, are they not?"

"Except when I look at you, dear. Then the pupil grows big with wonder at your beauty, and they are black."

"Sit down, Roger, and let us talk rationally. Tell me about your trip."

"It was a wearying, worrying trip. Let us not talk about it just yet."

"Tell me, then, your plans for the winter."

"You won't let me rest a moment longer in paradise? Very well, then. I will tell you what I had meant to do, and what I must do. I had planned to spend the lovely months of the fall with you here in Yariba; the winter at the North, attending to my business affairs, while my little girl was 'at home sewing long white seams,' and making ready for a marriage in the spring; the summer to be spent in travelling where my bride pleased, and then to settle in our home in the fall. But I have been forced to relinquish this. I can stay but a week with you here. Then I shall go to New Orleans for an indefinite time."

"To New Orleans! but why? What interests have you there?"

"No personal interests; and my going is a matter of duty, not of choice. You must know, Blythe, that the next Presidential campaign is to be a hardly contested one. The Democrats are determined to elect a Democratic President, by fair means or foul. In the South, where they have power, they can intimidate and crush the loyal Republican element, and they will do it mercilessly.* I have been living here, Blythe, in a dream—forgetting everything in the sweet madness of my love. But once away from you among men that are doing the world's work, I found the air filled with forebodings. It is a time when no honest man can shirk. I must do my part."

"But all this is extremely vague, Roger. What do you mean to do?"

"I mean to give the next year of my life to the service of my country. I shall go to Louisiana, and see with my own eyes how the campaign is conducted."

"Shall you make stump speeches," said Blythe, a little scornfully, "in the interests of the 'great and glorious Republican party?'"

"I shall make no effort to win Republican votes; but, by heaven! I will not see loyal men cowed or bullied as long as I have a voice!"

"What can one voice do?"

"It can make itself heard from Maine to Florida," said Roger Ellis.

"How very disagreeable all this is!" said Blythe, impatiently. "Oh, Mr. Ellis, I did hope that you were done with politics!"

"I shall never be a politician, Blythe, but I shall never be done with politics. My country is my religion. But come, my little girl, there are other things pleasanter to talk of in this first hour of meeting."

Blythe pressed his hand softly against her cheek, with a sudden sweet tenderness. "I could not love you more if you were twenty times a Democrat," she said, "and I am sure you will never do anything to hurt my country."

"My darling!" cried Ellis, with some emotion, "your country is my country, and mine is yours. I love the Union; and I hate and will fight remorselessly that old Bourbon element that would destroy

---

*Ellis's comments make it clear that this story takes place before the presidential election of 1876, which the Republican candidate, Rutherford B. Hayes, narrowly won after being awarded the contested votes of Louisiana, South Carolina, and Florida.

the Union to satisfy a desperate ambition; that would make your beautiful South an Egypt; that is and has always been opposed to progress in all its forms; that plays upon the passions of a low, unscrupulous class to whom murder is as easy as bird-shooting—"

"I don't know who these dreadful people are, Roger," interrupted Blythe, "nor where you find them. But I am sure you are talking very unpleasantly. My father and all his friends are Democrats. They seem to me to be gentlemen. And everybody knows that the Republican party in the South is made up of men of the lowest class and life."

"It is not a question of men, Blythe, but of great principles," said Roger; and then he changed the ungenial topic to one that filled the rest of the evening with its sweet repetitions and delightful mysteries of remembrance and anticipation.

The town clock was striking twelve as Mr. Ellis shut the Herndon gate behind him. It was a night to make one faint with beauty. Like a woman smiling in her lover's face, this little Southern town, set in the hills, revealed its tenderest fairness to the summer night. The large, low moon, and the few languid stars shone in a sky whose infinite distance rested rather than troubled the soul. The broad leaves of the chestnut and catalpa trees were glinted with gold; and high up in the air the cross on the church spire glittered tremblingly like an arrested prayer.

Roger Ellis walked slowly along the street, his eyes looking upward, his lips parted in a smile, his soul delicately poised between serenity and joy. He was brought to earth—almost literally—by stumbling against a something that lay under a tree on the sidewalk. The something rose and confronted him. It was not a mild-faced cow, but a little dark figure that Ellis recognized at once.

"Civil Rights Bill! what in the world are you doing here at this time of the night?"

"Howdy, Bister Ellis," said Bill, holding out his hand affably.

Bill was shivering. The catarrhal B was fitfully indicated in his speech, and Mr. Ellis, putting his hand on the lad's shoulder, found it damp.

"What the dickens does all this mean?" said he. "Speak out, you funny little forlorn mite of a boy."

"Nothin' much de batter," said Bill, with husky cheerfulness. "Mammy ducked me in de hoss-bond dis evenin', an' I cleared out."

"Ducked you in the horse-pond! What was that for?"

"Jes' de ole Satan in her, I reckon. I ain't a' been doin' nothin' out o' de way; you know dat, Bister Ellis."

"Oh, certainly, Bill," said Mr. Ellis, with his short laugh; "and did you mean to sleep all night under the tree?"

"Yessir; but it was kind o' coolish."

"I should think so. Come with me now, my lad. Take my hand, and let us walk fast."

As I write I wonder if any one who reads will feel the extreme lovableness of this man? if any one will say, "What a sweet and tender thing for him to do!" thinking of him as he hurried through the streets of Yariba, clasping a little chilled hand in his own, and talking cheerily to a tired child!

He took Bill to his hotel and to his room; he ordered a whiskey cocktail and made Bill drink it; he undressed the child and rubbed his numbed limbs; and ended by wrapping him round and round like a mummy in a blanket he pulled off the bed—smiling, as he did so, at the thought of the landlord's horror if he could look in upon his proceedings—and laying him on the lounge, where he soon fell asleep. His care, no doubt, saved Bill a fit of sickness; for, although the next morning he was so hoarse as not to be able to speak in his usual ringing treble, there were no feverish symptoms, and Ellis looked at him with all of a physician's satisfaction in his patient.

"I think, young man," he said, as Bill skipped around him a revived and grateful Bill—"I think I saved your life last night. *Ergo*, it ought to belong to me."

"Yes, Mars' Roger," said Bill, affectionately. "I'd be mighty proud to be your body-servant, sir."

"No, Bill; I rather fancy that there is the making of a man in you. And don't you ever call me Mars' Roger again. Should you like to go to the North and get an education?"

"I donno, sir," said Bill, doubtfully. "When I see Tom Tolliver a wrestlin' wid his books, and a cussin,' and a flingin' 'em across the room, it 'pears to me dar ain't much fun in gittin' educated. I'd rather be a clown in a circus."

"Bill, you are incorrigible. I shall have to help you in spite of yourself. But you wouldn't mind leaving Yariba, I suppose?"

"I reckon I wouldn't," said Bill, emphatically. "I'd rather ride on de kears dan to go to heaven."

Mr. Ellis was quite in earnest in his resolve to free Bill from Aunt Sally's malignant rule. It had long been on his mind, and it now occurred to him that he could connect Bill's interests with a scheme of benevolence that he had matured during his Northern tour.

The first step in Bill's behalf was to win Aunt Sally's consent to take him away. Directly after his breakfast he set off for the Tollivers, where he was received with great cordiality by Mrs. Tolliver.

"I'm right glad to see you back, Mr. Ellis," said the lady; "it seems like old times. I declare, we do miss the soldiers more and more every day. Mis' Tolliver is as cross as a bear without them, for he used to play cards with the colonel every evening, and that's just spoiled him for my game."

"I would not have intruded so early this morning," said Ellis, after a time, "except that I came on little Bill's account."

"And where is Bill?" cried Mrs. Tolliver. "Do you know that the poor child ran away last night? Aunt Sally treated him like a dog."

"I have heard about it."

"Yes, she got into one of her furies, and she snatched Bill up as if he had been a kitten—you know what a great, large, portly woman she is," said Mrs. Tolliver, with generous clearness; "and the next thing we knew she was down at the horse-pond, and had ducked him well before any of us could get to her. I gave her an up-and-down scolding, and told her if she couldn't behave herself she should walk right off this place; so she quieted down, and got supper as meekly as you please. When she brought in the hot muffins she looked so injured that I thought I would smooth the old lady down a little; so I said, 'What delicious muffins these are! Aunt Sally never fails on her muffins!' Aunt Sally tosses her head at this and says, 'Humph! I never fails on nothin' I tries to do, 'cep'n it's to drown a little nigger!' You ought to have heard her, Mr. Ellis. It was too funny for anything."

"I should think so," said Ellis, grimly.

"I sent Tom out after supper," continued Mrs. Tolliver, placidly, "to tell Bill to come and sleep in the house, for fear Aunt Sally should pounce on him again; but he couldn't find the child high nor low. I'm real glad you happened to stumble on him, Mr. Ellis."

Here Mr. Ellis briefly unfolded his plan for Bill's future; and Mrs. Tolliver, who, although a very naïve woman, was also a very polite one, did not express the surprise she felt, but declared that it would be "a great thing for Bill," and that she was sure Aunt Sally would consent.

"With your permission I will talk to Aunt Sally about it," said Ellis, rising.

"Come right through this way," said Mrs. Tolliver, passing through the hall to the back-door. "There's Aunt Sally in the yard; you can go out there, if you like—there are no dogs to fly at you."

A fire was burning in the yard, over which a great black kettle was set filled with boiling and bubbling suds. Aunt Sally stood by an old tree-stump, on whose smooth top a heap of motley garments were piled, that she was pounding with fierce blows from a "battling-stick" that she held in her hand. Whack! whack! the blows came down with unerring aim. Aunt Sally's lean arm, bared to the shoulder, seemed to describe a circle in the air—fine foam flew about her turbaned head.

"What in the world are you doing, Aunt Sally?" said Ellis, as she stopped an instant to give the clothes on the stump a turn.

"Lor', Mars' Ellis, is dat you? What a scare you give me, comin' up so sudden!"

Ellis repeated his query.

"What am I a doin'? Why, battlin' de close, to be sho'. I'se a old-fashioned Carliny nigger, I is, an' I sticks to de ole ways. None o' your scrubbin'-bo'des for my knuckles! I biles my close, an' battles 'em, an' dey's clean when *I* gits done wid 'em. Dat's Carliny way."

"And is it Carliny way," said Mr. Ellis, severely, "to dip children in horse-ponds and try to drown them?"

"Lor', how'd you hear dat? Well, I jes' tell you dat ar Bill is de provokin'est nigger dat de good Lord ever made. What d'ye think dat boy had done? He had tuk my best Sunday skiarf dat I wears wid my gauzlin gown, and ropped it roun' some miserbel new-born puppies! No wonder I ducked him. Pity de sinfulness couldn't be washed out o' him. Waste!—dat boy'll throw out more wid a teaspoon dan anybody kin bring in wid a shovel. He runs through my things as if dey was weeds. He ain't wuth his salt!"

"If that is the case," said Mr. Ellis, "perhaps you would be pleased to get rid of Bill for good and all."

This was the beginning of a negotiation that ended in the transfer of certain crisp bills from Ellis's pocket to Aunt Sally's bosom; and a formal written surrender of her grandchild, to which she affixed her mark, and which Tom Tolliver signed as a witness.

The next sight of interest afforded to Yariba was that of Civil Rights Bill, in a new suit of clothes, walking through the streets with an air of solemn dignity, followed by all the small boys of the town, evidently aching to "'eave 'arf a brick at him," and only restrained by fear of Mr. Ellis, whose eyes were twinkling behind him in mingled amusement and satisfaction.

CHAPTER XX

The First Faint Swerving
of the Heart

It was the grandmother who did it. Neither one of them ever knew this; but it was a fact that she brought about, indirectly, the first quarrel between Blythe and her lover. Blythe, who never lost an opportunity of praising Mr. Ellis in her grandmother's hearing, was speaking of his liberality of mind, his freedom from prejudice, his devotion to grand principles.

"Did you ever happen to tell him about your cousin, Dick Herndon?" said the old lady, carelessly.

"Why, no," said Blythe, in some surprise, as the question did not seem particularly relevant; "why should I?"

"Oh, for no reason, except that I should like to know what he would think of Dick's war career."

"I suppose he would think, as we all do, that Dick took an extreme course, but was almost justified in it by the terrible provocation. Mr. Ellis is not one," added Blythe, loftily, "to judge a man unjustly, because he happened to be on this side or the other."

Dick Herndon was a wild young fellow, who had covered himself with glory during the war as a guerilla captain. The notable thing about his mode of warfare was, *that he never took a prisoner.* Blythe could never forget one winter night, when, as bedtime drew near, there came a double rap at the front-door. Her father opened it cautiously, with a candle and a pistol in his hand—for those were troubled times—to see on the threshold the gray-coated forms of Dick Herndon and one of his comrades, who had ridden fast and far, and had stopped for a night's rest and food. She could never forget how they sat around the fire late into the dark hours of the new day, the grandmother leaning from one corner, herself crouching in another, and talked of battles, and flying rumors, and woeful deaths; nor how the firelight shone redly on the dark, thin face of the young guerilla captain, who was standing with his hand on his sword, as he said, "*Aunt Lucy, I have made a vow never to take another prisoner;*" nor how her mother's voice trembled as she said, "That is a dreadful vow, Dick; why did you make it?" nor the flash of passion, dimming the firelight, that kindled on Dick's face, as he replied, "How can you ask me, Aunt Herndon, when you know that my mother and sister live in New Orleans?"

It was long before Blythe understood the significance of these words, or the sombre pause that followed them; and when she did, it was to feel something like a thrill of pride in the young Southerner's desperate resolve, that seemed to her only a chivalrous, though exaggerated, vengeance for an insult offered to all women.

Dick had kept his word, and his name had become a terror through the state. In fact, his fame was so widespread that at the close of the war he had found it necessary to leave the country; and he was now in Brazil pursuing the peaceful avocation of a sheep-farmer, and much respected by his neighbors as a noble exile.

The grandmother's hint remained in Blythe's mind, and she took an early opportunity of telling Mr. Ellis about Dick. He had listened with an unmoved face, merely remarking that he was rather glad the young man had left the country.

"I shouldn't like to refuse my hand even to such an indefinite relation as a cousin by marriage," said he, dryly, "as I must have done, if, indeed, Mr. Dick Herndon had escaped hanging."

"But consider his terrible provocation, Roger," urged Blythe.

"I do not recognize that," said Mr. Ellis. "The war order in question was justifiable, necessary—emphatically, the right thing at the right time."*

---

*General Order Number 28, often known as the "woman order," was issued by General Benjamin Butler on May 15, 1862, to curb insults to Union soldiers. Outraged by the hostile behavior of southern women in occupied New Orleans, Butler ordered that any female insulting a Union soldier would be considered a "woman of the town plying her avocation."

Blythe grew white to the lips. It seemed as if her lover had struck her a blow.

"Roger, do you know what you are saying?"

"Why yes, dear. It is not a subject on which I could speak at random. You do not comprehend, Blythe, all that the American flag is to the men who offered their lives to save it. It has the magnificent sacredness of the Holy Grail; and when this flag was insulted, outraged, by the ill-bred women of a rebel city, it was right to give them a lesson that they would remember as long as the breath of life was in them."

Blythe had risen from her seat. She stood before Roger Ellis, cheeks and eyes blazing.

"And what could they do?" she said, with curling lips—"these terrible malignants, these powerful enemies, whom you did so well to fight?"

"Do? oh, a thousand petty atrocious things. It is astonishing," said Ellis, reflectively, "how many ingenious ways those New Orleans women devised to torment our soldiers. Nothing but the most rigorous measures would have answered with them. You cannot imagine, Blythe—"

"But I *can* imagine," said Blythe, interrupting him with impetuous haste; "you forget, Mr. Ellis, that I am twenty-two years old. The Northern troops were in Yariba half the time during the war, and we women of Yariba were not behind others in showing loyalty to our cause. When this house was taken for a hospital, and the Union flag hung over the porch, rather than walk under it I went out through the windows or jumped off the end of the porch. Had you seen me, and had I been ten years older—"

"Blythe, why torment yourself in this way? Let us be quietly thankful that I was not here, and that you are twenty-two instead of thirty-two years old."

"In any case, it should have been the same," said Blythe, waving him away as he approached her. "And you say that for such little, foolish outbreaks of a woman's feeling, that had no other vent—petty acts that should be no more regarded than a baby's slaps in a giant's face—that you would commend a base and terrible insult as a needed lesson!"

Then Mr. Ellis got up and made another little speech about the American flag; how it symbolized to him all that was sacred—all that other men found in religion, home, poetry, art. From this he branched off to some remarks on patriotism that would have done credit to a Fourth of July oration; and, returning to the subject in hand, he declared that events had proved the wisdom of the order in question, as it had taught the women to behave themselves.

Blythe had listened with growing irritation. To her excited fancy there was something fantastic about her lover—his bombastic tone, his iterated ideas. "Why, Blythe!" he broke off suddenly, "what a desperate little rebel you are, in spite of your liberal concession in accepting a Yankee lover!"

"You mistake me entirely," said the girl, proudly; "it is not as a Southerner I resent what you have said, but as a *woman*. I cannot bear it, Mr. Ellis!" and she made a sudden swift gesture of dismissal. "I should like to be alone."

It was Ellis's turn to doubt if his own ears might be trusted. He flashed a quiet glance at Blythe's burning face, but she stood there erect, passionately angry, but unmoved, like a frozen flame. He bowed profoundly and left the room.

Blythe cried much and slept little that night. She could not reconcile herself to a lowered ideal of her lover. Her family could but notice the following day that her eyelids were heavy and her cheeks pale; but she was too proud and too loyal to her lover to take any one into her confidence. They all knew, however, that something had happened, and the grandmother in her chamber rendered devout thanks to God.

In the afternoon Blythe essayed a little conversation with her father. "Papa," she said, leaning over the back of his chair so that he could not see her face, "what is a fanatic?"

"A fanatic, my dear," rejoined her father cheerfully, "a fanatic is a fool."

Two days passed, and it became evident to Blythe that if there was to be a reconciliation the advances must come from her. She was not sorry for this. It was a comfort to blame herself. She told her mother that she had turned Mr. Ellis out of the house, and saw with pleasure that lady's mortification and surprise. "But, Blythe," she said, "what had he said—what *could* he have said to lead you to such inexcusable rudeness?"

"I can't tell you, mamma; you would think less of him: though, after all, it was only a difference of opinion," said Blythe, generously.

"A difference of opinion! Oh, Blythe! and you have always prided yourself on being so impartial."

"I am, mother," said Blythe, naïvely; "but there is but one way of looking at this question."

"There must be," said Mrs. Herndon, laughing, "since you and Mr. Ellis differed about it."

"There is the puzzle," said Blythe with a sigh, "how he *could*— At any rate, mamma, I was so rude that I ought to write him a note and ask him to forgive me—don't you think so?"

"Most assuredly. I am perfectly ashamed, Blythe, when I think of the ill-breeding you showed. What will he think of the way you have been brought up?"

Another day of loneliness convinced Blythe that she could not give up her love. "The sweet habit of loving" had grown upon her, and she missed the close intimacy with an intellectual nature. But even as she wrote the note to bring him back she sighed, "It can never be quite the same again;" and she felt in a vague sort of way that it was a species of weakness to recall him. "I do it," she said, "to relieve my pain, just as I would go to a chloroform bottle if I had the toothache."

Mr. Ellis had not been so unhappy during the days of their estrangement as Blythe had been; he felt that he had sustained the cause of right under somewhat trying circumstances, and was stimulated by a martyr's glow. Still, he suffered; all the old sorrowful emotions that he had thought himself done with forever came rushing upon him, like a torrent too long dammed. He strolled about the woods, with Civil Rights Bill tramping laboriously after him; and he managed to blunt the edge of his feelings by giving that small youth much rambling information concerning genii, kobolds, and fairies. Finally he bethought himself of a visit to Mrs. Roy, who as yet remained ignorant of the good fortune awaiting her. Mr. Ellis, as I have said, had founded an orphan asylum at one period of his life. It had grown to be a large one, and Government had made it an appropriation. On his trip to the North he had found that there was a vacancy among its offices—the place of assistant seamstress—and it occurred to him that here was an opportunity to be of practical service to the melancholy Mrs. Roy. He found this tall dame very much as he had left her—depressed, yellow, and given to much talk and snuff.

"I manage to git on, sir," she said, "the neighbors is powerful good; but winter is comin', an' it just makes me sick to think about it."

Mr. Ellis then told her of the orphan asylum, and offered her the vacant place. She seemed grateful, but not surprised. Somebody always had managed her affairs for her: why should it not be so to the end?

"It's powerful good in you, Mr. Ellis," said she, "and I'll be thankful to take the place and keep things a-goin'. It'll come hard on me at first, I suppose, livin' at the North, with the climate an' ways so different, an' tramps murderin' you in your bed; but I s'pose I'll git used ter it."

"I think you will like it," said Ellis, with a fleeting smile; "it will be a good home for your children. They will get a plain education, and a chance to settle respectably in life."

"Yes, sir. I don't suppose their father will ever think of 'em again—po' innocents!"

"I will send a telegram to-night," said Ellis, "saying that you will take the place, and I think you had better leave as soon as possible. You will take a through train and have no trouble. I want to send Willy Tolliver with you. He can help you take care of the children."

"Bill Tolliver! Is he a-goin' to the asylum?"

"Yes."

"I thought folks at the North had all white servants," said Mrs. Roy; "and Bill is a shif'less little nigger anyhow, and can't be much good to nobody."

"I am not sending him as a servant, but as one of the children of the asylum."

"*What! you let in* niggers?"

"Why, my good woman, it is a colored orphan asylum. But they are not proud—they *let in* whites!"

Mrs. Roy, after looking at Mr. Ellis a moment in a stony sort of way, lifted up her voice and wept. "That it should come to this!" she sobbed—"to be insulted by a strange man and a Yankee! Oh, Jim, Jim! little did I think, when I married you, that marryin' would bring me to this. I would have you know, sir, that howsomever it be that I'm forsaken and po', I ain't quit off bein' *respectable;* an' I'll starve, if I must, but I won't let myself down to niggers—not quite yet. My family was always high-notioned, though we did live up the mountain an' didn't plant; but we owned niggers, an' if it hadn't a' been for the war that you an' sech as you brought upon us, a-plenty I would a' had to this day. I don't forgit the shirts, sir; an' I'll allow that you meant to be kind. But 'tain't to be expected that you could understand the feelin's of a Southern lady. I ain't ashamed of workin'; but I'll die in my tracks befo' I'll let my children associate with niggers; an' you can give that place to some Yankee woman who ain't above it, for poverty ain't took down *my* pride, Mr. Ellis!"

Mrs. Roy refreshed herself with a little snuff, and Mr. Ellis rose to go.

"Very well, madam," he said, somewhat roughly, "the place can readily be filled by some one, as you suggest, better fitted for it. I have only to wish you good-day."

So saying, Mr. Ellis shook from his feet the dust of the house of Roy, and walked away, not even stopping to speak to the Roy children, who were playing contentedly in the dirt with as many colored companions. He looked across the swelling fields to red-leaved woods, and stepped in the spreading gold of autumn's splendid sun; but his face was worn, his eyes tired, and there were lines of pain around his mouth. Once he sighed heavily, as if to relieve himself of an oppression, and murmured,

"And there was darkness over the land of Egypt—even darkness that might be felt."

But he found Blythe's note awaiting him at the hotel; and the transition from general woe to specific happiness was so violent that he could have scarcely been depressed, even had he known that the young lady was considering him as a bottle of chloroform.

CHAPTER XXI

A Bunch of Violets

Mrs. Oglethorpe had her reward. As soon as the regiments were settled in their winter-quarters, invitations poured upon her to visit her army friends in New Orleans; and she was not long in deciding to take a house there for the winter, nor in inviting Blythe Herndon and Betty Page to visit her. It was early in November that Mrs. Oglethorpe locked the door of her cottage in Yariba and went to New Orleans; six weeks later the two girls joined her.

They reached their journey's end at dusk; and the misty city showed little beauty to the eager young faces that pressed against the carriage panes, peering out with childlike interest. The carriage stopped before a house of which they could see nothing for the high wall that surrounded it. They pulled the rusty bell at the locked gate, and in a moment Peggy appeared—Peggy, as much beruffled as ever, and with a most elegant panier that showed she had not been a month in the neighborhood of Madame Olympe for nothing. Mrs. Oglethorpe greeted her "dear girls" with such effusive cordiality that they almost felt themselves back in Yariba; but her greetings were hardly over before she sent them to their rooms to dress for the evening. "I have invited a little company to meet you," she said.

"They will all be here," cried Betty, when they were alone in their room. "Oh, Blythe, isn't it lovely! Now tell me, dear, shall I do my hair low in a Grecian coil, or high with a plait on top?"

"Grecian coil, I think—you are so tall, you know."

"Yes," said Betty, doubtfully: "the *theory* of the Grecian coil is very fine; but, Blythe, do you know that I never have it so without a horrible suspicion that I look *flat-headed!*"

"You might pull out the crimps and make it fluffy on top," suggested Blythe, thoughtfully.

A rap at the door, and Peggy appeared.

"Here's sompen' one o' your beaux done sent you already, Miss Blythe. He's in a hurry, *he* is."

It was a basket of flowers—a careless confusion of violets and valley lilies—with a sealed note lying across them.

> My Darling,—You are making a poet of me. Last night, as I lay awake, thinking that another twenty-four hours would bring you to me, a sonnet came singing through my brain, that I send you now as my welcome:
>
> > I counted first the weeks, and then the days,
> > And now I count the hours that endless seem,
> > Ere thou wilt come again. As in a dream,
> > Or through an atmosphere of golden haze,
> > I see thee on those perilous iron ways,
> > As over mountain, valley, hill, and stream,
> > Those steeds with hearts of fire and breath of steam,
> > Are bearing thee, impatient of delays.
> > O Bird of Paradise, that comest flying—
> > Fast flying—flying to the sunny South,
> > Thou but returnest unto what is thine;
> > For as the sea, in dreamy silence lying,
> > Drinks the sweet waters from a river's mouth,
> > So I receive thy being into mine.
>
> There! that is your poem, for you have been its inspiration.
>
> "Outside, the sun is shining as if it were June—this is the rarest of days. Such, I say, as I look out on the beaming earth, has Blythe been to me. I owe to you, my beautiful comrade, my pure lover, more than you can ever know. A life-long gratitude is yours, won without a conscious effort, as the sun brings forth the violets, and does not know what a blessing it has been to them. But the violets

know what it is to be rescued from the cold grip of the frozen earth, and brought into fragrant life and the delirious joys of sunshine. And I know, my beautiful and bright and joy-giving Blythe, what your love has done for me. I bless you with my whole soul; every beat of my heart reverberates with benedictions.

"I cannot meet you at the station, Blythe. Miss Betty Page will be with you, and I don't believe I should have the strength of mind to refrain from taking you in my arms, though forty thousand Pages should stand ready to proclaim it. Then your lovely lips would take on that mutinous pout that it will take a great many years' kisses to make them forget. Many years' kisses! Blythe, Blythe, my fiery-souled and wilful and beloved child, do you know how humbly and how proudly I sign myself,

Your lover,
R. E.

"Oh, Betty, I am glad to be here!" said Blythe, with a long breath, folding the note and thrusting her face deep down into the sweet wet violets.

"I should think you might be," said Betty. "'Tisn't bad fun to have a devoted lover to send one violets and things."

"A poem, Betty," said Blythe, with a low laugh; "only think of that!"

"A poem!" cried Betty. "Oh! well, he copied it. My captain could do that much."

"*Copied* it! Indeed, he did no such thing! He composed it. It is a sonnet—fourteen lines, you know—and perfectly lovely!"

"Blythe, my dear, I've a new respect for you"—and Betty let fall her hair, that she had just combed up to the proper height. "I don't believe any other girl in Yariba ever had a poem written to her. It makes you feel like 'Mary in Heaven,' doesn't it? Now, dear, if you could come down to earth and tie this back hair—"

Blythe dressed herself slowly, and by the time she was ready to go down Mr. Ellis was announced. The young girl had a pretty way of stopping an instant on the threshold just before entering a room and looking in shyly. Ellis caught his breath as she stood at the door to-night. She wore a white woollen dress, from above which her face blossomed like a flower springing from the snow. Her lips were parted in a tender smile. Never had she seemed to him so winsome and so fair. He kissed her lips with a tenderness that she but half understood. Men and women love very differently; but I think the most exquisite feeling that a human nature can know is that of a man who clasps in his arms the woman that he loves. The keen joy, tempered by reverent wonder—the fine passion that would protect rather than exact—and above all, the rapturous certainty of possession—these are emotions that no woman ever quite comprehends.

"How brown you are, Roger!" cried Miss Blythe; "you are sunburnt, I do believe, and bearded like a pard. And oh, Roger, how absurdly happy you look!"

"Blythe, that look has *struck in* as unfadingly as if my head were an Easter egg and had been boiled in a piece of red calico. A raging toothache couldn't take it out. You must bear with it as best you can."

"If you can only repress it a little before people—"

"I will try—I will think on my latter end. But that won't do any good, for I hope to breathe my last sigh in your arms, my darling, and the thought is not a sad one."

"How I wish," said Blythe, pressing his hand to her cheek, "that we were to have this evening to ourselves. But Mrs. Oglethorpe has invited a lot of people to meet us."

"I feared as much, and came early to have a few minutes with you. Oh, my dear girl, I foresee all sorts of vexations and interruptions. I am busy from morning until night. I shall have to steal all the time I give you."

"But what are you doing, Roger?"

"At present I am trying to verify or disprove certain political outrages* that have been reported in Republican quarters and are carefully kept out of the newspapers. Witnesses pour in upon me. I listen to stories one hour, that make my blood run cold; and the next, to men who deny every word of them."

"How do you know which side to believe?"

"That is what I shall find out, if I have to travel the length and breadth of the State to do it," said Ellis, pressing his lips firmly together.

Outrages was the term often used for beatings, shootings, and other acts of violence and intimidation against the freedmen and other Republicans by various Democratic and white supremacist groups.

"Roger, why do you do all this? Do you know, it seems to me a sort of *detective* business," said Blythe, impatiently.

"My dear girl, I should much prefer going out with a musket on my shoulder; but that is not the way the fight is carried on to-day. I can only do my part by hunting down assassins, exposing trickery, and showing up fraud. It is not an agreeable business, but what would you? I cannot choose my work."

"I wish you were out of it," murmured Blythe.

"Remember, dear," said Ellis, "that I've the blood of the Scotch Covenanters in my veins, and it forces me to fight to the death for whatever cause I conceive to be just. I must throw whatever courage and ability I have on the side of the classes that cannot help themselves."

"If I were a man," said Blythe, "I would not touch such *pitch* as American politics."

"Blythe, it is a very false conception of politics that looks on it as an impure vocation. It arises from a natural disgust for the corrupt men who have made themselves prominent in public affairs. But should Miranda have forsworn love because Caliban had profaned its name? There are human beasts, and there are venal politicians, but there are also lovers and patriots. I don't think," he went on, laughing, "that women are ever very patriotic. They look with gentle pity on the foolish fellows who would give their lives for a strip of bunting. I give my word, Blythe, that when I was abroad I could never hear the word 'America' without a tingling of the blood. I passionately love the ideas that distinguish it from other nationalities. Only two things ever made me actually tremble with joy, with excess of love, in all my life—a woman's portrait and the American flag."

"Good heavens!" thought Blythe; "if the American flag is unfurled upon us we are undone!"

"A woman's portrait!" she cried; "perhaps I have a right to know a little more about that."

"Perhaps you don't remember a photograph you sent me in New York," he said, gayly. "It did not give me the light of your eyes, nor the glory of your hair; and yet it made such a light in my room that I had to draw the curtains, for fear people should think there was a conflagration inside and turn the fire-engines upon me."

"Oh, Roger, what a goose you are! I did not like that photograph at all. I had on my old blue."

"I am penetrated with awe," said Roger, "at that profound and unintelligible remark—*I had on my old blue.* Would you object to my writing it down in my note-book, under the head of metaphysics?"

"Be serious, Mr. Ellis. Come now, confess. Haven't you a dozen photographs of your sweethearts stuck around your walls with pins through their noses?"

"'Elegant idea!'" said Roger, "but I haven't. I've only one other picture of a woman—that is an ivorytype, a most beautiful picture of a most beautiful woman."

"Did you love her?"

"Yes, I loved her long and dearly, as the song says. I've nothing left of her now but a disagreeable memory—this picture and one letter, that I've kept principally for its literary excellence. She was a clever creature."

"Well, well," said Blythe, "I sha'n't be jealous. You had never seen me when you loved her. But I have never written you clever letters. Did you not make comparisons?"

"I did," said Roger, laughing; "and as I read your dear, formal little letters, beginning 'Dear Mr. Ellis,' I wanted to believe in God, that I might thank him that you were not as other women were. Your picture and the letter you sent me with it are on my heart, my darling; and though you turn me out-of-doors a dozen times over, I shall never give them back to you. I want them to moulder and mix with my dust. Hers I should have destroyed when I first won you, but I thought you might like to see them some day."

"The picture I should like to see very much; but the letter—oh no, Roger; it would not be right."

"She doesn't deserve the slightest consideration, my dear Blythe. Consider her as a woman in a book. At the very time when she was writing these letters to me—and I assure you that Sappho herself would have doffed her bonnet to her—she was carrying on impassioned love affairs with two other men, both intimate friends of mine."

"There is Betty's voice at the door!" cried Blythe, smoothing her slightly ruffled hair; and Miss Page came in pale and pretty, just as a peal at the bell announced other visitors.

Mr. Ellis had no further opportunity to speak with Blythe, except to make an engagement to take her to the French market the next morning before breakfast; for the room was soon crowded with the friends of the summer past, who gave warm greetings to both the pretty girls. Captain Silsby's figure was, of course, prominent among the officers. He had intended to be very dignified toward Miss Page, but he relented as he saw how his comrades crowded around her, and heard her pretty laugh rewarding their jokes, that he thought very stupid ones. Captain Silsby is, perhaps, not the first man who does not find out that a jewel is worth having until he sees its price affixed in a shop window.

Miss Page, after the two girls had gone to their room, expressed herself as highly delighted with the evening.

"I think we shall be great belles, Blythe," she remarked. "How they all crowded in this evening—even to the Great Panjandrum himself, with the little round button at the top."

"I suppose the Great Panjandrum is General Van der Meire?" said Blythe, laughing.

"Yes, ponderous old fellow! but his horses are simply superb. I do hope that he will ask me to ride."

"Captain Silsby seems entirely at your command."

"Yes," said Betty again, "and I shouldn't wonder, Blythe, if I were to have a—violet-sender before the winter is over."

"You don't mean that you would accept him?"

"Why not?"

"Oh, your principles, of course! Don't you remember the afternoon at the spring, when you launched out against me so furiously?"

"I don't remember," said Betty, innocently. "Did I say anything in particular? But I suppose I was rather intolerant, before I knew them so well."

"'Grown familiar with their hateful faces,
  You first endures, then pities, then embraces!'"
quoted Blythe, liberally.

"And then, Blythe," said Betty, meditatively, unlacing her boot, "I make distinctions. There are Yankees and Yankees. If Captain Silsby were a radical, I wouldn't think of him; but as he is not, I waste a thought on him now and then."

"General Van der Meire is a radical, and how delighted you are when he takes you to ride! And who was that young fellow you flirted with so desperately during the summer—alternating between him and Captain Silsby?"

"Lieutenant Gilbert?" suggested Betty.

"Yes; Mr. Ellis told me that his father is a great friend of Wendell Phillips, and this young fellow is an out-and-out radical himself."

"Oh, well, I only flirted with him," said Betty, briskly: "I never intended to marry him."

"I don't follow your reasoning, exactly; but for my part, I think it is just about as bad to make love to a man, as to marry him."

"Make love! as if I would do such a thing!" said Betty, with a yawn. "I only let them make love to me—there's all the difference in the world."

Chapter XXII

The French Market

To go to the French market in New Orleans, it is necessary to be ahead of the sun in rising; and Blythe looked like one of its advance beams, as she came into the room where Roger Ellis was awaiting her. Blythe had that beauty which is at its fairest in the searching morning hours.

"Here is an old friend of yours," said Mr. Ellis, leading forward a spruce young lad in a scarlet necktie, whom Blythe found no trouble in recognizing as Civil Rights Bill, in spite of his clean face and smart dress.

"He seems to have suffered a sea-change," said Blythe, laughing, as she shook hands. "Actually, he looks shy! How are you getting on, Bill?"

"Mighty well, thank you, Miss Blythe," returned Bill, in good English, and with an uneasy smile that was but the ghost of his former grin. "How are all the folks at home?"

"Very well, Bill. I saw Aunt Sally just before I left, and she told me to tell you 'Howdy' for her, and said that she wanted you to write her a letter and send her a new head-handkerchief."

"I suppose Bill is quite a hero in her eyes since he has left her?" said Mr. Ellis, as they walked away.

"Oh yes, indeed! I understand that she laments him as the comfort of her old age. I don't believe that your hold on the youth is very secure."

"I shall hold him fast enough. I've bought him, you know. Circumstance plays queer tricks with a man's principles. I *bought* the 'little Billee,' and paid for him in currency notes."

"And paid more than he is worth, I dare say," remarked Blythe.

"Not so, my Lady Blythe. I can't begin to tell you how fond I am of the lad. I brought him down here with me, intending to send him North the first opportunity that offered; but, really, he is such a comfort to me—such a faithful, affectionate little fellow—that I don't like to give him up."

Blythe was looking about her with interested eyes. They were almost the only persons in the street at this early morning hour. The pleasant air blew fresh against their faces with the softness of midsummer. The houses were solidly built, and were surrounded by the ever-blooming gardens, to which the warmth and moisture of the climate give a perpetual beauty.

"This is called the Garden District," said Ellis, "and is the least interesting because the newest and most American part of the city. You must see the French quarter—'le Carré de la Ville,' as the Creoles call it. It is the only place in the United States that I know of that gives one some idea of a European town. The streets are narrow and crooked, and all the names are foreign—Bourbon, Toulouse, Chartres, Royale, Dauphin, etc. It really is very quaint and interesting. You might imagine yourself in a sleepy old French town. And to add to the delusion, you will find people there who have never been in the part of the city made rude and Yankee-like by Americans; who boast that they have seen Paris the Beautiful, but never the vulgar part of New Orleans where the Yankees traffic and sell. Oh, it is a charming old city this! though its glory is passing away, and it will soon cease to be unique."

"How glad I am to be here!" said Blythe. "I hope it is an easy city to find one's way about in, for I mean to explore it thoroughly."

"You won't do much exploring alone," said Roger, pressing her hand against his arm; "you might easily lose yourself if you attempted it. All roads lead to the Levee, of course."

"Roger," said Blythe, with a blush, "I have heard of the Levee all my life, but I give you my word I don't know what it is."

He laughed gayly. "I am afraid you are shamming," he said, "in order to give me the pleasure of telling you something about your own Southern city; but know, my sly saint, that New Orleans differs from most seaport towns in that it has no wharves built out into the water, but the vessels and steamboats lie along a broad street called 'the Levee,' which in the season is covered with cotton bales and sugar hogsheads. This street follows the bend of the river on which the city is built, and from its shape comes the name 'Crescent City.' Other streets run from it, not parallel, but spreading out like the sticks of a fan."

"I should think that would be a confusing arrangement."

"So it is. You can never tell how far off the street may be that you knew, in the beginning of your walk, lay but a square to the right or left. Another puzzling peculiarity is, that a different name is often given to what would seem to be different parts of the same street. And all this goes to prove, sweetheart, that you must not go cruising about alone. If I can't go with you, take Civil Rights Bill. He will prove a vivacious and accurate guide. He knows the banks whereon the wild thyme grows just as well as if he had been a city *gamin* all his life."

They had passed the broad streets and were turning into the crooked, crowded ways where life was swarming busily. The chattering crowd were all going one way—toward the French market, whose long, low booths Blythe saw with the lively feeling of pleasure one experiences at any novel sight. It was a scene well worth looking at. Creoles, negroes, Mexicans, and French people crossed and recrossed each others' paths; pale Southern girls stood at the stalls, sipping the strong black coffee; children, fresh as the early dawn, ran about with their hands full of fruit. It was the busiest hour of the twenty-four. In the confusion of sounds Blythe could hardly distinguish any intelligible speech. The Gascon butchers, the Silician fruiterers, the Quadroon flower-merchants, and the old French women, in high white caps, who sold vegetables and rabbits, all seemed to think talk the soul of business, and chattered like so many monkeys on a branch, vying with each other in giving customers some trifle over their purchases, which they called *La Niappe*.

They wandered through the market, drinking coffee and buying flowers with the rest, until Blythe declared that the one had made her giddy, and that the other would soon need a basket to hold them.

"How soon are we going home, Roger?" she said.

"Oh, not for a long time yet. I shall take you to breakfast with me."

"Then all these lovely flowers will wither: let us send them home. Here, Bill, you take them—hold both hands. Now run home with them, and tell Miss Betty to put them into water. He may go, may he not, Roger?"

"The queen has spoken," said Roger, making a sign to Bill, and the little fellow darted away.

"Curious!" said Ellis, reflectively, "what a tone of command crept into your sweet Southern voice as you spoke to Bill! Now, a Yankee girl would perhaps have said, 'Please, Willy, will you take these flowers home for me?' But it comes as naturally for you to order as it does for him, poor little wretch, to obey."

"You ought to be glad of that," said Blythe. "You are training him to be a sort of confidential servant, are you not?"

"I am training him, Blythe, to be a *man*. He will rise to his level. If it is to be my master, well and good all the same."

"I hardly think that Bill will ever teach you anything. Where are we to breakfast, Roger?"

"I am going to take you to a queer little French restaurant near by, not known to more than half a hundred people in the city. Miss Betty Page probably would scorn to put the tip of her impertinent little nose inside of it; but you, my Blythe, will find eyes, nose, and palate alike delighted by the oddity, and cleanliness, and deliciousness of everything about it."

They had turned into a narrow, short street, at the foot of which a modest sign was swinging. A dingy figure of Napoleon was painted on it, underneath which the name "M. Costé" appeared in small black letters.

"Behold the restaurant of the Little Corporal!" said Ellis, waving his hand with an oratorical air. "Enter, mademoiselle."

Entering, they found a clean, sweet room with a sanded floor, and birds singing in the windows that looked out on beds of flowers. An old negro man, with snow-white hair, saluted Ellis with great dignity, and a nimble-footed *garçon*, whose name should have been Mercury, flung a smile at Blythe, placed a great bunch of scarlet radishes on the table, and asked for the gentleman's order, in one and the same instant of time.

"You shall have a regular French breakfast, dear," said Ellis, as Mercury flew away, "beginning with bread and radishes, changing your plate half a dozen times, and drinking, instead of tea or chocolate,

'A bottle of wine, to make you shine,'

and ending, if you like, with a cigarette."

"So I will!" cried Blythe. "My spirits rise at the prospect of such a delightful piece of wickedness."

"We will imagine ourselves in Paris on our wedding journey. No; on second thought, it shall not be Paris, but some little French town, like Barbazon or Morville, where the houses are old and steep-roofed, and the people, as fresh as the flowers in their fields, talk their *patois* around us, and won't understand a word when I say, 'My darling! My wife! I love you to madness!'"

"Eat your radishes!" cried Blythe, in a fright. "I can tell that yonder *garçon* is hearing and laughing at you by the way the parting of his back hair looks."

"Blythe, there will be no supercilious *garçon* to laugh at us in that little inn at Barbazon. There will be an old woman, with a face like scorched leather, and black eyes with a snap to them. She will say, 'What will it please monsieur and madame to order for breakfast?' and then she will go out and cook it herself, monsieur and madame not caring one jot how long she is about it—"

"Unless they are very hungry."

"—While they are feeding on meat that she knows not of. Blythe, my hand is under that newspaper; just slip yours into it for one second, that I may know if you are flesh and blood, and not a fair phantom that my own longing has conjured up."

"No phantom ever buttered bread with such deliberate energy as this, Mr. Ellis."

"I don't know. I had a dream the other night about Charlotte, in which she appeared as a ghost who went on cutting bread-and-butter in the sweet old way of life—only, to my horror, the loaf that she was slicing away was the head of Werther. To be sure, his head was a soft one—but what a vengeful ghost!"

The *garçon* coming with the breakfast, a new turn was given to the conversation.

"One reason why I like to come to this place," remarked Ellis, "is that they always let Willy sit at the table with me. Now, Blythe, why are you opening your blue eyes so wide?"

"Willy at the table with you!" repeated Blythe. "Now, Roger, isn't that carrying things a little too far?"

"My dear girl, if I had adopted one of the Roy children,

should you have thought it strange that I should have him at the table with me?"

Blythe was silent. After a moment's pause she said, "Roger, what are you going to do with Bill when we are—" she stopped with a lovely blush.

"When we are married, dear?" said Ellis, very gently: "why, nothing more than what I am doing now, aided by your lovely woman's influence."

"I hope you understand," said Blythe, looking down into her glass, "that I will not sit at table with him?"

"Blythe—"

"Please don't let us argue about it," said she, hastily. "I know all that you would say, and my reason tells me that you are right. I agree with you entirely in theory, but—I will *not* sit at the table with Civil Rights Bill!"

"Blythe, you remind me of the young man who turned upon the girl of his heart, as they sat on the settle, spooning sweetly—"

"How charmingly alliterative!"

—"With the question, 'Now, before this thing goes any farther, I want to know *who* is going to make the fires?'"

"I suppose I am rather premature," laughed Blythe. "There are more important questions to be settled before—"

"Before this Civil Rights Bill comes up between us," finished Ellis, with a smile. But Blythe noticed that a look of pain succeeded it.

Chapter XXIII

By the Tomb of the Faithful Slave

The winter that now opened for Blythe she remembered afterward as one recalls a night of fever and turbulent dreams. The days hurried by as never before in her uneventful life; for though New Orleans was far from being gay in this most sombre winter of eighteen hundred and seventy-six, the two girls from Yariba found living in it a very exciting affair. Blythe sometimes caught herself envying Betty Page, who walked about as if the very air exhilarated her, and grew prettier and saucier every day. If Mr. Swinburne had known the girls he would have added another verse to his "Ballad of Burdens," that he would have called "The Burden of Many Beaux;" for the officers were all more or less in love with them both, and pursued them with unflagging attentions. Nor was this the only world that opened to them. Blythe had letters from her grandmother to some of the old families in New Orleans, and in the finished charm of their courtly society she found the completest satisfaction that her winter afforded. Yet even this was marred when Roger Ellis's name began to be well and not favorably known among them, and she heard him spoken of with the careless contempt that places its object beyond the pale of honest hate, and is, of all tones the human voice can take, the most utterly disagreeable. Mr. Ellis had begun to be a rather conspicuous figure. Nobody seemed to know exactly what he was doing, but he was heard of now and then as making a speech at a negro meeting, or going up the river on a hunt for outrages instead of alligators, or talking on the street corners about the American flag, and the old Bourbon element (by which he did not mean whiskey) that was leading the country to ruin.

As for Blythe's interviews with her lover, they lacked the sweetness of past hours that had moved to the measure of the Sapphic Love Ode. A mania for letting Blythe know his opinions on all subjects appeared to have seized Mr. Ellis, and she felt sometimes as if she were being pelted with hailstones.

One Sunday afternoon they spent in an old French burying-ground. It was a dull old place in the heart of the city, surrounded by high walls that were devoted to the double purpose of guarding the enclosure and serving as a receptacle for the dead. They were very thick, and built in small compartments open on the inside, into each one of which a coffin could be shoved and the opening sealed up.

"I don't believe even Mrs. Dexter would call this an 'elegant idea,'" said Blythe, with a shudder. "I don't like to look at the walls, Roger; I should fancy a dead man in his shroud bursting through them and coming at me, if I were here alone. I should dash out my desperate brains for very fear of it. I do not feel that way in the least about the dear dead in the ground, over whom flowers are growing."

"There is something not altogether agreeable in the idea of being packed away as if you were a sardine," said Roger, laughing. "But I intend to be cremated, my dear, unless I die of a mysterious disease that will enable me to pay some pretty woman doctor the delicate attention of leaving her my remains for inside investigations."

"What ghastly talk!" and Blythe bent to examine an old tombstone on which was recorded the name and virtues of a faithful slave who had served his master's family for ninety years, during which time he had held in his arms the first-born of four generations.

"Let us rest here," said the young girl; and she seated herself on the low, flat tombstone, while Roger Ellis flung himself on the grass at her feet.

"There is a novel," he said, dreamily, "by Victor Cherbuliez, in which the hero, Prosper, a fascinating ne'er-do-well, determines on suicide; but, going to the top of a precipice from which he means to throw himself, he picks a little flower, the smell of which is so ineffably sweet that he decides not to renounce a life that still held such fine joys."

"As came to him through the nose," said Blythe, with a little scorn.

"And are not to be sneezed at," laughed Roger, "as if they were snuff. But I suppose the author meant to hint the folly of despair while any of our senses remained unimpaired. Suppose a man bereft of love, home, friends; life is worth the living if his digestion is still good. How much more if he has eyes for the glories of art, or ears for the ravishment of sound."

"This must be the reason," said Blythe, thoughtfully, "why we recover so soon from the death of one we have loved. The senses will enjoy, however much we may loathe ourselves for that enjoyment. But after all, Roger, I hate to think that you could be *forgetfully* happy if I were under one of these stones."

"Do not speak of such a thing here, Blythe. It makes me feel as if a lump of ice were pressed on my wrist: you know that cold, paralyzing sensation."

He raised himself on his elbow and looked up into her face—the pale Southern face, that did not flush so quickly now under his gaze. He wondered if she knew what his love was—the love that welled up and almost choked him at times—that was always with him, whether it rolled in tumultuous waves of passion or was at rest with tenderness. Other good hearts he might have won; but none other ever had power to make his own quiver in the silence of the night, in the shimmer of the dawn, in the sunshine of the day. It startled, it thrilled, it astounded him.

"Blythe," he murmured, "I thought that the genius of my heart was for suffering; you have taught me that it was for love."

"I wonder if you will always love me?" said Blythe; "if you won't change when you find out my faults?"

"If you have faults, sweetheart, I shall never scold you for them. If my heart-throbs don't wear them away, my temper shall never cut them away."

"It would be the proper thing," said Blythe, "for you to say I had no faults."

"But you know I never say the proper thing! Shall I say something truthful instead?"

"If you please."

"Here it is, then: Blythe, you do not love me a millionth part as much as I do you—that goes without saying. But further, I doubt sometimes if your real love-nature has ever been aroused."

"You have no right to say that!" cried Blythe, vehemently. "Are

179

we not engaged? Have I not—kissed you?" (This last in a very small whisper.)

Ellis laughed. "Ponder this orphic saying, my dear child: 'In the court of love, mistakes are not regarded as life-mortgages.' If ever you want to give me up, do not keep to me from any mistaken sense of duty. Sense of duty has done a great deal of mischief in this world. It is a rampant fiend that people mistake for a god, and build him altars out of ruined lives and broken hearts."

"How wildly you talk, Roger!"

"Then I will talk tamely. There is one reason, Blythe, why I am glad our marriage was postponed. I want you to see other men—to compare, to choose freely. If there is a man living who can win you from me, then he is the man whom you ought to marry. And remember this, dear: whatever sign of affection you have bestowed on me shall always be regarded as a *gift*—something to be grateful for; not as a claim on which to found dominion over you."

In spite of herself, Blythe's quick imagination caught at the idea he had suggested. "Suppose, after all, I have made a mistake," she whispered to herself; and side by side with the daring thought came another, veiled and blinded, indeed, but importunate for place— "If he knew me better than I myself—if he is so magnanimous as he says—he ought never to have kissed my lips, never have won my promise, until I had proved my own heart." But she thrust the thought from her, and only said lightly,

"You know, Roger, no one ever liked you as much as I do."

"I can't accuse you of talking wildly," said he, with a laugh; "there's no wild enthusiasm in that assurance of affection; and, by-the-way," he went on, sitting up and looking very animated, "I have the picture of my Sappho-sweetheart, and her last undestroyed letter. Should you like to see them?"

"Have you them with you?"

"Yes; I brought them to show you."

He drew a little packet from his waistcoat-pocket and handed it to Blythe. She looked at the picture without any emotion, although it was a much prettier face than her own. "But the letter, Roger—I ought not to read that."

"Imagine she has been dead for fifty years," he said, "and tell me what you think of it as a love-letter."

Blythe drew it out of the envelope with hesitating fingers, but after reading the first line her attention was absorbed. She read it to the end, and it dropped from her hand. If Ellis had looked at her face he would have been shocked. She felt as if the earth had slipped from her feet. The white butterflies were still flitting about, the birds singing from near and distant trees, but how her world had changed!

The letter was simply a passionate and extremely well-written love-letter.

> Come to my arms, my Antony,
> For the twilight shadows grow,
> And the tiger's ancient fierceness
> In my veins begins to flow.
> Come not cringing to sue me,
> Take me with triumph and power,
> As a warrior storms a fortress;
> I shall not shrink nor cower.

Story's Cleopatra might have been the model from which it had been written, and it was almost equally strong and fine. But its merit as a literary performance did not appeal to Blythe's sympathy. The irregular lines had seemed to reel across the page in a Bacchantic abandonment.

"It is little wonder," she said at last, "that you think I do not love you, if this is the sort of thing you like. It makes me *shiver* with shame for her—and for you.

"Blythe, what do you mean?" said Ellis, in genuine amazement. "It isn't possible that you are jealous! You women are queer creatures. If you like a man, you want to take out a patent on him."

But Blythe did not smile.

"Jealous! how little you understand!"

"I don't believe you understand yourself, dear child," he said, gravely.

"Why did you show it to me?" she cried, wringing her hands.

"It was nothing to me," he said, "except a brilliant letter. I thought it would interest you. I see that I have made a mistake."

Perhaps, were we to seek too curiously into motives, we should find in Mr. Ellis the slight vanity of wishing this proud Southern girl to know how he had been loved by a very brilliant woman. But he was sincere in regretting it. "Do not be jealous of my past, Blythe," he said. "Remember I was forty years old before I met you—and I was only flesh and blood, like other men. But I came to you with a heart as pure as your own."

"Jealous?" she repeated, "it is not that, Roger. But, don't you see—this seems to *vulgarize* our love? Oh, I can't talk about it!"

She felt a passionate sense of having been betrayed. She had fancied that she had revealed a whole world of new delights to her lover; but all the while she had only been following in a tame way the lead of another woman—other women, perhaps. The sacredness was all gone out of their love. She remembered the tears in his eyes the first night that he told her of his love—the tears that had turned the vibrating scale to the side of love. Good heavens! perhaps it was his way to shed tears on these occasions.

"How use doth breed a habit in a man!"
No wonder he talked love so well. Doubtless it is a matter of practice to become a lover, as it is to become a musician.

"Then we won't talk about it," said the voice of Mr. Ellis breaking upon her bitter thought. "See here, Blythe."

He had found a little hole in the side of the old tomb, and had crushed the letter and picture into a small package.

"I am going to put them in there," he said, "along with the dust of the faithful slave who held four first-borns in his arms. Come, dear, won't you say a *Requiescat?*"

She smiled faintly as he pushed them in with a long stick. "I think you are doing great dishonor to the faithful slave," she said.

"I can't understand your feeling," he said. "You knew long ago that I had loved other women."

"True," she said, "but I had never realized it." And poor Blythe will not be the last to find out that there are many things that must be realized before they can be comprehended.

"Why did you not marry her, Roger?" she said, after a while.

"She was married already," said Mr. Ellis, pensively.

Blythe pressed her hands down on the flat tombstone with a desperate sense of holding on—to something.

"She was married when she was sixteen," continued Roger, "by her parents, to a great brute of a man who had no more soul than—a centipede. He poisoned her life for her pretty effectually. In her heart-sickness she took to playing with love, until she rendered herself incapable of a real attachment. She flew from one excitement to another until she became a false and heartless creature unworthy of any man's love."

"But you loved her."

"Yes; I tried to save her. It was her last chance. But I met her too late. Her nature was thoroughly warped."

Now, if Roger Ellis, or any man, had confided to Blythe, as a fateful and tragic secret, the story of his love for a neglected and lovely creature whose husband was unworthy to kiss her shoe-tips, and had told it with a proper sense of its wild daring and romantic hopelessness, Blythe would have been the first to sympathize and glow with indignation against the unjust laws that pressed so heavily upon the better part of humanity; but the matter-of-fact way in which Roger Ellis mentioned that his Sappho was a married woman, was too much for Blythe's theoretic philosophy; and when Ellis went on—

"It was all the fault of her sinful marriage; and, by heaven! if I had fifty years to live I should organize a crusade against the corrupt system," she could only say, with the tears springing to her eyes. "Oh, Roger, this is worse than your African craze!"

Mr. Ellis laughed and caught Blythe's hands. "My dear girl," he said, "when you accepted me, you accepted a radical through and through. You cannot change me, dear. But I am not surprised at your feeling. What should you, a Southern child, brought up in the strictest school of conservatism, know of the great onward movements that owe their birth to radicalism?"

"I think, Roger," said Blythe "that you will make me a conservative in spite of myself."

"It is what you are, dear. But do you see this little shrub growing by the grave of the faithful slave? A year from now it will be tall enough to shake its leaves over the old tomb; another, and it will reach to your waist; a third, and we can hide our faces in its branches. *Growth*, dear child, is the law of life. You won't be exempt from it."

"I am not sure that I want to grow," said Blythe, with a troubled look.

CHAPTER XXIV

The Quadroon Ball

The year of eighteen hundred and seventy-six will be a deeply marked one in the annals of American history. It dawned in the North with the ringing of bells summoning all nations to witness America's prosperity, and to wonder at the swift glory that had crowned her youth; but in the South the Centennial Exposition was felt to be a much less important affair than the Presidential election. More especially in the Gulf States, where military rule had not yet been displaced, the party struggle of this year was looked forward to with a grim and terrible earnestness. The excitement in Louisiana culminated in its Crescent City; and not in its early years when its very existence was problematic—not in the awful time when the yellow horror of the pestilence enfolded it like a great vaporous serpent melting slowly into poisoned air—not when the Northern army held possession of it, and every day brought new hopes and fears—had the gay city known a time filled with such violent emotion as these winter months.

"The Southern people know how to suffer grandly!" said a prominent Louisiana gentleman, in speaking but recently of that eventful year; "but in the slavery to which they had been subjected since the war there was a sting of degradation that goaded them to a fury of resistance. Torn by party faction, her fair lands lying waste, an alien people on her soil who comprehended not her past nor cared for her future, our beautiful State turned like an animal at bay, and swore that the end of oppression had come. Her sons joined hands in a common cause; the same fire was kindled in every heart; their one hope and aim and resolve—*to free their mother State,* cost what it might. What a time it was! Men, women, and children talked politics; one breathed quickly walking among them; their passion charged the air."

Yet this strange Southern character! It is like a tapestry woven in brilliant hues, that, with a turn of the hand, shows a reverse side of sombre colors on a sanguinary ground. Mercurial and vivacious as they were resolute and violent, the people of New Orleans prepared for their annual play-day with the same zest and reckless liberality that had made their carnival pageant in the years past an evidence of exquisite tastes and a marvel of splendid effects.

It was a strange life for Blythe Herndon. She felt sometimes as if she were acting in some wild, fantastic tragedy. Nothing was real to her, though one emotion followed another, and her nerves were like quivering eyes bared to the sun. Roger Ellis did not have time to notice the subtle change. It is so gradual—the drifting away of a heart that has been ours. A word to-day, a look to-morrow, and a face that has been within the atmosphere of our breath, recedes slowly as if borne on waves, and is gone while we still dream of its kisses. Roger did see that Blythe was paler, quieter than she had been; he knew that she did not sympathize with his work; yet, with his own sublime faith in it, he believed that she would "grow" to its comprehension. He never spoke to her of what he was doing unless she questioned him; yet he was so often silent and preoccupied in her presence, that she knew his thoughts were wandering to some hateful subject that divided him from her. Once she had a glimpse of him among the people whose cause he upheld and in whose society he was working. There were quadroon balls given every fortnight in the city, and Mrs. Dexter had so often expressed a wish to know how they were carried on that the colonel made up a small party of intimate friends to look at one from the gallery of the hall in which it was given. It was somewhat hastily arranged, and Blythe had no opportunity to ask Mr. Ellis to join them. The ball was at its height just as they reached the hall. People of almost every color and nationality were dancing with an *abandon* due as much to the temperament of these Southern races as to the whiskey that circulated moderately. Some very beautiful quadroon girls, who would have been called white anywhere so long as they did not show their thumb-nails, attracted great attention by their graceful movements. The music was quick and irregular, and seemed much to the taste of the company. Now and then the leader, an old man with French and African blood in his veins, would sing out a verse of a song in negro-French that would elicit loud laughter and cries of *"Bis! bis! bis!"* from the dancers:

> "Mouché Préval,
> Li donné grand bal,
> Li fé nègue payé
> Pou santé ain pé.
> Dansé Calenda,
> Doun, doun, doun,
> Dansé Calenda,
> La, la, la!"

In one of the pauses of the music Blythe heard a laugh—the mellow, sympathetic laugh that she had once thought the pleasantest sound in the world. Almost at the same instant Betty Page, who was leaning over the gallery, exclaimed, "Look, Blythe! There is Roger Ellis!"

He was standing among a group of men who were talking noisily. One of them, a stalwart young negro, clapped Mr. Ellis familiarly on the back, as they looked down.

"He seems to be in very congenial company," remarked Miss Page. "I hope he won't see us."

He did see them, however, recognizing the ladies at once, although they were closely veiled. He came up to them, his face bright with pleasure at the unexpected meeting.

"It is worth looking at, isn't it?" he said. "I am sure none of you ever saw anything of this kind before."

"And I'm sure we never want to again," said Miss Page. "We only came out of curiosity—as we would have gone to any other monkey-show."

"These monkeys," said Roger Ellis, coolly, "are developing with uncommon rapidity. I shouldn't wonder if they got to be *men* even in your day, Miss Page.

> 'Dansé Calenda,
> Doun, doun, doun,
> Dansé Calenda,
> La, la, la!'"

"Do you understand the negro-French?" said Mr. Ellis, turning to Blythe. "It's easy, if you once get into it. Do you notice that white-haired fellow leaning against the post?"

"Yes."

"I must tell you something he said to me to-night. He is chief cook at one of the restaurants here, and has been a slave. I was dining there with some friends, and one of the *entrées* that he served was so particularly good that we sent for the old fellow to come in and have a glass of wine. Père Gabriel, as they call him, came in, bowing and pleased. We gave him a compliment and a toast. *'Ah! messhé!'* he said, alluding to the dish we had praised, *'c' n'est pas avec du syrop ié montré moi, ça!'* Which is to say, 'It was not with sugar (or soft words) that they taught me that.' Rather pathetic, wasn't it?

'Li donné soupé,
Pour nègue régalé,
So vié la musique,
Té bayé la colique.'"

"Really, Mr. Ellis," cried Miss Page, "I don't see how you could leave the charming society of your pathetic cook for our poor company."

He only smiled, and turned to Blythe with some low words of love that seemed to mix themselves oddly with the monotonous music:

'Dansé Calenda,
Doun, doun, doun,
Dansé Calenda,
La, la, la!'"

But she smiled back at him, and tried to be indifferent to the fact that he had on no gloves; and that Captain Silsby was scorning him for it, even as Betty Page was sneering at the anecdote of the "pathetic cook."

"See there, girls!" said Mrs. Oglethorpe, suddenly; "is not that the saddler who ran away from his wife in Yariba—Roy was his name, I believe—over there by the music-stand?"

"I never saw the man," said Blythe.

"That *is* he," said Roger Ellis: "I have recently made his acquaintance. He is still drinking out of the same glass of lemonade and eating off the same stick of candy with his beloved Ann Eliza."

"Oh, good heavens!" thought Blythe, turning cold; "in one minute more he will come out with some of his peculiar views to Mrs. Oglethorpe!"

She jumped up with such suddenness as to overturn her chair.

"Really, this air is insufferable!" she cried. "Do take me out, Mr. Ellis, to a place where I can breathe! I think a quadroon ball is like honey—a little more than a little is much too much."

"Suppose you let me take you home," said Roger, "and the others can follow when they are ready;" to which she gladly consented.

"How did you make Jim Roy's acquaintance?" she asked, as they walked toward home.

"He was a witness in a case that came up before one of our committees. I kept him after the others left, and attacked him in the most disinterested manner for going off and leaving Mrs. Roy with no money to buy her snuff. He unbosomed himself completely; said he led a dog's life of it with her. He is living in a little shanty up on the Bayou Têche. I stopped there one evening and made the acquaintance of the fair Ann Eliza. She made me a good cup of tea, and impressed me as being a very pretty and modest girl. Really, one can't wonder that he ran away from the melancholy Mrs. Roy."

Blythe gave a little groan, with the feeling that her views would have to put on seven-league boots to keep pace with Mr. Ellis's.

"I hope," said she, "that if you have any influence with this man, you will prevail on him to go back to his wife and children."

"Not I," said Mr. Ellis, cheerfully; "I'm all for Ann Eliza! But I'll tell you what I have done. I've told him that if he will enter into a written bond to send half his earnings to Mrs. Roy, I will help him to get a divorce that he may marry this girl."

"To leave her in turn, I suppose, when she gets to be a faded old scold."

"Oh! no man ever made a habit of that sort of thing," said Mr. Ellis, lightly, "except Blue-beard and the founder of your Church, the eighth Henry!"

"Jim Roy a witness!" burst out Blythe. "Roger, how can you believe anything he says, after the scandalous way in which he has acted?"

"I don't quite understand your logic, my dear Blythe," said he, laughing. "Does it follow with the unerring certainty of a marksman's aim that Jim Roy is a liar because he ran away from a wife he had ceased to love? That rather seems to me an evidence of his high moral truthfulness!"

"I suppose he is a good Republican when he is trying to take you in?" said Blythe, with more force than elegance.

"Yes," responded Mr. Ellis, with undiminished good-humor, "James seems to have struggled to the light."

"Everybody in Yariba will tell you that Jim Roy is a scamp," said Blythe, impressively; "and you will find out another thing— that it is only such men who belong to the radical party in the South."

"I dare say that it is only men who have little to lose who dare avow their honest convictions in this civilized country," said Mr. Ellis, giving Blythe's hand a gentle and provoking little pat.

CHAPTER XXV

Five Sides of a Question

It must not be supposed that Blythe Herndon was easily learning to unlove her lover. It was ebb and flow with the tides of her heart. In some exalted mood he would seem revealed to her so generous and tender and unselfish that her whole nature would turn to him with its old warmth; and his wit and brilliancy never failed to arouse her pride. In her moments of softened feeling, she longed passionately to put herself in harmony with his life; to enter into his thoughts, and share in his enthusiasms.

With all Blythe's pride she had more than usual humility. She was ready to acknowledge that Mr. Ellis's judgment was better than her own, and anxious to believe that his conclusions on all subjects were entirely right. But she had not that charming docility which in many women leads them to accept the *dictum* of the nearest man, as stolen goods are received—with no questions asked. My puzzled heroine had, in fact, just reached that point in mental growth where she asked to understand what she wished to believe; furthermore, she was developing the unfeminine power of looking at a question on more than one side—a power, by-the-way, not altogether to be desired by one who wishes to be a positive force in one day and generation, whatever it may be in the long run of the ages.

Miss Herndon made up her mind to decide on a political creed; and in spite of a hesitancy in presenting my Blythe to a not over-patient public in the character of a nuisance, I should like to tell how she went about it; for it has its humorous side, although the young lady was entirely serious.

"I know at least one ultra-Republican," she mused within herself, "and any number of ultra-Democrats. Then there is Colonel Dexter, who is a Republican, but not an extremist; and Van Tolliver, who matches him as a Democrat; and finally, Captain Silsby, who is indifferent to both sides alike. Now, these men are all honest, all clear-headed. I shall go to each one in turn, and say, 'Imagine I have just come to this earth from another planet, and explain to me all about American politics.' In this way I shall get on all sides and be able to form my own opinion."

Now, if there be any man who does not find something very pleasing in pretty Blythe's novel and ingenious plan for forming a political creed he may skip this chapter, for he will find it dull.

"Roger," she said one day, "I mean to study up this political question. Really, I don't yet know of any vital differences between the two parties. I am about as much a Republican as a Democrat."

"Don't pride yourself on that," said Ellis, smiling, and with a teasing tone of badinage. "Just let me whisper in your ear—and a very beautiful little ear it is—that that is only a confession, rather arrogantly made, of ignorance."

"Pray enlighten my ignorance," said Blythe, modestly, but with a high blush. "Imagine that I have just come from another plan—"

"My dear girl," interrupted Mr. Ellis, whose ears had only opened to the first half of Blythe's remark, "what would you have thought of a person who, when Luther was fighting the foes of free thought, had said that she was just as much a Catholic as a Protestant? or, during the war, that she was equally loyal to the North and to the South? Would you not have said that she did not know what her beautiful lips were talking about? Well, I can assure you there are differences as deep and far-reaching between Republicanism and Democracy as between the corner-stone of the Confederacy and Plymouth Rock."

"Explain the differences," said Blythe, with her finger on a point, as it were.

But Mr. Ellis got up and walked the length of the room; and when he spoke, it was in the voice usually reserved for remarks on the American flag.

"Blythe," he said, solemnly, "you must learn that there is a science and a religion in politics; and truth, in that as in every field of human thought and endeavor, must be sought with a humble and contrite spirit—with as earnest a desire to know truth for its own sake as fires the heart of the mystic or the soul of the man of science. To be very frank with you, my darling, you have not made the first step toward learning the truth in any science. It is not as a woman you must seek it; for truth is not a man, to be won by beauty or coquetry. But seek as a soul hungering and thirsting for it—ready to do and die for it. 'Whoso loveth father and mother more than me, is not worthy of me.' The great Man who said that was speaking of the truth. The small men who repeat it suppose he was a sublime egotist speaking of himself."

"This is very interesting," murmured Blythe. "I feel that I am assisting, as the French say, at an oration."

"I have sometimes wondered, Blythe, what different men would have said of the ground whereon Moses could not walk save with unsandaled feet. I think some of them would have called it in muddy weather a filthy arena; and others would have calculated that it was 'powerful po' land for cotton;' and most men would have called Moses a fanatic, because he saw more in it than they could see."

Here the talk was interrupted, rather to Blythe's relief, as it was getting nebulous.

"What I am after," she said to herself, plaintively, "are fixed facts. And Roger is so eloquent that it is very hard to get a fixed fact out of him. However, I shall have him to fall back on, in case the Democrats are too much for me."

The friends to whom Blythe applied, in turn, responded nobly to her appeal. It is never unpleasing to the masculine mind to lift the feminine into the region of high thought—especially into the cloud-capped region of "national affairs;" and it isn't every day that one gets a chance to enlighten a lovely young creature fresh from another planet.

And how much they found to say! how fruitful the subject! how varied its ramifications! Blythe had not been prepared for such wealth of discourse; and more than once she felt like the shuddering little fisherman who uncorked the tight little home in which an ungentle giant was packed away.

Among her Democratic friends was a man with a melancholy, rather poetic face, and a very gentle and musical voice. After going through the history of slavery in America, dwelling strongly on the assertion that it was only given up in Massachusetts after it had ceased to be profitable, he discoursed in this mild fashion: "And having satisfied their moral sense, sold their slaves, and pocketed the profits, our Northern brethren began to howl at their neighbors, and determined to advance the cause of Christ, as the Puritans called every scheme that suited their prejudices, by robbing them. And before our nation was a hundred years old, they had violated our glorious Constitution, and precipitated upon us a war in which they were spurred on by that hope of 'gaynful pilladge' that seems to find its natural home in the Puritan breast. Amidst blazing cities and the smoking ruin of desolated homes, the South succumbed to the force of superior numbers and superior resources, in a war characterized by atrocities that would shame Indian butchers. Having completed our ruin, they degraded us by placing over us as political masters the descendants of the Africans whom they kidnapped and solid into slavery. Think of it! We, in whose veins flows the blood of Surrey, of Raleigh, of Hampden, of the liberty-loving Huguenots, of the people of Normandy, Brittany, and the other heroic provinces of France, were subjected to the mastery of half a million brainless, brutal blacks, who were upheld by the bayonets of the Northern army! Well has it been called an act of savage, merciless revenge. Well has it been said that human nature was never before capable of so enormous, so abominable, and so infamous a crime."

"What a singular effect it has on them all!" mused Blythe. "They seem to jump on a platform, and address me as if I were an audience."

"Look at our Southern gentleman," continued her friend, "the finest product of civilization, the ornament and pride of the human race. But they've got one fault—they have borne insult and outrage with too grand a patience. Nothing saved the South from annihilation, after the war, but the Ku Klux Klan. And if we had not been so squeamish about mob-law—if we had hung a few dozen thieves and carpetbaggers to lamp-posts and trees—the South would have been free and prosperous to-day."

"Don't talk that way," said Blythe, vehemently. "It justifies the worst our enemies say of us. You ought to be ashamed of yourself! Suppose some Northern man heard you; he would be off and quote your words as representing Southern sentiment—and they do not, I am very sure."

"Why, Miss Blythe, I believe in law and order just as much as anybody; but there are times when a man with a shot-gun is of more use to his country than a lawyer. When scoundrels can commit every dastardly crime under heaven, and get clear of punishment by some infernal trickery, it is time for honest men to make laws that they can't skulk behind. Now, look at that Roger Ellis— a miserable Yankee, who is here for no other purpose than to stir up the evil passions of the negroes, and send home lying reports of outrages that he prompts or manufactures. He is the sort of man that ought to be knocked on the head and dropped into the river some dark night."

"Then you ought to be dropped with him," said Blythe, amiably, "for it is very clear that you are as much of a fanatic as he."

"There is no such thing as fanaticism in the cause of truth," rejoined her friend, with a grand air worthy of Roger himself.

The young girl repeated a part of this conversation to Mr. Ellis. "Now you see, Roger, what it is to be an extremist," said she; "he hates the Yankees as illogically as you do the 'rebels.' And the wonder to me is, that you, seeing, as you must, the silliness of fanaticism in others, can be a fanatic yourself."

"So you think me a fanatic, Blythe?" he said, with a half smile. "I wonder what you would say if you heard a genuine fanatic talk?"

"Tell me how he would talk. I want to hear all sides."

"I had better not. You are a Southern woman, and the fanatic wouldn't mince his words."

"Never mind that. I haven't any prejudices. Just imagine that I've come from another planet, and let your fanatic speak entirely in character."

"Very well, then; he would talk something in this way:

"'The war was a necessity—a growth. No statesmanship could do more than defer it.

"'The country exhibited the anomaly of two civilizations of extreme antagonisms growing up together. The most forcible people on earth were trying two experiments.

"'The Northern experiment was universal suffrage, universal freedom, universal education.

"'The Southern experiment was aristocracy founded on human slavery, universal ignorance, universal repression.

"'It did not matter that both experiments originated in a desire for profit.

"'The natural tendency of the North was to progress, enlightenment, freedom; of the South, to irresponsible power, license, narrowness—class to govern, a mass *to be* governed.

"'It is easier for man, when isolated, to revert to the savage than to progress in civilization.

"'The South isolated itself. It became savage. When the war came, it dropped the thin veneer of a false civilization, and donned paint and feathers.

"'The war rolled on. The innate tendency of the South to brutality was developed into its natural consequences. The laws of modern warfare were defied. Bands of murderers infested the country. Prisoners were starved—not in occasional instances, the accident of time or place, the fault of a fiendish keeper—but as a deliberate plan of the Southern leaders, to instil fear and to get rid of trouble—'"

Blythe put her hand to her lips to repress a passionate exclamation. "I *will* hear it out," she thought; "I brought it on myself."

"'The North was too mild,' continued Roger Ellis, who, perhaps, heard his own sharp, terse sentences with a certain degree of complacency. 'It should have treated the South as it would the shark or the tiger. It should have swept the South with the bosom of destruction—razed every house, burned every blade of grass, drowned opposition in blood. There should have been nothing left to fight.

"'As for reconstruction, the whole Southern country should have been reduced to a territorial condition—a ward of the nation, to be recognized when education and thrift had made it worthy of admission into a nation of freemen.'"

"That is enough," said Blythe, in a constrained voice; "you talk too well."

"My dear child, remember I was not talking in my own person. I only gave you—at your own request—an extreme Northern view, to set against that of your Democratic friend whom you have just quoted to me. You are not angry with me?"

"Oh no," said Blythe, recovering herself with an effort; "but sometimes I can hardly help feeling that you hate the Southern people."

Mr. Ellis looked hurt. "Blythe, you cannot mean that! Why, child, it is your battle I am fighting. As for assassins and bandits—yes, I hate them as they deserve. But are *they* the Southern people? Three hundred negroes were murdered in Mississippi and Louisiana during the last election campaign—"

"I do not believe it," said Blythe.

"It is a proven fact. But how should you know of these horrors, living in a civilized community, with all the papers silent or lying as to outrage, instigated by base political leaders?"

"It is a proven fact," retorted Blythe, "that one of the Vicksburg riots was instigated directly by the Republican governor, who said that the blood of twenty-five negroes would be the salvation of his party in Mississippi. Oh, Roger, how trying you are! You say that you do not hate the Southern people, yet in the next breath you say that we murder negroes—that our best men are base—that we are ignorant, uncivilized. Mr. Ellis, I know that I have a liberal mind. I believe in the Union—its theories of government—its future. But *you,* of all others, seem to narrow this feeling to a passionate love for the South—to a passionate resentment, as if I saw you strike my own mother. You make me as angry as one of Wendell Phillips's speeches. You know how cruel and bitter *he* is against us."

"My dear girl, neither Wendell Phillips nor any reformer ever thinks of people, but only of men as embodiments of ideas. The South, in the mind of Northern thinkers, means, not the Southern people, but the leaders and exponents of feudal as distinguished from popular or republican theories of government. These are the men who upheld slavery; who tried to create a damnable aristocratic order in the South; who ruined the land that fed them. It is they who have revived this sectional war. When they stop their insolence in Congress, their ostracism of Yankees—"

"Insolence, indeed!" cried Blythe, with an angry blush; "are you speaking of slaves, Mr. Ellis? Have not our Southern gentlemen a right to say what they choose in Congress? And it becomes *you,* indeed, to talk of ostracism of Yankees!"

Mr. Ellis came to Blythe, and took her hands in his strong, warm clasp: "My darling!" he said, with that peculiar tenderness of voice and eye that she could never quite resist, "you must not be angry with my plain-speaking; remember I am not arguing a question of North and South. There is a science which notes and directs the onward movements of the race; and he only is noble and of use to his age who aids the political and social elements that, on the whole, are travelling in the right way; and, more than that, who opposes whatever would retard the progress of his kind. In Italy the backward movement is called Popery; in France, Bourbonism; in England, Toryism; in America, Democracy. They are only different shapes and names for the same spirit—the spirit that once animated the past, and may have been of service then, but to-day is to be driven back, crushed, stamped into the sepulchre, whenever and wherever it rears its head."

Blythe's anger had passed: she began to laugh.

"I am just feeling my first throb of sympathy for General Grant," she said, gayly. "I know how he felt when he said, 'Let us have peace.'"

"Never mind, dear," he said, with a smile; "in after years you will be glad to have lived in just this tiresome and turbulent age; for the reconstruction era, with all its errors and follies and crimes, will be regarded as the auroral epoch of your beautiful South."

Blythe shook her head. "I am beginning, Roger, to have less confidence in your judgment than in your sincerity."

"And do you not think," said he, kissing the pink tips of Blythe's pretty fingers, "that if any fair Catholic of Luther's time had met a fiery Protestant and fallen in love with him, she would have had more confidence in his sincerity than in his judgment? We need not argue, fair Catholic—we look at things from an opposite point of view. To be sure, you are not an ultra-Catholic—hardly a Catholic at all—only a High-Church Episcopalian; but I am a Rationalist, you see, and have no more sympathy with Episcopalians, high or low-heeled, then with Jesuits or Inquisitors."

"Why don't you write a book, Roger?" said Blythe, languidly. "Your illustrations are so apt, and you have such a flow of language."

"Blythe, I am one of those men on whom pretty little sarcasms are thrown away—who make bouquets of them and send them back; so never hold your hand, dear."

"Well, well, you Quixotic goose of a Roger, why don't you like me better than your principles?" said Blythe, very softly, leaning her beautiful head toward his breast, and with a hint of passion in the upward look of her blue eyes that foolish Roger overlooked; for he patted her cheek in a meditative manner, and said:

"There must be pioneers of thought and of utterance. It is a hated but an honorable post. Some must be sacrificed; and I am ready to become one of the stepping-stones for my race to march over to the only heaven I know—an earth where justice reigns."

"I have not the faintest desire for such glory," said Blythe, sitting very erect, and with a little more color than usual in her cheeks; "so please understand that if asking me to become one with you you have any expectation that I shall be half the stepping-stone, I distinctly, finally, and forever decline that honor."

A fortnight later Van Tolliver came to New Orleans, and the young seeker after truth received her next political lesson from him. Van was an attractive talker. Equally free from rant or coldness, firm in opinion but modest of utterance, his words had a manly ring that could not fail of impressing the listener.

"I have accepted the consequences of the war," he said, "and mean to abide by them. I would not have the negro back in slavery if I could; and I don't want to deny him any rights that a free man ought to have. But as for having him to rule over us, that is a different thing. He is the tool of these miserable carpet-baggers, who have plundered the country steadily since the war, and who must be driven out, root and branch. The very essence of the Constitution is violated by their presence among us. Self-government is the very spirit of free institutions. We have been taxed and robbed and insulted long enough. We must get in a Democrat President next fall, who will free our country of its incubus, and then an era of prosperity will set in for the South."

"There is one subject, Van, that I should like to settle in my own mind," said Blythe: "What do you think of these outrages that they tell so much about? *Do* you think these dreadful stories are true?"

"You must take them with a good deal of dilution, Blythe."

"But even then, Van—"

"Well, yes," said Van, reluctantly; "I suppose some things have happened that we shall have to regret. But remember, every country has its lawless class; private vengeance is wreaked in many a case, and the motive covered with a political cloak. We can't always control the worst element of our population."

"But it seems to me, Van, that public sentiment ought to be strong enough to prevent repetition of these dreadful acts. But it isn't. People either deny them outright, or wink at them."

"I do not wish to excuse any act of violence," said Van, earnestly. "God knows, I would rather suffer a century than win even a just cause by a crime. But those upon whom oppression falls most heavily cannot always keep cool heads. And the provocation has been terrible. But there is fearful exaggeration in the stories you have heard—you may be very sure of that."

Colonel Dexter entered as Van had made his contribution to Blythe's confusion of ideas, and the discussion widened. Blythe was delighted to hear the two conservatives talk together. "Now I shall get the golden mean," she thought.

"The Democrats," said the colonel, "committed a political crime in the South; the Republicans, a political blunder. Both ruined their party. But our blunder—negro rule—is likely to be more disastrous to us than your crime—armed secession; because you've turned about, and we can't. It will ruin the North as well as the South. Now, the Republican party in the North is made up of our best people—church-going folk, thinkers, poets: you know this."

"Why, yes," said Van, "though our people generally don't realize it."

"No; because here we have a Peter's dream of a party—a blanket filled with animals clean and unclean, mostly the last; illiterate negroes, dishonest carpet-baggers, fanatics, office-seekers—so many that the few sensible men are crushed out, and the States are ruled by ignorance and greed and thievery. You've all had a turn. It makes me sick to think of it. Why the deuce, Van, didn't you Southern fellows go in at the close of the war and lead the blacks?"

"We had the misfortune to be gentlemen," said Van, quickly; and then he saw his error. But Blythe helped him out of his tongue-ditch by saying:

"But you know Mr. Ellis is a gentleman, Van, socially and by education; yet I have heard him say that he thought seriously of coming South after the war and making himself one of the leaders of the negro party."

"He is a *Northern* gentleman," said Van, seeing a chance for a masterly retreat from the inadvertent discourtesy of his speech. "He never held the relation of master to these people; and there is a wide difference between advocating the political claims of a class whom your education has taught you to regard as an oppressed people, and asking the boon of political support from men whom you once owned. We couldn't do it, colonel."

"The situation was full of difficulties," said the colonel, thoughtfully, "and a little of the wisdom of the serpent would have made things better for you. Uncommonly short-headed fellows you were. Look at one instance: your provisional government in Mississippi, under Johnson, passed a labor code* that practically restored sla-

---

*These labor laws, commonly referred to as the Black Codes, were a series of discriminatory laws passed in Mississippi late in 1865 to control the movements of freedmen. The freedmen were prohibited from renting land in rural areas and were required at the beginning of each year to have work permits or written proof of employment. Harsh vagrancy clauses punished any freedman without a job or who left his job; and apprenticeship clauses allowed African American children whose parents failed to support them to be bound out, often to their former owners.

very—that kicked over the fiat of emancipation. I don't wonder at it—don't blame you; it was a sort of guileless thing to do, you know. The anti-slavery power of the North was roused. They had to give the poor devils a weapon, or protection; the choice lay between universal suffrage and military rule."

"I should have preferred military rule."

"Perhaps, but that would have ended in destroying free institutions. So the Republicans decreed negro suffrage, as you call it; equal rights, as Ellis calls it; confusion worse confounded, I call it. And God knows how we shall ever get the muddle righted."

"By a Democratic National Administration," said Van, promptly.

"No; I think not. It is easy to know what we should have done. We should have waited and made education compulsory—no man, white or black, allowed to vote unless he could read; made more point of a citizen's duties and less of his rights. But that's past. We've done the mischief—we put the bull into the china shop. What we want now is a conservative Republican President, who will conciliate the alienated white South, do justice to the blacks, and bring things round to a normal state."

"You two gentlemen seem agreed on the vital points," said Blythe, "yet you belong to different parties. How is that?"

The colonel smiled. Van laughed.

"Oh, do speak freely!" urged Blythe. "You are too sensible to get angry about a political difference. And I do *so* want to understand this subject thoroughly."

"Go ahead, colonel," said Van; "fire away at my party, then I will have a shot at yours."

"Oh," said Colonel Dexter, good-naturedly, "be true to your traditions. The South fired first—we only answered back. Go on, Fort Sumter!"

"Very well," said Van, laughing. "But what is it you want to know, Blythe?"

"Oh, the particular reason why a Democrat should be elected next fall."

"I believe," said Van, "that a Democratic triumph only can restore the old harmony, because it is the only national party—the only party that maintains the good sound doctrine of self-government and home-rule, and that opposes centralization of power. It is the only party that upholds the rights of the States, and that has a traditional enmity to subsidies and extravagance of expenditure by the Federal Government. Besides, if your party were ever so sound in the faith, long rule necessarily engenders corruption; power becomes concentrated in a few hands; rings breed jobs; the caucus resolution silences the popular voice; we end in an oligarchy with the form of a democracy."

("What queer creatures men are," Blythe was thinking. "Who would think, to hear Van talk about politics, how crazy he was after Betty Page! And Colonel Dexter—how much better he looks than when he is fussing round his wife. They do not seem to strike realities until they talk to each other. I don't suppose a woman counts for much in any man's real life. She is a sort of side-issue—like Eve.")

"Well stated!" the colonel replied to Van; "now let me be as brief. Democracy talks nationality, and acts sectionality—that's history. The theory of State rights makes men not Americans, but Mississippians, Alabamians, Georgians, Carolinians—big boys proud of their village, not patriots proud of their country. Centralization means the majestic rule of a national government, instead of the squabbling orders of a provincial junto. Better subsidies for improvements that knit States together, than economies that hold them apart. Republicanism has never violated State rights; it doesn't take much stock in State prerogatives. Our party is not corrupt; there never was a purer party in history. It was not our fault that we were too strong. We didn't ask the Democrats to leave Congress and go out with their States, you know."

Blythe was a little tired. She found it impossible to sum up in her mind; she seemed farther than ever from a conclusion. It was a relief when Captain Silsby's card was brought in. She felt a desire to be frivolous.

"Oh, captain," she said, as he entered, "our friends here are trying to teach me the real difference between the Republican and Democratic party. Now, *what* is it?"

"Ins and outs," said the captain, indifferently. "We-uns and you-uns—office-seekers and office-holders—house of have and house of want—every man for his place and the devil take the hindmost, on the election returns."

"And what is your political creed?"

"To go for good men, snap your fingers at parties, and hurrah for the side that is up. It's all the same, you know. It's a game of see-saw. It doesn't put a stop to the country's growing-pains. Do I make myself understood, Miss Herndon?"

"Perfectly. I think you must be rather a comfortable person to live with. Such easy philosophy! The Vicar of Bray over again!"

"The Vicar of Bray I have not met," murmured the captain, "though there are ordinary fellows, even in the army, who do it. But if you think I would do to live with, please consider me at your feet, Miss Herndon."

"What creed should you like me to adopt, Roger?" she said, at last, "if I could make a choice?"

"Any but my own," he said, laughing. "It's only egotism to adore a feminine likeness of one's self. Choose the worst if possible. I don't want you to be too perfect; and there's a zest in ideas all awry, when they're held in a head covered with golden plaits, and uttered by lips lovelier than ever Paris kissed."

Blythe felt that Roger did not understand her; and she wrote in her journal: "My plan has been an utter failure. I am frightened at myself. I am getting to have a sort of—of—disdain of people who have opinions. I can't find anything to put in the place that I emptied of my prejudices. Indifference is benumbing. I feel languid and worn—averse to thinking out things. What a state of mind! It is only a ghost or a pig—who has a right to be indifferent to human affairs. But how is one ever to really *know* anything, unless he has lived from the beginning of time?

"I wish I had not come from the other planet. I believe I am less strong than I thought myself."

CHAPTER XXVI

The Carnival

Shrove Tuesday fell, this year, on the last day of February—the

> "one day more,
> We add to it one year in four."

It was brilliant with sunshine, as a Carnival-day should be; and from the flush of its dawn the streets were crowded with people giving themselves up to the spirit of the festival with all the joyous surrender of a Southern race.

Our friends were assembled on a Canal Street balcony, from which the younger members of the party could hardly be persuaded to stir even for luncheon or dinner, so delightful was the scene to their unaccustomed eyes. Mary Barton, who had been spending the week before Mardi-Gras with Mrs. Dexter, was among them, and kisses, bouquets, and bon-bons were flung upward by the gay masqueraders as the three pretty faces peeped over the balcony. Each one of the girls looked particularly happy, and they looked exactly as they felt, which relieves me of the necessity of making a not entirely novel remark about masks and faces that the day might suggest. Each one, of course, had her especial and private reason for being happy. Miss Page was thinking of a dress of pale yellow silk that had come forth a miracle from Olympe's hands, and was to be worn at the Carnival ball; Mary Barton felt as Taglioni looked when she poised herself on the tips of her toes and seemed just ready to spring into the air as her natural home; this was because Van had happened to be in New Orleans ever since she had been there, and had seemed delightfully indifferent to his old love; and Blythe Herndon was happy because Mr. Ellis was with her, and in his sunniest, wittiest mood. She forgot for a moment that a jarring word had ever been spoken between them; and the regrets that had haunted her of late like spectres grew too pale to be seen in the sunshine of his tenderness.

The day passed quickly. Its long hours seemed to melt into one splendid point of time, so changeless was the vision of undulating crowds, of glittering processions, and grotesque disguises.

Late in the afternoon the girls disappeared long enough to make their toilets for the evening, coming back with soft dark shawls wrapped about them, concealing their ball-dresses and heightening the rosy loveliness of their faces.

Blythe leaned against a vine-wreathed pillar, apart from the rest, waiting the return of her lover in a state of dreamy content. It was her last day in New Orleans; she was to leave for Yariba with Mary Barton on the morning of Ash-Wednesday. "The last day and the happiest," she whispered to herself. Roger had been so lovely all day. He had said charming things of the joyous grace of the Southern people at play; he had not so much as hinted that the world held an assassin, a bandit, or an American flag; he had laughed with the others when Satan and his imps passed along the street, the Returning-board and the Louisiana Senate being prominent and horrible among the devils of his majesty's court.

"Why does he stay away so long?" murmured Blythe, and a thought of Rosalind passed through her mind—"Come woo me, woo me; for I am in holiday humor, and like enough to consent."

But her mood in nowise resembled that of the vivacious, masquerading maid. She had eaten nothing all day, and for all her dinner had drunk a cup of strong coffee dashed with a glass of Cognac. The powerful stimulant had set her nerves to vibrating tremulously. A penetrating languor diffused itself subtilely through her frame. She could close her eyes and imagine herself with warm arms of love about her, floating to the pale heights of distant stars.

"Blythe!"

She turned her head and Roger Ellis was beside her. She held out her hand with a lovely, lingering smile. The shawl had slipped from her shoulders, and he kissed it passionately as he folded it about her bare, beautiful neck.

"Oh, my love! my love!" he whispered, as their hands met, and their eyes shone on each other through the dusk, "how completely you have wrapped me in your heart!"

As the darkness deepened, the crowd grew denser and more quiet. An expectant hush thrilled the vast multitude. They awaited the great event of the day—the coming of the "Mystick Krewe." Suddenly, with a wild burst of music and a blaze of golden light, the splendid vision pierced the dusk. The History of the Jews was the theme chosen for illustration: a series of pictures from the beginning of things in the idyllic garden, to the destruction of Jerusalem by the Roman soldiers; grouped on wide slow-moving floats with a dramatic perception, a splendor and exactness of costuming, that lifted them into the region of high art, and made one sigh that their passing should be so brief.

"Who would have thought that the Bible could be so interesting!" cried Betty Page. "I declare, I shall enjoy reading it after this, for it will remind me of this beautiful night."

"This beautiful night!" echoed Blythe, softly, leaning toward her lover; "and it is but just begun."

It was not the ball, however, to which she looked forward as the evening's crowning glory. True, she was going; but after the tableaux and the first dance Mr. Ellis was to bring her home, and spend the evening with her alone.

"And you may stay until Mrs. Oglethorpe and Betty come back from the ball," she had said, recklessly, "whatever that hour may be!"

As soon as the last float had passed the ladies were hurried to their carriages and driven to the Grand Opera–house. At the door they were forced to part from their escorts, as the best seats were all reserved for ladies, and the gentlemen, without exception, must be "gallery gods" for the nonce.

"Remember," said Blythe, to Mr. Ellis, as they stood at the door, "you are to come for me after the first dance. I shall be with Mrs. Oglethorpe."

At this moment a ragged figure pushed its way through the crowd to where Mr. Ellis stood and thrust a folded paper into his hand. Blythe had no time to ask what it was, as the crowd hurried her and her friends to their places.

The tableaux were over; the "Mystick Krewe" had come from behind the curtain, and, still masked, were selecting their partners for the first dance. Blythe had been chosen by no less a person than the mighty Moses. They had just taken their places on the floor, and she was idly trying to recognize a friend behind the long beard of the Lawgiver, when she saw Roger Ellis hurrying toward her.

"One moment, darling," he said in a low voice, drawing her a little to one side; "I have some bad news—I must leave you."

"*Leave me—to-night?*"

"I *must*, Blythe. I have just received intelligence of a secret meeting in the lower part of the city that it is absolutely necessary I should attend."

"But, Roger, have you forgotten that I go to-morrow—that this is our last evening?"

"Oh, my darling, do you think I *want* to leave you? It distracts me. But it is so plainly my duty, that I should be a coward to hesitate. I will come back if I can. At least you shall see me the first thing to-morrow."

The music struck up with a deafening crash. Moses extended his venerable hand.

"Good-bye, darling! darling! darling!" murmured Ellis.

He will never forget that moment of his life; he will never forget how she looked as she stood there, white like a lily, with the glory of color around her, and the sound of music swelling above her low, sweet tones; nor the deepening look of pain on her delicate, wistful, lovely face, as she held one hand half out to him in unconscious appeal, and resigned the other to the impatient clasp of her masked partner. She was swept from him, and the next moment he was in the street.

Nor will Blythe forget that night. She crushed the bewildered pain at her heart. Like all proud, hurt creatures, she strove to hide her wound. A brilliant color leaped to her cheek, light to her eyes, and repartee to her tongue. She was a new being. She outshone Betty Page, and for the first time in her life was a belle. Her mother would scarcely have known her; her father would never have been so proud of his child.

At last it was over. Pale and drooping, she sat by the fire in her room, wondering if she should ever sleep again, when Betty Page came in, radiant as the sun.

"Blythe Herndon!" she cried; "pinch me and see if I am real. I am going to Europe."

"So am I," said Blythe, dreamily—"when I die."

"I am going in three months' time!"

"As companion to some rich old lady?"

"As companion to Captain Silsby, my dear. I have accepted him. He is to get a six months' leave. We are to be married in April, go to the Exposition, and from there to Europe. Oh, Blythe, think of Paris! Now *do* tell me that I am the luckiest girl under the sun!"

"You are, dear—if you love him."

"Oh, I love him well enough—not madly, you know. I'm not romantic. But then, neither is he. He isn't a poem-writer, like your Mr. Ellis—but I'm not a poem-reader. We *suit* each other, don't you see, Blythe? and there's everything in that."

"Yes, I think there is," said Blythe, slowly.

"It was all settled to-night. This dress was too much for him," said Betty, smoothing out her yellow skirts. "I knew it would be. And Europe was too much for me. There isn't another girl in Yariba who ever went to Europe for a bridal tour. Blythe, suppose you and Mr. Ellis get married at the same time. Think what a sensation a double wedding would make in poky old Yariba, and let us all go to Europe together. Propose it to him, will you, Blythe?"

"Hardly!"

"Well, what difference would it make? You really mean to marry him, don't you?"

"I don't know, Betty," said Blythe, wearily, walking to the window, and looking up to the sky, from which the pale stars were beginning to fade in the dawn of Ash-Wednesday morning. The city had grown still as sleep; but as she stood there she heard the striking of a distant clock, and a belated Frenchman passed under her window, who had probably taken his little glass of absinthe, and was declaiming Victor Hugo in high, shrieking tones:

> "L'avenir! l'avenir! mystère!
> Toutes les choses de la terre,
> Gloire, fortune militaire,
> Couronne éclatante des rois;
> Victoire aux ailes embrasées
> Illusions realisées,
> Ne sont jamais sur nous posées,
> Que comme l'oiseau sur nos toits."

CHAPTER XXVII

Be Happy and Forget Me

"We twain shall not re-measure
The ways which left us twain."

Mr. Ellis did not make his appearance the next morning; but Civil Rights Bill came with a note of explanation and regret, that Blythe read with a slight, bitter smile, and to which she returned no answer.

"You look like a ghost," said Mrs. Oglethorpe, as she kissed her young guest good-bye. "I am afraid the winter has been too much for you."

"She needs Yariba air," said Van Tolliver, who was to escort the two girls home.

"Yes," said Blythe, "I shall be glad to get back to Yariba, although I have enjoyed my visit so much; but I did not know I was so fond of the dear old place. I am sure I shall want to kiss the very cows by the Spring!"

Squire Barton was waiting for the girls in a light wagon at the railway station; and he drove them home in fine style, laughing all the way at their raptures in getting back to Yariba.

"You'd have thought they had been gone seven years," he said to his wife. "When they got to the Spring, they must get out and walk; and who should come along but old Riddleback, the jugman, you know, and what must both those girls do but stop and shake hands with the old Dutchman, as if he had been kin to them!

You never saw an old fellow so taken aback: you see, he didn't even know they had been away!"

"How does Blythe look?" asked Mrs. Barton.

"She looks sick; she looks as if she needs a good deal of *mother*," said the honest old squire, giving his wife a sounding kiss.

"The trip seems to have agreed with Mary," said Mrs. Barton, fondly. "I never saw her look so well in my life."

"Oh, I enjoyed every moment of the time," said Mary, with a deep blush, as if she had made a most compromising statement. "Still, I am very glad to be at home again."

"Ah, yes," said the squire; "there's no place like Yariba. The man or woman that can't be happy in Yariba can't be happy anywhere on God's green earth."

"It seems to me, father, that I have heard you say something like that before," said Mary, slyly.

"Perhaps you have, child. It has occurred to me more than once," said the placid squire.

One person in Blythe's family rejoiced over her altered looks—that was the grandmother. She saw that she was unhappy; she felt that there was trouble between her and Mr. Ellis; and again she thanked God in a devout spirit.

Betty Page came home with her brave bridal garments, and was married in the spring, with a string of bridesmaids as long as the tail of a Highland chieftain attending her. She was brilliantly happy. There had never been anything in Yariba as fine as her wedding. She had originated the daring novelty of being married in a dress the color of the peach-blooms, while all her bridesmaids appeared in white.

"It will be very effective," she had said to Blythe, "and no one will have a chance to say that Captain Silsby has got a White Elephant on his hands—you know how immense I am in white."

"Happy pair!" wrote Mr. Ellis; "I am almost tempted to envy them. When I think of the summer we too might have had in the shadow of some cool, far-off foreign mountains, and the summer I *must* have here in this hot, wretched country, filling my soul with horrors, life seems just a little hard; but here I feel my duty lies, and not even you, my Blythe, could tempt me out of its path."

Sensational articles appeared from time to time in the Northern papers, giving Mr. Ellis's name as authority for terrific stories of Southern outrages. A deep and bitter feeling against him was aroused in Yariba. The *Yariba Advocate* came out in a scathing editorial headed "Human Vipers," that was very much admired throughout the county. Mrs. Oglethorpe gave a dinner-party, and solemnly assured her friends that she had turned the cold shoulder to him just as soon as she found out what he was doing in New Orleans. Mr. Shepherd said that nothing was too infamous to expect from a man of his loose religious views. Mrs. Roy made the tour of the town, with a basket on her arm for stray contributions, and told the story of her acquaintanceship with Mr. Ellis, not omitting to say that "she mistrusted the man as soon as she clapped her eyes on him, but he seemed so anxious to do something for her that she thought it would be ungenerous to refuse." Squire Barton, ever good-natured, undertook a word in his defence.

"You must consider how a man's made," he said. "Now, Ellis can't help being what he is, any more than a June bug can help its smell. But, then"—reflectively—"I can't say that I like having a June bug rubbed under my nose."

Mrs. Tolliver declared that for her part she always would say that Mr. Ellis was a kind, good man; that Mis' Tolliver said he was as weak as mush; but she thought it was just a sign of his generous nature that he was so easily taken in by the negroes, who would lie just for the fun of it; but, to be sure, how was he to know that?

All this was trifling enough; but it was gall and wormwood to a girl like Blythe Herndon, whose most ardent desire was to be proud of her lover. She never failed to defend him, but it grew to be a tiresome business; and day after day, walking by the spring, climbing the hill, sewing or pretending to read, the same old wearying train of thought passed through her mind—"Do I love him? Did I ever love him? And if so, could my heart turn from him now, whatever he might do?"

She read his impassioned letters, remembering how she had read the first of them with blushes and thrills of shy delight; but now her heart beat not faster, nor did her cheek change its even pallor. She wondered if it were so in all love; if passion were as short-lived as a flower held in a warm hand; or if, as Mr. Ellis had sometimes said, her deepest feeling had never been aroused. This thought came to her with mingled pain and consolation—consolation that she might still believe in love as a reality, not as a dream of her imagination; pain, desperate pain, that she had wasted herself so recklessly before the true love came. She felt it a solemn and a shameful thing to break an engagement that had been sealed by such kisses as lovers give. "Unless I loved Roger Ellis," she said to herself, "I am too indelicate and obtuse a creature to live upon the earth, or some fine instinct would have held me back. And yet, if I have exhausted so soon the finest and divinest passion that a human heart can know, then life is a cheat and a lie, and I don't want to live any longer."

In truth, Blythe was unfortunately constituted. Her intellect was eager and aspiring, her soul delicate and sensitive, but her physical temperament was cold. To hold dominion over such a woman it was absolutely essential to keep her intellectual admiration. The man who could do this might pass his life in the delusion that she adored his person.

Heart-sickness seizes strongly on young souls; and Blythe grew hollow-eyed and thin. If she had talked to any one of her trouble it would have been easier to bear; but she made no confidant, not even of Mary Barton, who, through some unknown influence, was growing tenderer and sweeter every day. And now a very novel experience came to her—she began to like going to church. Service was held every afternoon at six, and after a long day of tiresome thought it was peace and quiet pleasure to glide into the little church where scarcely more than two or three were gathered together, and listen to the familiar words of prayer as the long aisles grew misty in the twilight, and the fading sunbeams rested on the communion altar, or flickered at play with the black lettering of a tablet "to the beloved and blessed memory" of a pastor who had died among his people. There was good singing in the church at Yariba, and all her life long Blythe will remember those evening hymns, and that stole like perfume into her soul—

> "Softly now the light of day
> Fades upon my sight away;
> Now from care, from labor free,
> Lord, I would commune with thee,"

Or,

> "Lord, dismiss us with thy blessing,
> Fill our hearts with joy and peace"—

sweet, soothing strains that she could not hear without a faint trembling at the heart, and a slow coming of tears to her blue eyes.

Every one noticed the change in Blythe Herndon, and every one liked her softened manner. She took more interest in every-day matters. In her intercourse with Roger Ellis she had heard so many fine abstractions and glittering theories, that it was with a sense of actual relief that she listened to Mrs. Dering's gentle account of the sufferings of Carrie's twins when they were five days old, or heard Mrs. Barton tell of a silk quilt she had just finished in the bird's-nest pattern, for which she had been saving the pieces twenty-five years.

Sometimes she wondered vaguely at herself. "I seem to be crystallizing in a new mould," she said; "or is it that I am just finding out what I really am?" She had been called romantic, but the most romantic expression of love had failed to satisfy her; she had thought herself liberal-minded, but her lover seemed to her a fanatic, and she was not liberal enough to be indifferent to it; she had been impatient of the commonplace, yet she was so commonplace as to desire a smooth and comfortable life; she had openly declared her scorn of "the prosaic and narrow teachings" of her early life, but their influences held her as tenaciously as the earth holds the roots of a flower, while its blossoms may be blown to the winds.

During all this time she had written short, cold letters at long intervals to Roger Ellis: finally there came from him a passionate appeal for her confidence.

"My darling," he wrote, "you do not understand my love. It has gone away up beyond the table-lands of pleasure to the summits of the soul where selfishness cannot live. Its one desire is for your happiness. Nothing could drive me from you, or cause me to be less than your truest friend. The one thing I could not bear would be to make you my wife and find that I failed to satisfy every part of your nature. For a long time, my precious child, I have seen that you were wavering and in doubt. Now, before you write to me again, look deep into your heart, and in making your decision do not think of me. Only selfish or weak souls suffer long. I should find in life duties enough to prevent me becoming a cynical or a sad man; and in study, in travel, in friendship fill the years with beauty. And I should never think of you but with gratitude—recalling you as the radiant angel that threw open the barred gates of my heart and filled it with perfumes, and the light that only shines from a nature that is pure and noble, and imperial in its power to bless."

One more week for her slow-forming resolve to crystallize, and Blythe wrote:

> Your letter has given me courage to write what is in my heart. I must give you up. I do not love you any more.

You will think that I never did, or I could not be so weak as to fall away from you now. I do not know. It is only of late that I have begun to study myself, and I cannot tell whether I have loved you as much as I can love, or whether it was a mistake from the first, and I was simply flattered by your beautiful words, and beguiled by beautiful love. Only this much is now clear to me—that when I think of a future with you, it is with sadness and unrest. I feel like one launching out on a wild sea. I dread your influence over me. I do not wish to turn away from all the sweet teachings of my father and my mother and my early youth. There could be no harmony in our lives. You may be right; but you are at the end of things, I at the beginning. If ever I come to where you are, it must be by my own slow steps. I cannot jump such a space. Since you came South the last time I have had one shock after another.

I have tried to be faithful to you. I know that you are noble, and nothing shall ever make me doubt that you are true. But I should not know how to live with one who despises what I feel dimly I ought to revere, and who was always running a tilt against things that a giant could not shake. The world is so full of beauty! and the good God who holds it in the hollow of his hand will in his own time turn its evil into good.

This letter will sound hard, and cold, and cruel; but I cannot help it. I seem to have lost all feeling—but I have suffered. I know the day would come when you, so brilliant and advanced, would regret having a wife like me— that is the one comfort.

I have sinned toward you; but I did not know myself. I know that you will forgive me, and I pray that you may be happy and forget me.

Emma Blythe Herndon.

It was done. She took the letter to the office and posted it herself, a cold shudder quivering through her body, as she dropped it into the box, as if a little snake had slipped through her fingers.

Then she walked home, the gray twilight folding itself about her, her heart all desolate and empty, like a room from which a dead body has been taken to its grave.

She took her place at the tea-table, cold, pale, and preoccupied. Her mother pressed her to drink a glass of iced tea that she had prepared for her; the grandmother watched her keenly. When she rose from the table, she stood a moment leaning lightly on her chair, and said,

"I don't wish any questions asked about it, but I must tell you all that I have broken my engagement with Mr. Ellis."

She started out with a fleet step; but turned when the incautious Jimmie waved his fork and called out, "Hooray for you, Blythe! I didn't think you would bring that black radical into our family!"

"I don't suppose it's any use trying to make any of you understand," she burst out, the red color flaming over her face, "but I will tell you that I do not give him up because he is a radical. I am a radical myself!" cried poor Blythe, in one last despairing effort of loyalty toward her lover—"at least, just as much as I am anything. I have examined the record of the Democratic party, and I've no respect for it—no, papa, not one bit. And I don't want you ever to hint that I gave him up because of his politics, or because of his being a Northern man. It is simply that we don't suit each other— that's all there is about it." And catching her breath in one quick sob that she could not keep back, Blythe went out of the room.

And all of them at the table smiled at each other with the most heartfelt satisfaction, and applauded the child's good-sense in having come to her decision without any pressure from outside.

"The thought of this marriage has long been obnoxious to me," said Mr. Herndon; "but I had given my word, and besides, I knew opposition would only make matters worse. I've found out one thing about Blythe; if you give her her head—let her do exactly as she chooses—she is sure to bring up all right."

"What a sad experience for the poor child!" said the mother, with tears in her eyes.

"It is I who have saved her!" said the grandmother's solemn, exultant voice; "my prayers have been answered;" and she clasped her hands over her heart as if to still its agitated beatings.

"I don't know how you could pray for our dear girl's misery!" said Mrs. Herndon, a little angrily.

"Oh, she will get over it," said the grandmother. "I shall give her my solitaire," she added, solemnly: "and oh, Archer, I do hope this will be a lesson to you."

Mr. Herndon laughed, and patted his wife on the cheek.

"Never fear, Lucy," he said, gently, "she will get over it—not for a little while, perhaps, but in time for the Christmas parties."

And then Jimmie piped in with the tender appreciation of youth:

"She is like the old hen in my First Reader—'The old hen is ill. She is too ill to scratch. But she is not so ill as to die.'"

And so Blythe's love-affair was lightly dismissed.

But later the grandmother crept into Blythe's room. She was sitting by the window, without a light. The moonlight poured its flood upon her pale gold hair, that floated all unbound around her slight figure. Her eyes were closed. Her face leaned against the window-pane. And when her grandmother tried to fit the ring on her slim finger she pushed it back. "Take it away," she said, drearily; "I do not want it. Oh, my heart is sore!"

And the old lady went out and left her alone with her grief.

CHAPTER XXVIII

Gods and Men, We Are All Deluded Thus!

The long summer had passed drearily enough to Roger Ellis, and a great sorrow was in store for him. There had not been the yellow-fever panic, that usually empties the city as the dreaded fall months approach; yet fever is always lurking in the low Southern country, where a city seems to have been built especially to provide it victims, and each year it ends the tale of some doomed life. And this year, unused to the hot climate, pining for the hills, weakened by a mental activity to which he had been a stranger in all his idle, easy life, poor little Civil Rights Bill was stricken down. For weeks the fever burned in his veins, and Mr. Ellis sorrowfully watched beside him, aided by one of the good Sisters who choose so hard a path to heaven.

How the sick child raved! He fancied himself back in Yariba, and with incessant, untiring energy lived over his old life. He would sing wild snatches of song in a voice alternately faint and shrill; sometimes repeating one verse again and again in a high, swinging melody, that will ring in Roger Ellis's ears through many a summer day to come.

The sun shone like heated brass in the heavens; the earth seemed to swoon beneath; and Bill's talk was of mountains and cool streams—of picking blue flowers under the trees of Mount Sano, and diving for moss in the clearest waves of the spring.

He would have intervals of semi-consciousness, in which he would beg Mr. Ellis to talk to him.

"Tell me about the railroads, and the genii. Don't you r'member, Mr. Ellis? you said it was your fairy story."

And Ellis would try to recall some of the old fanciful talk with which he had striven to arouse Bill to intellectual effort:

"Down in the depths of the earth, genii dig metals, separate them, burn them, torture them in a thousand shapes; then they stretch them out like ribbons across valleys, over plains, through mountains—"

"Through the cold hearts of mountains," said Bill, with a child's tenacious memory.

"—Through the cold hearts of mountains, until cities are knit like beads on a string."

"Cities like beads," repeated the weak little voice. "Oh, me, me, what a great hot bead this one is!" and he threw his restless arms against the great palm-leaf fan that the quiet nun moved with tireless hand at his side.

"Mr. Ellis!"

"Well, Bill?"

"It's a long way, ain't it?"

"What, my poor child?"

"To go to all the beads—all in this world. It's such a big world, you know. I uster think Yariba was pretty big. I've learned a heap since then," said Bill, with a faint smile of pride.

"Yes, Willy, it is a long way," said Mr. Ellis, wishing now, sorrowfully, that he had never taken the poor dying child from the woods and mountains of his home.

"I reckon it takes all of a man's life—till he is old and white-headed—to see everything," said Bill; "and oh, me, me!"—with the little sigh of weariness that recurred so often in his talk—"how tired anybody must get of goin', goin', goin'—never stoppin' to rest! Don't you ever get tired, Mr. Ellis?"

"Yes, Bill; God knows I do—tired enough to wish to die rather than to live."

"Am I goin' to die?" said Bill, in a low, awed whisper.

"I don't know, my poor boy. I hope not—I hope not! I want you to stay with me."

"I know," said Bill, looking up at him with big, loving eyes, "you was goin' to make a man of me."

"I uster think"—he went on after a pause—"that when you got old, and blind, and deaf, maybe—'cause there's a good many old men in Yariba like that—that I could wait on you, and be a sight o' comfort to you. I just tell you the truth, me, befo' I was too sick, every night when I come to bed I could see myself tall an' straight as Mars' Van Tolliver; an' you, with your hair all white, a-leanin' on me, an' us a-walkin' in the sunshine."

Mr. Ellis turned his face away, and his form shook with sobs.

"But I s'pose you'll have Miss Blythe, won't you, Mr. Ellis?"

"I don't know, Bill. I think sometimes that she doesn't love me a great deal; not as much as you do."

"Of course I love you—I belongs to you. An' ain't you the only person that ever keered a button whether I was alive or dead? Oh, Mr. Ellis, don't let me die!" and Bill clung to him with a frightened look in his eyes.

"I saw a dead baby once," he whispered—"little Becky, they called her. She was kind of foolish—never did have sense—and everybody said it was good for her to die an' go to heaven. I wonder where heaven is!"

Mr. Ellis was silent. His eyes met those of the nun, across the bed. A look of deep pity dawned in her face. She leaned forward and held a crucifix before Bill's eyes, murmuring a prayer.

"I dunno about it all," said the obstinate little heathen. "I'll b'lieve whatever Mr. Ellis says about it."

"Bill, child, you will soon know more than I or any living man can tell you."

"You don't think I'll go to hell?" he said, with a quick convulsive shudder.

"*No*, Bill, don't be afraid of that. If there is a heaven, it will open fast enough to a poor child like you."

This was their last talk. Delirium came back, and then the fatal signs of approaching death. The fever had left him. Exhausted and almost lifeless, his eyes followed Mr. Ellis about the room with pitiful persistence. It was night, and a cooling rain dashed against the windows. Bill slumbered lightly.

"Pray," said Mr. Ellis, fixing his sad eyes on the nun's passionless face, "pray—that he may not suffer at the last."

At the morning's dawn he opened his eyes gently, and with yearning, loving gratitude in their expression.

"Thank you, sir!" he said, faintly. "You've been mighty good to me. I'm sorry I couldn't grow up to be a man. Tell Tom and mammy, and all the boys good-bye."

The breath grew fainter—the eyes dulled.

"Bill!" cried Mr. Ellis.

Both hands gropingly sought Roger's.

"Good-bye—I'm not afraid. I'll—tell—God—how good—"

And so saying, poor little Civil Rights Bill passed out of a life that had not been over kind, to another all bordered with rolling clouds that faith claims to penetrate, and see beyond them a glory that is everlasting.

Ellis buried his dead; and came back from the funeral, at which he had been the one mourner, to find a letter from Blythe awaiting him. He took it up with a passionate throb of hope. He read it.

The damp, warm wind blew in at the open window. The moon rose; and moon, and stars, and rising sun looked in upon a man who sat by the table, his face buried in his hands, while the only sound was the tossing of an open letter that the breeze blew about on the floor.

But to him the silence was filled with sound: echoing like drum-taps, hollow and clear, through his soul, rang the words conse-crated long ago to Blythe in the garden of roses:

> "Singing how down the vale of Menalus,
> I pursued a maiden, and I clasped—a reed.
> Gods and men, we are all deluded thus!—
> It breaks in our bosom—and then, we bleed."

He made no attempt to change her decision: he felt that it would be a useless pain. In his heart he vowed to her an eternal service of friendship; and then he took up his life, to make of it what he could. It is not difficult to foretell his future. Men who have a talent for crusades always find enough to do.

> "For the wrong that needs resistance,
> For the cause that lacks assistance,"

is the motto he has inscribed on his banner; and, whether foolishly or grandly, he will sacrifice himself as long as a heart beats in his breast. He may love again; but, ah! never again one so fresh and fair as the Southern girl whose love he won and lost in a land of dreams.

And Blythe? Young and beautiful and sad-hearted, she sits by her window, and watches ghosts go by, and tells herself that her romance is ended before her life is well begun. Other women than Blythe have made their sad little moans, and have lived to smile at them. But of one thing be sure: never again will she know the fresh, ethereal madness that, like the Holy Ghost to the kneeling Virgin, comes but once to the human heart, and is called first love. Wider, deeper, richer joys may wait for her in the coming years, like undiscovered stars that earthly eyes have not yet seen; but I who write, alike with you who read, can only guess at what the future holds—for the story of her life is not yet told.

THE END